P9-DBT-557

DISCARD

EVERY KIND OF WANTING

EVERY KIND OF WANTING

A NOVEL

GINA FRANGELLO

COUNTERPOINT • BERKELEY

FOR ALICIA, GIVER OF IMPROBABLE GIFTS,
PORT IN EVERY STORM, BFA.

Library of Congress Cataloging-in-Publication Data

Names: Frangello, Gina, author.
Title: Every kind of wanting : a novel / Gina Frangello.
Description: Berkeley : Counterpoint Press, [2016]
Identifiers: LCCN 2016020227 | ISBN 9781619027220 (hardcover)
Subjects: LCSH: Interpersonal relations—Fiction. | Married people—Fiction. | Conception—Fiction. | Domestic fiction. | BISAC: FICTION / Literary.
Classification: LCC PS3606.R3757 E94 2016 | DDC 813/.6—dc23
LC record available at https://lccn.loc.gov/2016020227

Cover design by Jarrod Taylor
Interior design by Domini Dragoone

ISBN 978-1-61902-722-0

COUNTERPOINT
2560 Ninth Street, Suite 318
Berkeley, CA 94710
www.counterpointpress.com

Printed in the United States of America
Distributed by Publishers Group West

10 9 8 7 6 5 4 3 2 1

ACT III

PRIVATE BEASTS

ACT I

THE COMMUNITY BABY

ACT II

COMMUNISTS IN THE FUNHOUSE

ACT IV

STRONG'S LANDING

ACT III

PRIVATE BEASTS

VERY EARLY IN MY LIFE,
IT WAS TOO LATE.
—MARGUERITE DURAS

LINA

You think you know our story, Nick, but that would imply that I was capable of honesty. You think our stories are some joint thing, a common narrative on which we, the coconspirators, would agree, but you don't know anything yet.

One thing you taught me is that all empathy involves a kind of method acting. You used to say I was a natural actress, but with bipolar as rapid-cycling and tidal as mine, maybe inhabiting alternate states isn't particularly foreign. Plenty of days, I can wake up in a hypomanic groove, cylinders firing with crystalline clarity all morning, then crash into a blackhearted, apathetic depression by evening where my brain feels wrapped in gauze, and come 1:00 a.m., facing another manic, sleepless night, I'm ready to peel the paint from the walls, mentally ricocheting around like a fruit fly that can't land, head blaring, trying to benzo myself into sleep or stupor and hoping the ride will be less wild tomorrow, unsure of who I'll be.

I love all the versions of you, you used to tell me, my pluralities for the first time not an embarrassing liability. But if characters are supposed to be consistent, I'm damned from the outset. Maybe I'll have an easier time with the rest of you than I do with myself.

I don't know my brother's husband's sister well, but I've been around her, I don't have to conjure her from scratch. You've met her plenty of times, so that's something, too. For our purposes here, let's call her Gretchen. Did you ever visit her old house? I didn't, but I bet we can both imagine it, in the shiny North Shore suburbs of Chicago. We both know what that kitchen looked like, right? Viking stove nobody ever cooked in: check. Gretchen's marriage was unraveling just as all of this was beginning, so of everyone, perhaps she should have known better. But she loved her brother, Chad, who loved my brother, Miguel, who once upon a time knew Emily, before she was your wife. The story of how they all came together again is random, as chaotic as everything that happens in our lives, and yet not: *we* were their intersection, Nick. We are to blame, for life, for death, for everything.

Besides, if even one person had known better, where would I be now?

Still, there you have them: our ensemble cast. The movers and shakers of the Community Baby Plan. All the pieces on the board now. Who will be the queen; who will be the knight; who will be the pawn?

Isabel is still in the shadows, I know. I'm aiming for that Virginia Woolf thing, that "absent presence," but all I really know for sure is blank space. An Isabel in dirty cotton underpants, left behind. A tragic thirteen-year-old pawn, protecting Mami, the queen, when that's not *half* the picture, has nothing to do with the Isabel I grew up longing for and reacting against. Isabel, who had nothing to do with these one-big-happy-commune surrogacy plans, who would have been appalled if anyone had possessed the nerve to breathe a word of it to her. And yet her body in many ways is ground zero—for what came before us and what came after. The damage and the beauty that, in turn, was waiting for us all.

We live every day on top of fault lines, Nick—well, I don't need to tell you that. What I mean is that maybe *everybody* does, at every moment, and it's just that some people don't hide it well—we wear visible rifts and fissures on our skin and in our eyes, in our disreputable professions and fringe lifestyles and mile-long medical charts. For others, the shifting plates are way below ground, biding time where no one can see them, everything on the surface Stepford-pretty while underneath, forces are brewing that can swallow entire cities whole.

I'm trying to wrap my head around what lies beneath. Around what people who are not like me might call the Truth. But for me, truth only ever slides around like the mercury from a broken thermometer, ricocheting inside a white sink—truth offers two choices: touch it and be poisoned, or watch it wash down the drain.

You may think that because of my "episodes" I can't be trusted with our story—that I'm too damaged. But *all* stories are altered by perspective—and you would never say that anyway. That's just my own voice, or maybe Isabel's, still talking to me inside my head. Besides, with our cast, it's easy to see how things could go awry. And so they did.

All the texts I sent you the night I left Bebe are still on my phone. I don't have a wife or two sons; I don't even have a girlfriend anymore: I have no reason to delete anything. I allowed my phone to run out of batteries and stashed it in a drawer with my Self-Destruction Survival Kit. The needle, the lighter, the spoon. They've been in the same bag for six years; most nights, I don't give them a second thought. My dead phone, though, has become an increasingly noisy siren; it glows like something radioactive, I can't keep it quiet in my head. I've thrown the power cord away, but I swear I feel like I could plug my fingers in a socket and light up the History of Us. How many "load earlier messages" would I have to scroll through to get to our beginning? How many new texts would I find from you, after I let my phone go dark and abandoned you to the nightmare ensuing? Would yours be as frantic as the ones I sent you that last night?

I need you.

They spiraled out from there, longer, messier, but always between us, things came back to the same starting point:

Nick? I need you.

The first time I told you I wanted you to hit me, I asked, "Do you have a problem with that?" You laughed and said, "I'm guessing you haven't met many people who had a problem with that." But you'd be surprised. You said, "The thing is, I don't know how to hurt someone without *hurting* them," then caught me off guard by offering, "You could show me first, on me, what you like." Bebe always maintained that the recommendation of "tops" trying things out on themselves first to "know how it feels" was idiotic—if she doesn't experience pain as pleasure, how would burning herself, or testing a cane on her skin, give her a clue about my experience? It would only suck. But when I parroted her words to tell you I wasn't interested in topping, that it would ruin the dynamic so that when you did it to me it wouldn't feel real, you said, "Those are just labels, that's a load of shit—we're both here. *We're* real."

You'd say I'm hiding behind sex again, bringing all that up at a time like this. But what I'm trying to say is: we *were* real, Nick. I'm afraid by the time you're done reading this, you'll think we were nothing but a game to me, a challenge or a role-play or a means to an end. This is the part where usually I cut my losses and run. There are only so many options, only so many potential outcomes to any story. Heartbeats can be rectified. Your heart is still beating out in the world, and I am here, without you, without Bebe, and I can cling to this new thing with both hands or I can just let go.

There are so many things I need to tell you here, before I can tell you the one thing you really need to know. But try showing me a story that isn't about secrets, the sins of the fathers. That isn't about desire, lies, family, loss, and what it takes to survive. You show me any tangled knot of people that doesn't simultaneously exemplify both loyalty and betrayal. Is a baby any different than a lover when it comes to the endless, unwinnable war over who owns love? You show me anything worth losing, Nick, that doesn't at some point give way to jealousy, entitlement, possession, even if that's exactly what we were all trying to avoid.

ACT I

THE COMMUNITY BABY

YOU CAN DRIVE THE DEVIL OUT OF YOUR GARDEN BUT YOU WILL FIND HIM AGAIN IN THE GARDEN OF YOUR SON.

—JOHANN HEINRICH PESTALOZZI

GRETCHEN

Something is wrong with Gretchen's son Gray when he sits down in the breakfast nook. He looks different, alien, but Gretchen can't place it. She keeps staring at him and it's like she's taken someone else's black coat accidentally in the pile of coats at a party, when she's a little bit drunk and the coat looks like hers and maybe is even the same designer but something is implacably wrong. She watches Gray as though feeling inside the pockets of this wrong coat, hoping for some evidence of its wrongness or, better yet, clues to whom it actually belongs.

Troy saunters into the room for coffee, looking sexy and angular and hateful like someone who would be cast to play a Nazi in a miniseries, and takes one look at Gray and says, "Where the hell are his eyebrows?"

"Huh?" Gretchen says.

"Why doesn't our kid have eyebrows?" Troy snaps, and they both turn back to Gray, who is shoveling cereal into his mouth. For an instant, their eyes meet above his head in a rare moment of collusion: Is it possible that Gray has *never* had eyebrows? Has he been eyebrowless from the get-go, and somehow Gretchen and Troy forgot to . . . *notice* until now?

Gretchen glances at a photograph on the hutch of the three of them in better-if-still-not-good times, when Gray was maybe three, and no—thank God!—there are his eyebrows in the photograph. Kind of pale, but definitely present. She says, "Uh, Gray, honey. Did something happen to your face?"

"Did something happen to my face," Gray states in that inflectionless way of his.

"Yes. Your face."

"Your eyebrows!" Troy says. "For Christ's sake, Gretch, be specific at least, what are you trying to say? Are you asking him if he's had a facelift? Are you asking if he has a black eye? Say what you mean!"

"Your eyebrows." Gretchen feels herself turning red. "Where did they . . . go?"

Gray laughs.

"Did you shave your eyebrows, honey?"

Gray spits milk and cereal chunks into his bowl, giggling. "No!"

She and Troy are both on him now, standing above him, handling his face, searching for clues. There are still some strays protruding from his fair skin, which is reddish around where the missing hair should be. Troy pokes her too hard in the arm and mouths, *What the fuck?*, but Gretchen says quietly, "Gray, did you *pull* your eyebrows out?"

"Why are you yelling?" shouts Gray.

"I'm not yelling, honey."

"Stop yelling at me!" Gray bolts from the table, knocking some of the milk from his bowl.

"Oh my God," Gretchen says to Troy. "What are we going to do?"

"Do you have an eyebrow pencil?" Troy asks.

"No, I don't. Do *you*?"

"Why would I—what's wrong with my eyebrows?"

"I don't understand how he did it," Gretchen says. "Did he spend all night pinching his little eyebrow hairs one by one and yanking them out at the root? Why would he do that? I didn't even know that was possible."

"I love how in Gray's moment of crisis," Troy says, "you manage to twist this around so that you're implying that something is wrong with my eyebrows."

Gretchen huffs out of the room. Troy doesn't follow her; she can hear him pouring coffee into his portable mug and then, seconds later, exiting into the garage—its door rising—presumably on his way to the gym, where he goes every morning (or pretends to go every morning). Gretchen heads upstairs to Gray's bedroom, some of the wind stupidly taken out of her sails by the fact that Troy didn't chase her. The last two years of her life have been marked by more Bette Davis exits than the whole forty years prior, but now that she is thinking of it, not one such departure has ever been met with anyone pursuing her. She leaves rooms in a thunder but no one ever seems to care that she is gone.

Inside Gray's bedroom, he is playing with a model of the Titanic. These models—he has seven or eight of them—are not really toys; they're expensive and kind of fragile and clunky—but since discovering the Titanic, Gray has taken little interest in anything else. After having spent the bulk of preschool and pre-K being the subject of parent-teacher meetings because he seemed wholly disinterested in learning the alphabet, suddenly, still months shy of his sixth birthday, Gray knows how to read at a fourth-grade level and spends his every free moment on the family room computer researching ship disasters and writing by hand elaborate lists of the names of every ship whose sinking has ever been documented. Gretchen is alternately thrilled by his precocious reading skills and . . . well, utterly creeped out.

"You need to get ready for school," Gretchen tells him. He fails to look up. "You still have to go to school today. If the other kids make fun of you about your eyebrows . . ." She wants to say, *Then maybe you shouldn't have fucking yanked them out of your head*, but instead makes herself say, "I'm sure Daddy will have an eyebrow pencil for you by the time he gets home tonight."

"I'm ready," Gray says. "You're the one in your pajamas."

Gretchen looks down at her body. She's wearing a nightgown, but she drives Gray to school and was just planning to put her raincoat on over it, which she thinks he should know by now, so he must just be acting rude intentionally, copying the way Troy talks to her. Still, shamed, she stalks into her own bedroom to put on sweats (Troy would say *these* are pajamas, too, although he just left the house in track pants for the gym. *You aren't going to the gym*, he would counter if she said that). They're already late—they are late to school pretty much every day—but Gretchen can't stop herself from sinking onto her bed and plugging into her iPhone: *kid pulls out his eyebrows.*

WebMD says: *Trichotillomania is a type of impulse-control disorder. Impulse-control disorders are mental illnesses that involve the repeated failure to resist impulses, or urges, to act in ways that are dangerous or harmful. People with these disorders know that they can hurt themselves or others by acting on the impulses, but they cannot stop themselves.*

Fuck. Fuck fuck fuck fuck.

She catches a glimpse of herself in the mirror: her Middle American embarrassing sweatpants, her disheveled hair, her own pale eyebrows that could be absent when glimpsed through a mirror all the way across the room—evidence that, clearly, an eyebrow pencil *should* be in her repertoire.

The thing about getting your child to school so ungodly early in the morning is that, if you have a Normal Child, you are probably desperate to get their loud, messy, sticky little personage out of your house to get some peace and quiet. Whereas Gretchen could go about her business and not hear from Gray for the rest of the day while he played with his overpriced models, chronicled marine disasters, and engaged in "failure to resist impulses." As a baby, he never cried, even when he was hungry. It was like owning a fish; Gretchen sometimes feared: if you forgot to feed it, it sent no signals, it just . . . died. She was often nervous that something would happen to Gray on her watch—that he didn't seem to have the proper instincts of self-preservation and that she was, in the business of keeping him alive, more alone than she was supposed to be.

On that note, she stands with renewed purpose. At least at school, presumably, someone will notice if he attempts to scalp himself.

Gretchen's parents have taken, in their advancing age, to throwing parties in the daytime. It's her mother's sixty-fifth birthday, and her parents are hosting an adults-only luncheon at the country club, which is an excruciatingly specific insult to Gretchen, given that Gray is the only child in the family, the only one they had to go out of their way to make sure was not in attendance. Gretchen is galled, though not enough so to lose awareness that she is also relieved to be there alone—Troy wouldn't dream of coming these days—unencumbered of either. Her mother will be irritated that Gretchen is wearing a pantsuit to her party, but cocktail dresses make Gretchen feel like a transvestite. She is nearly six feet tall, thick-calved, hearty, suggestive of appetites. Her mother has often cautioned her never to wear her hair pulled back, lest she resemble a Polish cleaning woman. When she was young she was a tennis jock, skilled enough to excuse her lack of daintiness, and even to play professionally—briefly, but long enough to become acquainted with legions of other low-tier pros like herself and to marry one. Now she works with numbers, though to describe exactly how would be sadistically dull.

Her parents and all of their friends are socially unbearable, but Gretchen's brother Chad will save the day. Even if this were not a major birthday, she and Chad have long understood, as most children raised by Money do, the unspoken, nonnegotiable requirement that they put in an appearance *anywhere* to which their parents extend an invitation. It is the old-money equivalent of aspiring Mafiosos kissing a ring.

Standing alone waiting for her brother to arrive, armed only with her second vodka tonic and leaning against a baby grand, Gretchen feels the anticipatory shiver of what she is about to do once Chad arrives. She feels like a spy with a secret, in a delicious way that temporarily eclipses the infuriating secrets Troy has lately imposed on her life. It thrills her to imagine how scandalized all the geriatric, Republican guests would be if they knew that she, in her sensible pantsuit, with her sensible accounting job and sensible mid-length bob, is planning to give her gay brother her eggs so that he and his (foreign-born! Latino!) partner can procreate. Her stomach tilts and pitches with the anxiety of her own heroism. Albeit, the intimacy implied by egg-gifting weirdly exceeds her actual shared history with her brother, which in childhood was comprised mainly of being shuffled around by separate nannies to their separately overscheduled activities. She is one year older and has no memories of Chad as a baby—her dominant recollection of his significance in her early life is speculating with her junior high friends as to when he would make a grand revelation of the obvious and come out of the closet. She began expecting this by the time Chad was eleven, and by the time it occurred, when he was twenty-two, even their father had figured it out, though their mother still cried as though being filmed by *Candid Camera: Disgraced WASPs Edition*.

Chad is late . . . typical of him, a workaholic, like their father once was, like Gretchen herself has become in an effort to avoid Troy. Signal her third drink, consumed alone, and with it, Third Drink Thoughts. Chad's partner Miguel (they say "husband," but let's face it, their marriage is not legal—not that Gretchen *agrees* with that, but still, it's not) thinks it is a secret that he believes Gretchen to be a lesbian, but it is nothing resembling a secret, and it annoys her.

Gretchen is not a lesbian—is not even colorfully bi despite her athleticism and attendance at Wellesley, where being bi for a semester seemed part of the undergrad prereq curriculum for females in the late eighties. Lately, she barely feels heterosexual, either, however, and would classify her sexual orientation as Done With It, Frankly. If only Miguel knew the ferocity with which she once wanted Troy: a wanton, out-of-character lust that now feels embarrassing enough to strangle her. She imagines Troy laughing about it with his friends—Gretchen's desperately whorish behavior during their courtship—but in reality, she doubts she ever comes up in his private conversations at all.

Recently, in Troy's "personal" account, she found confusing credit card payments to what seemed to be an interactive Russian porn site. Her ire was raised, her righteous indignation sparked, and like a fool in a horror flick who doesn't know when to flee the house, she went prying around in the figurative basement looking for the monster. Turns out, Troy has spent some four grand on an (specifically Soviet) escort service. Gretchen and Troy have not made love for more than two years. But . . . Russians? Where did *that* come from?

It is unclear how one should proceed in such circumstances. Gretchen does not have a prenup, though everyone told her to get one, even her mother, who never says anything that later proves true. When she and Troy met thirteen years ago, he was intimidatingly handsome and wickedly funny and made her yell things while coming that were worse than an all-pants wardrobe, manners wise. He was talented in bed the way Gretchen now supposes it benefits a sociopath to be. If she kicks him to the curb, he will take half her money and might sue for custody of Gray. She has meant to consult a shark attorney to investigate her options, but in order to find an attorney who would be suitable in her family's eyes, Gretchen would have to ask around and get referrals, which would mean admitting her predicament to at least one other human being. Therefore, she has mainly just gone to work and crunched numbers, and taken copious amounts of Valium while drinking Ketel One on the sofa in her home office, in between chauffeuring Gray to his many over-scheduled activities, all of which seem to go more badly for him than Gretchen recalls anything ever going for *her* as a child, or even for Chad. Other children do not like Gray, and Gray does not seem to like them, either. Toileting accidents are involved. Biting.

This not having eyebrows thing is surely not going to help.

Her anticipation and the vodka have morphed from titillation into full-on roiling nausea.

Enter Chad.

Gretchen sees Chad's and Miguel's shirts before she sees *them*, exactly. These shirts are all French cuffs and collars that do not lie down in the traditional manner; they boast thick stripes and paisleys of untraditional hues. They are pretty garments, but the boys should not be wearing them on the same day: there is something Teletubbies about it. Both Chad and the usually subdued Miguel seem unfeasibly delighted to see her, which hints that they may have been discussing the egg matter all the way from the city. They hug her and beam, as though something wildly interesting will be said, though Gretchen is not a cornucopia of fascinating tidbits, and Miguel, while known to mutter amusingly snide comments, usually does so low under his breath so that no one else can hear.

Fine then, if it is all but a foregone conclusion, Gretchen will be interesting. Finally, she has something to say.

"So, I've thought it over," she begins with pep-squad-level cheer, "and why not? I don't see why not! You want some of my eggs, you can have them—they're yours."

But Miguel's brow furrows in confusion. It is immediately clear that his only context for "eggs" involves Sunday brunch. Chad, on the other hand, is tearing up.

"This is so incredibly generous of you," Chad says, hugging her again. "Honestly, Miguel, can you *believe* this? I don't even know what to say, Gret—you're amazing! Thank you! Isn't she amazing, honey?"

"She's amazing," Miguel concurs, deadpan. "But. Uh. What are we supposed to do with an egg? Build a laboratory in our house and hatch it?"

"Oh, there are gestational surrogates, honey," Chad says, his eyes catching light like small marbles.

"Surrogates?" Miguel snorts. "You mean, like, impoverished people renting their wombs because it's illegal to actually sell your organs?"

Disappointment bubbles in Gretchen's throat, blindsiding her. Her goofball brother came with a hand out for her eggs, without even *mentioning* it to the other baby daddy? Jesus, her family. Though honestly, when Chad first brought this up on the phone a week ago, it never occurred to Gretchen that *she* would agree. The matter struck her as one it was only polite to feign thinking on for some time, as a show of seriousness, yet then to decline as simply being "too much"—something surely no one, even her brother, could begrudge. But stealthily in the ensuing days, an axis shifted. Why would she deny her sweet brother a chance to be a father? Why would she deny Gray the chance for other children in the family? Why would she deny *herself* the chance to do something useful—something unusual and positive and colorful—for once? As quickly as desire assaulted her, however, Miguel has nixed it, and Gretchen feels alone in a hallway all over again, inconsequential, a replay of her morning. She gulps the dregs of her drink in confusion and shame.

"Chad only said *eggs*," she explains to Miguel haltingly. "He never mentioned anything about the rest of the nine yards. He never said anything about . . . carrying it. I mean . . ." She remembers the phrase: *too much*. Maybe everything *is* clicking into place as it's meant to—this was a crazy thing to want, even momentarily.

"Chad only said?" Miguel repeats. "Like, as in, Chad *asked*? Chad . . . asked for your eggs, and never . . . thought to tell me?"

"There's nothing disreputable about surrogacy," Chad says as though Miguel isn't speaking. "Women who aren't able to carry a pregnancy to term hire surrogates all the time. It's a perfectly legitimate way to bring in extra income."

"Wow," Miguel says. "Somebody's been doing his homework on the sly."

"So I take it you guys have never talked about this," Gretchen says, feeling her head bobbing in a nod. "Um. Having children?"

"We've talked about it," Chad says at the exact same instant Miguel says, "Why would we have talked about that?"

"Well," Gretchen says, louder than her usual voice. "This isn't awkward at all. I'm so glad I brought it up."

Miguel seems to come to his senses. She watches something pass across his dark eyes and ease his highly arched and decadently sensual brows. He is too handsome to strike her as entirely trustworthy, the irony of which is not lost on her since she, too, married an untrustworthily handsome man. She is not sure what she thinks Miguel might be up to, but a face like that is often attached to something nefarious.

"God," Miguel says. "I'm being a total jerk. Gret, you're a rock star, it's unbelievable of you to offer us your eggs, it's, seriously—it's the nicest thing anyone has ever . . . I mean, who *does* that? You're amazing—" He draws in breath jaggedly, like someone whose ribs are broken. "I'm sure there's a perfectly good explanation for why Chad attempted to reproduce without consulting me. Probably just a small crack addiction or something—a minor annoyance—nothing that can't be cured by a stint in . . . where do you people go? Hazelton?"

"Well, Silver Hill is better," Gretchen says earnestly.

Chad elbows her.

"I'm just not sure I get it," Gretchen continues, stepping away from Chad. "You guys had more guests at your ceremony than Troy and I did. What was all that *for* if not to signal to the world that it's all right to have kids? Why else would anyone get married?"

"Plenty of people get married and don't have children," says Miguel, who is from someplace in Latin America that Gretchen can never remember and has probably never met any such person in his entire life.

"But," Chad bursts in, "we've never had an opportunity like this before, either. We always assumed we'd have to adopt, and one of us would have to pretend to be a single straight man or something, and probably be investigated as a potential pedophile running a sex-slave racket—it's not like we can just walk into any agency and say, 'Hi, my husband and I would like to adopt a desirably young and healthy infant,' waving a rainbow flag. We never really considered it because it seemed like a really . . . uphill climb."

"*That's* why we didn't consider it?" Miguel asks. He doesn't sound sarcastic anymore. He sounds genuinely confused.

Gretchen waves her empty glass subtly. There is a bar, but if she waves her glass like so for a while, someone will appear and take it from her hand and reappear with a fresh vodka tonic. She has a feeling that she should be uncomfortable, but what Chad is saying makes so much sense that she just turns to Miguel and lays a reassuring hand on his arm.

"You have to understand," she explains. "You may not realize this because of how driven he is at his job, but on a very fundamental level, Chad and I were taught that we would never have to work at anything. If something seems like it would be a lot of work, it must be the wrong direction, clearly, and you should just give up now and redirect."

"That's not what I meant!" Chad protests. "What are you, Emma Goldman—you're always acting like we're so psychologically challenged just because we didn't grow up with dirt floors like Miguel. What you're saying isn't true at all."

Miguel, though, nods. He places his hand on Chad's arm so that they are standing there, a chain of people with reassuring hands upon each other's arms, and empty drink glasses dangling from the hands not busy with reassurance, waiting for automatic refills. "Yeah, Chad," Miguel says, smiling almost sweetly. "It really, really is."

MIGUEL

How does a man decide to become a father, when for as long as he can remember, fathers have been everything he hates and fears?

If fatherhood is nothing Miguel is practiced at, seething he has made his life's art. He starts with Chad, of course. Entitled, feckless Chad, who understands nothing of the wildly infinite variables of things that can go wrong in life, who barrels forward, who never *asks*. Chad, who was raised by a parade of nannies his eccentric (read: batshit) mother often fired for reasons having to do with an irrational belief that they were moving her furniture around, and yet he seems to have emerged unscathed. This always baffled Miguel in a good way—proof of Chad's elementally positive nature—but now it enrages him.

"You work ninety hours a week," he rails, unprompted, in the middle of *The Daily Show*. "You'd be a plantation daddy. Who do you think is going to raise this fictitious kid of ours?"

Chad regards him like a floor where the shards from a recently broken glass have been swept up, but you never know what may still lurk, too small to be seen. "Um," he counters, hedging, "because the thing is, lots of parents have . . . jobs?"

Miguel can't pin down the language for his minefield of emotions. As the days pass since Gretchen's offer, he oscillates between taciturn and snarky, withholds sex like a 1950s wife, makes biting comments about Chad in front of others. He is an asshole. He is obsessed.

He wants the baby. He is terrified of the baby. He has never been around a baby in his entire adult life. Everything else in his midst has become porous and insubstantial.

How can it be that he has gone forty years without the slightest inkling to parent—without the most cursory interest in babies—and now this? His desire can only be likened to what it felt like to long for male bodies in the 1980s as a closeted high school student: dark, dangerous, all-consuming, bottomlessly hungry. Babies are pink- and blue-clad, powdery-smelling, tender things, but the teeth of Miguel's need are sharp. This is proof (*why* is this proof? Being gay certainly turned out nowhere near as catastrophically as he feared) that he should avoid fatherhood altogether, that he doesn't have the proper wiring.

Guerra men are crazy. Guerra men are violent. Miguel is the last Guerra man standing. Guerra men should not attempt to raise any defenseless beings just to fuck them up; the lineage should die with Miguel altogether.

Of course, the fictional baby could be a girl. But Guerra women aren't much better. Mami's all right, but that's because she's not a Guerra by blood. Miguel is sandwiched between two women of epic demons: Isabel, his elder sister, and Angelina, aka Lina, Miguel's younger sister . . . sort of.

Chad shows attempts at understanding. "I know you didn't have the happiest childhood." His hand rubs circles on Miguel's back and it is all Miguel can do not to buck him off. "I know your father died young and you never really had a male role model. I know a traditional nuclear family was never anything you wanted, exactly."

Miguel seethes in his thrashing, unnamed wanting. The mountain of truths Chad does not know, forever looming in their distance, can only be called Miguel's fault.

The family's progression to dirt had been in stages. First, when Papi worked, there were cracked stucco walls, crumbly concrete floors, dirt only on the roads. But by the time Miguel started school, Papi slept during the day, and floors and roads had become indistinguishable. Mountains lay forever on the horizon, no matter where they moved: San Felipe, Caracas. "Chicago is flat," Mami said over and over of the city where she'd been raised. She'd left to follow Papi—also an American, by way of Cuba—down to Venezuela, where some cousin wanted to go into business with him, before Miguel was even born. That short-term venture was far behind them now, lost in the dust of their perpetual movement. "Chicago is flat," Mami always said, but their family never went to the mountains; peaks simply loomed like a taunt. People in the mythic Chicago were better off that they did not know the beauty they were missing.

Isbael, thirteen, and Miguel, nine, shared the tiny second bedroom, slept together in one bed. Isabel complained that Miguel slept too close, made her sweat in her sleep until her hair frizzed, but whenever he woke in the night, Isabel's arm was slung over him protectively, and he loved the slick of her skin glued against his. Their bed was where he felt the safest. Lately, whenever Papi was home, Miguel had to sleep in the living room on two wicker chairs pushed together to make a bed, because Papi said Isabel was too old to share with a boy. When Mami was alone with the children, she did not care where Miguel slept. Her own bed had space, but Mami cried in the night, and Isabel told Miguel they needed the quiet of their own room so they could do well in school. Miguel knew they both found school an effortless refuge, were fluent in two languages and could see math inside their heads, so Isabel's words were obviously a euphemism for some other reason they should not go into Mami's room. Miguel had a dim awareness that children should not witness their parents' tears, but Mami had been crying for so long that this seemed to him like something said in church, a pretty symbol that had no bearing on reality.

In the small yard out back, vegetables grew, but not well. Mami was an American city girl; the way her tomatoes bruised and caved in as if under a hex was the cause of many fights. Afterward, Isabel would say of Mami, Su piel se ha puesto como estos tomates—algun dia, el se la comera tambien. *Miguel was afraid of this image of his father wolfing down his mother's tendered skin in lieu of her faulty tomatoes, but he couldn't concentrate on that fear because there were too many mistakes to work to keep from making, or he would become the target of Papi's anger. Nothing he did was ever right. Papi railed at Mami that the house was a mess and beat her for it, but if Miguel tried to help his mother clean, Papi said Mami was making him into a girl, and hit them both. Only Isabel was unafraid of Papi. She provoked. When he passed out, she laid handkerchiefs over his face to watch them soar.*

In the beginning of Caracas, when Papi would disappear for a few days, Miguel was suffused with giddiness, like Christmas morning the one time they'd visited Abuela in Chicago, when Papi was still working and they had saved money all year for the airplane. Lately, when Papi disappeared, it was for longer, and they grew hungry. When Papi was home and beat Mami, sometimes Mami cried, but those tears made sense because she was being struck. When Papi was gone and Mami cried alone in her small room, behind the red curtain, her tears seemed more ominous. Isabel would stand twisting her hands just outside the curtain, like a bride hesitating to cross the threshold. Other times she mocked just out of Mami's earshot, Aye, my children are starving, what will I do, they're going to drop dead right in front of my eyes, poor me, poor me, I would go and get a job but then who would cry in my bedroom all day long, sweet Jesus, this is a full-time job, you know! *until Miguel was choking with laughter. The hunger scraped in Miguel's stomach and made concentration difficult, but he carried awareness that it was not* starvation—*that he was not yet willing to trade other luxuries for food.*

Once, the wicker chairs separated while Miguel tried to sleep on them, and Miguel, half-somnolent, spread his thin blanket onto the dirt floor and fell back asleep. He woke to an itching on his back that, when scratched, lurched around inside his T-shirt like a camel's hump wanting independence. His screaming woke Mami, but she was too afraid of the rat to touch Miguel—she kept approaching, lunging back—so Isabel straddled him, yanked the garment over his head with one swift motion so forceful that, released, he fell back against the dirt with a thud. Looming above him, moonlight haloing her curls the color of dead leaves, Isabel touched his face only once before standing. The rat had scuttled away, gone before they could even think to get a broom, to corner and kill it as Papi sometimes did—not that they were up to the task. In Mami's bedroom, Papi snored on, unconcerned with their daily trials and fears. Miguel's back stung like being belted whenever he or Isabel misbehaved. Once, Isabel had borne the brunt, but lately Papi had noticed that she often lied for Miguel, claimed his crimes as her own, so now Papi simply beat them both, shouting that he couldn't trust their confessions.

When Papi didn't come home from the bar, Miguel could crawl into the safe bed with his sister. How long did it take before that balance shifted, before his stomach's scraping expanded, conquered the cheap, defenseless terrain of his heart so that happiness meant nothing anymore and all he could think of was food? Nights of crying in bed, Isabel alternatingly trying to comfort him and curling up in a tight ball, her knees pressed to the wall, her own sobs swallowed and muffled. Then, though every day had seemed to last a year, the hunger itself waned, and neither affection nor food compelled him anymore.

Papi had been gone longer than a month, this time—it was nearly Miguel's tenth birthday. They had all grown thin enough that their hipbones jutted like small missiles through their thin clothes; Miguel's elbows and knees were wider than the limbs they held together. When there was anything to eat, Mami and Isabel both attempted to give him more than they took for themselves, but the smell of food had started to make water rise into his mouth in a tidal wave of nausea. He coughed constantly, as though the dirt had invaded his lungs, the spasms tapping his energy so that running outside with his friends seemed something he had done in another, carefree lifetime. Both Miguel and Isabel missed school for so many consecutive days that returning felt almost pointless. Toward the End of Papi, Mami took Miguel into her bed even though Isabel had long prohibited this, and Miguel began to hate Isabel a little for having made it seem like such a big deal, because now he knew, when he did not want to know, that if Mami had taken him in then something ordinarily just wrong *had become* dire.

Toward the End of Papi, Mami, with her desperate city-girl mind, thought to make little fake bouquets of flowers out of cloth and paper: an entrepreneur. She filled baskets with them and cajoled Isabel to carry them door-to-door to sell like a gypsy, as if the neighbors were not almost as poor. That was the only time Miguel saw Isabel cry, refusing to go out into the street with the bouquets, humiliated. "Do you want your baby brother to starve?" Mami shouted, but Isabel sat immobile, staring at some stain on the wall. That was the only time Mami got Papi's belt, waving it like a cowboy swinging a rodeo lasso, her hysteria contrasting Isabel's rigid calm. She lunged at Isabel, snapping the belt without bothering to fold it over in her hand the way Papi did—even Miguel understood that she would lack precision. Her blows hit Isabel in all the wrong spots: her ear; her schoolbooks, the small of her back. Isabel yelped and swung back at the belt with her hands, though she did not try to run—Mami kept swinging until both were sobbing; Isabel curled into herself on the bed, not resisting the blows anymore, just allowing the belt to have its way.

"No one will buy them from me,*" Mami finally begged, all the violence in her exhausted. She leaned against the doorframe, breathing heavy. "You see the way they look at me. They'll laugh in my face."*

"If you send me out there," Isabel said, panting, "I'll throw those hideous flowers away and let some man buy my *flower instead. Even that would have more dignity."*

When he offered to take the flowers himself, Mami hesitated, but Isabel said, "No, it's better, you'll see," and thrust the basket into his hand. He despised her as he trudged door-to-door, feeling himself hover above his own dizzy body, listening to himself recite what Mami had told Isabel to say and aware in some crevice of his mind that every time someone pressed a coin into his palm, it meant one thing: a nine-year-old boy peddling homemade bouquets was such a shameful thing that even his impoverished neighbors had taken pity, overcome with gratitude that they themselves had not yet fallen so low.

When he returned home, there was enough money for butter, sugar, and corn flour: the buttered arepas were their meals, and for desert they sprinkled sugar on top.

But aren't these stories absurd? They're a goddamn "Save the Children" ad, played in the middle of the night when no one is watching TV. They're the tortured, white-guilt fantasies of the PC kids Miguel went to college with in the late eighties, who earnestly attended anti-apartheid meetings as though Midwestern teenagers possessed any ability to impact change in South Africa. Who would possibly *believe* this melodrama: The alcoholic, machismo father with the iron fist; long-suffering, passively weeping mother? The *rat*, for god's sake! Surely Miguel's memory is faulty, has fallen prey to embellishment.

Yet some thirty years after standing, basket in hand, at the head of his street in Caracas, where he felt himself lift out of his body for the first time, Miguel will tell Chad, "When I was a little boy, I used to eat sticks of butter," in some attempt at an explanation for why he does not want Gretchen's eggs. And poor Chad will listen, rapt, probably thinking this some quaint Venezuelan custom, understanding nothing.

All couples have their own language, and Miguel and Chad's has become one devoid of causality. In the early years of their courtship, Chad always held Miguel's hands across the table at restaurants, despite any protests Miguel might kick up, then flawlessly schmoozed his way into complimentary desert and champagne. His casual logic ("Why are gay patrons so afraid to show a little affection when the chef is obviously a queen and so are all the waiters?") seemed to cause the world to click into place around them, adapting to Common Sense According to Chad. Chad called himself a "historic preservationist" by trade, but what buildings he owned—under the auspices of his real-estate-mogul father—were comprised mainly of Section 8 housing in Englewood, one of the roughest neighborhoods on the South Side: his daily work of collecting rent from tenants or supervising workmen's restoration projects commonly consisted of having guns pulled on him, his car being vandalized, and getting punched in the face when someone couldn't pay or when he interrupted people turning tricks or dealing drugs in his unoccupied buildings. It was work Miguel would have joined the freaking military or monkhood before undertaking, but Chad called it his "passion," appeared for their every date (twice with blackened eyes, several times with mangled car) flawlessly cheerful, bubbling with enthusiasm. Miguel assumed this façade would crack once they moved in together, but it . . . didn't. Even up close and intimate, Chad really *was* the idealistic urban hero he was portrayed as in local newspaper and NPR-affiliate features: a crowd-pleasingly handsome blond Ken-doll half the gay community lusted after in the final summer of the 1990s when Chad, inexplicably, took an interest in moody Miguel and upended Miguel's life for the better.

And so, as years went by, Miguel continued to speak in light sentences, as he would to a lover of a different tongue. It has proven a relief, really, to present this partial version of himself, to live on the bright surface of things instead of the ugly, murky depths. "I was the first in my family to go to college," Miguel says, omitting, *I'd already slashed my wrists twice and hoped a dose of university liberalism could save me.* "Then I moved to Barcelona to improve my Spanish," he continues, without, *Travel or Prozac—the only two things that could get me out of bed after college.* "But I ran out of money, so I came home," he concludes, instead of, *I failed in starving myself to death or catching AIDS, and I'd lost the balls for outright suicide, so I didn't know what else to do.* "Love you," he dutifully chirps every night before bed, even adding, "honey," though once he would not have been caught dead.

Behind every word, every half-truth is: *Help—teach me how to be like you.*

How a man decides to become a father: because the best thing he has ever known in his life—his partner of ten years—wants it with such a boundless exuberance that eventually Miguel relents, against all his better judgments, against all his mountainous superstitions of something secretly rotten at his genetic core. How a man decides to become a father: when the will *to oppose* has been worn out of him for so many years that he capitulates, just as he did to that basket of chintzy bouquets—succumbs to Chad's coaxing hands under the blanket, to Chad's laughter, to Chad's plans for a nursery, to Chad's gentle mocking of Miguel's "adorable" third-world guilt over hiring a nanny. One day, Miguel comes home with a book of baby names A-Z, and says only, with twinges of joy and terror in equal measure, "Oh, fuck it. Why the hell not?"

A series of dinners with potential carriers ensues. But it is 2008 and everyone these days is having babies; it's hard to find an empty womb. The first Lesbian Couple they approach have spit out two already, alternating the load between them, and the moment Miguel and Chad broach the topic, it's revealed that they are knocked up with a third, skewing the balance. "We should do it next year," one member of the Lesbian Couple quips, "just to even things out," but of course they are joking. More smiles, more laughs, *Oh you'll be such great dads!* The first Single Woman they ask, teetering precariously at the tipping point between party girl and spinster, squeals over an expensive sushi dinner, gushing, "I've always wanted to experience pregnancy!" She has had a lot of sake and her cheeks are pink, her voice a breathless combination of 1940s films and faux-British accent à la Madonna, although she was raised on the west side of Chicago. She strikes Miguel as a bad actress cast in the role of their lives. Chad presses her, "You could move in with us if you wanted, while you were pregnant. Save money on rent, besides what we'd pay you. You could be like an aunt to the baby—we'd all be like family—we already are." This isn't technically true. She is a peripheral friend; they see her at parties—it is only that, being childless, parties are plentiful. She doesn't live in their *house*. But the train is moving too fast to slam on the brakes now without doing significant damage. It rolls on its own momentum such that locking down a womb for Gretchen's egg (and Miguel's sperm, obviously: it can't be Chad's or the baby would have two heads) has started to seem essential to the very fate of the world. At home they no longer debate whether they should be doing this, but fall into bed frantic with plotting, each day a womb has failed to be procured. The Single Woman's enthusiasm is a good sign; her pink cheeks are a good sign; her demented desire to go through the medieval hell of pregnancy is definitely a good sign, if not a great indicator of sanity, irrelevant since her genes are not involved. Chad can promise her a Mormon marriage and all Miguel will do is nod and smile.

Everyone they've asked is really too old, but they don't *know* any young people other than Lina, Miguel's notoriously unstable younger sister, who Chad vetoed out of the gate. "Listen," he said, though he didn't have to say it, Miguel knew. "I love Lina, but she's a drug addict. There is no fucking way, honey. Please don't take offense." Miguel was, frankly, relieved. It wasn't that he thought Lina would run out to score heroin with their child in her womb—that was a brief period (what was it about *that was a brief period* that Chad failed to understand?), and she has been her version of clean for almost six years. It's more that because Lina's body is her trade—stripping, now this crazy burlesque thing—Miguel is afraid she would flat out say no. Lina is the only member of his family who has never rejected him outright, and he is embarrassed to admit how badly he needs to keep it that way. They *can't* ask Lina's lover Bebe. She and Lina have been together since Lina was Bebe's student at UIC, dazzled by Bebe's proficiency with French feminist theory—then, before the term was over, by Bebe's even greater proficiency with restraints and riding crops. Still, even if after five years Bebe is family, Miguel has the impression that any kinship she nurses toward him does not extend to her body being treated as a waiting room by "the patriarchy." On a list of women they know, scrawled in Chad's neat-yet-immature handwriting, Miguel sees next to Bebe's name: *femi-nazi.* (Next to Angelina's, simply: *crazy.*) To ask them both—the ideologue and the stripper—could constitute a double rejection beyond endurance.

Plus, Bebe is a decade older than Lina, adding to their constituent of the middle-aged.

Beside Miguel's older sister Isabel's name, Chad has written: *pushing menopause + thinks we're going to hell.*

What to leave in and what to omit? The logistics of planning consume them.

The baby track, it turns out, is a virtual *labyrinth* of tracks: soon they have gone to see six properties for sale, and Chad has zeroed in obsessively on one historic mansion in Wicker Park selling for "about a million dollars less than it's worth" because of the small matter of a termite infestation. The floors will need to be gutted, but most of the vintage features are restorable and could remain intact: Chad's wet dream. The $1.5 million asking price is so far beyond what they can afford that at first Miguel thinks Chad is joking. Of course, he thought this when Gretchen offered them her eggs, too. Gutting eggs from a woman; gutting floors from a house: same difference. Miguel's sense of humor is failing him—he can no longer trust it as a gauge of reality.

"As soon as I inherit the business," Chad reasons, "we'll be collecting about two million dollars a *month*."

Chad's father, Charles Merry, is not even seventy. He still puts in a full day's work on every day he doesn't put in a full day's golf. He hosts Republican fundraisers at which he smokes pot in the bathroom. Chad's paternal grandmother is 101 years old. On this trajectory, Miguel reasons they will be inheriting the Merry's realty empire around the time their hypothetical baby hits college.

The Single Woman gets back to them on the same day Chad puts in an offer on Termite Mansion. "I thought I could do it," she weeps into the phone, and Miguel curses Chad silently for working late, as usual, so that he had to take this call—"but I can't."

"It's okay," he tells her, though it is anything but okay and he hates her now: How dare she not want to waste the next year of her life for his convenience? He finds himself unsavory. "Please don't worry about it . . . it's a lot to ask."

"I guess I have to come to terms with the fact that I'll never have a baby," she says, sniffing what he cannot help but believe is theatrically. People do not need to sniff that loud.

"I'm sorry to have brought all this up for you," Miguel manages. The alarm signals that come with open displays of emotion flash so bright behind his eyes that Chad may come home to find him passed out, still holding the phone. "We'll pursue our other options. You were just the first person we wanted to ask," he tacks on, because Chad has stipulated that they should tell everybody that.

What to leave in, what to omit? This track plays on repeat for weeks. Requests, met with incredulously awkward giggles or tearful refusals. It is as though they are collecting every "no" a man would normally receive from women over a lifetime of trying to bed them, all at once—it is as though a man cannot get out of this life without his quota of Nos.

Meanwhile, Miguel has never seen so many pregnant women. They are everywhere: at Starbuck's, in restaurants, even at the Board of Trade where Miguel works, and where women are a rare exotic breed.

Miguel's sonofabitch father, Javier Guerra, had no trouble making babies. Rumor was he had bastards all over Caracas. And although the situations are not remotely similar, something in Miguel that has been seething for thirty-one years, since the End of Papi, begins, slowly, to give way to grief.

Mami was looking for Miguel's shoes. Why she thought they'd be in her bedroom, Miguel couldn't guess. She had to take Miguel to the doctor to have his foot put in a cast; now that they had food at home, Mami was determined to send him back to school, so Miguel claimed a hurt foot to avoid it. When he kept the story going, Mami dragged him to the clinic. None of Miguel's friends ever went to the doctor; why did he have to be the one with a crazy mother from Chicago? Over Miguel's squirming protests, the doctor pried at him with fingers greasy from other people's sweat, proclaimed the cartilage on the ball of his foot "cracked." Mami, bubbling with doctor-faith that would later become minister-faith, meant to drag Miguel back to have his foot obscured in plaster so the doctor could grow more fat and rich.

"Wait here," Mami told him, tiptoeing into her room to search for the shoes. Behind the red curtain, Papi was passed out. He was back from wherever he'd been the past month and a half, still in the shirt he'd been wearing when he left. Miguel heard the clumsy thud of keys, bottles falling on dirt. He waited, full of hatred for the doctor and Mami, who never saw people for what they were.

"Thieving whore—you think you can trap me by hiding my keys?" Behind the red curtain, Papi's heavy feet made hollow echoes against the dirt; Mami's steps were too light to be heard until she burst through the fabric, black hair trailing, almost knocking Miguel over as she fled. Papi pursued her to the yard, where the neighbors on both sides were out

tending their gardens: watering, weeding, gathering—things his mother, the doctor-believer, did not know how to do properly. The neighbors turned their lazy eyes to Papi. He was just violent enough to be a bit of novelty, even in their violence-splattered lives. Papi caught Mami's hair in a fist; like a yo-yo, her face made contact with Papi's curled knuckles, which were perpetually split and purple, like a woman's hidden parts. Mami's bones made a louder noise than feet on dirt, but her muffled cry was similar: an echo inside her own chest. Miguel buried his head in his knees. Let him stop now, God, let him stop now, I promise I'll go to the doctor like Mami wants.

Then: Isabel's screams. Isabel, running from the front yard. Mami was on her knees, one catching the hem of her dress taut and hunching her over, the fabric too stiff to stretch. Papi held her hair at the scalp, no movement permitted. Mami had become a twig, easy to crack, from saving flour, butter, and sugar for Miguel. Through her skin, sharp bones. The crunching of knuckle on jaw, knuckle on shoulder blade, knuckle on teeth. Blood on Papi's hand. Was that where the purple came from—dried blood and dirt, never washed from some other beating? In the past month, had Papi been at some other lady's house, as Isabel always said, collecting blood to stain his jagged fingers? Or was the discoloration merely an aging man's decay, waiting for Miguel someday, too? Now, Isabel in the yard, a whirlwind in bare feet, shaking the fence. The neighbors stared: the girl was too proud, she and her American mother both. Ayudenla! Ayuden a mi mami, ayudenla! *Who did the child think she was, asking they get involved? That man was crazy—they had enough troubles of their own.*

"Isabel!" Mami's voice, weak but rising like a sharp note, stilling the air. "Go in the house!" The neighbors did not comprehend English, Mami's command a reassuring proof of her otherness, her lesser-than-their-own humanity. "Take Miguel inside—now!"

Limbs flew. Isabel, soaring through the air with the grace of a savage ballerina in grand jeté—landing in a jumble of limbs on her father's back, all gnarled ponytail, bare thighs, and dirty cotton underpants. Papi reeled; at thirteen, Isabel was a woman already, breasts and substance; he collapsed to his knees, flung her off by bending over so she flipped like TV kung fu: back against dirt, dress above her hips, collar still in Papi's grip. Mami scampered to her feet, gathered Miguel tight—she did not seem to know her face was pulpy. The neighbors glanced at one another, worried. Would the snotty American lady go away and leave him to beat the girl for show? They did not want to see him beat the little girl.

From the ground, Isabel shouted, phlegm and authority: "Mami—take him, take *him!"*

By the sockets of his left arm, Mami dragged. Around to the front of the house, down the street, farther, farther. Where could they be going? Mami almost never went anywhere; her prospective destination was a mystery. Maybe she would make the doctor look at her face, too, along with Miguel's phantomly damaged foot. They traveled away, *off the block, clutching to each other, a beast with four legs—Mami did not stop pulling until Miguel was uncertain where he was. He shivered in the burning sunlight, felt boneless and floppy with exhaustion; though he was nearly as tall as she was, his mother hoisted him on her sharp hip and carried him onward, as if on legs made of steel. The color of the sun was different now, a furious light trying to break through the shadows of evening's approach. They stood on an unknown corner, strangers glancing now and then at them, though as with the neighbors nobody approached or intervened. Mami's face was a fighter's, her nose broken, so much blood down the front of her that Miguel's left side, where she'd held him, was drenched in it. For once, she was not crying.*

The next week, she and Miguel would go to the doctor and the doctor would say of Mami's nose, Sorry, nothing we can do for you, *while Miguel's healthy foot twitched in its cast.*

The week after that, Papi would be dead.

Since being a stripper apparently wasn't bizarre enough for Lina, now she is playing the role of a shrink in a zombie burlesque. None of the rest of the Guerra clan would be caught dead, so it is on Miguel—who has over the past decade become something like the family ambassador to the country of Crazy Lina—to purchase tickets and go watch his younger sister swath her nudity in a white sheet she maneuvers like a juggler, daring it to fall. She is the star of the play—the romantic lead.

The play has been going on for a couple of months now, but Miguel was not exactly frantic to get here. This is the final night, so it was now or never. There have been, unfeasibly, fantastic reviews, starred recommendations everywhere. A production of the same show has started in Minneapolis, which is not exactly the same as being picked up by HBO, but is admittedly quite a bit better than the hurling of rotten tomatoes Miguel originally envisioned. There are murmurs of New York—of finding a bigger theater in Chicago and reopening . . . it may all be talk, but Miguel is still eating humble pie.

Just as she had never shown the slightest indication of being a dyke prior to moving in with Bebe, likewise Lina, who unbeknownst to their mother started stripping when she was twenty, never mentioned any desire to act. One day, about four months ago, she was shopping at Trader Joe's when a random man approached her and asked if she was an actress. It seemed such an obvious pickup line that Miguel objected when Lina called him afterward to say she was going to "audition" for the guy. The play itself sounded so demented, Miguel couldn't believe it wasn't a scam. *Zombies*, Lina explained (as though she were someone who often began sentences with the word *zombies*), attack a psychiatric hospital and naturally eat the brains of those interned there, but then the zombies begin to exhibit signs of the psychiatric diseases of the patients whose brains they devoured. "This is the stupidest thing I have ever heard," Miguel kept saying. "You're going to end up chained to a wall while this so-called writer/

director does experiments on you in his basement—he's going to eat *your* brain." He'd assumed the whole shebang was taking place in the back room of a dive bar, and when Lina mentioned a smallish but reputable theater in the North Center area—one Miguel had once bought Chad a subscription to for Christmas—he scoffed, even though he knew she wasn't lying.

"Way to be supportive, big brother," Lina said. "You're going to make me crush and cook all Mami's morphine and shoot it into my neck just to drown out your negativity."

"You have neck-shooting paraphernalia lying around the house, do you?" Miguel asked, what he hoped was lightly.

"Sure," Lina said; he heard her dragging on her cigarette. "I keep everything I need for one shot. This shit is a *choice*, or it isn't real."

"That sounds profoundly masochistic."

Her laugh came as an indelicate snort.

A generation removed when they were kids, his younger sister—thirty, twice-divorced, twelve-stepping her ass off, and living with a lesbian-chic English professor—has become his closest friend. As such, their low-level enabling of one another's vices and weaknesses is an unspoken given, hence Miguel said nothing to the effect that taking the morphine pills their mother was supposed to use for her sciatica (but Mami would have nothing to do with them—left "perfectly good drugs" to rot) was not exactly *clean*. He also said nothing because *he* kept half the pills for himself—or what Lina, who had absconded with the original bottle, passed off as "half." Plus, whereas everyone else in his family has either implicitly or explicitly made clear that his homosexuality is an abomination, Lina has admiringly followed in Miguel's footsteps in choosing a same-sex partner, the way one might go to med school if one's successful older sibling happened to be a doctor.

Now his baby sister is backstage, presumably engaging in last-minute tactics to keep her violently white sheet from exposing her inside holes and cracks to the audience while she pirouettes around like a lunatic. Miguel chain-smokes outside until he has no choice but to go to his seat in the front row with Chad.

"You're cute," Chad says, leafing through the program without looking at it. "You're ready to jump out of your skin. The protective *papi* with a baseball bat at the front door when some jerk comes to pick up your little *hija* for her first date."

"I cannot believe this is happening," Miguel says.

"I don't understand how you can not see how awesome this is," Chad says sadly.

The house lights have dimmed and people are mildly quiet. Suddenly, Miguel feels a repeated whacking on his shoulder. He turns around.

"Mike!" The woman behind him stage-whispers, shaking his shoulder now. "Holy smoke! I can't believe it's you."

Miguel *knows* her; it isn't that he doesn't know her. It is only that he can't place anything that *matters* about this fact, like how they are acquainted, or her name.

"Heeey," he drawls, quiet but with an upward lilt to his voice, cautious. "So great to see you. Uh." He elbows Chad, taking a chance. "This is my husband, Chad."

"Oh my god," the woman says, laughing. "The stud of Lane Tech, secretly batting for the other team all along. Wow, what a relief—I was so in love with you—I was going to have to go home and cry into my pillow tonight now that I'd seen you and you're still so hot!"

Jesus Christ. It is *Emily.*

Miguel fights a sudden impulse to stand up, half fling himself across the chair backs that separate them, and embrace her.

Someone has come out onstage. Emily pats his shoulder, nodding, gesturing with quick sweeping motions of her fingers that he should look forward, at the stage. In this gesture he sees that she is a mother now, and wonders how many children she has.

Emily—a mother. Emily, a grown woman. Not that Miguel has thought of her often, but on the occasions he has, she was of course locked into his memory as a teenage girl. Never exactly *beautiful*, there was something about her at seventeen, a wounded charm that men universally find appealing. Her skirts were always too short, and she was endlessly pulling them down as though someone else had dressed her and she was surprised by their length. When harsh winds blew, as they all walked west on Addison past the stadium to hang in the McDonald's parking lot, pouring stolen booze into soda cups and getting shit-faced through straws, Emily used to hold on to his arm, and once, in the most evil stretch of winter, he'd seen a gust blow her on her stupid, precarious heels along an ice patch until she fell on her bony ass, literally *knocked over by the wind.* Her best friend, a flagrantly confident and intellectual girl of that rare high school breed that makes bookish asexuality look chic, had been a closer friend of his, but that girl had disappeared east after high school, into the kind of bright new Ivy League life that entails dropping all your spic and white-trash friends from the Midwest. Without her as the glue, he and Emily quickly lost touch. Miguel has a sudden flash of one night at an underage dance club, letting Emily give him hickeys all over his neck while they were both drunk on watermelon schnapps. He is pretty certain they never had sex, as he doled out intercourse judiciously, only when something needed to be proven beyond a doubt. Emily was not that kind of girl: the kind who demanded proof of anything. She was the sort who waited to be *taken*—who seemed, in the way so many young girls do, that it was not worthy of particular speculation, somewhat destined for ruin. She drank a lot in the daytime, did more cocaine than the rest of their crowd, though it was 1985, 1986, and of course when it came to cocaine, everyone did *some*, then. He turns to face the stage, but in his mind there is still Emily, wearing her adult skin. The new Her doesn't suit her. He feels discombobulated, wants to turn around to verify that it *is* her: her Emily-bones under this new, expansive flesh and Earth Mama attire. Her hair, which was short, spikey, and dark when he knew her, is long and flaxen, and he realizes with some alarm that this is her *real* hair—that the dark version was just some Goth kid thing, and his Emily is a blonde.

His Emily? Well, no one was ever really "his," back then. He was in the closet, his life a general fraud. He recalls one cringingly embarrassing phone call with Emily, in which he attempted to "open up" and ended up talking about how he wanted to kill himself. He had the conversation while sitting on the bathroom floor of his mother's house, the phone cord smashed in the closed door. His suicidal ideation could not have had any sensible context to Emily, since nobody knew he was gay. He was handsome (even he can see this in retrospect), got straight As, had friends and girlfriends, was scholarship bound. But his vague past in Venezuela, his dead father, his too-religious Latino family—four generations of women—all crammed together in one apartment with a perpetually barking, enraged Chihuahua, apparently seemed context enough. He remembers it being strange to him that she never questioned *why* he might wish to die. Perhaps there was some fundamental lack in him that was visible to others, even if he himself thought the trouble lay elsewhere, in mere sexual preference. Even now, he blushes in the dark theater, hoping Emily does not remember that call.

Later, he stands outside the theater smoking with Emily's husband, Nick—the dude who picked up Lina in a Trader Joe's. Nick wrote this . . . *play*, if that's the right word . . . this cacophonously hilarious, possibly slightly brilliant *thing* they have just seen. He collaborated with an all-female burlesque troupe on the choreography, but the stage play is all *his*, and after spending some fifteen minutes with Nick, this no longer seems surprising. Nick also acts, playing not the co-lead—the zombie with whom Lina's shrink falls in love, who coincidentally has bipolar disorder, like Lina herself—but a more minor character, an agoraphobic zombie who convinces the others to remain in the hospital indefinitely, sitting out the apocalypse raging outside its walls until an angry mob of humans finally shows up in the final act, attacking the zombies, who have come to only want to paint and read poetry and have sex.

"So do the zombies take their meds?" Miguel asks.

"That's what they need the *shrink* for, mate, it's why they originally keep her alive when she shows up!" Nick answers in a near brogue, despite the fact that, being married to Emily, he has probably lived in Chicago for a damn long time. He proceeds to give Miguel a chronicle of the various zombies' prescription cocktails, none of which Miguel can recall actually being mentioned *in* the play, lighting one cigarette off the other the entire time until Miguel thinks his own lungs may spontaneously begin to bleed.

He isn't sure if Nick's hair *always* looks like this, or if it's a short-term thing, for the part.

Though they've been standing together for less than half an hour, Miguel feels a strange fondness for Nick that people, especially heterosexual men, rarely elicit in him. In a decade of working at the Federal Reserve building, he has not once had a smoking buddy whose company he actually sought on breaks, whose cigarette habits he would time his own around, but if Nick worked with him, he would go outside to smoke when Nick did. This surprises him, though it is not exactly unsettling. Maybe it's the accent. Though it isn't that he wants to *fuck* Nick; hippie boys were never his thing, even in college—even in Barcelona. Nick seems like the kind of androgynous man who once got a lot of pussy. His hair is the deep auburn of a woman or an Irish Setter, his eyes green as gems; he's elvish in an Orlando Bloom rather than a Santa's helper kind of way. He and Emily must have made an unsettlingly sexy couple, once upon a time. They have two sons now, one almost fifteen—as old as the marriage—and the other only seven, and every time either boy is mentioned in conversation, Nick's already-animated face brightens like a floodlight. He has an ease around fags uncommon in straight men, irrespective of their politics; maybe he used to blow guys on a Dublin commune in the name of free love, if that hair isn't just for this part.

"I'm quitting smoking tomorrow," Nick says, sucking on the cigarette like a joint. He rolls his own. Miguel is smoking one of his, too, and it is giving him a beautiful head rush.

"Sure you are. Yep. Me too."

"Seriously. Em gave me until the closing. My number's up."

"I told Chad I'll quit smoking when he loses twenty pounds," Miguel says. A wave of anxiety instantly washes over him. Chad is less overweight than Emily's become, and Nick may think he's making a dig.

"Well," says Nick, not biting, "if I end up with a tracheotomy, Jay'll start taking me in for *show-and-tell*." He laughs to himself. "They call it *show-and-share* now." He presses his throat, which is encircled with two chunky necklaces, and mimics a trach voice: "Hi, kids, I'm here for show-and-share. Just say no to smoking, or you'll end up with a glory hole in your neck." He flicks his butt to the curb. "Seriously, Em'll refuse to fuck me if I don't quit. The candy store or the tobacco store is closing down—you know, man, no contest."

Miguel feels his eyes blinking rapidly, bats away some smoke.

Emily and Chad come outside together arm in arm, like French schoolgirls. "But why did you only ask lesbians and single women?" Emily is saying. "Are you afraid breeder DNA is going to, like, infect your kid or something?"

Chad giggles. He puts his hand lightly on Miguel's arm, and Miguel stubs the Nick-rolled cigarette against the brick wall of the building. "Well, that was a consideration," Chad says. "But really, just, you know, what man would say *yes* to something like that, right? I mean, if a woman had a husband, he'd never go for it—carrying some other man's baby for nine months . . . why *would* any man go along with that?"

"That's funny," Emily says. "Nick would go along with it. Wouldn't you, Nick?"

"I have no fucking idea what you people are talking about."

"These guys," she tells him. "They want to have a baby. Chad's sister is giving them the eggs, but she doesn't want to carry the pregnancy. They need a gestational surrogate. We should do it, don't you think?" She turns to Miguel. "I love being pregnant."

"Oh yikes," Chad rushes—"No, I . . ." he looks at Nick, almost imploringly. "That's not why I told her about it . . . I was just making conversation. I mean, you don't even know us."

"Miguel knows me," Emily says. "We haven't seen each other in a long time, but he knows me better than most people in my life do now, actually. People know each other differently in high school. No one knows each other that way at fortysomething. We're all too busy—it'd be an imposition. When's the last time you had a real phone conversation? In high school, I used to spend six hours a night on the phone. I don't even talk to Nick for six hours a night, and we live together!"

"When we were long distance," Nick says, "we'd talk so long we'd fall asleep with the phones in our hands. I had to crash in my car for a month—my phone bill was so high I got evicted."

Miguel is not sure if he is relieved or crushed to see the conversation back on the ground of phone bills.

"I love being pregnant," Emily says again. "It suits me. Everyone said so, didn't they, Nick?"

"I don't know about everyone," Nick says. "It suited you, *I* thought, yeah. You glowed. I always thought that was bullshit. Pregnant women looked the opposite of glowing to me—like chalk, or wax, something . . . flame resistant. Then I saw Emily carrying Miles, before we even *knew* yet, and something was . . . different about her. It was incredible."

"We should do it," Emily says. "You guys would be great parents. Wouldn't they, Nick?"

"Look," Chad says, and he seems, to Miguel's ears, more alarmed than is anywhere near normal for him. "I'm sure you don't need to be pregnant for Nick to think you glow!"

Nick laughs at this. "Hey," he says, "if she digs being pregnant so much, that's up to Emily, it's her body." He looks at Miguel, and there is a strange intimacy to the look, as though everyone is speaking in code and Miguel is the decoder. "But is there, you know, money in this or something? Like, you rent the space? Is that how this works? Because that's a little creepy. I wouldn't be into that."

"We were . . . expecting to pay, yes."

Nick shrugs. "They have professionals, from what I understand, for this sort of thing."

"But you want it to be someone you trust," Emily protests. "Not some stranger. *That'd* be creepy—a stranger carrying your baby. We wouldn't have to take money. Just the expenses and stuff like that—I wasn't saying it for the money—Nick and I don't care about things like that. I'd just . . ." When she smiles, Miguel sees some old fragility in the curve of her lips. The smile conveys some need, but he doesn't know her well enough anymore to read the source. She says, "I'd just . . . it'd make me feel incredible, actually, to help someone else have that."

"*Really*?" Chad asks, and Miguel does know *him* well enough that the alarm in Chad's voice a moment before makes utter sense to him. They have, this past month, run into dead end after brick wall after cliff's edge. Their hopes rise and fall. They are dashed against rocks. They are emotionally exhausted. They were fools to think they could have this. They live in a world where it is okay to hold hands at a restaurant; where they don't fear having their asses kicked or being murdered just for being *together*, and this allowed them to become smug. Their hope has battered too hard, lately, against the glass ceiling of what they will be permitted. *Hope*, Chad has discovered—which Miguel knew all along—is dangerous.

"If you want to," Emily's saying, just as Lina comes out onto the street, Bebe not here tonight, just Lina dressed in low-slung button-fly men's Levi's and a black dago tee that falls low on her braless breasts and reveals an ill-chosen tattoo of her first ex-husband's initials: *JJ*. She takes the fresh cigarette out of Nick's hand without asking and takes a drag, and Miguel thinks instantly, *Oh fuck*, though Emily doesn't even blink. "I'd be honored," Emily is saying. "God, it'd be so fun!" Other people are filing out thinly after Lina; the party must be breaking up; they've been out here a long time, even though it's ostensibly Nick's party.

"Did you hear?" Nick says to Lina, but loudly enough that the others turn to look at him—he's an actor and knows how to project his voice; he's the writer and they are all used to memorizing his words. "My wife's having a baby, but don't worry, it's not mine."

It seems, to Miguel, a punch line that could go either way. People could grow uncomfortable, look at the floor, glare at Emily, wait breathlessly for some messy marital scene. Miguel himself isn't sure, even, how to react. But no, this crowd *knows* Nick, and not a single person seems to take the words amiss, and everyone laughs, except Lina, who drags from the cigarette and seems, in her strange way, to have already taken this random development as a forgone conclusion.

LINA

You text me the day after the play's closing party. Your wife isn't pregnant yet; she's just talking. Gretchen's eggs are still inside her own skin, and she knows nothing yet about regret, about plotting treason or staging a coup. She knows nothing yet about watching her own bright future belong to other people, because she can't see the future. No, today, Nick, everyone is still happy, bubbling with prospects, what could possibly go wrong?

A fucking lot can go wrong. Starting with this:

Your text reads, *I miss you! Let's get together! Now!*

I am, to put it mildly, startled. It's noon. I've only been awake for an hour. It's a Wednesday, and I know you've been up since 7:00 a.m. to make breakfast and take Jay to school; I know that Miles rides the bus somewhere you describe as *far-a-fucking-way* to go to a performing arts school where he studies drama, like everyone in your family for so many generations that you can't count back to before the Ryans were actors. I know more about your daily schedule than I do anyone's but Bebe's—certainly more than about any of the women's Bebe and I bring home. Still, I keep looking at your text, as if expecting the words to rearrange to say something more expected. I'm used to your guileless exuberance, the way you make no effort to "act cool" by appearing indifferent about people, but I have to admit I always thought *that*, actually, was part of your shtick: the guy who's so cool he doesn't have to play it cool. After the closing party I didn't think I'd ever hear from you again.

Much less the next day, with an invitation to get together in person, immediately, with exclamation points.

I had figured . . . well, I figured you were like me. That whatever circumstances you happened to be in, you zeroed in on the most kindred spirit in that particular room and charmed them and made them your best friend for the hour waiting at the dentist's office, the three days of jury duty, the months of rehearsing and performing a play, the year of dancing at a skanky west-side strip club, the four years of college. Then, you left whatever environs in which you shared a connection with that person, and you were on to the next place, the next kindred spirit, the next performance. That was who I thought you were, and I had no problem with it. I liked being the chosen recipient of your particular nature, for a finite period of time. I liked the juxtaposition of intense intimacy and implicit transience. I am good at intensity. I am not good at permanence.

I text back, *Sure let's find a date next week that will work*, thinking to put you off. I don't want to see you, though I realize this seems nuts since seeing you was always my favorite thing about the play. But for some reason now I feel anxious and smothered, uncertain what to do.

Probably you find this offensive, if you're reading this now. Like I'm negating what things were like between us from the beginning. The minute I saw you again in the produce aisle, I *wanted* to be your friend. People talk a lot about that instant sense of "recognition," and I know it sounds cheesy, but I felt as though instead of asking me to be in a burlesque zombie play, you had suddenly revealed to me that we had the same father and were secret siblings. It wasn't because you had already seen me naked, because everyone has already seen me naked. It was . . . something else. You were dressed strange as hell in some contrasting striped-plaid combo of wrinkled and too-big clothes, but even in the dim lighting, buried under fabric, the ethereal grace of your bones was evident and you looked *brighter*, differently lit than the rest of the room. You seemed almost to give off sparks, as though trying to break past your own essential physical barriers, too big to contain yourself.

We were already setting the stage for lies that day. The lie of "how we met," it turned out, would set the stage for everything.

What you and I told everyone: that you approached me at total random in a Trader Joe's and asked me to audition for your play.

The truth: we had met, first, at the club, years before. Well . . . *met* may be too strong a word; we had seen each other in that dimly lit room, sporadically, for months—months in which you started frequenting a strip club in the afternoon, on days you didn't teach, Jay finally in full-day kindergarten. The club, it turned out, was near a rinky-dink theater putting on one of your plays, and you were "in the neighborhood" for rehearsals, but in all human history no one has ever gone to watch naked women dancing because they were *in the neighborhood* of anything. You stopped coming by when your show ended, maybe a full year before I quit and the club faded into our mutual rearview. We were not *friends* there; you never paid me for anything extra; I don't believe we ever had a conversation. You were not the first customer from the club I'd run into in my ordinary life—others had recognized me, known me by my stage name and tried to talk to me, and I spurned them, kept my boundaries erected around me tight. But when you and I saw each other, both of us rummaging over little prepackaged salads, our faces mutually lit up in a way suggestive of something entirely other than what we were. We smiled nakedly as though running into our first crush from grade school. I said, "I love your hair long like that," and you grabbed the top of my arm abruptly in a way that should have freaked me out and said, the first time I heard your accent, "I've grown it for a play I'm in—you should be in it too!" We both laughed then because the suggestion was so absurd, but suddenly you were writing your phone number down on my hand, a move so girl-like it allowed me to pretend you couldn't possibly be a threat to anything. "It's a zombie burlesque," you explained, still holding my wrist, and I said, "Are you fucking with me?" and you said, "I wrote it!" and I said, "You *are* fucking with me," and you said, "Come audition—I want you for the part of the psychiatrist, the lead," and I said, "Oh, you do not want me to play a shrink, I hate shrinks," and you said, "Brilliant, now I *really* want you for the part."

Later we would fail to realize that the fake version of our meeting made it sound like you were so instantly attracted to me that you approached a total stranger. The real version was *less* sexual somehow, but not necessarily better. The real version was that you saw me as someone who already knew your secrets. We were lying for one another before we had a reason.

Another true thing: if that hadn't happened, your wife would never have seen my brother again. In a way, your going into a strip club—your sitting at the bar with your back turned most times to the stage, looking exactly like a certain kind of man does in such places: like he is trying to find the Exit sign to his life—was the real beginning.

From the first, we were always next to one another on rehearsal breaks; we sat together on steps and curbs and tables, our knees touching, passing cigarettes and laughter back and forth. You reminded me of my brother, if my brother would ever actually *talk* to people in a real way. The same dry, almost pathological irreverence. If anything, we had the familiarity of people who had been lovers long ago but that was all over now: you spoke of your kids and of Emily with an easy grace, as though I were another man or your sister. You told me how hot Bebe was and then spun a once-upon-a-time story about your efforts to get a hot lesbian from London to go out with you, and how as a result you ended up fucking a slew of lesbians because you were always following her around like a dog.

"Some of her friends were bi or took pity on me, and I got used to the first I heard in the morning being, *I can't believe I slept with a bloke.*" You loved being the boy the lesbians passed around—they even had a slogan: *Miss dick? Call Nick.* You had beautiful lips, they agreed, and a phenomenal tongue, longer and stronger than most women's. *Stick out your tongue*, one would command if a new woman dropped by the table. *Show her, Nick, move it around.* And you'd do so, delighted. *Go on*, they'd urge the new girl, *give him a try, he's an honorary dyke.* And another would say, *Let's not push it—maybe a human vibrator*, and they'd all laugh. "I'd sit there," you told me, sometime during our first week of rehearsal, "and feel myself floating away and melting into the bar seat simultaneously. It was the happiest I'd ever been."

I thought you were the most charming man I had ever met.

Now, looking down at this unexpected text stream, this invitation to . . . *get together* . . . I'm thinking clearly my judgment was fucked up as usual. Maybe Bebe was right and sex is what you've wanted from me all along. Maybe your wife is having some midlife crisis and wants to start swinging with girls, and you've mistaken the things I've disclosed about Bebe's and my life for an open-admissions welcome mat. But Bebe doesn't miss dick or need Nick. She might let *Emily* in the bed, but I have no interest in your wife. I don't want to be her friend. I want, though, with sudden ferocity, to be yours—not at rehearsals, during finite times in a finite space, but for real.

You text, *You going on auditions all this week, then? I hope you get them all.*

I have, for the record, never even *been* on an audition other than for you. I quit the club when we started rehearsals, only kept up dancing at sporadic lesbian nights before that faded out, too. I graduated from college more than two years ago, but I've never sent out resumes or gone on a job interview. It's not like I'm hell-bent on being an *actress*, so why would I go on auditions? I text back, *Yes, a few . . . thanks!*

Em really wants to have your brother's kid. She was up all night talking about it. So I guess we're gonna be related, so to speak. Maybe we'll be spending every Thanksgiving together, Aunt Lina. I make a mean tofurkey.

I press "contact" on the phone and call you instead of texting back. As you answer in a startled voice, I say, like I'm on to you, "Oh, so *that's* why you want to meet. The surrogacy scheme."

"It's like we struck gold," you say. "Now we have, like, an excuse to keep in touch. We're going to be family, almost. I was feeling so awful about how much I was going to miss you when the play ended. And then this came out of nowhere, like fate. Now we can just keep *going*."

What are you talking about? If you hadn't texted me, would I ever even have thought of you again? "Keep going *where*?" I ask, my voice gentler now, almost cautious.

"Cuba?" you ask, and I laugh, something like terror, something like joy catching in my throat. "But for the moment, I bet you haven't had coffee yet, slacker girl. Filter, in an hour?"

And I guess, in retrospect, right at the moment when everything begins to come together is also precisely the moment when everything starts to fall apart.

GRETCHEN

Suddenly Chad is the cruise director of Gretchen's life. Going through pregnancy herself and then nursing a newborn was less demanding than her brother has become, calling her daily with litanies of insurance information and the surrogate's, Emily's, work schedule, which Gretchen must accommodate: Emily needs to be knocked up in October so that she can deliver in the summer when she's off work, *chop chop*. On what she has started to think of as an impulsive move born of cocktails on an empty stomach and the despair of being in a roomful of senior-citizen WASPs, Gretchen now shoots Pergonal into her thighs until she is bruised like a junkie. The hormones make her skin break out, and Troy is horrified. "You should start going into Neiman's to get your makeup professionally done," he tells her. "The only time your makeup has ever looked good was at our wedding."

Neiman Marcus is not even open at 8:00 a.m. Even Jennifer Fucking Aniston surely doesn't have a professional makeup job at the crack of dawn, daily. Gretchen wrestles with whether Troy truly means what he suggests—whether this is what he considers a viable option—or if he is only striving to be cruel. When she repeats his remarks to Chad, her brother says, "His shiftless ass lives off our money and he can't even pretend to be polite?" as though Troy's feigning niceness out of greed would be a perfectly acceptable solution. Chad adds, "God, I hate conflict—I don't know how you handle it, Gret."

Today is her phone interview with the psychiatrist. "Say as little as possible," Miguel coached her, missteps apparently a given should she give herself free reign. *His* interview has already taken place. The fertility center takes care of all these details: attorneys for the surrogate, the egg donor, the dads. A contract has been drawn up in which Gretchen is to relinquish her legal claims on the child—another contract for the surrogate, stipulating not just her lack of rights to the baby, but what kind of compensation she will receive. The going market rate seems to be about thirty grand, but this Emily woman will not accept more than ten. "She isn't doing it for the money," Chad says, as though this makes sense. What the hell *else* would the girl be doing it for? She's an old friend of Miguel's, but Gretchen has known Miguel for ten years and never heard of Emily until now, so how good a friend can she possibly be? The situation is inexplicable. Gretchen is donating an egg to her *brother.* The offspring will be part of the Merry clan. Even if the situation in which she's found herself makes little sense to her on an emotional level, it sounds sensible on paper.

"Are you on good terms with your parents?" the psychiatrist asks on the phone, and Gretchen resists the urge to say, "Define good." Clearly that would not fall under saying as little as possible. "Very good terms," Gretchen says dutifully. "We're a close-knit family. My parents are very involved with my son."

It is all true. Truth floats on the surface of things, with subtext beneath, hanging off the various words like a diagramed sentence.

Very good terms.

(We lie to each other about everything and therefore everyone is comfortable and happy.)

(*Happy*, of course, being a euphemism for a lack of anxiety.)

(Anxiety, of course, being controlled by various prescription pills.)

(Which, of course, my husband refuses to take, and instead kicks the dog when his anxiety reaches unmanageable proportions.)

(Unmanageable proportions occurring, that is, mainly every day.)

(Including for the dog, who has taken to pissing on the carpet.)

(Which causes my husband to kick it.)

(Did you mention my parents? Oh, yes, we're on very good terms.)

We're a close-knit family.

(My mother is an annoying person, so her so-called friends can only tolerate her in small doses, and therefore the lion's share of coping with her is left to the nuclear family.)

(By which I mean *me*, since my father is off playing golf and having martini lunches, and my brother is, despite being gay, still of the male persuasion and therefore mainly useless.)

(Every time the phone rings, my husband says, "There's fucking Elaine, ringing her bell." Now when the phone rings, Gray says, "There's Grandma! Ringing her bell!")

(Yes, we managed to eliminate the "fucking Elaine" part, after Troy washed Gray's mouth out with soap the first time he said it, even though Gray was only repeating what he'd heard his father say.)

(Did I mention that "repeating" is a bit of an issue around here? As in, my son is a parrot. If you read him the Gettysburg Address, he'd be walking around the house reciting it from memory within half an hour.)

(Instead, most of what he repeats consists of imperatives that I should get my makeup done at Neiman's and that the dog is a filthy animal bringing diseases into the house, even though it never ventures farther than our backyard.)

(I suppose at least Gray only got his mouth washed out with soap and didn't get kicked.)

(Although for the remainder of the night, I thought obsessively of that movie with Farrah Fawcett, *The Burning Bed*, and how immensely satisfying it would be to burn the house down while Troy was asleep . . . how all I would need to do is send Gray out for a sleepover and we'd be all set . . .)

(Except Gray has no friends at whose houses he could sleep.)

(And I'd have to leave the dog inside and let it be burned to a crisp, since evacuating the pets is one of the surest signs that arson has been committed.)

(Which might not be the worst thing, except that Gray is more attached to that pissing dog than he is to us.)

My parents are very involved with my son.

(No subtext here, stupid. Don't you recognize sarcasm?)

The interview is mostly painless. Gretchen ignores the ringing doorbell to complete the call and hangs up relatively certain she has not sabotaged Chad's and Miguel's hopes of parenthood. She trots to the door to see if there's any sign of who was there and finds a package at her feet from UPS. The address label reads *Troy Underwood*, but this stops Gretchen not at all. Any package in the mail is a golden opportunity. Perhaps it will be an inflatable doll with a Russian flag right above its vagina! Then she could photograph it and give it to her future shark attorney to keep in her hypothetical divorce file, which is becoming, in her mind, as crowded as a hope chest. She rips open the packaging.

At first, she has no idea what the thing is. It looks like an oversized flashlight, like something you might bring on a camping trip, which makes no sense given Troy, who would probably wear Prada on a camping trip, except that he would never go on a camping trip . . . for God's sake, even when he has been on vacation somewhere like the Four Seasons Punta Mita, he spreads all his luggage out in the garage on Hefty bags and airs it out for a full twenty-four hours to let the germs dissipate before he will permit it back inside the house.

Only when Gretchen reads the warranty information does she realize that what she's holding is a blue light—the kind used in forensics on TV crime dramas. Instantly, a shudder runs through her. Jesus Christ. Troy must be planning to kill her for the insurance money and then use this to make sure he's eliminated all the evidence. Frantically, she checks the receipt to see if he used his credit card—if he's left a trail of evidence. He has. For some reason this makes Gretchen's heart steady just a touch, though her hand is still gripping the wall. That fucktard. Just let him try and kill her. She will call Chad and tell him about the blue light so that Troy's stupid ass will be busted and sent to prison the moment she turns up missing . . .

It takes thirty seconds or so to realize that she—dead in this scenario—does not exactly emerge triumphant. Gretchen marches into Troy's study—

(*Study* being a euphemism, since Troy does not work other than the occasional crappy product endorsements of has-been athletes, and since he has never, in their entire marriage, read a book . . .)

—she does not knock, just bursts in. Troy is at the computer, though not doing anything useful to her future divorce case like jacking off to Cold War porn; he seems to be browsing the *Travel & Leisure* website, and he doesn't look up when she enters.

"What the fuck is this?" she demands, throwing the blue light half across the room at his desk, where it knocks down a photo of Gray.

Troy jumps . . . but in only a second his alarm turns to enthusiasm as he grabs for the light. "What's the matter with you?" he says. "Why would you throw something with glass and batteries? I paid three hundred bucks for this. Do you have to run around like some parody of a hysterical woman every single minute of every single day?"

"Why are you ordering a blue light for three hundred dollars off the Internet?" Gretchen demands. "What do you need a blue light for? Are you planning to bury bodies in the basement?"

Troy is grinning. He stands, holding the light out to her like an offering, despite having just called her hysterical. "It's for the dog!" he explains, bouncing up and down a little in his mirth. "I just *know* those carpet cleaners haven't gotten everything out. Those guys were careless, you could tell by just looking at them, it was like Cheech and Chong came to clean the rugs . . . I can still smell urine hanging in the air—I *know* the carpets are still contaminated. So we can have them come back and *show* them all the spots they missed, and then we'll have them redo it and check again with the light while they're still here. We won't stop until all the piss is gone."

It is possible, Gretchen realizes, that the scenario in which Troy was planning to murder her was preferable to this. "You have totally lost your mind."

"Why?" Troy says pleasantly. "Look, just because you don't care anything about personal hygiene—I mean, fine, maybe that's why you have acne like a thirteen-year-old. Excuse me if I don't want to walk around a river of dog piss in my own house."

"I have acne because I'm on freaking hormone shots!" Gretchen hears her voice, hysterical, just like he said. "I'm trying to help my brother have a baby! I have other things to think about besides whether the dog has an accident and some shadow of a shadow of a germ hasn't been eliminated even though we've had the carpet professionally shampooed *twice*!"

"Fine," Troy says. "Go ahead and eat your lunch straight off the piss-soaked carpet for all I care, but I happen to be concerned for my son's safety and would rather he not get some disease from an outdoor animal urinating in his house."

"Carrot is not an outdoor animal!" Gretchen screams again. "*All* dogs go outdoors to go to the bathroom! The fact that we let Carrot into the yard does not make him an outdoor animal! You don't even make any sense! It's like you're just on some campaign to drive me insane."

Troy snorts. "You don't seem to need any help on that front."

Gretchen feels a series of small explosions going off inside her brain. She is dimly aware of biting the insides of her cheeks so hard that she can taste a metallic pre-blood along her tongue. She and Troy are supposed to attend one of her biggest client's weddings tonight. They will not know many people there, but it will be an outstanding opportunity to drum up new business, given that she will be introduced to everyone by her professional capacity (*This is my accountant, Gretchen Underwood*) . . . and Gretchen cannot show up stag. If she picks up the blue light right now and makes sure to rectify her error of *not* damaging it, by proceeding to beat Troy about the head and shoulders with it, she will look like: a) a pathetic old spinster at the wedding or b) a predatory woman out to have affairs with all the other women's husbands should they hire her to do their books.

(Not that she is much of a threat, with her adolescent acne and her mannish pantsuits . . .)

Still, a husband is a vital necessity at such affairs. And if her days of having a husband are numbered, she needs to score all the clients she can—in between rushing into the bathroom to stab her leg with a needle and elevate her risk of cancer with hormones, that is, so that her brother can have the bright new start to his life that Gretchen, once upon a time, believed she was having when, in the eleventh hour of her youth, she got pregnant with Gray. She is not sure whether she pities Chad and Miguel or whether she wants to kill them with envy. Something is clearly wrong: with her, with this egg-donating master plan. *Don't think, don't think. If you slow down to think, you are doomed . . .*

Instead, she storms out of Troy's office, poor terrorized Carrot scuttling out of her way in the kitchen as though expecting a foot to the ribs. Against the kitchen counter, Gretchen leans, gasping irrationally. She needs a glass of wine. But even as she is thinking this thought, she walks right past the wine rack to the freezer, where the old bottle of Ketel One has barely an inch left, but a new bottle rests beside it, frosty and untouched. Gray will not be out of the Day School for four hours. She has time, before she has to drive.

MIGUEL

Miguel is ordering his Paxil off the Internet, with no idea that a gun is about to be introduced into Act I that will later, more than once, attempt to shoot him in the face. He's in a pair of boxer shorts, looking casually gorgeous to no one except his litter of drooling bulldogs, thrilled out of his mind—in his misanthropic way that doesn't include actual giddiness—to be home alone while Chad is as usual working. He almost doesn't pick up the ringing phone, as he tends to pick up only for Lina. Then he remembers that these days people are constantly calling to discuss Important Matters, so he relents as though Chad is watching him, saying, "Yeah?" into the receiver.

"Good morning, Miguel," says Christine, their coordinator at the fertility clinic, as soon as she's able to ascertain that she doesn't have the wrong number. "I don't know how to tell you this, but your tests came back and it seems you have syphilis."

For a long stretch, Miguel hears himself not saying anything. He would like to hang up, but Chad would kill him if he hung up on Christine. Finally he sighs. "Of course I do."

"You mean you already knew?" she asks.

He sighs again. She will conclude that one of the symptoms of syphilis is sighing. "No. I had no idea. I mean—you know, it's one more thing."

"One more thing," Christine repeats.

"One more thing that's gone wrong," Miguel explains.

"Did something else go wrong?" she asks, her voice elevating in concern. "Is something wrong with the surrogate?"

Miguel sighs again. He smacks himself in the head so that his ear bangs a little against the phone.

"Well," he quips, "at least it's not AIDS! Syphilis—the kinder and gentler STD." He laughs a goofy falsetto into the phone, then stops abruptly. "So, uh . . . what am I supposed to *do*?"

"You need to call your doctor." Now it is Christine's turn to lapse into silence, panic rising in Miguel's throat so that by the time she speaks again, he is almost gagging on sudden fear. "They can treat it with antibiotics. It shouldn't be a big deal for you. Once it's all cleared up, you can come back and we can get things back on track."

"Wait a second . . ." He has to cough, to speak around all the lumps. "What do you *mean*, once it's all cleared up?"

"Mmm. Well. Yes . . . you can't donate sperm with an active case of syphilis, Miguel. It's against the law."

"My sperm is against the law?"

"Sure. Or, what I mean to say, it's against our policies. The FDA, strictly speaking, says it's legal as long as the surrogate is informed and consents, but that's a can of worms we don't want to get into. It's our policy not to get involved with cases like that. Anyway, the antibiotics take three to six months to take full effect. You go in for some shots, is my understanding of it. It's simple. You'll always have the marker for syphilis, but once you're considered cured we can proceed."

"God," he says, "of course I have to be cured first, otherwise Emily could get infected, too."

"Well, not exactly," Christine says. "Generally speaking, in an implantation like this, there isn't actual transmission to the surrogate. Statistically."

"Oh. Well, that's good—really good—so she might still . . ." *My STD'd ass may not completely scare her away is what I mean, Christine.* He tries, "So I need to be cured so the *baby* doesn't get it."

"Sure," Christine says. "Nobody wants that. They say that's not really a risk, though. Statistically again, I mean. I did some research today, before I called you."

The moment reeks weirdly of Kafka. "So I have syphilis," he recaps. "But I have no symptoms. And the surrogate can't get it. And statistically, the fetus is safe, too. And the FDA is A-okay with my sperm. But you—*you* guys, the *agency*—you're going to hold me up six months, because that's the . . . policy?"

"Everyone wants to be safe here," Christine reiterates.

"But Emily and Gretchen are almost ready. They're stuffing themselves full of hormones *now.* Emily has to be pregnant by the end of October . . ."

"You know," Christine says, "I'm surprised that a woman who's had two children of her own thinks that things can be timed down to the precise second that way. That just isn't the way pregnancy works."

Miguel stares at his computer screen. Indian Paxil stares back. He watches his hand on the mouse, clicking to increase his dosage.

"You can't always plan these things," Christine continues. "Obstacles occur. This, for example. Syphilis is . . . an obstacle. People need to be flexible. Family planning isn't an exact science."

This seems a bizarre declaration from someone whose living is made scheduling desperate couples into the precise time slots in which they will be fertilized, but Miguel lets it stand.

"There has to be another solution," he says. "I'm not sure . . . if I have to wait six months, I'm not sure they'd both still be on board."

"Sure, sure, I understand, yes, of course. Well, clearly you could try to find another agency that will . . . work within these parameters, though I have to be honest, I'm not hopeful about that . . . I imagine most feel exactly as we do. Or"—her voice brightens—"you could simply get another sperm donor. Maybe that would even make things more equal . . . then the offspring wouldn't be your biological child but not Chad's. Since his sister's the egg donor—well, do you have a brother?"

A world in which the Guerra family had another male offspring seems so far from the one he recognizes that Miguel laughs.

Silence again from Christine. Miguel has worn the welcome off this conversation, he knows. He remembers vaguely reading somewhere that syphilis was possibly responsible for a wide array of cultural catastrophes, from cases of female "hysteria" to the witch trials. The syphilitics were mad—it drove you crazy and there was no stopping the train to crazy town back then.

"Uh, look. Do you know how long I've *had* this? Do you know . . . I mean, does it say?"

"I have no idea," Christine says. "But Chad should be tested, too, of course. Even though he didn't need medical screening for the surrogacy, he'll obviously need treatment if you've passed this to him." She pauses. "I'm sorry—that was insensitive. We don't know the origins, of course. He could be the one who passed it to you."

The moment Christine is off the phone, Miguel has already progressed from being desperate to get rid of her to wanting her back. Something horrible looms in the background of this moment, and solitude only encourages its approach. He sits, still in the same chair he'd been lounging in when the call came, the same Indian drug website up on his browser, the same dogs asleep on the same drool-ridden floor at his feet. If he can divorce the fact that his STD has apparently derailed his and Chad's plans for parenthood, and completely inconvenienced at least one woman (Gretchen's eggs, he supposes, can be harvested for future use, so maybe she has not gone through all this in vain), he has to admit that he does not particularly *care* that he has syphilis. This seems strange—strange enough that he actually does a kind of bullshit-detection test on himself, to see if he's in some kind of denial. But no. Syphilis . . . whatever. Miguel has always half-expected to die of AIDS, and syphilis is anticlimactic and, it seems, fairly inconsequential. If the syphilis were responsible for his . . . let's say *lack of mental stability* . . . then his father wouldn't have been an abusive drunk who drove his car off a bridge in Caracas, and Isabel wouldn't be such a religious fanatic that she converted to Eastern Orthodox and bought some apple orchard in Northern Michigan (Midwestern apple orchards being a bastion for the Latino Eastern Orthodox community? The juxtaposition of these actions seems oxymoronic to Miguel) and virtually disowned every member of their family, including Mami, who is not exactly a heathen herself. If syphilis were responsible for whatever is wrong with Miguel's brain, then Lina wouldn't have been a twice-divorced addict by the time she was twenty-five or now in a relationship with a stern mommy figure (not that he's judging). Unless somehow Mami was sprinkling syphilis germs on the arepas when he was a child, STDs have nothing to do with whatever is wrong with the Family Guerra.

Fine, then: syphilis.

Miguel does not even bother, yet, reaching for the phone to call his doctor. He certainly is in no hurry to call Chad and confess to how he's ruined everything, either. He sits in this same chair, staring at this same screen, wondering why everything—everything—seems changed.

Chad should be tested, too, of course . . .

Miguel tries, with some difficulty, to remember the various guys he fucked in the 1990s. Really, though, there is no need: he has already concluded that his former lover, Tomas, with whom he lived in states of rhapsody and heartbreak during one absurd year in Barcelona, is the clear culprit. Tomas was a slut, and his slutty ways broke Miguel's heart into messy, humiliating pieces, and it is almost fitting that he has left Miguel this symbolic albatross to drag around for the next decade, hence sabotaging his efforts at fatherhood. Tomas would laugh wickedly could he see this. Except stupid Tomas is probably dead by now—he, Miguel would place money on it, would have found a way to contract AIDS . . . or if not, some hot-headed Spaniard would have murdered him for fucking his: a) lover, b) son. Tomas had a doomed air about him. Even as he thinks this, Miguel realizes that everyone he ever loved prior to Chad possessed a doomed air, yet most of them are still alive, and that at a certain age that air passes from romantic to fucked up to simply desperate. He finds himself hoping fervently that Tomas is dead, rather than an embarrassing old troll.

Everyone important is gone. He and Emily, who were joined by mutual friendship with a more powerful personality, are now stuck with only each other in this absurdist play that will have resulted in him having syphilis and her having wasted her time. He and Tomas once seemed capable of writing their love across the sky, except that it turned out Tomas was offering himself to half of Barcelona, and now here is Miguel, with Chad . . . sweet Chad.

Middle age: a B movie hobbled together from scenes on the cutting room floor, populated by extras who never get a billing.

Somehow, a baby was supposed to help that. Somehow, Termite Mansion was supposed to make that all right. He and Chad would become shimmering again. The numbness would go away. Life would throb with significance.

"I have syphilis," Miguel says to the empty room, followed by a cackle. One of the bulldogs raises its sleepy head in jerky alarm. "I have syphilis, but it doesn't *mean* anything."

He knows he has calls to make. Injections to receive. News to break. He sits, unmoving, staring at the phone.

Caracas had a speed-of-light gossip grapevine, but Mami was no part of it. They would hear about Isabel only much later, from "Tía," an elderly widow in need of caretaking, with whom they were living by then. Tía rarely left the house—her legs were too bad, swollen most days to resemble elongated watermelons—and she could not afford a telephone. She was old enough that her husband and most of her friends were dead, but somehow everyone knew her. Mami had shown up on her doorstep with Miguel half-hidden in shame behind her body, after two nights on the street.

It was not, Miguel would often remind himself later, that his mother had made no effort *to reunite with Isabel: by the time they ended up with Tía they had circled back to the house twice, in an attempt to find her. Neither visit had yielded anyone at home. The house, which Mami would not let Miguel enter, was upended like a TV police search had taken place within. Mami stole scraps of food from her own kitchen, but they couldn't stay long—"He must have taken Isabel with him, wherever he went,* el perro, *to make sure she didn't run off." For a man who abandoned so easily, Papi was terrified of being left—even Miguel remembered that the earliest fights he'd heard between his parents had concerned Mami wanting to go home to Chicago and her mother. Miguel thought they should arm themselves with kitchen knives, wait until Papi stumbled drunkenly through the door, and bring Isabel with them by force, but Mami, when he suggested this, said, "Violence is not the answer, Miguel—don't grow up to be the kind of man your father is," and Miguel's body flooded with confusion. If he were the man his father was, he would leave Isabel to rot. Except Papi was not doing that, apparently, but guarding her like a secret talisman. This was how it was with Mami: when they spoke to one another, the words never seemed to hit the mark; both he and his mother fired a mix of Spanish and English back and forth, yet words fizzled out and deflated between them so that they could not seem to grasp one another's meaning. There was a world between the man his father was and being a sobbing victim behind a red curtain, but Miguel did not know how to express this. Mami coaxed him to eat their own stolen food, under a palm tree in the shade, no longer in plain sight of the house. They waited and watched, and one of the old ladies who had bought Miguel's bouquets eventually came to where they huddled and told Mami that Tía was no longer able to care for herself, was in a bad way, but the house was hers, Tía's husband had paid for it.*

They stood in Tía's doorway, but still Mami could not seem to find words. Tía's house had a proper floor, though it was uneven and buckled. "I can clean," Mami said at last, not even properly introducing herself; Miguel was uncertain whether they had ever met. "I can cook, I can sew, I am strong." Tía had few teeth and her watermelon legs, and Miguel stood behind his mother as Tía explained that she had no money and was not looking to hire anyone—the suggestion was patently preposterous, even to Miguel, yet Tía's voice held no mockery or malice; she explained somberly, as though Mami had come making a sensible inquiry. "I don't need money," Mami qualified, which seemed a gross misrepresentation. "Just my son, if there's a place on the floor someplace out of your way where he could sleep."

Miguel imagined Mami sleeping in the yard like a dog, and for a moment bile rose in his throat to protest that he would stay with her, wherever she went. But two nights in the park with wet grass beneath his back held his tongue. People were so easy to crack. He would sell his mother for one night in this watermelon-witch's home. Who was he, later, to criticize Mami for saving herself instead of Isabel?

Of course Tía had not put Mami in the yard. Within the week, they were all like family, in a new world where family *had the meaning it should have; where family did not come with purple knuckles. His mother's words did not misfire to Tía. They sat late into the night drinking coffee and laughing grimly, their stories of men's fists also teaching Miguel a narrative about his father that his mother would have gone to the grave never sharing with him directly. As an adult, he would own no photographs of his father, but through his mother's stories to Tía he would know—in a way he had not been able to recognize as a child, when his father bore the face of a monster—that Papi had been beautiful, educated with two years of college, wrote poetry, fell prey to mysterious "black fits" that, at first, the drinking eased, enabling him to stop weeping, to get out of bed and go to work to feed his children. That somehow the fits and the drinking eventually became indistinguishable, and the rage he had once turned inward he began to direct at Mami.*

Was Miguel not supposed to say, here in this house his mother kept spotlessly clean as she never had their own, that it was time to go back again for Isabel? Was he supposed to assume that one of the neighbors would tell Isabel where they'd gone, and she would get here on her own? Of course someone would tell her. Everyone *would know by now that they were here. There were no mysteries, and the same old lady who had whispered in Mami's ear would whisper in Isabel's, wouldn't she? Miguel said nothing. He went to school steadily for a week, nearly two, but Isabel was never in the schoolyard. For all he knew, Mami was checking their old house daily; perhaps she and Tía failed to mention it as some effort at protection. Miguel lay awake nights on Tía's sofa—Mami slept with Tía in her old marital bed, in the house's one bedroom. Tía and her husband had been unable to have children, "But now," Tía said, her eyes misting over, "I am blessed with a daughter and a grandchild."*

Two, *Miguel thought.* Two. *Days spread out on the horizon. Thirteen years old, when they had lived at home, had seemed reassuringly old and wise to Miguel. Now, at Tía's, he began to realize for the first time how* young *Isabel truly was, though he did not yet understand that with every subsequent year of his life, his missing sister would seem still younger . . .*

"How did your father drive his car off a bridge?" Chad would ask him, twenty years later, in the first year of their courtship.

And it was the old rhythm of Mami's words to Tía that made that unspoken narrative finally take shape before Miguel's eyes—the fits, the poetry, Papi's remorse over his family's exodus—that for the first time made him understand.

The morning after learning of his status as a syphilitic, Miguel is walking from the El stop to the Federal Reserve building, wearing his winter coat for the first time this fall, and by the time he gets to the revolving glass doors every inch of his exposed skin is red and itchy. His hands, the worst, are covered in hives. He has to get through a metal detector to get in the building, even though 9/11 was seven years ago and Chicago has long since gotten over itself as the center of anything. His hands, swiping his ID badge through security, look red and vaguely elephantine. Not scratching himself in public like a monkey takes heroic effort. Every place air has touched his skin not just itches but *burns*. He nurses a residual fear from the 1980s that whenever he has anything resembling a lesion on his skin, people will think he has AIDS—it's hard not to envision men in hazmat suits tackling him, taking him to some underground quarantine; panic rises in his throat, or maybe something *else* is happening to his throat, which feels thick, coated, plugged. He usually arrives at work early enough to hit the gym before the open, but today he didn't—still, he races for the Fed's gym, to which he has free access, moving straight to the locker room, mechanically undressing, careful not to appear frantic. He turns his shower as hot as it can go, which in this context is *not very*. Still, the tepid heat and moist, trapped air feel like a balm.

The hot water doesn't make the hives disappear, but Miguel can feel the situation deescalating, no longer getting worse. His skin still looks wrong, but the unbearable sensations have ceased, and the steam seems to be reaching a deeper place in his lungs, his inhales hitting bottom. He leans against the wall of the shower. He is almost uncannily healthy, other than his lifelong migraines and his recent status as a syphilitic. He has never been allergic to anything. Still, suddenly he *knows*. In college he majored in math; he thinks in patterns; logic is his friend. The writing is on the wall, even if it is insane and written in Greek. He has suddenly become allergic to cold.

GRETCHEN

Gretchen gets her medical tests done at the Highland Park branch of the Fertility Center, so she's the one who points out to the others how close the men's restroom is to the sperm donation area. Lately, Gretchen thinks like a criminal. Her mind runs on a perpetual loop of plotting. If *she* had ordered a blue light in the mail, she would know damn well what to do with it. Instead, she finds herself meeting the usual suspects of this community-baby business at the ungodly hour of 7:00 a.m., for the very first appointment of the day, when the center will be less crowded, lessening the danger of accidental bystanders impeding their master plan. This was Nick's—the surrogate's Irish husband's—idea. "See," he says to Miguel, smacking him on the arm like a brother at the entrance to the empty men's restroom. "What did I say? Who the fuck would come here this early? Maybe a few desperate women, sure, but no man would drag his ass here at seven to jerk off in a cup."

"I did," Miguel mumbles miserably, slinking inside. Nick motions enthusiastically for Chad to go into the bathroom, too. Gretchen feels her face warm like a hot pad.

"The honeymoon suite," Nick says, bowing. "You kids have fun now."

Chad loiters awkwardly outside the door, clearly shocked, unsure whether to join Miguel. They all stand for a moment, an unnecessarily large gaggle in the otherwise deserted hallway. Finally, Gretchen pushes her brother into the men's john and yanks Emily and Nick forward by the arms like children. Enough already.

Inside the office, one lone patient, a woman in professional attire, perches anxiously on one of the sofas, crossing and uncrossing her ankles, awaiting whatever important fertility procedure prior to whatever important business meeting.

"You *were* right, honey," Emily stage-whispers to Nick, with a tone of surprise appropriate to any man ever being right about anything.

Gretchen strides over to the receptionist. There is no appreciable age difference between herself and this couple, but she feels like she could be Emily and Nick's mother. In part, it's their clothing. Emily is wearing some facsimile of parachute pants, tied-dyed, and a baggy T-shirt under which she clearly sports no bra, despite the fact that she's packing on enough extra pounds to have raised a couple of cup sizes from what her breasts must have once been, and is deflated a bit from nursing. Her blond hair is in loose, messy braids, and there is something childlike about her, like a Nordic exchange student, that makes Gretchen want to both smack her and protect her. Nick, on the other hand, looks like something you might need to protect Emily *from*. He's got on a crazy purple shirt—something out of *Saturday Night Fever*, or later, with more irony, *Pulp Fiction*. It's open to nearly the middle of his hairless chest and again at the very bottom, tails flapping, as if he literally forgot to button it, and visible through the gaping neck are a freaky assortment of necklaces, one of which seems to have an animal tooth on the end of it—Gretchen doesn't care to look too closely. The bottoms of Nick's pants drag on the ground so that the ends have frayed and little wisps of fabric follow him like the train of a veil. That Technicolor red hair stands on end in seventeen different directions, and he smells profoundly of smoke and man-skin. Gretchen would lay odds this guy has never owned a stick of deodorant in his life. The young receptionist is staring openly at him, and Gretchen sees both Nick and Emily notice this, and recognition churns in her gut. Although as straggly boho as she and Troy are suburban preppy, *this* coupleship dynamic is one she knows well. In their own hippie-dippie sphere, Gretchen can recognize that Nick would be considered devastatingly hot, just like Troy is in hers. Emily, like Gretchen, will have long since grown accustomed to other women checking him out in her presence, sizing her up as not much of a threat, and flirting with him right under his wife's nose.

"This is Nick Ryan," Gretchen barks at the dumb receptionist. "The *sperm* donor. He's here to give his *sperm*."

From behind her, Emily does herself no favors by tittering.

"Nicholas Owen Ryan," the receptionist recites, smirking. "It's like three first names."

"Handy for my multiple personality disorder," Nick quips, taking the clipboard the receptionist holds out and then plonking his bony ass down in the middle of two chairs, taking them both in a way Gretchen finds incensing. Never mind that the waiting room is virtually empty.

Emily is still standing next to Gretchen. She's made some audible snort of disgust that Gretchen assumed was directed at the salivating receptionist, but when Gretchen looks her way, Emily—as if waiting for this cue—purses her lips and whispers derisively of Nick, "That's not even his real name."

Gretchen has no idea what to make of this.

Nick's cell phone rings. He answers it loudly, barking things into it like, "What do you mean?" and, "No, you'd better not choose that one, just hold on a minute," until he finally shrugs helplessly at the receptionist, running his free hand through his deranged hair, and says, "I'm going to take this in the hall."

Gretchen hears him in the hallway. Yep, he's an actor all right. He doesn't drop the charade the moment the office door is closed, but keeps conducting the makeshift conversation, one-sidedly, making sure to project his voice. "I told you last month that we needed to change this routine," he says with agitation. "This bullshit is going to cost me a fortune!" Emily sits meekly in her chair, holding Nick's clipboard on her lap, smiling secretly like the Mona Fucking Lisa. Her ability at deception is quieter than Nick's, but equally unflappable.

After some time, Nick strides back in, cell phone still in his hand but hanging loosely at his side. "Sorry about that," he says loudly, as though the entire room has been following his predicament—which, of course, they have. "Where was I? Oh yeah, the part where I was about to say I don't need any magazines, I've brought my beautiful wife with me."

Emily snorts in her chair. "Gretchen and I will be *right here*, waiting." Then, getting so into the game that Gretchen wonders if Emily has genuinely forgotten what they're actually doing, Emily continues, "Anyway, you have an iPhone. "

"How's the Wi-Fi in here?" Nick asks the receptionist, who stammers, "Not that great, actually . . . um . . . but we do . . . have magazines, I mean."

An awkward beat, during which Gretchen half-expects the receptionist to offer to accompany Nick herself. Then, "What did they used to tell brides?" Nick says abruptly. "Close your eyes and think of England?"

He palms the cup and he's off.

Gretchen and Emily sit, not speaking. If screens above their heads could translate their thoughts into pictures, then on both screens Nick would be backing up to the door of the men's restroom while still loudly blathering on his cell phone, until he had bumped the door open just a crack, and the hand of Chad or Miguel slipped him a fat syringe, which Nick would quickly pocket in those oversized pants. Now, inside the "donation area," he would be seen carefully opening his donation cup and then shooting the contents of Miguel's sperm inside it, shaking the last vestiges loose. On the screen above Emily's head, the short film might end there. On the screen above Gretchen's head, Nick would then take a moment to flip through one of the pussy magazines.

When Nick reappears, Emily booms, "Oh, you're back—great job!" Gretchen recognizes this, too: the voice of a woman who talks to children all day. Who has forgotten that saying "great job!" isn't the best response to male ejaculation—even fake ejaculation.

"Yep," Nick says nonchalantly. "I'm nearly forty. I've got this skill in the bag."

The receptionist laughs, then averts her eyes.

They are already out of the office, out to the car where Chad and Miguel are waiting, before it occurs to Gretchen to wonder why she came. The guys and Emily high-five each other across the front and back seats like a sports team, whooping, "Operation Switcheroo complete!" and, "Mission accomplished!" Chad says the word champagne. They all holler things at once. Nick says, "What's a little syphilis between friends?" and even Miguel seems almost mirthful, chortling with the rest of them, Chad throwing out names of suburban restaurants where mimosas and bloody marys might be procured before licensing hours in exchange for a fat tip.

"You can drop me on the way," Gretchen says, and she regrets it even as she's saying it, but she can't stop herself. "I have a lot of work to do. I can't go drinking before 8:00 a.m."

"Party pooper!" Chad boos and hisses. They seem drunk already. The merriment is oppressive.

"No, really," Gretchen says. "Sorry. I'm on a deadline."

Chad takes a turn that indicates he's heading back to her house. They all sit quietly for a while. Chad's Sirius radio is blasting ABBA, and Gretchen would bet her ass the hippies aren't happy about it, but they're both too polite to say anything. She's not wild about ABBA, either—*really*, just because they're gay? Is it absolutely imperative that everybody drink the goddamn Kool-Aid about goddamn everything? Gretchen is already thinking about the Ketel in her freezer—better than mimosas anyway—when she hears Emily murmur "yikes" under her breath. When Gretchen looks, Nick has the fouled syringe in his hand, Miguel's seed still clinging to its plastic sides like residual salad dressing in a bowl. "Hey," he says, "can I throw this out now, or did you guys want to keep it as a souvenir?"

LINA

The evening after your wife first hears my brother's baby's heartbeat, Bebe and I are sitting at another overpriced restaurant, pushing the only vegetarian entrees on the menu around on our plates. Since I've stopped stripping, we are at a lack for things to do socially. We aren't foodies. She doesn't like movies or TV. I've been reading more or less continually for the past five years, but when we try to talk about books, it doesn't go well. It turns out there is a lot we don't agree on, in the texts on our bookshelves, in the text of our lives. Bebe was all for it when I left the testosterone-laden club I'd danced at for years—we didn't need the money, she said; she was fine with supporting us—but when I stopped performing even on lesbian nights, on BDSM night at our own favorite bar, something shifted. It was, in a sense I'm not quite sure I can convey, almost as though she were Simone de Beauvoir, and had written a book—a treatise on our own lives—and I were Nelson Algren, and had publicly trashed her in a scathing review. I have undermined something carefully and artfully constructed between us, and in its wake is a tension neither of us dare acknowledge, a hole in the shape of my previous sexuality, conspicuous in its blankness.

I'm no longer what she signed up for. When we got together, I was a twenty-four-year-old tough-girl stripper who had never read anything, who approached middle class and intellectual culture as though I were an alien who required an earthling guide to help decipher the simplest customs. Somehow I have turned into a well-read thirty-year-old skeptic of our shared manifesto; I've become some twisted version of a frustrated housewife, full of disgruntlement and thrashing-but-diffuse want. Sex hasn't been that great lately. I would say Bebe's losing interest in me, but I know I lost interest first in *being* the person in whom she was interested. I've shed my skin again, but what's underneath the sloughed-off epidermis is raw and unformed still.

"Miguel and Chad want us to go to Mami's for dinner tomorrow," I say. "I think they're going to announce the pregnancy, but they don't know we know, so act surprised."

"But we're already going there for Thanksgiving!" Bebe drains her wine in alarm. "I am going to poke my eye out with a fork if I have to hear anything more about that fucking baby. Why do I give a fuck about its every development?"

"Apparently you don't," I say. "Whatever, never mind."

"What? You want to *go*?"

"I don't care about going."

"You just want to go in case Nick is invited, too," she informs me. "Because he has such an obvious crush on you. You miss stripping—you miss being the object of the male gaze, so now you're looking for it in individual men. Which, I hope you realize, means now those men have power over you. If you need them to want you for you to feel good about yourself, then *they* hold the cards. When you had their desire collectively, in an environment you controlled, *you* were in power, but now it's the opposite."

I mean . . . what does a person possibly respond to something like this?

"I wasn't thinking in terms of power," I try. "Nick is kind of my friend. Emily's a cool person. She's having my brother's baby. I *like* my brother. I'd like to give him the chance to actually *tell* me he's having a kid—I'm not sure that correlates to my addiction to the male gaze, or whatever, Bebe, but fine, if you want to frame it that way, I don't think I was in control at the club, either. I think it just turns you on to think I was. But whatever."

"You've just said *whatever* about eight times," she says, sighing with impatience because I believe myself to be intelligent, when that was never what she wanted from me.

When I was dancing, Bebe liked to come into the club with her friends from the English Department. Most of our lesbian friends never dug the club—some came in once or twice for the novelty, but that was years ago. I remember the first time a few of them showed up, they looked like either the bachelorette party for a dyke wedding, or like they might be planning to stage a half-assed political protest in the middle of my set. Bebe's colleagues, though, are a nerdy, bookish lot, and going to the club made them feel cool and subversive. They believed my working there meant I was a sexual outlaw, like someone Kathy Acker would write about, or at least like Madonna, exploiting myself before the patriarchy could and turning a profit at its expense. Maybe it sounds like I'm mocking it now, but the truth is that after all I had been through by the time I met Bebe, being seen through this flattering lens was like salve on a burn. America, the land of reinvention. I was a feminist heroine; I was subverting the patriarchy; yeah, that's the ticket. "Look at these poor men with their throbbing hard-ons and open wallets," Bebe would scoff into her bourbon. "They think they're the spectators in the zoo, but who's really inside the cage? They're helpless before the primal female energy here. They worship and fear the cunt." Here I should stipulate that English Department men adore it when women talk that way. They love to use the word *cunt* in group discourse. They read books published by FC2; they read feminist theory; they talk about "the hysterics" as though they were a radical activist collective. They all have hip glasses, wimpy or doughy physiques, and are at least ten years older than I am. Bebe's academic friends always acted stupidly excited to see me and disproportionately fond of me, though none of the women ever engaged me in an actual conversation even when my clothes were on, and the men who did seemed to forget that Bebe's words about the zoo applied to them, too.

My zucchini florets look, in fact, like some abstract sculpture of a cunt. I sever one with my fork. "If strippers have so much power, you'd have been one yourself. You're the one who wants to rule the world, not me."

I expect Bebe to tell me that I'm acting like a twelve-year-old, pitching a tantrum. I half expect, even, for her to tell me that I'm getting a caning to remind me of my place, which honestly would be a relief, since even though it would be humiliating it would give us something to *do*. I used to beg her to settle any dispute that way—I even wanted to sign a contract to that effect—but she found the plan impractical. She never struck me in anger. "I'm only turned on when I'm happy," she explained patiently. "I don't *want* you when you've pissed me off." Now she sighs contemplatively. "I don't know, Lina, I guess you can't be empowered by something you yourself don't find empowering. If you want to see yourself as a pawn, then you'll always be one. I'm not trying to say I'd rather be a stripper than a *professor*. But I don't see how it's any more demeaning than having to ask every customer if they'd like apple pie with that, wearing a paper hat. All unskilled labor is run by someone else's rules. The patriarchy runs McDonald's, too. At least you were affirming a sex-positive politics—maybe it was activism on a small scale, but you weren't just sitting around the apartment *not stripping*. Now you just seem like you're slut-shaming yourself all of a sudden, for no apparent reason."

Stripping, or wearing a paper hat. These are what my lover thinks my options are.

But a contrarian even to my *thoughts*, Bebe ventures helpfully, "Why don't you go to grad school?"

She's *right*, but instead of admitting it I say, "Most occupations are only based on some illusion of bullshit need—they just require still *more* occupations to keep bolstering that false economy of needs. Grad school is the absolute perfect illustration of that."

She stares back at me, looking dismal.

"And by the way, 'the patriarchy' just means *life*." I turn away, watching a black woman in a slithery green dress stride toward the restrooms, which of course in a place like this are single occupancy, hence meaning I am trapped at the table with Bebe and my own petulance. I hear her mutter, "Jesus."

I guess this is what people call "growing apart."

It seems to be what couples do. This is a developmental stage, like recognizing yourself in a mirror or the ability to think critically. Usually, this seems to be the stage when couples decide to have a baby, which renews their common ground on a lease of eighteen years, prolonged if they have more than one, guaranteeing them something to talk about for perpetuity. They may not always agree on parenting issues any more than Bebe and I always agree on books we read, but unlike the case with a book, the two people in question are the only people on the planet who will ever be as interested or invested in that particular baby as the other one is, which is, I suppose, what is called "incentive" to stay together.

But you would know more about this than I do.

All at once, an existence that revolves around being "transgressive" and making some kind of political statement with my life feels to me like living nonstop at a cocktail party or an activists' rally, at which people happen not to be wearing clothes. I am bored out of my mind. I am sick of rhetoric and dogma. I'm not sure what intimacy is, exactly—it wasn't my house growing up; it sure as hell wasn't either of my husbands—but I am getting the feeling this is not it, either.

For the moment, I don't move out because I have no money, and if I moved out I'd have to go back to stripping, since it's the only gainful employment I have ever actually held.

Why Bebe doesn't ditch my ass, on the other hand, is beyond me. Perhaps she thinks I am just going through a phase. Perhaps she feels sorry for me. Perhaps she is just waiting to find someone better. Perhaps, even though I am annoying her within an inch of her life, she really believes she is in love.

As we say in the Program: you always go out before you go out.

MIGUEL

Miguel summons what is left of his family for dinner, so that he and Chad can make their grand announcement. Isabel, her husband, and their grown daughter have all fled the state of Illinois, so Miguel and Lina are all Mami and her American husband, Carlos, have left. Essentially, the Christian, married, normally procreating Guerra child gathered up her family and abandoned Mami with the two queers. It could not possibly be funnier, with the drawback that Mami does not possess much of a sense of humor about anything, especially this.

It's been decades since Miguel has stepped into his mother's home without Fox News blaring. Carlos is so perpetually engaged in some manner of home renovation that, in the rules of any logical universe, he and Mami should be living in the Taj Mahal by now, and yet every time Miguel comes over, the ramshackle little A-frame, with its aluminum siding and tiny cement steps, always looks the same.

"A celebratory dinner," Miguel said when he called his mother. Then, as if this clarified things: "We're celebrating."

Lina must have forced Bebe to attend. Miguel came out a decade and a half before Lina took up with a woman, which should have paved the way, but in fact Bebe has had a much rockier road with

Mami than Chad ever suffered. Even Carlos loves Chad. When Chad enters the house, hugs and exclamations of delight fly. Mami has a tendency to look at Bebe as though her hair is on fire.

The smell of rice and beans permeates the walls so thoroughly that it would take a gut rehab to remove it.

In the silence, Bebe's leather pants crackle and stick and make wild suction noises against the plastic sofa covering. Bebe crosses and uncrosses her legs, provoking the noise. The pants are brown and loose, not really Whore of Babylon at all . . . Bebe wears them with a plain black T-shirt and a pair of Chuck Taylors. There is something Euro about Bebe, although she was raised in St. Louis. She exudes sex and arrogance in proportions normally reserved for the French. Every time her leather rubs the plastic, Mami flinches.

"So!" Lina hurls her body forward toward Miguel, violently enough that her small breasts brush her thighs. "What are we celebrating?"

"Oh," Miguel says, alarmed. "I was going to announce it at dinner."

Carlos is in the yard grilling burgers. It's almost Thanksgiving, and forty degrees outside.

"The last time I tried to use the grill," Mami tells them, "I opened the lid and there was a rat inside."

"Jesus!" Lina says. "I hope you bought a new grill. I hope you're not grilling the burgers on top of rat feces."

"Oh, the rat was dead," Mami says, as though this explains everything.

"You don't eat meat anyway," Miguel says. "Carlos could have stuck the rat carcass into the food processer and be serving it to us as burgers tonight and all you're going to have is the salad, so what do you care?"

"I washed the grill with bleach," Mami says, frowning. "I wore gloves—aye, Miguel, your sister's right, if you breathe in the . . . the rodent's poop, you know? You can die from that, they say." She fusses with the ends of her orangutan-colored hair, which loans her dark skin a vicariously orange hue. "Your body shuts down and they can't save you, once it's in your lungs."

"That's an old wives' tale," Miguel says. "That doesn't happen."

"Yes it does." Bebe, of course. "Your mother means the hantavirus. It's rare in the United States, but there have actually been a couple cases in Illinois. They *can* save you if they catch it early, but it's usually fatal because early symptoms are like the flu and people don't get treatment." Good Christ. How does Bebe *know* this? How exactly does the hantavirus relate to Derrida? She stops talking, but none of them have wine glasses to busy themselves with, so after a moment, Bebe seems unable to resist and blurts, "I don't know why you'd assume it was an *old wives' tale*, Miguel, whatever *that's* supposed to mean anyway."

"Sexist pig," Lina says. Then, in the deadpan of a radio announcer: "Miguel—he's part of the problem, not the solution."

Chad, Miguel, Lina, and even Bebe laugh. Mami stares, which makes Miguel and Lina laugh harder.

Carlos comes in with a steaming plate of burgers and a giant, Jimmy Carter grin. This puts Lina straight onto the floor, convulsing with mirth. Carlos and Mami exchange terrified glances.

At the kitchen table, Chad hits his fork against his water glass as though inviting a bride and groom to kiss. "Well," he says loudly despite no need for this ceremony, the six of them knee-to-knee under the small table—"We have a big announcement to make. Honey, do you want to tell them?"

Miguel takes a giant bite of his bleach burger—the hantavirus would be a welcome distraction right now. "Go ahead," he says with his mouth full.

"Go ahead, Chad," Lina concurs; she has Miguel's back, or she's just impatient for the news, who knows? "You don't need to defer to Miguel—he can't tell a story anyway—you're part of the family. Isn't he, Mami?"

"Of course!" Mami booms without irony, which Miguel can't help but think isn't exactly the reaction Lina wanted, though she'd deny it.

"So! Okay! Well!" Chad spreads his arms, though he has to do this carefully to keep from knocking food out of Bebe's and Carlos's hands. "The thing is . . . Miguel and I are going to be parents. My sister donated the egg, and we've been working with a gestational surrogate to carry the pregnancy to term. The procedure was a success . . . the in vitro fertilization, I mean, straight out of the gate, the first time, which is . . . isn't that *rare*, Miguel?" When Miguel responds by chewing, Chad forges on, "They told us it was lucky, but Emily, she's had two other children and *loves* being pregnant—they say the previous pregnancies of the surrogate don't matter, but how can that possibly be true, I think it *has* to have helped. Anyway, we kept quiet about it at first, which wasn't easy. In case, you know, just *in case*. But she went in for her first ultrasound and everything looks perfect . . . we're at five weeks now . . . she's five weeks pregnant." He pauses, looking at Lina for help. "With *our baby*!"

"Oh my god! That's so amazing!" Lina is smiling, but abruptly Miguel notices that the smile is the same one she's been wearing all night; it is her formal smile, a perfect curved U of gleaming white teeth, and not her wilder one where the gums show above her top teeth and she throws her head back so you can see the tendons of her neck and the inside of her mouth. Lina wasn't impatient *for* the news, he realizes; she was impatient for the news to be out in the open so they could *discuss* it. She already knew. Except that Miguel has said nothing about it to her since she overheard the casual, strange discussion outside the theater on closing night . . . he assumed she'd have concluded by now that it was all some perverse joke . . . god knows he and Chad thought as much when they went home that night, until Emily called them the very next morning, gushing with plans, Nick still asleep but, she promised, "totally on board." Anyway, that zombie-burlesque hocus-pocus is over now, so it's not like Lina's seeing Nick at rehearsals and performances . . .

"Congratulations," Bebe says.

Chad's theatrical Face of Happiness has gone on a beat too long in the face of Mami's silence. Lina hugs him across Bebe's body, putting him out of his misery, crooning, "I'm so thrilled for you guys—you're going to be the best parents."

Mami and Carlos are both looking at their plates. This *has* to be one of those moments in which Miguel is being paranoid—is imagining some horrible slight that is too spectacular to exist in nature. He looks back and forth between his mother and his stepfather. He realizes, in a flash of horror, that the identical look of hysterical joy Chad's face sported a moment ago is still arranged across his own features, waiting—waiting—

"Mmm," Mami says to Carlos, as though thinking on a weighty problem. "These burgers are delicious. I'm sorry I forgot to buy the ketchup."

The police showed up at Tía's door in the middle of the night to say that Papi was dead. Even though Miguel slept no more than a dozen feet from the front door, he didn't rouse, so he had to hear the details—Papi's car careening into the Guaire River—from Mami the next morning. Neither he nor his mother wept, though Miguel felt prickingly self-conscious, like Mami might expect some show of emotion he was incapable of mustering. He needn't have worried: after her few cursory sentences of explanation, Mami never wished to speak of Papi's death again, and treated any curiosity from Miguel as a personal affront.

Time collapsed, then expanded in the days following Papi's death. Miguel followed Mami around the small house pestering, "They're sure Isabel wasn't in the car? Where did they take Isabel, then? Are you sure she wasn't in the car and they just won't tell you because they don't want you to be upset?" until his mother, who had never shouted at him in his ten years, screeched, "Listen to yourself, as if the police care about upsetting the likes of me—are you stupid or something!"

Their father was dead, but somehow nothing changed. Mami and Tía gritted their teeth and carried on. Reclaiming the family's shitty little house after Papi's death was never even presented as an option: after only two weeks, Tía's was simply where they lived now.

And then, there was Isabel. Could it have been, as Miguel remembers it, as much as a month later? Surely not. Only suddenly, as though she had been delivered by gypsies in the night—as though all important news arrived in the dead of night while he slept—there was Isabel one morning, the house thick with implicit knowledge that she, too, lived here now. No one seemed surprised to see her but Miguel.

In the time warp of memory, Miguel has no recollection of ever, in the ensuing months, "finding out" about Isabel's pregnancy. Only of his self-contained older sister abruptly being swollen beyond comfort, bedridden on sweaty sheets, and of her shrieks, which he could hear from outdoors where they'd chased him, when she delivered. His warrior sister, who never wept or pleaded when Papi beat them, sounded like an animal skewered by spears. Afterward, there was a baby: a scrawny, black-eyed baby who cried as though she thought she lived in a mansion where people could escape her. Miguel had little interest in her—then, or during the ensuing eight years they lived together, before he departed for college.

How long, though, did they live with Tía? It couldn't have been more than a year, could it? Long enough for a pregnancy to come to term; long enough that Isabel was supposed to be in her first year of high school, though she never so much as reported for her first day. Miguel left the house in the morning to the baby's screams and came home to them after school, taking to the streets to avoid both the howling infant and the silent anger of his mother and older sister, which seemed to him a form of ominous telepathic communication between them. He had no friends on this new street, so he mostly walked around alone, taunted by the other children for having a sister who was a whore, who had borne a nasty bastard, for his dead drunken father and the fact that he and his mother were "charity" Tía had taken in like stray cats. Or maybe he was taunted that way only once, and it seems, now, to have happened over and over again, Miguel riding a carousel of torment in memory. Maybe mainly, he was invisible, learning to tuck himself into corners and shadows, wondering at the life that had accidentally become his and wondering if he really existed.

And then, he and Mami were on a plane to Chicago, with Isabel's baby.

Then, he and Mami were in a frozen, gray city, throwing themselves on the mercy of an abuela *Miguel scarcely remembered: Mami's stern mother, who'd always known that Mami should not marry Papi or move to Venezuela or do any of the things she'd done. Isabel was not with them on the plane—not with them in Chicago—remained behind with Tía, who had not even seemed to* like *her much. From what little Miguel could garner, Isabel was cooking and cleaning for the old woman instead of going to school—but why, if the baby was in Chicago, was Isabel not in school?* Why *was Isabel not on that plane?*

The story wafted through Miguel's fingers like smoke. How much of it was even real? How much was illusory—some recurring nightmare made fact? These were the facts: Baby Angelina, Miguel, and Mami—who was now Angelina's "Mami," too—lived in Chicago, Illinois; Miguel, and later Angelina, attended a Chicago public school and were United States citizens; still, Isabel was nowhere to be seen.

After leaving Mami and Carlos: drinking at the Violet Hour cocktail lounge. Old-fashioned cocktails in fancy glasses litter the table (Lina's soda water and lime could be mistaken for a G&T), along with Bebe's vintage cigarette holder, containing a cigarette, unlit, since smoking has been illegal in bars in Chicago for two years. Miguel recalls something about Bebe once making a New Year's resolution that she would "never touch a cigarette with these hands again," but that since she could not survive even the first twenty-four hours of withdrawal, she promptly began using a cigarette holder she'd once bought to complement a flapper costume for a Halloween party. Now, Miguel's sister is not just a sub in the bedroom but also puts the cigarettes inside Bebe's holder for her, at which point Bebe is free to smoke *without her hands touching a cigarette.* Despite the preposterous hypocrisy of this, Bebe happens to look hot with a vintage cigarette holder, especially given the Violet Hour's speakeasy theme and the juxtaposition of this femme affectation against the butch of her distressed brown leather pants and Chuck Taylors . . . and despite also looking, on another level, of course ridiculous.

Miguel feels acutely aware that something is different than it usually is when he goes out with his sister and her girlfriend—that he feels less uncomfortable than normal, and for an instant he thinks that this must be what fatherhood is all about: a sudden comfort in your own skin and in the world. Then he realizes what it actually is: this is the first time he's ever been out with Lina and Bebe wherein his little sister's petite, curvy body is not all but draped over her lover's, and instead Lina and Bebe are sitting upright in the booth like normal people rather than nearly humping dogs. The realization, while it should come as a relief, disheartens him. Although normally he finds their excessive sexuality showy and a bit immature, as though they have to make a political statement of their coupledom every waking moment lest any passing stranger commit the egregious error of mistaking them for "just friends," the fact that they are sitting like two self-contained entities, not even touching, makes him . . . sad. Is it the seven-year itch, arriving slightly early? Did they have a fight on the way to Mami's and Carlos's, in the car? Is boredom and distance the inevitable condition of coupledom and his sister has finally caught humanity's universal disease? He liked it better when they were making out and talking about the differences between rattan and rawhide canes and bringing him and Chad a "violet wand" as a gift—a positively horrifying contraption that looked to Miguel like something the welder chick from *Flashdance* should be using at work, and not anything he wanted near his naked body. Still.

Chad is saying, "I'm not sure you two understand—I mean, that went really *really* well with Wanda and Carlos tonight. When we told *my* parents last night, we were stupid enough to bring the sonogram with us, and when we showed it to them, they thought it was an ultrasound of another *bulldog* puppy—"

"Which," Miguel hears himself interrupt, "your parents instantly started *screaming* about and jumping up and down, so that was surreal in a whole other fucking manner—"

Chad clarifies, "My mom was squealing, 'Oh, look at my little grandpuppy.'"

Miguel says, "Gretchen started laughing at her idiocy, and Elaine was all, 'Just because you don't like dogs, Gretchen, doesn't mean the rest of us are as coldhearted as you are.' I had to start shouting and waving the sonogram around being all, 'This is not a picture of a puppy fetus . . .' I'm basically standing on a chair with a megaphone, like, 'That is a human fetus, folks!' I'm like, 'Gretchen donated her eggs to us so that's her egg and my sperm and *behold the fucking human fetus*. You know, the thing you don't think women should have the right to abort because it is so human? That thing you just mistook for a dog is our *baby*.'"

Chad says, "Upon which my mother started to cry . . . which we think, for just about one moronic second, is because she's so happy for us . . ."

"But no," Miguel says. "Suddenly Elaine is on Gretchen, hugging her and weeping and jumping up and down pretty much exactly like she did for the puppies, squeaking, 'You're going to be a mommy!'"

Chad says, "My father is literally opening champagne."

"Both of them are fawning all over Gretchen," Miguel explains, "and they're alternating between telling her what a heroic saint she is for helping us, then saying how she's going to have a baby, as though they've completely missed the part where she's not the one who's pregnant."

Chad: "Or that Miguel's sperm has anything to do with it."

Miguel: "Or that we're the ones who are going to be raising the child."

Chad: "But they're pouring champagne!"

Lina has barely moved during this entire exchange. Finally, she shifts positions, folds her legs under her like a child, leans into the table. "So in a nutshell, Gretchen's a saint for helping you," she says, "but you don't really *exist*, so she's heroically helping you in the abstract, because really the baby is still *hers*."

Miguel and Chad shout together, "Exactly!"

"Well," Bebe says, rolling her cigarette holder around between her fingers. "At least they didn't try to put ketchup on the sonogram, which I think your mother and Carlos would have done if they could have gotten away with it."

Lina snorts. "And then poured some bleach on it."

Chad says to Miguel, "At least nobody cried at your house."

"At least at *your* house we got champagne!"

Bebe says, "You should really tell your parents to get a water filter, Lina."

"Bebe, you just ate a bleached rat for dinner, I do not think the water is your biggest problem right now." Lina sighs, slamming her seltzer like a shot. "I should tell my parents to buy a goddamn case of Jameson so that going to their house wouldn't be so unbearable. At least for the rest of you."

As if on cue, everyone drinks deeply.

"Technically," Lina says, "neither one of them is actually my parent anyway, so really they should be Miguel's problem."

"I'm the boy," Miguel says flatly. "Boys are never stuck with the parents."

"No, *I'm* the boy, because I'm the only member of the entire family who eats pussy."

Bebe laughs. "I hate to break it to you both, but Isabel is the boy, because she moved away and doesn't give a fuck what any of you think."

"Okay, kids, okay!" Chad claps like a kindergarten teacher calling for attention; the motion strikes Miguel as queenie and dorky at once, and annoys him, though perhaps not as much as his own annoyance annoys him. "This does not need to devolve into a debate over . . . uh . . . pussy—"

"How would you know, Chad?" Lina says, leaning languidly into Bebe now, as though some ice has been broken. "You haven't ever even been near one!"

"Is that *true*?" Bebe demands.

Miguel stands up, grabbing his sister by her bony arm. "I think it's time for a smoke break."

By the time Isabel arrived in Chicago, Miguel's luck had shifted.

The gap between the Isabel years comprised more than half a decade, from the time Miguel was ten until he was sixteen. During these years, Isabel herself had morphed in his memory, too: a shapeshifter, with no transitions between. At Papi's house, she had been a child: hairless, odorless, all sinewy androgynous muscles and no pores. Then there was Isabel pregnant, on Tía's bed, seeming to fester inside her own body's juices, bloated and greasy and sick. Miguel could not hold other images of her intact for long—Isabel wavered, drifted beyond his gaze until he could no longer see her: his sister, his surrogate mother, his savior, simply . . . gone.

The Isabel who finally came to Chicago was close to twenty years old, and a different breed from any Miguel had encountered. He was a junior in high school and had long since stopped wondering at the narrative of his sister's shadowy life in Caracas. If anything, the past they shared felt increasingly like a photo album of somebody else's bad vacation, to which he had been repeatedly subjected. In her absence, he had become Someone Else. The once-defining features of his identity felt upended, the arc of his story entirely different in the new light of his teenage homosexuality. He had, at ten, been an immigrant. His English had been patchy; his mother astronomically poor and laboring at a factory while he cared for the still-infant Angelina and did most of the household chores. Mami worked herself raw and aged ten years in two before she met Carlos, another drunk, Christ, the women in his family. But life held surprises even in the most hopeless clichés, and Carlos, a bit younger than Mami's thirty-five years, got sober and found God and married Mami, getting a second job to move them all out of their dank apartment with bars on its windows and into a modest ranch house on Chicago's mostly white North Side.

What did identity *mean? Miguel, at ten, had seemed defined by his foreignness, by being below the poverty line, so much dust from Caracas still clinging to his skin. This condition had seemed permanent. Now, at sixteen, he was called "Mike" by his friends and was on the swim team and it turned out that—completely ill-suited to his reclusive, self-conscious, wildly cynical personality—he happened to be good looking, and girls flocked his way, and where girls flocked, guys soon followed. Popular white guys befriended him, and closeted Miguel found himself devirginizing cheerleaders in his spare time . . . an unpleasant job he believed he should consider himself lucky to have. His parents—for he had come, despite rarely conversing with him, to consider Carlos essentially his dad—went to church with embarrassing daily frequency, which seemed a weirdly Hispanic thing to do unless you lived in the Deep South. But in "Mike's" new world, being Hispanic wasn't necessarily a liability. It was Chicago, and in his high school of more than five thousand kids, people came in a rainbow of hues. There was no viable way he could "come out" while living at home with Mami and Carlos, whose church believed faggots would rot in hell, but in just over a year, Miguel would be college bound, probably on some full-ride scholarship. The lens through which he was going to view the world was not yet* set, *but he was beginning to see glimmers that, through some lenses, being gay near the end of the century was No Big Fucking Deal.*

It was to this Chicago that Isabel arrived: a grown woman, with a hint of Frida Kahlo dark hair over her sensuous lips and neither the little-girl clothes nor the maternity smocks he remembered. Her hair spilled like a wavy black sea down her back; her petite body was composed of hairpin curves; her skin seemed to glow with perpetual fever. She radiated sex, even if Miguel suspected that his male friends wouldn't understand the primal nature of her appeal, since they all fell over one another to go out with the most crowd-pleasing girls, the girls nobody could criticize. High school boys love nothing more than a blandly flawless girl, and Isabel's beauty didn't lie in the realm of conformity—she looked like the object of a Neruda poem, the star of an Almodóvar film. Isabel arrived, and with her a vortex of activity. Mami introduced her around the church community. Mami, Carlos, and Abuela all spoke of sending Isabel to Bible study to help her find a good man, and to improve her English so she could get a job if the man was not so good as all that. By her twenty-first birthday, she would be married to Eddie, desperate to cleave from Mami's home, but Miguel yet didn't know, when she arrived, that she would join him in stampeding for the door.

Angelina was in kindergarten when she "met" Isabel for the first time. Nobody ever directly referenced Isabel having given birth to her, much less hounded Isabel anymore to confess what perro *she'd allowed to lie with her and spoil her so young. Angelina had always called Miguel's mother "Mami," and even Carlos "Papi," unlike Miguel. It wasn't a* secret *that Isabel was the biological mother, exactly: Angelina knew, had grown up with the knowledge, just . . . abstractly.*

There had been a story—a sweeping, tragic story in a faraway land, involving starvation and addiction and violence and unwed pregnancy and death—and remarkably, Miguel had been a character in that drama, had owned his bit part like everything he was. But like Mami and Carlos's church no longer seemed to represent the entire world, so it was easy for that other life to seem a closed door, where now this—*dancing on a platform at the underage dance club, Medusa's, and wondering if that guy meant to touch his ass or if it was only crowded up here, and did his friends see the hot guy brush his ass, and Emily was wasted tonight and he might have to let her kiss him if she tried, and Ministry blaring and Violent Femmes blaring and* One, one, one cause you left me and two, two, two for my family, *and three was for loneliness the world was lonely but here was a platform amidst other young thrashing bodies, and this . . .*

This was where he lived now.

GRETCHEN

Gretchen is walking Carrot when the call comes from the Day School. "Hello, Mrs. Underwood!" chirps the voice of the school social worker. "I just wanted to give you the good news that we managed to schedule Gray's evaluation for immediately after school today—I'm really sorry for the delay."

Gretchen stops walking; Carrot jerks at her arm. "Evaluation," she parrots, sounding like Gray. "Do you mean about that eyebrow thing?"

"Um . . . what eyebrow thing would you be referring to?"

"I've lost track of this evaluation," Gretchen plows on, as though it is an email she has accidentally deleted. "I'm not showing anything for that."

"I apologize," the social worker says. Her name is Debbie or Amy or something like that. "Mr. Underwood called me a couple of weeks ago about Gray's problems with soccer. He asked for a gross motor skills evaluation, and our physical education team and occupational therapist have had some trouble coordinating until today."

"Problems with soccer?" Then: "*Seriously*?"

"Mr. Underwood was concerned about the fact that Gray isn't able to kick the ball from a running start . . . that he seems to be behind his peers developmentally."

"In *soccer*."

"Yes, kicking the ball from a—"

"A running start," Gretchen finishes. "Yeah, I heard you. I'm just confused. Gray isn't in AYSO or anything. Is there some partnership the Day School has going on with the US Olympic soccer team that I was unaware of? I didn't know that advanced ball-kicking skills were a requirement for the successful completion of kindergarten. Or, for that matter, *life*."

Debbie/Amy doesn't laugh. "Gross motor skills delays can be indicative of larger problems," she says soberly.

Larger problems. Gretchen falls silent, chastened. She listens to Debbie/Amy tell her the time of the evaluation and obediently mutters, "I'll be there."

And so it is that Gretchen finds herself sitting in the bleachers behind glass while an entire ring of adults in turn kicks balls at Gray. Poor Gray, delicate in his robin's-egg-blue school uniform, stands at one end of the gymnasium, attempting to volley their balls back with his goofy little feet. Under his Nikes and socks, Gretchen can imagine his toes: the way the second and third toes aren't entirely separate but seem, under his nearly translucent toe skin, connected by one curving, U-shaped bone. Gretchen remembers one drowsy morning in the early days of Gray's infancy, when she was still attempting the madness of breast-feeding and lived with a pump attached to her as though she were a cow with udders, lying in bed with Gray at her breast and bringing his tiny feet to her mouth and practically making out with them in her bliss—kissing that particular misshapen toe bone over and over again and cooing, *My wishbone baby. Who's my wishbone baby?* In the humid, jock-strap-smelling bleachers, her eyes begin to smart and her armpits dampen under her coat so rapidly that she has to remove it and she can smell herself rising up in the air: some animal smell of remorse and trapped fear. That is the only time Gretchen can recall ever having kissed her son's feet, and while—well—perhaps it is no more a requirement of life to go around kissing toes than it is to be a soccer all-star, suddenly it seems to her that she has done something horribly, irreparably wrong.

Since the implantation—Emily's implantation with *her* egg—it has been this way: getting misty-eyed at commercials with babies in them, finding herself smiling at babies in Whole Foods when normally she finds other people's children annoying. At first, she believed it was the hormones; God knows they'd pumped her with enough of them to turn anyone psycho. But the hormones have got to be out of her system by now, and since Emily's first sonogram . . . since the detection of the heartbeat formed from Gretchen's middle-aged egg and Miguel's syphilitic sperm, she has only been more of a wreck.

Down on the floor, Gray misses ball after ball. It's uncanny. Gretchen works with statistical probability, and the only way a kid misses this many easy balls is if he's cast to play the dweeby foreign exchange student in a John Hughes film. She hears the muffle of shouted commands through the glass as though Gray and the faculty are underwater. There are bleachers on the main floor of the gymnasium but they made her come up here because they said her presence "might make Gray nervous." But Gray obviously *is* nervous: he has six adults barking orders at him in a semicircle, sending balls speeding his way. Wait—just a second ago, these balls looked "easy" to Gretchen. *Make up your mind.* But Gray is her *baby*, out there. He looks confused, and once or twice he falls. The gym teacher goes and helps him to his feet, and seems to be explaining something to him, but then there they go again with the balls. *Zoom, bam, pop!* like some demented Batman cartoon. Gray tries—Gretchen *sees him trying*—but he only manages to kick one kind of off to the side, and the others simply hit his left leg or get tangled under his feet and he falls again. Gretchen jumps to her feet. When he looks up, he is crying.

Rushing down the bleacher stairs, she is already bellowing, "That's enough!" *That is enough, Debbie/Amy; that is enough, All People Who Consider Physical Education a Real Teaching Field and work out their childhood bullying issues by going into it; that is enough, Troy, you manipulative, Munchausen-by-proxy sonofabitch—let's see your ass come out here and kick these balls!* Except of course Troy can probably kick a ball plenty. He was a tennis pro; his hand-eye coordination is exemplary—surely his graceful feet follow suit. Gretchen bursts into the main gymnasium, coat under her arm, huffing, "Enough!" and remarkably, they all turn to look at her, acknowledge her Bette Davis theatrics involving doors. Remarkably, she is invisible only inside the confines of her own house.

"Mrs. Underwood," Amy/Debbie squeaks. Her real name, Gretchen learned upon arrival, is Shana—but fuck it. "Mrs. Underwood, I realize it can be hard to—"

But then Gray is on her. Hurtling across the gymnasium floor at a speed Gretchen would bet none of this posse has ever seen him move, he flings himself into his mother's arms sobbing, and instantly Gretchen shields him from the team's further gaze with her coat, wrapped around him so that her body and the coat form a protective barrier between Gray and the world.

"I told you on the phone that I thought this was ridiculous," she says quietly now. "My husband and I are going through a divorce, and the only reason he even called this meeting with you was to spite me, because that's the kind of person he is. The kind who tortures a shy, unathletic little boy—his own son—for sport just to inconvenience and embarrass me."

Amy/Debbie: "Mrs. Underwood, when we're embarrassed of our children's delays, we don't give the child a chance to get the proper intervention that allows them to reach their full potential."

"Oh, you misunderstand me," Gretchen says. She is breathing heavily from heat and an unusual influx of emotion. "I'm only embarrassed for all of *you*. Not that Gray isn't headed for the soccer championship! Not that he doesn't act just like the other kids you teach. You all whisper about being 'on the spectrum,' but those kids are the same ones who have been making scientific discoveries and advancing civilization since time began. If you have something to say, just say it. Don't stand around hurling balls at a five-year-old like you're stoning someone to death in Afghanistan. I don't know how you people can even keep straight faces—can you see yourselves, for God's sake!"

She keeps Gray under her coat as she sweeps toward the door. His clutzy little feet that couldn't kick the easiest balls in the world ten minutes before manage to keep up perfectly.

The hours that follow are not dissimilar from how Gretchen imagines people may act when they are preparing to go into the witness protection program. It's only early December—they will easily be wearing winter coats for four months—but Gretchen packs some spring clothes in her own suitcase and Gray's. She slams her laptop shut and shoves it, and all the secret folders with Russian escort receipts and clandestine credit card bills that she has been compiling for the hypothetical shark, underneath the spare tire in her trunk. When she thinks she has enough in her possession to board an ocean liner for a round-the-world tour, she and Gray drive to her parents' house, one mile away.

What does she expect is going to happen now? Does she think Troy will murder Gray for screwing up his soccer assessment? Does she think he will kill *her* for intervening? She remembers the blue light. No—as usual with Troy, the punishment will not be meted out in the expected form.

The Day School is as incestuous and gossipy as a small-town church. The moment Shana sees Troy, he will realize that Gretchen referred to their until-today-fictitious divorce proceedings, about which he has heard nothing. And by the time he hears the news, in terms of the larger Day School population, he will be the last to know.

The Underwoods are getting a divorce.

He must have a younger woman—she's really let herself go since the kid.

Gretchen parks in her parents' wide, pristine driveway. She has a copy of their garage door opener but is too lazy to use it. She remembers her phone call convincing Miguel and Chad's social worker of what a tight-knit family they all are, and yes: maybe all of this—her living a mile from the house she grew up in; her having her parents' garage opener and front door key—maybe this would all be touching and tender if only she actually *liked* her parents. Instead, it seems glaringly dysfunctional.

Naomi gets the front door. Naomi is her mother's cleaning woman. The Merrys insist that she comes three times a week, but whenever Gretchen goes there—*whenever* the fuck Gretchen goes to their house—Naomi is always there, so Gretchen assumes that in this context, *three* means *five*, with occasional weekend emergencies.

"Hey, little man!" Naomi says jubilantly, even though Gray has never said hello back to her in his life.

"Is my mother here?" Gretchen says.

"Oh sure," Naomi says. "You missed lunch, but the hippie girl, she brought a cake, and they're still going strong."

Gretchen heads through the foyer, following the sound of voices. And yes, sure enough there they are by the fire in the great room, already having abandoned the dining room or wherever they may have taken lunch. Elaine Merry, Chad, and pregnant Emily, somehow already showing signs of ripeness, all sit with luscious little slices of what smells like a ginger cake balanced precariously on their knees, coffees on coasters on the side tables.

"Oh my God!" Chad croons. "I'm so glad you could make it!"

"You must be," Gretchen says. "Especially since I wasn't invited."

"Invited?" Chad asks back, blank, as though she was simply supposed to divine that they were here and show up. Which, she supposes, she has.

"Look at your son!" Emily says. "He's still a wee! Jay is getting so big—second grade now. I need a scrumptious little one like this guy!"

It seems an odd thing for a pregnant woman to say. Gretchen stands dumbly, unaware of what the protocol for response is in this Brave New World of community childbirth. It would be fair to say that nothing in her day is lining up with the rote series of responses she has been trained to give in all situations. It would be fair to say that nothing in her upbringing has quite prepared her for seeing her son surrounded by a team of adults attacking him with balls for his "own good," or another woman sitting in her mother's house, her belly full of cake and Gretchen's progeny.

"I'm getting a divorce," she says.

"Halleluiah!" Chad cries out, as Elaine begins to cry and Emily gasps awkwardly. Gray makes no indication he has even heard her. He is wandering around the periphery of the room, talking to himself, counting—his own steps? Decorative teaspoons hung on the wall? Slats of wood on the floor? It is impossible to tell.

"I was wondering if Gray and I could stay here. It wouldn't interfere with getting him to school since it's so close, but I just . . . I don't want to stay in the same house as Troy once he finds out."

"He's supposed to leave," Chad says. "He's the man."

"Nominally, yes," Gretchen mutters, and Emily unexpectedly cackles.

"Possession is nine-tenths of the law," Chad continues. "You can't leave or he'll get your house."

"I don't care about my house," Gretchen says.

"Gretchen!" Elaine's voice is hush-hush like the way people used to say "cancer" in the seventies. "That is your son's home. What do you think you're going to do, live at Cabrini-Green?"

"Oh, for God's sake, Mom. Cabrini-Green doesn't even exist anymore."

"Sure it does," Chad says. "They've been tearing it down for years, but it's still there—I pass it all the time."

"Nobody lives there anymore, Chad."

"I see people all over the place," Chad insists.

"Naomi!" Elaine calls loudly. "Does Cabrini-Green still exist?"

"Mom!" Gretchen and Chad screech together.

"What?" Elaine asks. "You two seem very opinionated on the matter, so we should ask someone who would know."

"Jesus Christ!" Chad shouts, flapping his hands. "Mom! The woman lives in Rogers Park! She's from Barbados! She's probably never even heard of Cabrini-Green!"

"Then why are you so worried I'll offend her?" Elaine asks.

Naomi appears at the doorway. "Capital Grille," she says mildly. "You like I should call them up and make sure they still exist? What time you like the reservation?"

Elaine, Gretchen, Chad, and Emily all exchange glances. Apparently they are going to downtown Chicago for dinner. "Maybe seven," Gretchen says weakly. "We don't want to keep Gray out too late."

Naomi shuffles away. Chad stage-whispers, "Time for Old Naomi there to get a hearing aid!" and Gretchen and Elaine dissolve into goofy, tension-breaking laughter. Only Emily mutters, unsmiling, under her breath, "Not with you people around."

Here they are, then, upstairs at the Capital Grille, overlooking the rainy visage of Rush Street below: shoppers and diners in expensive black coats that just barely stand out among the gray early evening. Charles Merry and Miguel have both come to meet them on this madcap impulse to dine downtown on a Tuesday night, and so—rather, it seems, than admit to her husband that they had been in the process of interrogating Naomi about life in the projects—the occasion has been dubbed a "divorce party" for Gretchen. Miguel, who is an unsettlingly good artist and used to, apparently, study at the Art Institute before settling into progressively more lucrative and mind-numbingly dull options like actuarial mathematics and finance, has brought Gretchen a homemade card for the occasion. The top reads "Gretchen Unbound" and it features a cartoon strip of Gretchen in various dominatrix-like situations, clad in a bustier and bossing around musclemen. It is adorable and funny and infinitely depressing. And a little bizarre.

Of course, not as bizarre as the fact that Emily is still *here*. No one ever mentioned her leaving, and so she was simply piled into the car and ferried along, Chad even insisting she invite her husband, although the man thankfully had the decency to decline, saying Miles and Jay had "a lot of homework." So here is Emily, who Gretchen is starting to believe has a talent for insinuating herself, sitting between Charles and Elaine Merry, as though they have taken stock of their gay son, their soon-to-be-divorced daughter, and silent, sullen Gray, and traded up.

"What can we use against him?" Charles Merry says into his second Grey Goose martini. Steaks have not yet arrived. "Listen, this one here"—he points at Gray—"is young as hell, custody gets dirty these days, father's rights, all that shit, pardon my French, Emily sweetheart." Gretchen looks at Gray to see how Granddad's "French" is sitting on *his* ears, but Gray is playing Tiny Towers on Gretchen's iPhone and doesn't seem to know he isn't home alone in his bedroom. "Illinois is a no-fault divorce state so it won't matter if he's banging the secretary, he could still end up with the kid."

"Troy doesn't have a secretary, Dad. He'd need a *job* for that, remember?"

"Are you sure you really need to leave him, Gret? Because we could end up paying him off for the rest of our lives in alimony, you know? Then he has a kid with some other bimbo and next thing you know, that kid's living on Gray's money. I'm just being practical. You can't move Old McEnroe into the bedroom down the hall and just not talk much? Don't ask, don't tell, that's how we did it in my time."

It is shaping up to be this kind of day: the kind where everything you were ever taught not to do seems moot. Gretchen says, "He's been paying for escorts and I have evidence. I'm guessing we could probably use *that* against him. Even in a state with no-fault divorce, hookers are still illegal last I checked."

"Snap!" cries Chad. He isn't even drinking. There is no logical explanation.

"Prostitutes!" Elaine cries at the same instant. She bursts into tears again, her hand going to Emily's abdomen as if on instinct. "Darling! The baby! Gretchen's eggs could have AIDS!"

"I'm pretty sure they do a thorough testing for sexually transmitted diseases at the fertility center," Miguel mutters into his scotch.

"Can we be sure?" Elaine persists. "Emily, you *must* go in and make sure." Then, as if this is actually an afterthought, Elaine fingers the sharp bottoms of her blond bob and adds, "You should be tested, too, Gretchen, dear."

"I'll call tomorrow," Gretchen says, shooting daggers in Emily's direction lest she protest or contradict.

Steaks, doled out like playing cards to everyone at the table, even Gray. Gretchen is pretty sure she remembers Emily and Nick being vegetarians, but Emily beams down at her slab of meat as though she could mainline the iron into her veins. Pregnancy does strange things to the appetite, Gretchen knows: with Gray, she craved tuna so intensely that she once ate a party-sized vat of tuna salad from Whole Foods, and afterward her OB-GYN scolded her about her mercury intake until Gretchen slunk home in tears. Still, Gretchen has a strong feeling Emily chows down carnivorously whenever Nick's back is turned—a belief that makes her strangely happy.

In Gray's hands, Gretchen's cell phone has been pinging wildly with the sound of incoming texts. She's been ignoring it, fearing it's someone from the Day School calling to expel Gray, which would be at once an immense relief and a significant dilemma: Where the hell would he go when it is nearly winter break; would he fail kindergarten and have to repeat it? But staring at her son, Gretchen realizes this would probably be a great thing for Gray. Everyone says boys who are on the younger side should start kindergarten as late as possible, and Gray won't even be six until July—some of the kids in his class have been six since September. Maybe this whole debacle is just some factor of ten months. Maybe if Gray were in kindergarten again next year, he would miraculously have no problems socially. Maybe amongst the apish brutes in public school, he would seem advanced and be the teacher's pet. She gently extracts her phone from his intent grip.

There are eleven texts from Troy. Nine say, *Where r u?* The next two say, *Where the fuck r u?*

The last one has added: *I am going to call the police and have you arrested for kidnapping.*

Gretchen stares at her iPhone screen.

"You know, darling," her mother says to Gretchen across the table, "Your handbag is supposed to be worn in the spring. It's not season appropriate."

Gretchen feels her eyes blinking rapidly.

"Well," Emily interjects, as though she is someone who understands about seasonal handbags, "It hasn't snowed yet this year."

"But you see, there's both the floral pattern *and* the fact that it's made of nylon," Elaine continues, Vanna White gesturing towards the fabric of Gretchen's Kate Spade. Emily may be bearing her grandchild but this is a serious matter. "It doesn't go with winter outerwear at all. You could bring it on a cruise in the winter, but even then I would say it's more day than evening."

"It was daytime when I got to your house and got abducted for dinner so that Naomi wouldn't know we were a bunch of racists," Gretchen says.

"Racists?" Gretchen's father's neck double-takes dramatically. "Why would Naomi think a thing like that? She's practically family!"

This sends Miguel chortling into his martini.

Gretchen says, "Then why isn't she here at dinner?"

"Oh, for God's sake, Gret," Chad says. "Let it go. This is Mom and Dad you're talking to. The freaking Black Panthers wouldn't have any luck here. You don't see me having a conniption fit that they donated to McCain, do you? We'd have been rounded up to the gas chambers right next to Naomi if that old fart had died and Sarah Palin became our president, but hey, that's fine if my parents don't care about my human rights—we wouldn't want to ruin a good steak."

"Gas chambers?" Elaine squeals. "Charles, what is he talking about?"

The expression on Emily's slightly bloated face makes it clear she has been duly punished for intruding on Gretchen's divorce party.

Gretchen texts back, *As you have probably heard around town by now, we are getting a divorce. Be packed and gone by the time Gray and I return this weekend. I will pay for your hotel room. Hasta la vista, baby.*

Chad, Miguel, and Emily have remained in the city, so it is only Gretchen, an exhausted Gray, and the inebriated Merrys by the time they arrive back in Winnetka. After Charles parks (no one should have let him drive, yet Gretchen didn't even suggest relieving him of the keys), Gretchen goes to her car in the driveway to get her luggage, but before she even lifts the door, she sees through the back window of her Lexus SUV that the trunk is empty, and she dutifully follows her parents into the house. Once in the great room, however, she sees her bags are not *there*, either. Maybe Naomi took them up to the guest room already? But no, as Gretchen trots around the house—nonchalant at first and then with increasing urgency—she realizes they are simply nowhere to be found. Did she leave them at her house: packed bags sitting at the front door when Troy arrived home? Is this why he was threatening to have her arrested for kidnapping? She'd been so sure that everyone at the Day School would have already informed him of her divorce proclamation, but what if . . . well, what if no one had? What if no one wanted to get involved, and now she has just texted Troy some insane shit and left packed bags sitting in their foyer? Although she's not certain why this would be a disaster exactly (she has wanted this divorce for two years), she finds herself embarrassed, her stomach churning like a blender. Leaving Gray in front of the TV, she goes back to the driveway and flings open her trunk as though she may find the hulking bags actually sitting there after all, unnoticeable through the window.

Then she sees it. A Post-it note with the words *Hasta la vista my ass, bitch.*

The carpeting in the trunk is askew. Gretchen hurls it back, undigested steak rising up in her throat. There, under her spare tire where her laptop and file folders should be: nothing.

Nothing.

This cannot be happening. Gretchen stands in the driveway, heart hammering in her temples. How the hell did he even find her car—well, no duh, he always says how codependent she is on her parents, where else would she be? Troy has, of course, a spare key to her Lexus. She imagines him, circling like a big cat of prey. He has, Gretchen would put money on it, never changed a tire in his life. Yet still she can envision the maniacal light going on behind Troy's piercing blue eyes as it suddenly occurred to him to lift the carpet in the trunk and plumb the bowels of the vehicle. But . . . who would *think* of something like that? What kind of person . . . Gretchen stands with her hands to her mouth, for the first time realizing what she is dealing with here, horrified, waiting to wake up, waiting for the credits to this horror film of her life to roll.

She retches in the driveway, but nothing comes up.

Hasta la vista my ass, bitch.

Gretchen has spent two years worrying about appearances. She has worried about showing up stag at work parties like a husband-stealing predator, or worse, being an object of pity—the mannish middle-aged woman with her unusual, borderline-autistic son—while Troy would be out partying it up with Fine Young Things. But no, she was wrong: that is not what Troy will be doing. And all at once it occurs to her: if Troy weren't living precisely the life he wanted and intended on living, then he—an unnervingly handsome former athlete—would have divorced *her*, an heiress with her large feet and wrong-seasoned handbags. No, Troy has had a plan. The plan, it abruptly occurs to Gretchen, implied so much gratitude on her part for his mere presence that she would never actually expect anything of him: a steady job, civil conversation, sex, reasonable co-parenting, a lack of blue lights. She has been imagining that Troy was just tired of her, might be glad to let her go . . . but Troy was tired of her from the onset and that had done nothing to stop his calculated plan. Divorcing her would entail losing half the money, losing social connections, cachet. How has it never dawned on her that Troy . . . wanted these things? At the prospect of their being taken away, taken away by *Gretchen*, she is pretty sure Russian hookers and nights out clubbing are the last thing on Troy's mind.

Her husband is gearing up for war.

Charles and Elaine Merry do not have separate bedrooms, although in most other ways their relationship seems to hold the distance Charles was referring to at dinner. Gretchen stands on the outside of their bedroom door, contemplating a knock. She knows that at some point in her childhood, she must have knocked on her parents' bedroom door seeking comfort, but if this is true she has no recollection. For a time they had a string of nannies who lived with them. One was an actual au pair, from France, but she was much younger than the rest and didn't last long. Gretchen remembers Chad harassing the nannies with his constant chatter and neediness—that he stalked them through the house babbling and seeking attention. He had long, elaborate bedtime rituals. Gretchen does not remember particularly desiring the affection of her nannies—in her memory, she always retained a strange awareness that the nannies were only being paid to love her, and that in their real lives, who knew? She remembers being curious as to whether they had boyfriends. One had children who lived with her mother in Mexico, and the children were approximately Gretchen's and Chad's ages. It seems unlikely that Charles and Elaine Merry ever had knocks on their nuptial door in the middle of the night. When Gray was born, everyone advised Gretchen to hire a night nurse, and so she had—it was the way things were done. Now it occurs to her that perhaps if she had tended to her own child in the dead of night, Gray would be more interactive with her now. She knows, in some pit of her stomach, that this is not true exactly: that the disconnect between Gray and the world is something genetic, chemical—the words "on the spectrum" loom—but for a moment it feels agonizing and delicious to imagine that the blame is simply her own, and that had she stood up to her parents and what seemed to be "the world" and kept her own nipple in her child's mouth instead of some stranger feeding him a sterilized bottle full of pumped milk, everything could be different.

Different how? Different like pumping her egg into a stranger's body and giving that away, too?

On the other end of the door, at her tentative knock, her mother calls a bright, "Come in!"

Gretchen feels her feet wading through the plush, cream-colored carpet. Her mother is in bed, in crisp white pajamas with bright peonies popping vibrantly all over them. Her father is in the bathroom, brushing his teeth with the door open.

She explains the situation calmly. Her mother is an extremely excitable person—is, let's face it, a crazy person, although the source of this "insanity" feels nebulous: there is no diagnosis, and Gretchen does not recall her mother being batshit when she was a child, merely preoccupied and flighty, like so many of the women in their circle. She conveys the facts, slowly and with some redundancy. Troy has been increasingly difficult at home. He berates her and calls her names, even in front of Gray. He spends her money in dishonest ways, attempting to hide grand purchases from her. While searching for proof of his financial duplicity, she found this matter of the Soviets. Troy has been abusing Carrot, and as she understands it, animal cruelty is a sign of sociopathy. Then, the soccer balls that broke the camel's back. "I didn't know what else to do," she says, and the plaintiveness in her voice makes her cringe. "I didn't mean to make trouble." And she explains about the pillaged trunk, as though explaining an assault on her body, even though Troy always accused her, just like he did *about* her body, that she didn't take good enough care of the car. "It's all gone," she concludes. "Every single thing I've piled up to use against him, he has it now. And that means he knows all my intentions, and he's the one with the upper hand."

Her father stands in the hallway between walk-in his-and-hers closets, a towel in his hands. "It's simple," he says. "Go home."

"Now wait a minute, Charles," her mother says. "I don't understand. How can Troy have the upper hand? He hasn't held a steady job in years. An attorney can track down credit card statements pretty easily. I don't see how this changes anything. Gretchen, honey, it seems to me you just stay the course and proceed with the divorce. This thievery thing is just . . . a minor inconvenience."

"I don't know . . ." Gretchen falters. "He says I'm depressed. He says I . . ." Her eyes flood and she looks in the other direction until she can swallow it down. "He says I drink too much. He says I'm a cold mother, and that I'm hysterical, and my medicine cabinet looks like

Valley of the Dolls, and you can tell just by looking at me that I'm not creating a thriving environment for Gray."

Her parents stare at her. Neither one says a word.

"I *am* drinking too much," she blurts. "He's right. I'm to blame." She's sobbing now, unable to stop.

"Oh, honey!" her mother cries. "Who doesn't drink too much? That's nonsense. We all need a little help. *Everyone's* to blame!"

"It's not nonsense, Elaine," her father barks back. "More than half of the fathers who pursue custody get it. That clown wants a buy-off. Write him a check for a cool mil and see how fast he's out of our hair. Well, I'll be damned if I'm going to give in. He wants the kid so much, let him have him. What's *he* going to do with a kid? Call his bluff, I say."

Gretchen steps backward. "You want me to . . . give him Gray to prove a point?"

"Oh, bullshit," her father says. "He'll have him back on your doorstep with packed bags inside of a month."

"Raising a child is very hard," agrees her mother, who never raised a child in her life.

"This is probably always what he was after," her father says, swiping a fist in the air. "I said it from the beginning—he saw dollar signs and went after them. Oh, he had that act down while he needed it, but I'm surprised he stuck around this long—Gray is, what, three, four? I thought he'd take a hike and sue for alimony the minute the kid was born."

"He's five and a half," Gretchen says pointlessly.

Another round of silence.

"I think," Gretchen says, "I need to sleep on all this."

"Good idea," her father says, striding toward the bed.

"I've asked Naomi to come back early to make pancakes for Gray!" her mother booms cheerily. "We can find the cookie cutters and make Mickey Mouse ears."

"Great," Gretchen says. "Um. Thanks."

She stands in the hallway taking gasping breaths of air, trying to survey her situation:

1) *Her father believes Troy never really loved her and was after the family's money from the start.*
2) *This would be more infuriating and less humiliating if Gretchen did not believe the same exact thing.*
3) *Neither of her parents seems even mildly concerned about her alcohol and pill intake.*
4) *She has imminent plans to pop a Xanax and pour a drink.*
5) *In her father's mind, Gray makes a very fine bargaining tool . . .*
6) *. . . but is definitely not worth the "cool mil" that would make Troy go away.*
7) *Gretchen going home and admitting defeat would make things infinitely easier on everyone.*

She thinks of Carrot, home alone with Troy tonight, and realizes:

8) *There is clearly something wrong with her, leaving a helpless animal in the house to suffer Troy's wrath.*

Would it have killed her to bring the fucking dog?

Back in her room, Xanax swallowed dry and no alcohol yet, she calls Chad's cell.

"Listen," she begins when he answers the phone, "I'm not sure what to do next. I can't stand it here . . . Mom and Dad will make me into Lizzie Borden before Christmas. I don't even know if I should bring Gray back to that school, Chad—it's the fucking Stepford Children over there . . . could we just come and stay with you and Miguel until something shifts?"

"Oh, honey, sure, of course," Chad coos. "Don't worry about a thing. I mean, the baby isn't born until July, you could stay for months before then if you need to."

"No, no, don't worry, I'd never stay that long," she says. "Just a couple of weeks at most, I mean, until—" And all at once she freezes. "But wait. You mean . . . if the baby was born . . . I mean . . . would we not be able to stay then?"

"What do you mean?" Chad asks. "You just said you'd never stay that long."

"But what if, like, instead of staying now, I wanted—I needed to stay then. Like in July or August. Would that still be all right?"

"Well sure," Chad says slowly. "You'd be welcome to stay with us for a couple of weeks like you're talking about any time, Gret, you know that."

She feels that creeping sense of paranoia, like she's acting crazy—the way she tends to feel when talking to Troy—but now she can't let it go.

"But not longer," she says.

"Longer?" Chad asks. "How much longer? Why would it be longer?"

"What I'm just trying to ascertain," she says flatly, and all the tentativeness is gone from her voice, "is whether by giving you one of my eggs, I've just made myself and my son *less* welcome in your house instead of more."

"Gretchen!" Chad sounds genuinely alarmed; he sounds like their mother. "Of course not!"

"So," she persists, "just to be clear, if the baby were already born, and say Troy were to start draining all my money on a horrific divorce, and Mom and Dad were being . . . *Mom and Dad*, and were an unfit environment for anyone to live in unless they're hoping to gear up the incentive to eat a gun . . . in circumstances like that, Chad, if my son and I needed a place to stay, you and Miguel would welcome us, to come and live with you and the baby."

"I don't know what's happening here," Chad says. She hears, in the background, Miguel saying something like *What's going on?* Everywhere, couples are making their decisions two by two, like animals on Noah's Ark; she is the only single. There is no man casually brushing his teeth in her bathroom; there is no voice over her shoulder asking *What's going on?* when she is in distress. She is in this alone—and Gray being Gray, his growing up may do little to rectify this fact, and Troy being Troy, any notions she ever held about not being alone in the past have only ever been an illusion.

"Gret," Chad says slowly. "I know you're having a rough day. I'm just not sure what you're talking about here. Listen—I'm not trying to be rude—but Miguel and I barely *see* you. You live in Winnetka. You send your kid to the school you and I went to and belong to the country club. Before tonight I don't know when the last time I saw you in the city was. I'm not even sure Gray remembers Miguel's *name*, Gretchen . . . since when are you interested in, like, living with us in Wicker Park, among the tattooed hipster contingent? I'm just trying to be clear . . . why you would even be *asking* me this? I thought you were talking about this week—but instead suddenly you're talking about summer? Because that isn't what we agreed to, and I just want to be clear . . . but Miguel and I aren't thinking about our child having a mother. That isn't what the arrangement was going to be. That isn't what any of the documents we signed stipulate. We weren't planning on you living in our house and the baby calling you Mommy. Just to be totally clear—should we be concerned about this? We were thinking that this child would be . . . well . . . *ours*."

And it flashes on her then, like she is Mildred Pierce standing outside the window of her daughter's house—she can see it all: Troy, ripping her son from her arms so that she sees him a couple of days a week, like a distant aunt; Miguel and Chad with *their* baby—her *daughter*, maybe, and a sob catches in Gretchen's throat—in a home in the city at which she is only welcome on Christmas and Easter.

What the fuck has she done?

Exhaustion slams into her with a tidal force. She suddenly wants off this phone more than she has ever wanted anything in her life. "I think," she says to Chad, struggling to keep her voice even, "I'm just very emotional tonight. Troy broke into my car and stole my computer and some documents. He seems to be gearing up for a fight, and I don't know what he's after. Dad thinks it's money, but I'm not convinced. Maybe it's Gray . . . but maybe . . . Chad, I think he just wants to *destroy* me in some way. And I'm not even sure why."

"Okay," Chad says, his voice friendlier again, but still cautious. "Just try to breathe. Troy is a loser, Gret. A judge would see through him. I don't think you have anything to worry about. If we all have his number, so will anyone smart enough to be a judge."

But I didn't have his number, she wants to say.

"You're right," she manages. "I really need to sleep. I'll keep you posted, okay?"

"Of course," Chad says. "We all love you. We've got your back."

Sure. As long as I don't want anything to do with the baby I gave you, you do.

She barely notices hanging up the phone, her feet moving automatically toward the hallway, the stairs, until she is standing in front of her parents' liquor cabinet. She stares at it for a while: the vodka in particular seems alight among the other bottles; they have both Ketel One *and* Grey Goose. She imagines herself grabbing a glass and pouring it halfway full and the buzzy warmth sliding over her like an electric blanket, but like the things she imagined saying to her brother, this picture stays in her head, and she keeps walking, grabbing her handbag from the table in the foyer, and heading back out to her car.

For a moment, she imagines a bomb going off the moment she turns the ignition. But of course, Troy is not even capable of holding down employment; he doesn't build bombs in his spare time. She has to get a grip. She drives.

This is all her own fault, and that is the story of her life, really. Who would marry this man—this shiftless and cruelly opportunistic kicker of dogs? She has spent her life looking for love in impossible places, not even smart enough to seek it in the arms of nannies who might truly have cared, but instead living like some codependent little groupie of her parents her entire adult life, searching for some intimacy of which they are clearly incapable. Earlier today, she and Gray seemed to have a breakthrough of sorts, him sobbing and clinging to her under her coat, but she knows her son well enough to realize that already, for him, it is like this never transpired. In the morning, he will eat his Mickey Mouse–shaped pancakes without even talking to her—his mind will spin in a million orbits, inaccessible. Now Chad and Miguel will have her child—this potential new beginning—because she just *gave it away*, signed her name on every dotted line. Under her own forty-two-year-old skin, her eggs are gone: kept in a fertility center as the property of her brother and his not-quite husband.

His not-quite husband. Not that she agrees with that. Not that she agrees with that at all. But she . . . she is the mother. She is the biological mother of the baby silly, intrusive Emily is carrying, whereas Chad and Miguel are not even allowed to get married, are not even allowed to adopt. What does it matter what lines on which she has signed her name? She is the *mother.*

Her father wants her to go back to Troy and act like none of this ever happened. Her brother wants her to play nice, to stay in Winnetka, to selflessly sign over her future to him no matter what Troy has in store for her and Gray. But if Gretchen does these things, soon bottles of vodka and bottles of pills will cease to even feel like an escape, and will just become a matter of course. If she continues to just do whatever is "expected" of her, she will either end up as crazy as her mother—as Troy accuses her of being—or she will end up dead. No matter what happens next, there is no going back to her former life. She is already on the other side of a divide she didn't know existed until today.

She wants more. An end to invisibility. She is hungry . . . for the first time in longer than she can remember, she . . . *wants*, ravenously.

At the front door of her own house, she stands quietly for a moment, listening inside. The windows are dark. It is unrealistic to think Troy would be sitting in the pitch blackness waiting for her, ready to pounce. Obviously he has gone to bed. She will go inside and get Carrot, and then she will be gone. Her parents will never tolerate Carrot staying in their house, and she cannot stand the thought, now, of going to Chad and Miguel's, but in the morning when Gray sees Carrot his eyes will light up, and when Troy's feet seek the dog to kick, that outlet for his frustration will be gone.

She hears whines to her left and realizes—of course—Troy has put Carrot in the garage for the night. He has always said the dog should sleep in the garage, not on Gray's bed. He has Gray taking allergy medicine that Gretchen suspects he doesn't even need, to protect him from the filthy dog dander that Gretchen—the unfit mother—allows into his bed. Gretchen rushes to her car and sticks her key back in the ignition, pushes the garage door switch. Inside, Carrot is jumping up and down in the cage they use when they take him to the groomer or the kennel if they go on vacation. It is a freakishly big cage, though Carrot is a small dog—if Carrot were brighter, Gretchen is fairly certain he might even be able to wriggle out between the bars. But it would take eellike ingenuity, and Carrot is a stupid and trusting beast, despite his anxiety issues. At seeing Gretchen, he runs in a circle inside the cage, and Gretchen goes to lift the cage and drag it to her car when she suddenly realizes: she does not *need* to bring the cage. She can allow Carrot and his "toxic" dander *inside her car.* If, in the poor dog's piteous excitement at being inside a car uncaged, he pisses on her leather seats, she can just wet-wipe the mess right up: no blue light needed.

Gretchen crouches and unlocks Carrot's cage. Her heart is thrumming, every fiber of her waiting for the garage door that adjoins to the house to fling open, and Troy to be standing there, having heard the door rise. Maybe he will kill her. She *doubts* it, but men have killed women for less. Still she finds, strangely, perhaps insanely, that even if Troy showed up at the door with a gun, there is no way she is leaving without her dog.

The cage door is open, but for a moment Carrot freezes, continuing to stand inside the door and whine. "Come on," Gretchen baby-talks, "come on, you stupid little dog, come on." Still, Carrot only tips his head to stare at her, apparently afraid to leave the cage. Who knows what lurks out there? Maybe there will be a shoe to his ribs. Maybe it will be a trick. Gretchen gets down onto her knees, then flat on her stomach on the garage floor, inserting both her head and arms into the cage to stroke Carrot's fur. "It's okay," she says to him, weeping stupidly at the beautiful sight of his black doggy eyes. "I know I've let you down." Twitchy under her hands, Carrot begins licking her face, which is more, she knows, than her own son can manage in terms of affection. "I know you're not the best dog going," she whispers while Carrot licks her tears, "but you're *my* dog, and I'm getting you out of here. Mommy's got you, Carrot, you dope, come *on*."

But in the end, she doesn't get up right away, and her shoulders are blocking the entrance to the cage so that Carrot cannot actually get out. In the end, when she finally sits up, she has to pull him out with her by force, because he has forgotten that she wanted him to leave, and has been happy in his confined space licking her face and under her hands. Gretchen's back hurts and her black coat is full of short, bristly white fur impossible to brush off with her hands, and Carrot's trembling little body radiates heat in her arms as she carries him to the car.

MIGUEL

Nick wasn't kidding—Emily *glows*. She already had this sort of Swedish-farm-wife thing going on—so radically different from the wan-Goth thing she had in high school that Miguel feels spatially disoriented in her presence—but now, seven weeks into the pregnancy, she seems lit from within, the way a pervert might imagine Joan of Arc. It's only been days since their dinner with the Merrys at the Capital Grille downtown, but Emily's rosy light has increased even since then. She burns.

"You know that in France, they tell you to only have two glasses of wine with dinner when you're pregnant," she says, leaning back in her chair and patting her belly. "In the UK, they say not to have more than two drinks a week. I drank with both of my boys, but if you guys aren't comfortable with it, it doesn't mean anything to me—I can give it up."

Miguel and Chad look at one another quickly. Are they supposed to care about this? At Emily and Nick's dining room table—also populated by their son Miles, fourteen—Emily is the only one in possession of a uterus. Without speaking, a consensus is reached.

"Whatever works for you," Chad says.

"Emily's not much of a drinker anyway," Nick says. "She just likes scandalizing servers by ordering champagne in the last trimester. Half the time she makes me drink it once it shows up."

"This time, I can freak them out even more by telling them it's not my baby," says Emily gleefully.

"Or *mine*."

"Great," Miles says. He's an alarmingly good-looking kid, a debut-film teen version of the delicate-featured twentysomething British movie stars Miguel occasionally jerks off to. "So I'm not going to be able to go anywhere with you guys until after this kid is born, is what you're saying."

"I feel like I want to tell everyone," Emily goes on. "It's just so exciting. I feel like we're finally *doing* something, you know? Nick and I are always so agitated by what complacent jerks everyone seems to be . . . we're always complaining about this and that injustice. But we never do much about it—what can we do, you know? We have no money . . . we're not really political. We just sit outside the thing and say how it should be different. Now this *will* be different."

Nick glances at her, and Miguel can tell he's attempting some manner of wordless, marital communication, like Miguel and Chad had about whether or not Emily should be permitted to drink while carrying their progeny, but Emily is smiling happily and doesn't meet his eyes. Nick clears his throat. "Yeah, well, it's a *baby*," he says. "It's not going to undo history. It's not going to close Guantanamo. Chad and Miguel aren't making a political statement—they're just trying to become parents."

Emily blushes. It's a sight to behold, given her already ruddy complexion. Miguel agrees with everything Nick just said, but still, he'd like to deck him for humiliating Emily.

"I get it, though," Miguel says, and his words surprise him even as he's forming them. "I've been feeling this sense of being part of something, too. Just before all this happened, like, the day I found out about the . . ." He looks at Miles and shrugs. "The things that made the switcheroo necessary . . . you know? I was feeling like, what's the point anyway? Why bring more children into the world—what's so great about the world? Just so they can get old and die, too? And it's not like—believe me, I'm not exactly disavowed of that notion or anything. It's not like I've had some meaning-of-life revelation. But lately, I feel . . . connected to things, in a way I didn't before—like my life matters. Excited, Em, like you said. I feel really . . . *awake*, if that makes sense."

"Yes," Emily gushes. "That's it exactly. I mean—I know your motivations for having a child are exactly the same as any couple's—as Nick's and mine were—I didn't mean—"

"Well," Nick says, putting his hand on Miles's shoulder. "The same as with *Jay*, you mean. This guy here was just an accident."

Emily's brows gather while Miles and Nick laugh.

"I was a broken condom," Miles says.

Nick looks at Miguel—that way he has of making things seem like a conspiracy, of drawing you into an illicit intimacy—and in the look Miguel discerns that there was no condom involved, that probably Nick and Emily were just a traveling one-night stand or a booty call in the middle of the night, high, after some club closed down. This fits with the Emily he used to know more than a philanthropic farm wife does, and makes him suddenly happy. Just like that, he likes Nick again.

He likes their house, too. There's a cozy quality to the chaos. Their stuff all looks cheap, but not in the plastic-coated, plywood way of Mami's and Carlos's furniture. Everything seems to languish in a state of pretty decay, romantic like an artist's garret. There are piles of books and loose stacks of paper under the windows just feet from the dining room table. There's a bookcase in the small dining room, too, so that the table barely fits. Albums and CDs take up an additional wall of the living room as though Emily and Nick have never heard of iPods. Even the handsome Miles looks like an arty prop, in a moth-eaten sweater like someone's professorial grandfather might wear, and glasses with a heavy, tortoiseshell top frame, the bottoms rimless. This place is definitely an Abercrombie- and Ikea-free zone. While they don't actually have any milk crates functioning as end tables or candles stuck into wine bottles, Miguel is still reminded of his apartment with Tomas in Barcelona . . . of smoking together on their crumbling-stone balcony with the wrought-iron rail he sometimes bent Tomas over in the dark; of the stained art-museum postcards taped all over those Spanish walls.

Later, on the porch swing, he and Nick flick cigarette butts into a pottery vase that must contain four hundred such old filters, swollen with rainwater from last night's storm. Down the street, some kids play on a felled tree that's still lying in the middle of the road.

"Weird that nobody came to take that away," Miguel says, gesturing at the tree.

"Take what away?" Nick asks, although he's facing the tree and seems to be looking directly at it.

Miguel doesn't answer. He's taking in Nick's nose: an older version of Miles's. Emily's is upturned and perky, but Nick and Miles have aquiline noses, delicate and perfect at the bridge, with nostrils that flare just slightly, enough that something vaguely feral messes up their elegance.

"So you're embarrassing your son with your hippie ways," he says, and Nick snorts out of the nose Miguel isn't supposed to be analyzing this way.

"Poor kid," he says. "He doesn't even know from hippies, apparently. His mother's the assistant principle of a fucking *charter* school. It's not exactly Woodstock over here."

"Yeah, well, I don't know. Pacifist zombies, bearing someone else's child. I think you might be able to apply for the hippie card and not be turned down."

"Point well taken."

Miguel's throat itches from the cold air; still, he is about to test the waters, to say, *So, have you talked to my sister lately?* He feels foolish. He's not certain *what* he aims to test. Lina is a lesbian now. Still, the "now" implies bi rather than homo sexuality, doesn't it? But come on: Lina couldn't have ever been *attracted* to those other guys—Javier, the Joke from the Hood who even had the same name as Papi as though Lina was painting some sign over everyone's heads that said, *Behold while I make the worst possible self-destructive choice and fuck you all.* (Albeit, every fucking Cuban man is named Javier—Javiers are crawling out of the woodwork, should a girl happen to need one for her Oedipal dysfunctions.) Then, Javier's Replacement, which is how Miguel thinks of Lina's second marriage to some unsuspecting slacker who looked like Shaggy from Scooby Doo and let Lina live with him while she fought it out with Javier, slept around, and nursed a massive drug habit—from inception to annulment (instigated by Shaggy, on the grounds of Lina's addiction, since Lina herself, high or clean, couldn't have given a rat's ass whether the marriage "counted"), it all lasted under a year. Still, his sister's ambiguous sexuality aside, with the way Nick talks about his "glowing" wife it's not an *affair* that he's suspicious of, precisely. So, what? Is he afraid, in some junior high way, that Lina is closer to Nick and Emily than he is—that they are closer to her? His motives make no sense to him, so he holds his tongue.

Which feels swollen and itchy in his mouth, like it's being dive-bombed by mosquitos.

"What's up?" Nick says. "You're looking a little *Flowers for Algernon*, man."

Miguel startles, barks a laugh. He's been chewing his tongue, trying to figure out what's wrong with it, if anything's wrong with it—trying to assess whether he's having an attack. It's not *that* cold outside today, above freezing. Still, it's December and he's not wearing a coat.

"Just chilly," he says. "Better go inside."

Chad and Emily are on the sofa looking at photographs—Miles must have fled for refuge in his room. Emily turns the pages of the album spread jointly across her own and Chad's knees, and they look up at the sound of the door: four blue eyes in unison. Although Emily's hair is bone straight, Chad's in blond ringlets, they could be siblings, even twins. They have the same poreless skin and guileless innocence, an attractiveness Miguel hates himself a little for thinking of as *bland*. Which is crazy since, if Emily's aesthetics diverge greatly from her former self, then Chad looks—with the exception of a few pounds—almost exactly the same as the day Miguel said "I do."

"We have ice cream!" Emily bounds from the sofa. "It's ginger-orange. Homemade."

Nick made the dinner—couscous with some kind of caramelized onions and eggplant, with goat cheese; it was slightly ugly to look at but spectacular—and now homemade ice cream? Miguel and Chad have not used their kitchen to cook a meal since the new millennium. Clearly they should be the ones giving a baby to Emily and Nick, not the other way around.

They sit sipping French press coffee and eating ice cream out of faded, mildly chipped Moroccan bowls. All the poetry of this night seems in danger of killing him.

Miguel's throat still itches; his tongue is still acting up. He chugs his scalding coffee and chases the burn with a big, unpoetic gulp of the heavenly ice cream for balance.

And that quickly, all air is gone.

He tries to breathe in but no: the passageway has closed. He hears his own wheezy gasp . . . some trickle of breath that must be escaping his lungs, and before he even knows what is happening his arms are flailing, knocking the precious little bowls off the table: he clutches the tablecloth (batik, something straight from *Out of Africa*) and runs, crazily, wildly, round the room.

Chad, Emily, Nick, making noises like, *Ohmigod, are you okay?* and *Holy shit, what's wrong?* and *Babe, what the fuck should we do?*

"I'm calling 9-1-1," Emily says, loud and clear, waving the cordless phone in Miguel's face, which he sees only dimly, through stars popping in front of his eyes.

All at once, Nick is on him, and for a second Miguel has the consciousness to think the poor guy may be about to try to perform the Heimlich or mouth-to-mouth, unable to accept that their dinner guest, and the father of their collective child, is allergic to the fucking cold. Then it's like Nick isn't there anymore at all. The weight of him is off Miguel's abdomen, where Nick had leaned an arm, and instead the world is gray and floaty, and he is gray and floaty in it—

Then: color, noise, flooding, wowowow—

He's sitting upright, though he doesn't remember how he got there. The world zooms at him loudly, colors vibrantly psychedelic. "What's going on?" he shouts, his voice a volume he's maybe never heard it. Under the raw bones of his chest, his heart races.

"Me, you, and syringes, my friend," Nick says, holding up what looks like a long tube. "Meet Jay's EpiPen."

"EpiPen?" Miguel murmurs, voice breaking midway.

"Jay has asthma," Emily says. "And all kinds of food allergies. They say it's not part of his cerebral palsy—they say it's a totally separate thing and really common now, with kids, but I don't know . . ." She looks down. "We have to carry EpiPens everywhere."

"Reason for my man purse," Nick says, gesturing at his ratty messenger bag.

Staring at Miguel, all three manage grins to indicate gladness that Miguel has not ruined the night by being dead.

"Never a dull moment around you two," Chad booms to their hosts.

"Us?" Nick says. "*This* guy's the one who keeps getting, like, syphilis and falling on the ground choking. Jesus Christ. Can't take you anywhere."

Miguel feels himself laugh, although his head is still roaring.

"We should probably go to the ER," Emily says. "You should be checked out."

This gets Miguel to his feet. "Oh, no, that's not necessary," he says. "I'll make an appointment with my doctor tomorrow. I should probably . . . I guess request one of those Epi things for myself."

"Honey," Chad says, "maybe you should see some kind of specialist."

"I don't think they have specialists for people who are allergic to the cold, Chad."

"Don't kid yourself," Chad says. "If you can charge money for it, there's a specialist for everything."

Suddenly they are at the door. Everyone is hugging. Everyone is filled with miraculous relief and affection, like prisoners who have just orchestrated an elaborate breakout and now find themselves bidding adieu on the other side of a river, safe from the law. Things, lately, are absurd. For the past decade, Miguel has done nothing much more complex than go to work every day, come home, order dinner, watch TV, or attend some party or fundraiser or theater performance that Chad insisted on dragging him to, then falling into his increasingly platonic bed. The days have blurred together in a not-unpleasant fugue of sameness. If all the world's a stage, Miguel was one of those serving as the requisite audience. No drama for him. He'd had enough in his first thirty years to last him, thank you very much. Now, lately, he suddenly feels the stage under his feet again. It may be a comedy of errors, but he is the star of his own life again.

"Next time we'll pad the walls," Nick calls after them, holding up a bowl fragment.

"And put away the breakables," follows Emily.

It may be all the adrenaline from the EpiPen, but Miguel would have to label the warm rush he's feeling as *happiness*.

One morning, the smell of Mami's overly strong coffee still hanging in the air, Miguel found himself alone in the kitchen with Isabel—unusual in their house populated by five people. Miguel was obsessing about the night before, about having his cock sucked for the first time, by another lifeguard at a beach party, their intertwined bodies pressed flat as possible against the pier in the dark so no one would see them in the distance, images and sensations playing in a loop in his mind, when abruptly Isabel said, "Do you know if somebody has a criminal record in another country, do they still have one in the United States, or is it gone?"

Miguel sat up straighter, and just like that it was all back: Caracas, Papi, the constant air of a danger that had nothing to do with pleasure, with parties, with clandestine desire.

"You mean you*?" he stammered. "Have? A criminal record?"*

"I don't know," Isabel said. "I'm not sure."

"Uh. How can a person not be sure if they have a criminal record, exactly?"

"You know." She shrugged, and her shoulders beneath her sleeveless nightgown looked as though she had applied some kind of shimmery body lotion to them, but that was just the way she looked; while other people were matte, Isabel was glossy. "From when they finally found me and picked me up off the street to tell me Papi had died—when they made me go back to Mami."

Miguel had no idea what this meant. In his family, though, he had learned to approach truth sideways and with eyes averted, like one might a dangerous animal accidentally set loose. What was his sister doing being "picked up off the street"? He never permitted himself to think of it consciously . . . but of course it made sense: if she wasn't with them *after Papi's death, she must have been . . .* alone. *He took slow, invisible inhales as though if his older sister noticed him breathing it might be incriminating. But wait . . . Caracas cops were not such a considerate breed as to go hunting for a thirteen-year-old girl for who knows how long, to personally tell her about her father's fatal accident. They had come to the door for Mami. How would they know which of the children had been sleeping in a bedroom that night? Why would they have targeted Isabel in particular and gone looking to retrieve her?*

He said, circuitously, to keep her talking, "I don't think being on the street is, on its own, cause for a permanent record. You were underage, for starters. It would have been expunged when you turned eighteen, even if it were a crime . . . which I don't think it is."

"Yeah, I guess you're right," she said, voice slow and cautious, and he got the feeling that she was playing the same game he was.

"What I don't understand," he continued, "is why you didn't just come to Tía's. From the beginning—were you afraid our father would come there to find you and, like, kill us all? I mean, he must have known Mami was there and he never showed up." But he felt the blood rushing to his face and his casual tone faltering, even as it happened. "I've never understood exactly how it became your job to keep Papi from the rest of us. It was like you and Mami had some unspoken conspiracy but . . . I mean, you were thirteen."

Isabel wrapped her arms around herself and rubbed up and down the sides of her arms with her hands. She made a noise in the back of her throat that sounded like a laugh, if a grim one.

"I knew I wasn't welcome at Tía's, Miguel, let's just put it that way."

"What, because you were pregnant? Mami knew about that already?"

"Something like that," Isabel said. He could hear the warning in her voice, not to cross the next line. He remembered a time when there hadn't been lines between Isabel and himself, when lines were between Them and the rest of the world. Who was he kidding, though? He'd sold those days down the river long ago. That scared boy cozying up to Isabel's prematurely maternal body in their piece-of-shit house—it wasn't even a house; it was a freaking shanty!—that kid was dead.

"I'm sure you don't have a criminal record," he said, using a tone as though she were still thirteen, and he the older brother suddenly. "You're probably just lucky the cops picked you up when they did. I'm sure they were only trying to help. I hardly think you won't be able to get a job in Chicago because of the Caracas police. Getting your GED is probably . . . um . . . a bigger concern, if I had to put my money on it."

She watched him for a long time, not moving the cup from her lips but not drinking. He watched her head bob in a slow nod. Her eyes looked moist, and he felt vaguely guilty as he got up and went to the shower, though from then on, if anything, Isabel was warmer toward him, more like a real sister again, some ice broken. But she never mentioned the police, living on the streets, or any of the things that had lingered unsaid between them, again.

And this is of course how it happens. This is the lesson Miguel should have learned at ten years old—the lesson he failed to learn when marrying Chad, in some blind belief that Chad's relentless optimism could remake him. But he is a Guerra: a fool who never learns from his mistakes. Because although Miguel does not believe in any god, or bullshit like karma or fate, one thing he does know beyond a doubt: if you dare to open yourself to that trickster, Happiness, it is an open dare for misfortune to find you.

Maybe he and Chad see the voicemail light blinking when they get home from Nick and Emily's. Maybe they do, but Miguel has just almost died, and they have earned *The Daily Show* on TiVo; they don't check it. Miguel is not a brain surgeon on call—his cell phone is . . . *somewhere.* He is asleep before Jon Stewart's "Moment of Zen," waking some nebulous hours later to a first frost on the windows and a relentlessly ringing phone. Beneath his cottony haze lurks a memory of the phone ringing, too, in some diffuse "before" time, while he was in the land of sleep—he can't be sure. It's barely 8:00 a.m., and Chad hasn't even stirred. The machine picks up, so Miguel rolls groggily over onto his stomach again.

"Miguel." It's Lina's voice. "What the fuck, where *are* you? I've been trying your cell all night, too. Listen." But what follows is silence; what follows silence is a jagged breath clogged with sobs. "I didn't want to say this on your machine before, but . . . shit. Isabel has cancer. Ovarian. I don't know much more, we found out last night—Eddie called Mami, but Isabel won't take our calls so we can't talk to her. I'm on my way to pick Mami up now to drive to Charlevoix. It's not good, Miguel. Eddie says it's already spread."

Chad, now, is sitting up, too, his hands over his mouth, saying, "Oh my god, aren't you going to pick up?" but Lina's voice is gone, it's too late. Miguel and Chad sit together in the bed, staring at the phone as though perhaps, if Miguel never stands up, never crosses the room to call Lina back, this may not be happening; this may not be real. *Let me be dreaming*, Miguel thinks nonsensically, but that has never done him any good: in none of his worst nightmares has he ever been dreaming. No lightning bolt came hurling from the sky for *him*—his husband is huddled next to him; his baby has a heartbeat; he survived the attack of the killer ice cream—but meanwhile Isabel, who saved them all, may be dying.

ACT II

COMMUNISTS IN THE FUNHOUSE

THERE ARE ALWAYS TWO DEATHS,
THE REAL ONE AND THE
ONE PEOPLE KNOW ABOUT.

—JEAN RHYS

EMILY

Emily's car is in the shop so she has to take the CTA back from work, just pregnant enough to feel bloated and nauseous, not pregnant enough to be given a seat, the whole ride home on her tired feet, the sticky stench of children on her skin. This is the irony of her life, a not-funny irony that has started to feel like a sick joke: Emily has realized that she hates most children, and she can't get away from children, and she can't get away from the self she is who hates children, which is a self she didn't know she was, back when she decided to become a teacher, back when she decided not to abort Miles at twenty-five when she found herself knocked up and thought it would be a grand adventure. She grew up listening to her bitter mother talk about how she wished abortion had been legal when she got pregnant with Emily, because she would have had one, and back then Emily imagined herself the complete antithesis of her mother: while her mother was selfish and had no filter, was constantly spewing bile into the world and spreading her legs for strangers, Emily would be loving, giving, altruistic, perfect. She would marry at a respectably young age and be a good mother and not fuck around. She would work in a selfless profession "doing good." She would finish college and make money and not subject her children to a roach-infested apartment or sit around in a half-open robe on weekend mornings diatribing about the fantasy of legal abortions—a necessity in her mother's mind because she had been stupid enough to marry a car-thief junkie who liked to smack her around. Emily married a man from Ireland, which connoted class and culture and the opposite of everything her mother was. Nick was from a theater family and had lived all over the world. They would have a baby and she would be a teacher and everything would be as far from that stench of bottom-rung-blue-collar bitterness as Emily could get without leaving Chicago, where her upwardly mobile career was already underway. She was convinced of her every oncoming happiness.

Now here she is on a fucking CTA bus, in the snow, with the smell of wet leave-in conditioner clinging to the hair of various passengers, turning her pregnant stomach, hating where she's come from, hating where she's standing, dreading her arrival home. All day long, children want a piece of her, with their infinite neediness, their black holes of selfishness that make Emily's mother look like a giver. Children are the most narcissistic creatures in the entire universe and nobody forewarns you about that. Now Emily pities her mother, who is of course dead, who died youngish hauling around an oxygen tank because she wouldn't give up smoking despite her CPD—now Emily thinks about her mother having to live with *her*, Young Emily, an Emily who must have been as self-absorbed as these legions of children at her job, as her own sons are at home, and she feels surprised her mother didn't give her over to foster care and go on with her life, since nobody was really . . . looking.

If nobody was looking at Emily, what might she do?

But everyone is always looking at Emily. No, not here on this bus—but that's only because Jay isn't here with her. When he is, they are the object of constant scrutiny, judgment, pity: everyone writes their own story onto Emily, the long-suffering saintly mother of the palely luminous Disabled Boy who says sweet, precocious things to strangers that set Emily's teeth on edge. Jay, like his father, never knows when to shut up. He invites people into their periphery with his big mouth, as though his gait and leg braces and arm crutches don't do enough to assure Emily's privacy is constantly being invaded. At work, since she finally, after years of night classes, got out of the classroom and became an administrator and got a vice principal gig that allows her family to have purchased a pitifully mediocre west-side house and stop having to rent, people are watching her more than ever. Leader of a brave new charter school! But all children despise a vice principal. The vice principal is like the bad cop of childhood, and gets all the dirty work and none of the rewards. She spends her day "punishing" revolting children, and no longer has any real access to the few exceptionally delightful ones that made being a classroom teacher—at times—bearable. Her day revolves around the little vipers of the school, and then she goes home and has to put on her saintly disabled-child's-mother hat, and put up with Miles and Jay both also treating her like a bad cop of sorts, taking her for granted, wanting her to serve their every need until Nick comes home and they can ignore her. The money is never enough (the car in the shop again! This fucking CTA bus! Who rides the CTA at forty? She is a vice principal, for God's sake!), and now here she is, trying to scrounge a little more since Nick can't be counted on to do it—here she is in the ultimate irony in her perpetual clawing desire to flee from the Velcro needs of unappealing children: pregnant again.

Everybody tells you that you will grow up and realize your mother was right. Emily has the strong feeling that, as an adult, despite her mother's lack of formal education and the constant stale smoke of her cigarettes (Nick is no better in the latter), she would actually enjoy her mother's company now, more than she enjoys just about anyone else's. She misses her mother, in yet another thing that could be filed under Irony, since she did nothing but try to distance herself and say snotty sanctimonious things to her mother when she was living, but now she misses her like a hole torn into the fabric of the universe: like the one thing that was honest in a whole inextricable system of lies. To her mother, Emily could finally have told the truth and her mother would have laughed, would have no doubt mocked her for getting off her high horse at last, but her mother would also have been relieved and agreed with her every word.

Your husband is a useless loser, her mother would have said. *That accent doesn't save him from anything. He cheats on you, you know. For that, he should at least have a real job.*

You're going to be saddled with that Jay for the rest of your life, her mother would have said. *You'll never be free of him, and he'll suck you dry until you die. You should have had that amnio, and then you should have had an abortion. What were you trying to prove?*

You couldn't pay me to be pregnant again, her mother would have said. *But since they are paying you, make sure you get your money's worth. They're rich men. Don't let it stop at some one-time fee. Play it smart and you'll get more. Use your head for once and think it through.*

The bus stops several blocks from Emily's house. She gets off and walks in the petering snow, hair flattening against her head, bile perpetually at her throat from the smell of the world: exhaust fumes, fast food chains, human sweat. Jay smells, sticky and sour, but Miles, despite his beauty, smells worse: all man pits and fouled gym socks and clandestine cigarettes, his things everywhere in Emily's space, and when she shouts at him that he smells terrible and to do something about himself, Nick (who doesn't even use deodorant, for Christ's sake) says she's being cruel and that she should listen to herself, and who talks to their kid that way?

Who talks to their kid that way?

Not a man who's never had to work a real day in his life and has her taking care of everything for him, apparently.

The fetus inside her is *already* sucking her dry, making the world an even harder place, but she'll be rid of it soon enough and maybe if her (dead) mother is right, the benefits of having done this can somehow extend. Emily isn't sure she has anything resembling a solid plan, but she is working on it. She has another thirty-three weeks to figure this out. Planning has never been her strong suit, obviously, or she wouldn't be living here in this bullshit life of hers, but that's the whole point, isn't it? It is never too late for reinvention.

At approximately 6:00 p.m.—Nick having dropped Jay off after school but then disappeared again to wherever the hell he goes that Emily doesn't really care about—she flicks the garbage disposal switch up, and the kitchen explodes. Black tar-water, with chunks of hostile goo like sewage, flies like a geyser from the adjacent bowl's drain. Predictably, Jay screams. Emily darts out of the way, though not fast enough to prevent debris from splotching onto her clothes. Jay remains next to the sink as it bubbles and spurts, so that, by the time Emily regains her senses and lurches forward shouting, "Fucking fuck!" to herself, to flick off the disposal switch, her disabled son is covered in filth.

She stands, breathing hard. It is possible that, had Jay attempted to avoid the spray, he would have fallen. It is not that she wants her son to fall. Clearly—she exhales; she inhales—she does not want her son to *fall*. It is simply that it isn't right for a person to just stand there, inert, while being defiled by toxic, flying liquid. Jay is conditioned to Nick jumping in immediately, scooping him up, removing him from every challenge. He has become passive, as though he doesn't have legs, when he . . . *has legs*. He has to walk around at school, obviously; he is in a mainstream classroom, and if suddenly sewage water began flooding the classroom, Jay would get to his feet like every other kid and haul ass. But not here at home, no. Because Nick spoils him, babies him, caters to his every possible desire whenever, of course, Nick happens to be around, which is not that often, and then when he's gone—like now—look at Jay, look at what Nick has created.

Jay says, "Mommy, you swore. You have to give money to the jar!"

This bullshit idea: another one of Nick's. Nick, who cannot get through a full sentence without expletives when the children aren't around—who has never used the term "make love" in his entire adult life and, every time he expects Emily to put out, has to say "fuck." Nick suggested the Swear Jar, which of course he only did so as to be constantly penalized for the boys' amusement, and then to have them end up with a bunch of cash at the end that they had not earned in any productive way other than listening to their father curse.

"I have to go down to the basement," Emily tells Jay.

She says this because the last time the garbage disposal acted up, it turned out that it was . . . let's see if she can even get this straight . . . not connected somehow to the main sewage line, and was, in actuality, just dumping the family's disposal debris into a reservoir under their house. In that case, Emily did not learn about the problem via an explosion of filth, but because the festering liquid trash reservoir had become more or less a swimming pool for all the neighborhood rats, and some started coming up through the drains and strolling around her kitchen. She saw one—this must have been two years ago—just sauntering, fat and urban and slimy, out of Miles's bedroom while Miles was sleeping, the rat meandering around her kitchen. They found three, in the end, living inside their house, before finally getting some plumber they could not remotely afford to come and eliminate the rat pond from the goddamn *Deer Hunter* from beneath their house. After which, Nick brought home two cats, as "protection" from any further vermin invasion. Now Emily has to take a Claritin every day—she has had to switch to Benadryl since this pregnancy because Claritin isn't allowed, and the Benadryl makes her sleepy—for the sake of these two overweight cats, whose water bowl Nick has never changed in two years, having what seems to be an earnest belief that they can "drink out of the toilet like normal cats," and, when Emily protests that this is positively disgusting, he has said, "There are four of us showering—all they have to do is go into the shower, it's always wet as hell in there." The conversations they have had about the cats' water bowl have, clearly, been more time consuming than it would have been for Nick to change the bowl.

"Can I come to the basement?" Jay says, excited. Emily rarely goes into the basement. It's like all of a sudden their house has become a scary movie. The basement!

"You should go wipe yourself off in the tub and change into some clean pajamas," Emily tells him, trying to keep her voice smooth.

"Maybe the tub will do like the garbage disposal," Jay says. "Maybe we shouldn't run the water. I should come to the basement."

It's like he and Nick share the same brain: always churning, manipulative, with a warped idea of what constitutes "fun."

"Whatever," Emily says, "come to the basement, fine, I don't care."

Of course she shouldn't have said it. It takes Jay about fifteen minutes to get down the stairs. He's slight as a bird and normally she might get impatient and carry him, but she is pregnant now and he is covered in globular slime, so that is not going to happen.

In the basement, what did she expect: a floor-to-ceiling huddle of rats? It's unclear. What she sees, however, is gray sludge all over the hallway, emanating from the furnace room and leaking out from the back of the washer.

Is this even *related*? Does the washer—does the furnace room for that matter—have anything to do with the kitchen sink and garbage disposal? How is Emily supposed to know this? People know such things—Nick knows them—but it is unclear to her where they were when they acquired this type of knowledge, and why she was never at that place. How does Nick, whose parents were warring, adulterous actors in a small Irish town, possess a knowledge about the invisible workings of plumbing and electricity and how to fix a roof? By no description of his father would that man have known such things or, even if he had, imparted them to his son. He was the sort of man, if

Nick's stories are to be believed, who hired a hooker to devirginize his son on his sixteenth birthday, except of course that Nick was already not a virgin, and he also fancies himself a feminist, and so he spent his hour *talking* to the hooker, which, from what Emily knows of sixteen-year-old boys, must have been a fairly more significant chore for that poor whore than just screwing him—an act that would likely have taken three and a half minutes tops.

Where *is* Nick? With the kitchen looking like the setting for his insipid zombie play and the basement looking like the film set of *The Blob*—where is he? But who ever knows where Nick is? Nick sits around the house all day "writing" while the boys are in school, picks Jay up every day faithfully, but then takes off again once Miles gets home to watch his brother, gallivanting around with his writing group or his actors or whatever woman on whom he currently has a puppy dog crush, showing up an hour or two before Jay's bedtime, just in time to turn on the charm and act like the perfect father and make both boys howl in laughter, after Emily has already done all the hard shit.

"I can't handle this," Emily says sharply to Jay, who is saying, "Woah!" "Let's just go back upstairs. Clearly we have to call somebody."

"Maybe I can fix it," Jay says. He is seven. He means what he is saying because children are stupid, and nobody knows that better than the vice principal of an elementary school. Jay's heart is enormous, Emily will give him that, but almost every single thing that comes out of his mouth is delusional and takes her energy to perpetually deflect in her Vice Principal Voice, without screaming in his face to shut up.

"You can't fix it, Jay. It's too complex, and the mess might be contaminated and bad for your health, and I need to go upstairs and clean up because I'm pregnant and I can't swim around in Chernobyl water with Chad and Miguel's fetus inside me. Let's go."

Jay, clearly, has no idea what Chernobyl is, but since nothing she says is as important to him as the fantasies inside his head, or as what his father says, he doesn't ask.

Back upstairs, it's a crapshoot. Dare Emily turn on the water in the shower? What will come out of there if she does? But what else are she and Jay supposed to do? They're filthy. He still has homework. Dinner was mid-prep, but now splattered, too, with the blobs of disposal gunk. Miles is in his room with the door shut, listening to music on his headphones like he always does, and has no idea that any of this is even happening. His mother and Jay could be on fire, and until he smelled the smoke he wouldn't have a clue. There is absolutely no point in calling for his assistance, because he is even more useless than his father, in that his father *knows* how to do shit but simply doesn't do it, whereas Miles doesn't know how to do anything except play on his iPhone.

Thank God the water from the shower is normal. She strips Jay's repulsive little clothes off his skinny body and ushers him to his shower chair, into the steam, rushing his fouled attire to his laundry bin and then taking off her own clothes right there in his bedroom and adding them to the mix. Since Jay is in the shower and Miles is in his bedroom and Nick is nowhere to be found, she walks naked back to her bedroom and puts on a robe, the bottom of which parts a little already from the pregnancy, despite how early it is, necessitating that she put on some granny underwear lest she flash the boys. With Miles, she barely showed until the fifth month. With each pregnancy, you pop sooner, and plus of course she is old, and whereas she weighed 115 pounds when she got pregnant with Miles, she is now 152 pounds pre-pregnancy, and things just don't work the same way they used to.

Her brain is on spin cycle, calculating costs. What if the basement isn't related to the garbage disposal and they have to fix them both? Maybe Nick can fix the disposal himself. He can get down under the sink and open up the drain and do Boy Things that make the world operate normally again. He is missing and she wants to kill him, but he is in some ways still useful. He takes Jay—and even often Miles—to school early in the morning despite being a nocturnal creature who rarely falls asleep himself before 4:00 a.m. He does this without complaint, sparing the family the expense of hiring a nanny for Jay, since Emily needs to be at work too early for her to also take him to school. Combined over time since Miles was young, this has saved . . . a lot of money Emily cannot quite calculate, as math is not her strong suit, but given how broke they perpetually are, surely the expenditure of that money would have qualified as a Problem.

It has become this: she has to go over the ways in which Nick is useful, in order to act friendly toward him when he saunters in. He can take the car in to be serviced. He knows when it is time to get filters changed and what to do about "the gutters" on a house. It is important to stipulate that he is mostly inadequate at doing any of these things in a timely manner, i.e., never before they malfunction in some way, but again, his knowledge of how things function—whereas to Emily the world appears to work "as if by magic"—has no doubt saved astronomical sums of money over the past fifteen years.

He is emotionally proprietary with the boys, which sounds like it should be a con but in actuality means Emily has rarely had to engage in endlessly repetitive bedtime rituals, never had to read the Harry Potter books, and gets to do her own administrative work at night when Nick is entertaining Jay and attempting to have deep, meaningful talks with Miles. Emily ponders this, in her cheap terrycloth robe, trying for more positive Nick attributes. There was a time at which she could have made a list four miles long and rhapsodized about him until people's eyes glazed. But everything that was once a wildly euphoric pro has now turned into a con, somehow. Everything has turned upside down, not suddenly, but over a slow, unstoppable landslide for years . . .

His looks, his accent—God, were those plusses at one time. What it felt like, to be the white-trash daughter of a neighborhood slut, walking around with such a pretty Irish lad on her arm, making her seem special. But it's not fair, is it, what happens to men vs. women over time? Emily has had two children—the process of which began immediately at the onset of their marriage—and while she put on nearly forty pounds and watched her body and face go slack from working ten-hour days and bringing work home and taking care of the house and the boys and eating leftover Annie's shells and cheese, Nick did what men . . . do . . . some men, that certain kind of man, and continued to grow in attractiveness so that an adorableness in him that was charming and endearing at twenty-four has blossomed into full-fledged (and calculated) sexual charisma that every woman they encounter, everywhere they go, notices. He is flirted with by waitresses, checkout girls, receptionists, even her friends, flagrantly, right in front of her face. And of course he fucking loves it. He can't even pretend not to notice, to politely ignore it. He hams it up incorrigibly, like a politician kissing babies or Johnny Depp making a visit to a middle-aged suburban ladies' book club.

Plus, what good does being hot even do when you're not that great in bed? When their chemistry began radically fizzling out after Jay's birth, Nick, being Nick, decided that they should "be real" about it and get the spark back by talking honestly about their fantasies with one another. They were drunk, which had been the case throughout most of their early dating, and when their happiness pitched a sharp downward spiral—if Emily thought too closely on this, it had happened, really, before she was even pregnant with Jay—for a while she and Nick tried to self-medicate back to bliss with copious evening cocktails, even though both had lost the zeal for it. Emily thought the divulge-your-innermost-fantasy stuff might be funny—might be *fun.* She was embarrassingly truthful, confessing that her earliest masturbatory forays had been to a) the fantasy that she was Marie Osmond and that she and Donnie were having an incestuous affair, and the Osmond family had implanted cameras in her closet to try to catch them, and b) fantasies of being seduced by Damien—the adult version, not the creepy tricycle-riding kid—from *The Omen*. Nick was the type of man to whom you could say such things without the fear that he would judge you, and Emily felt a kind of transcendent giddiness at first confessing these ridiculous—but in her youth truly powerful—fantasies that had informed, somehow in ways she couldn't place, her adult sexuality.

Then it was Nick's turn. And he said he had always fantasized about being forced to wear a floral apron and clean the house of a powerful woman, and lay her clothes out in the morning, and keep her house while she was out working, and then be her sexual slave at night, doing anything she might possibly desire for her pleasure. He mentioned something he called "male chastity" and this fantasy Powerful Woman—did he mean *Emily*?!—controlling when he was permitted to orgasm, while she could come as often as she liked, and of her "punishing him" with increased denial or maybe even humiliating tasks if he disobeyed and jerked off.

Oh my fucking God.

Okay . . . it wasn't really true. Nick was pretty good in bed, as long as you didn't allow yourself to think about *any of the above*. He had a reliably functional cock; he fucked for a normative period of time; he knew how to go down on a woman like nobody's business, which she didn't really like to dwell on since she knew he had obscene amounts of experience in this regard . . . he was an attentive lover, a good lover . . . except for the fact that, apparently, rather than pushing his dick into her vagina and creating the appropriate friction that made them both feel good, he would rather be . . . in an apron not being allowed to come and then getting "punished" (did he mean cleaning the kitchen floor with a toothbrush?) if he transgressed.

As though Emily didn't spend her entire day at school dealing with errant children and their necessary punishments and calling their parents and delivering stern-but-artificially-loving scoldings. As though she wanted to come home and do this, too!

And if they made love and he didn't orgasm, how was anyone supposed to know when they were "done"? Some people have real jobs and things to do . . .

A floral apron!

Let's be clear here: Nick *sucks* at cleaning the house. Let's be clear here: Emily would dearly love to be able to afford a cleaning woman, if her husband weren't sitting around teaching one adjunct class per semester to the tune of five grand each, and writing plays that turn out to be zombie-apocalypse burlesque farces. She is a busy woman and has no fondness of cleaning. Let's be clear here: Emily is no prude and if some naked dude wants to wear an apron and clean her house from top to bottom so that she could lick the floors, that guy is welcome to call her and as long as the children aren't home, he can have at it! But when you have been married to someone since 1993, you know the difference between what gets their dick hard and what they are actually capable of *doing*, and Nick is not capable of picking up his socks, much less scrubbing her toilet daily, or ever, in his entire life, putting away a load of laundry, which, should he attempt it, he would only make her sit there explaining to him where everything "goes," even though they have lived in this house for the exact same amount of time and she has no mysterious, Pentagon-code-cracking organizational system that should make any of it less than self-evident. She knows that what Nick *really* meant by this crazy, somewhat disturbing fantasy is that he wanted her to dress him up and have him *pretend* to clean shit, for twenty minutes or so, before she endlessly played with his dick and denied him orgasms, then, while he happily fell asleep in his apron, she would go and do the real housework, with her sore, cramped hands.

Nick has never once "laid out her clothes," even though she goes to work every single morning to support their family, presumably like the woman in the fantasy, though of course that woman probably has no kids. By "laying out her clothes," what he apparently means is hitting the snooze button thirteen times, so that he doesn't have to wake up to take the boys to school until Emily is on her way out the door, dressed just fine on her own, thanks, like a normal person anyway.

Is this the kind of thing he does then, with his frequent crushes he doesn't think she notices? Emily . . . isn't sure. What's more, she isn't sure how much she cares. He makes pretty frequent overtures toward sex at home, although not since the pregnancy, which is fine with her. It's been years since he mentioned this "chastity" thing, and from what Emily can tell, he still likes to shoot his wad at least once a week into her, mainly at night in bed when the boys are asleep, and when Emily would like to be sleeping, too. In this sense, his desire and frequency since around the time of Jay's birth seems more consistent with long-married middle-agers than with a man having frequent hot-and-heavy affairs, who might either overcompensate with hypersexuality or spurn her altogether, so Emily has deduced that Nick's tendency to fall into infatuations at the drop of a hat is mainly just an extension of his *fantasy* life, like the floral apron. Which, on measure, is . . . more pro than con, she supposes. Her many resentments have built such that it's hard to really . . . *want* him, exactly . . . but she has also gained weight and spends most of her day around children and women, and it is somewhat gratifying to know that this good-looking Irish guy all the waitresses flirt with still wants to stick it in her and get off.

Or at least it had seemed to Emily prior to the Question of Lina.

By 7:00 p.m., Emily is on her knees, sponging and mopping and slopping up the grotesque horror show that has become her kitchen, when the phone rings. She lunges for it with her filthy cleaning gloves, immediately regretting having done so because now she will have to take a Q-tip dipped in cleaning fluid and cleanse around all the different buttons on the phone, but she presumes it's probably Nick, and she is not so far gone in this cleaning process that he couldn't help her if she told him to get his ass home right now. Nick is profoundly averse to confrontation, and if Emily were to raise her voice and say something like, *Get your ass home now and help me*, he would come home immediately. He doesn't, however, find anger an attractive quality, and can become petulant and taciturn if she uses it on him too much, making her feel again like she is dealing with one of the kids at school, so she has to be judicious in her blowups, and most likely, *The entire house seems to have exploded sewage, it's horrible*, would be enough to get him here. She begins her conversation, "You won't believe . . ."

But in her tizzy, she hasn't checked caller ID, and it's Chad on the other end of the line.

"Oh my God, what? Are you okay?"

Emily sighs. Chad is dear. She likes that he asked "you" instead of "the baby." She likes it even if he doesn't mean it. Who ever told this generation of educated Americans that they were supposed to say everything the way they mean it? What is *wrong* with people? Don't they care about how they are being perceived? Chad, Emily has noted, seems to understand about "appearances" and manners. This is probably because he's so rich, though Emily was raised by a single mother below the poverty line and she, too, understands, so perhaps this is just called Intelligence.

After Chad thanks her again profusely for "saving Miguel's life last night," she gives him a quick but theatrical rundown of the disrepair that is her home. Chad is a good audience. He gasps at all the right moments and laughs at her jokes. He isn't like Nick, who would be running his hands like a maniac through his shambolic hair, swearing under his breath, worrying about money he does nothing to provide, and going to pop an Ativan before doing anything useful.

"Okay," Chad is saying, laughing like this is all a very good joke, "so as soon as your son is out of the shower, you guys go out and buy some hazmat suits. Meanwhile, I'll send over one of my crews first thing in the morning and get it all straightened out. Don't bother cleaning before then because they'll just make more of a mess. Barb can come and clean it all up once they're done."

"Barb?" Emily says. *Crews. Straightened out.*

"Our cleaning woman," Chad says. "It's bizarre, actually, because Miguel and I have had four different cleaning women since we met, and every single one of them has been named Barb."

Emily has no idea what to say to this.

"They're all Polish!" Chad hoots, by way of explanation.

Emily thinks: *Barbara Streisand. Barbara Kingsolver.* Though she went to public schools in Chicago—as of course did Miguel—so she knows a thing or two about *Polish*, which in Chicago is as strong an ethnic block as African American. The Poles are cliquish and obsessed with their culture, and tend toward political conservatism, speaking Polish at home until the day they die, and owning cleaning services, and none of it makes any sense to her, as they often have blond hair and blue eyes and look exactly like the people who run America, but they apparently patently refuse, preferring to go to their Polish dance parties on the weekend and scrubbing other people's floors.

"Okay," she says. She intrinsically understands that Barb is being "comped" to her, like a man in the olden days loaning out his wife to repay a debt. She is fine with this. Chad will compensate or not compensate Barb, but the upshot is the same for Emily. About the "crew," however, she is skeptical. "Are you going to send me some kind of estimate for the plumbing work?" she says casually. "I'm sure your crew is amazing, but Nick and I may not be able to afford . . . a crew. We might, like, need some guy with a plumber's crack from Craigslist or something."

"Are you crazy?" Chad says. "You're not paying! Good lord! Do you want me to come pick you up right now and get you out of there? Nick can watch the kids, right? We can go somewhere and drink umbrella drinks—they can make yours a virgin if you like. Miguel says tiki lounges are all the rage, even though he never wants to go out and only says that to make me feel old and square."

Emily laughs genuinely now. She likes sickly sweet umbrella drinks, which Nick thinks are ridiculous. She likes tiki lounges, having frequented them in the 1980s with her fake ID. She likes Chad, and only in this moment does she realize that *something* is clicking into place just as she thought it would. Something she was afraid to articulate, even to herself, because it seemed . . . misguided. But it is happening—she is only seven weeks pregnant, and already it is *working*.

If someone had injected her with truth serum the night she badgered Nick that they should have Chad and Miguel's child for what was clearly no logical reason, her not having seen Miguel for some twenty years and their already having their hands full between her demanding career and Jay, what Emily would have said (and what it was absolutely imperative that she hide from everyone on the planet, especially Nick but perhaps also herself) was that she had made the offer because she was afraid Lina was *different* to Nick, and Miguel was Lina's sister, and Emily wanted to insinuate herself into this potentially problematic situation and thereby control it. She was so acclimated to Nick's crushes that they barely fazed her anymore—maybe, even, they alleviated a certain pressure on her to pretend to be more interested in him than she really was, and allowed their marriage to function more smoothly. But throughout the months of the ridiculous zombie play, something was . . . happening. Nick talked about Lina almost constantly at home. *Lina said this, Lina said that*. And about two weeks before the closing-night party, he had told her, in his guileless Nick way, that Lina was making him "love and understand himself more" and that their friendship had been a powerfully positive force "of self-acceptance" in his life and that he was really going to miss it.

Love and understand himself more?

How exactly was some thirty-year-old stripper assisting her husband with "self-acceptance"?

And did he think she didn't understand that the sentence *I am really going to miss it* translated directly, in man-speak, to *I am going to continue my involvement with this woman*?

There was simply no way on the planet that Nick was going to be permitted—after all she had done for him—to abandon and humiliate her that way, in front of everyone.

Lina was, apparently, a lesbian. As such, Emily had avoided fighting with Nick about the friendship, for fear of appearing controlling and possessive in ways that were the opposite of "self-acceptance" and whatever the hell else he thought Lina was selling. But Nick used to fuck a lot of lesbians. That sounded weird—none of the lesbians Emily knew went off for the occasional roll in the hay with a dude—but it was one of the stories she had heard him tell over and over and over again until it had gone from the height of charisma to making her want to put a fork in her eye: when he lived in London, after fleeing his oppressively small Irish town, he went through a period wherein he fell in company with a group of hot lipstick lesbians, and more than half their number at one time or another took him to bed, almost all but the one he was actually there to stalk and believed himself in love with.

So Lina was a lesbian. That was supposed to make her safe. But with Nick, nothing was "normal." Everything was zombie plays and no income and coming and going at will and confessions about floral aprons and sudden comments that were truly so uproariously funny that their sons thought he was a rock star.

So: a baby. For nine months—for longer—she would be able to "keep tabs" on Nick and Lina via Miguel, her old friend. She would be the do-gooder carrying their baby, and even Nick, with his man-brain, would be too ashamed to fuck one of the baby daddies' trampy little sisters, with the tacky tit tattoo. She would nip this nonsense in the bud, and Lina could crawl back under the little ghetto rock from whence she came, a rock not unlike those Emily's mother had once lived under, though Emily's mother had not been smart enough to strip and turn her tackiness into an economic commodity: she and Emily had just lived in squalor while Mom gave it away for free.

"Miles!" she calls loudly, not bothering to knock on his door. "You're watching your brother until Dad gets home, okay? I'm going out to talk some business with Chad."

"'Kay," Miles calls from behind his door.

Emily almost calls back that when Nick gets home, he should not clean the kitchen because Polish Barb is on it . . . but then she changes her mind. Why *shouldn't* Nick clean the kitchen? If "the crew" makes another mess tomorrow, Barb will take care of that, Chad said. There's no reason they have to *begin* with a mess. Why shouldn't Nick do something useful?

She scrambles out of her too-tight robe, puts on tights and a skirt and a boxy turtleneck, wets her hair to make sure nothing of Chernobyl is still living in it and combs it out and braids it. She puts on some bright pink lipstick (Nick doesn't like her lipstick; he prefers red).

She waits at the door, like on a date, the feeling still bubbling inside her that somehow *it has worked.*

What? *What* worked? She and Nick have only agreed to take ten thousand dollars for the surrogacy. The boys offered thirty—thirty!—but Nick said he wouldn't go along if they took that much, and at first Emily argued, but then something began to settle in her: a kind of dangerously hopeful epiphany.

By looking like she was "not doing it for the money," she was making it less of a business transaction. She was getting in Chad's and Miguel's permanent good graces. She was the hero of the story . . .

Chad and Miguel—poverty-stricken Miguel from their high school days—are almost unfeasibly wealthy men. Chad owns hundreds of properties. Hundreds. They just bought one of those historic mansions lining Wicker Park. Chad's family has houses and condos in Wisconsin, Miami, Puerto Vallarta, Scottsdale. In taking only one-third the money they were offering her, Emily was actually . . . opening the door to more, if she played her cards right. If she became a friend. The kind of friend everyone knows isn't a gold digger, and therefore asks to hold the gold.

"Where are you going, Mommy?" Jay says, standing in his hooded towel. "I'm hungry."

"Well, clearly I can't cook in that train wreck of a kitchen," Emily snaps. "When your father gets home, have him run out and pick something up for you."

"Where are you going?"

"Out with Chad."

"About the baby?" Jay asks.

"Yes, about the baby." Emily checks behind the curtain for the lights of Chad's car.

"Are you going to like the new baby more than me?" Jay says, behind her.

Emily snorts. "It's not my baby. I don't like the new baby in any particular way."

"I'm still your baby, then?" Jay asks, and Emily immediately thinks of how Nick coddles him. A child with special needs shouldn't talk this way—shouldn't behave immaturely for his age—it only encourages his being teased.

"You will always be my youngest child, yes," Emily corrects. "You aren't a baby, but you are not in competition with this baby, if that's what you're asking, because this baby is not mine, and is nothing to me." Then, seeing headlights approaching, she adds, "We don't say that to other people because it's rude. It's my job to keep this baby safe. But it is a business transaction and I want to do a good job, just like I would do a good job at the school where I work. It's not about you."

"Oh," Jay says.

Emily races out the door, not kissing him good-bye, because she has confirmed that he is not in competition with the baby, but she doesn't wish to reward his clingy behavior, so she has done quite enough. She goes more slowly down her front stairs so that Chad will see she is "being careful" and doing a good job, just like she said. She gets into his car (he drives a dump, unbefitting of his economic status) and experiences herself as lighter than she has felt in ages, almost girlish in her excitement, like on a first date, the entire world of possibilities spread at her feet.

Because sometimes, just sometimes, after a lifetime of stupid mistakes, you finally do something right and get a do-over. And here is Chad, smiling, and that—it is suddenly abundantly clear to Emily—is exactly what this is.

LINA

On Beaver Island, it's like the world ends every winter. The drive from Chicago is seven hours just to get to Charlevoix, where then you have to wait to catch a two-plus-hour ferry to the island. By early December, this usually means waiting overnight, because the ferries don't take off every few hours like in the summer. By January, the ferry won't run at all, and the island will be in quarantine all winter long aside from its tiny, exorbitantly priced airport. This poses logistical problems Mami and I cannot wrap our minds around. We are from the city. When it snows in Chicago, the plows are out on the streets at 4:00 a.m. The city never shuts down. On Beaver Island, the island residents could be cannibalizing one another for all the contact they have with the outside world. How is Isabel supposed to get advanced medical treatment in a place where even the Internet can only be accessed at the library, which is hardly ever open, so people congregate in the parking lot trying to get online? It's like Isabel has gotten cancer on Little House on the Goddamn Prairie.

Mami sobs for the seven-hour ride, which is something people say but I fucking mean it. Her stamina is impressive. She wails like a banshee, like an Indian bride set on fire and going down with her husband, like she is immolating inside my car. I have no idea what to do with her. The history between Mami and Isabel feels like a minefield. I am one of the mines buried under the ground, and I don't know what to do with myself. I would like to make it easier on them and bury the evidence of my existence, but instead I am driving the car. There is no articulating how much I would like to shut up my mother who is not my mother; how much I would like a Jameson and a handful of Oxys; how much I would like to slice a razor or a knife along the tender inside of my arms; how much I wish Miguel were in the car with me. I am ready to explode, but when I look in the rearview mirror I look normal, and the schism unsettles me further. I'm wearing lipstick because I'm apparently an asshole. I swerve around and nearly get us killed half a dozen times, but Mami's hysteria is not feigned; she doesn't suddenly sit upright and chide me for my careless driving—she is the real deal of grief and doesn't even notice trucks blowing their foghorns at my incompetency.

I have only been to Charlevoix once, in the summertime of 2005 when it was bursting with cheesy Midwestern tourists and preppy boat people stuffing their faces with fudge and ice cream, strolling around browsing sweatshirt shops and the one decent bookstore. It's a ghost town in December. Little restaurants litter the main street along the waterfront, and inside any single one of them I could order a glass of wine—nothing radical, just a discreet glass of Pinot Noir, an appropriate letting off of steam for a woman whose sister/mother is living on a soon-to-be-quarantined island with metastasized cancer—a nice warm red to pair with cold Michigan air. Mami, I should stipulate, has no comprehension of twelve-step programs, though of course being Baptist she does not drink. I could order a glass of wine in her presence and she would notice this even less than the trucks that nearly killed us on the highway. This is important: I want you to know that I could have ordered a glass of wine, but didn't. I will always want someone to give me a medal for that, every single day of my life, even though it's childish and I don't deserve a medal for living inside my own head instead of making myself disappear. Don't other people have to live inside their heads, too? But this is a slippery slope of rationalizations: Are the other people here, in this quaint tourist joint off-season, fighting to quell the perpetual roar of their brains? Do their heads sound like mine? Are their sisters dying? Are their sisters their mothers?

All addicts, under layers of self-loathing and shame so thick you can't reach the skin, have hearts beating with belief in their own exceptionalism. *I am the piece of shit at the center of the universe.* The reward for sobriety is supposed to be an ability to face myself in a mirror. Problem is, there are a lot of ways to be ashamed in a mirror. You don't have to be drunk or high, as you and I have both discovered, Nick. I say this now to be collusive with you, because I love when we are coconspirators, but really I have always known this. All it takes is noticing that I took the time not only to put on dark red Chanel lipstick before leaving to drive my grieving mother to my dying sister on her quarantined island, but to *reapply* said lipstick in the toilet of some gas station where I texted you, *Kill me now. Get ammo and scale some tree and put a bullet in my brain like a sniper when I can't see it coming, you'd be doing me a favor.* And you texted me, *You're talking to the wrong guy*, and I started laughing hard because you told me once that every single sentence in the universe can be answered with one of the following statements: *I don't know*, and, *You're talking to the wrong guy*, and I'd been trying to think of exceptions ever since but couldn't. I texted back, *Oh I'm talking to the right guy all right. You're my idea man.* And you wrote, *I'm so sorry sweet girl. I'm no good with a gun but I've got your back.*

We are weeks away from sleeping together, though we don't know it. I may be an asshole, but I am not yet the villain of any larger story. Right now we are merely (merely?) best friends, in a kind of delighted, over-the-top way of two kids who meet on the first day of summer camp and immediately recognize one another as fellow troublemakers. You have a wife and two sons, one of whom has cerebral palsy;

I have two divorces, a lover who treats sex like her personal Mount Everest, and a family history that reads like some amalgamation of Shakespeare, Freud, and a telenovela. But none of that particularly matters because the artsy white guy and the exotically ethnic lesbian are a recognizable (even cliché) friend pairing in tribes like ours, and so we make a kind of sense, and no one has thought to question us yet.

I don't order the wine, Nick.

Mami and I have missed that day's ferry by a good stretch, so we share a tiny motel room off the main drag, at a place called Villa Moderne. Several letters in the sign fail to light up and cannot be seen in the dark so that the sign reads "Vi la M dern." That is good enough for us.

"No offense, but I'm not going to be able to sleep if you're crying all night long," I whisper to Mami in the motel office. "We should probably get two rooms." But Mami has her Stranger Smile plastered on her face, her White Person Smile, even if the white person in question is only a townie high school boy, and she asks for one room, pays cash like a fugitive. I don't speak up to change anything. In our room, Mami tries to call Isabel again without avail, sobs her way through some basic cable, and falls asleep before 10:00 p.m., the room now quieter in the end than my Chicago apartment, few cars even on the road. Still, I'm nocturnal. I text back and forth with you like we always do late at night, smoking on the rocking chairs in front of the motel with my mother's down coat wrapped around my pajamas. I exhale smoke and visible breath into the sharp air, with no idea that you and I will soon be at this motel together, because how on earth would I know something like that? I don't know yet that, if Time is an illusion, then right now you and I are already tangled on the bed of the room around the corner; that we are already on these wooden rockers sharing one of my cigarettes with the filter ripped off. We have seen each other nearly every single day for half a year or so, but other than the casually tight hugs you give everyone and the way we pass cigarettes between us savoring the imprint of one another's mouths, we have never touched. You have a crush on me, in a way befitting a long-married man on his "safe" dyke friend; you have a crush on me, in a way befitting my constant need to be perceived and desired; we are both happy with this arrangement, this titillating, nonthreatening arrangement; these are the stories I tell myself.

But what does it matter what I believe, when it's already clear that I am a person not to be trusted about anything? What does that matter when Mami and I don't even have any idea how to get Isabel off the island to a hospital? Part of what is wrong with me is that I have no perspective.

Isabel's husband meets us at the ferry. Mami is seasick from the December waves. She's been orange for about a decade now, which Miguel and I can never figure out—she is not the type to go to tanning beds; maybe a self-tanning cream or something?—but under the orange, green around her gills now, too. Mami is some kind of rainbow, staggering down the metal staircase and pouring herself out into the parking lot, into Edwin's arms. Edwin Martinez is not That Kind of Latino, but Mami doesn't care; she doesn't understand the difference and touches him all the time, gesturing with her hands in his face, raising her voice and pantomiming emotions with her eyes and mouth until Eddie looks dizzy. He keeps making small, jerky motions that I know indicate a desire to move us into his truck, parked on the other side of the metal chains cordoning off the ferry, but I don't follow him. I stand there passive-aggressively clutching my luggage and leave the two of them to fend for themselves, speaking their amalgamation of Spanish and English and yet having no idea how to bridge a gulf of translation. It takes Eddie ten minutes in the whipping wind to get Mami across the lot and inside the truck. Normally I would be chewing my own leg off to get out of the cold but I'm numb. I should sit between them, as the youngest, but I don't want to press up against Eddie so I let Mami crawl over, her short legs barely enabling her to get inside the truck's cab. I lean my cheek into the frosty window and try to stop the jackhammer noise in my skull, like icing a wound, but neither Mami nor my head will quiet down.

Sloptown Road. My biological mother lives on Sloptown Road.

Her house is one of the prettiest on the island, though, outside of some of the really fancy ones on Donegal Bay. The house has a name, "Strong's Landing," origins unclear, but it used to be a B&B by the same name. It sits on a twenty-acre apple orchard, with wooded trails in the back. It's the oldest still-lived-in log cabin on the island or something, too, although most of the house is a new expansion, and only the little living room with the potbellied stove and one upstairs bedroom still have the original log walls. When I came that one time three years ago in the summer, the outside of the house exploded with flowers in that deliberately haphazard way of an overgrown English garden. Isabel's pretty, old-fashioned pink bicycle was propped against the house amidst a tangle of flowers, and I would borrow it and ride to the beach, where I could look out at one of the lighthouses and see the ferries coming in. Even in high season the island had a deserted feel; every time a car passed me on the road, the driver would wave, as though stunned to have encountered another human being. In the mornings, I would ride Isabel's pink bike to the tiny airport, down a long unpaved, gravelly road canopied by trees growing from either side and touching in the middle. The bike and the trees made me feel like I was in the South of France, in some foreign film, rather than in Upper Michigan where the best place in town to get breakfast was some weird little joint attached to an airstrip. People with private planes would fly in, eat breakfast, and fly out. It was some kind of Thing, the waitress explained; this was something rich people with planes did, not just here but other places, too. They flew places and ate at airport restaurants and got back in their planes.

It occurs to me that I am making it sound like I did all of this *alone*, but of course you know I don't like doing anything alone. Miguel was with me, riding Eddie's bike and "making peace" after more than five year's relative estrangement with Isabel, following her crazy bullshit around his wedding. Isabel and Miguel were flawlessly polite to one another, as though cast in a BBC miniseries about English servants with stiff upper lips and perfect manners. Nothing of substance was ever discussed, and although we were all adults, mainly the trip consisted of the illusion that Miguel and I were constantly sneaking out of the house to smoke. Miguel called Eddie's bike the Hobbit Bike, and late in the trip his back went out from taking it around everywhere on the bumpy roads. We would sit at the outdoor picnic tables of the airport restaurant and smoke our lungs raw and drink coffee and I guess eat. We would talk like Miguel and I do: like every word is a secret of great import, though really we did nothing but gripe about our repressed, religious family and trade stories about our sex lives, our laughs always dry and under our breaths.

In December, there is no pink bike propped against the house. I didn't bring my car over on the ferry from Charlevoix because vehicle transport has to be arranged ahead of time and Mami and I came too much on the spur of the moment, but all at once I realize what a mistake this was: Eddie's truck is a stick, and town is something like two miles away. Whatever flowers still exist are dead for the winter, and Isabel may not live to see them bloom again. I hate the fucking flowers anyway, the way they die and come back to life unscathed. They are like me that way, maybe. In December, with no bike and a useless truck and already frigid temperatures, I am trapped at Strong's Landing until Mami consents to leave or Isabel consents to come with us to Chicago.

We enter through the back, just like last time I was here. Two rocking chairs sit on the porch, which looks out onto the high grass and the apple orchard. I don't want to admit this—because the consensus in my family is that Isabel is deranged to live out here—but I understand the magic of this place. There are no mountains or other dramatic landscape, yet Isabel's backyard is one of the most beautiful places on earth. If I were an artist, this would be an amazing place to paint; if I were a mother, I would want to picnic in this backyard with my children, on a giant white blanket. But I am none of those things.

Eddie puts Mami's bag down inside the house and says, "Isabel is sleeping," and bolts upstairs. Mami and I look at one another, and her eyes well up again but this time I know it isn't the cancer. In a normal house, the mother would rush up the stairs and embrace her sick daughter; the daughter would be waiting and fall into her mother's arms. But with Isabel, none of the normal rules of life have ever applied, and as always Mami and I are left standing here holding the bags, with each other as a consolation prize.

As I go up that tomb-like staircase with walls on either side of my body, you should know my heart is flipping in my chest like a fish. I'm afraid to look at Isabel. I don't know what to expect. I haven't seen Isabel in three years. Is it strange to say that the fact that she is my mother seems more acute the less I see of her? That when she briefly lived in the house with me, then just across the city, she was playing the role of my older sister, and consequently I rarely considered the alternative?

Mami doesn't climb the stairs with me. Even in this, they are in a contest of wills. At the top of the staircase I turn left and I am in her doorway. Maybe one of the other two bedrooms is an office now. All the doors are shut. Bebe closes her office door, too, when she works, sometimes ten or twelve hours a day, coming out only for tea and granola bars. I am never allowed to enter without knocking and waiting for her voice to grant permission. In my childhood, doors were never closed unless someone was taking a shit. Once Miguel left for college, Mami and I often didn't even close the door to pee when Carlos was at work. We kept right on talking over the stream. No one had an "office." Mami and Carlos even slept with their bedroom door open, with an implication that they never had sex, though I now realize that who knows, they could have been fucking on the dining room table while I was out (always out) with my legs in the air in Javier's orange Corvette. Middle-class people don't realize that they invented the closed door.

I rap on Isabel's distressed wooden door so hard I hear Mami downstairs mutter "Aye" in nervous shock. Isabel's voice takes longer to say, "Yes?"

"We're here." I'm talking as I open the door, like people do on television, but the truth is I'm not looking at her yet.

"I told her not to come."

When I finally see her it's this crazy overlapping of horror and relief and old obsessive analysis. Isabel is a chameleon. In my youth—when she arrived in Chicago during my sixth year of life—she was a hot Puerto Rican chica. She wore tight jeans and low-cut shirts and that fucking hair, Jesus that hair. She looked like Frida Kahlo in a Guess jeans ad. She was short like Mami and I are, but she had more substance, more heft, real tits and ass and flesh that always seemed dewy like someone was following her around with a bottle of mist. The last time I saw her, by contrast, in 2005, she was wearing an oversized floral dress and zebra-print wellies and had a hoe in her hands. Her hair was still long and flowing over her shoulders but she didn't lacquer or style it and the effect was weirdly more sexual than her teased look of old. The first thing I see now is that her hair is flapper short, razor blunt around her jaw, and that she has lost so much weight she has almost no breasts. Isabel has always had the darkest skin in the family but she looks strangely white in the wintery sunlight spotlighting her bed.

"What do you mean you told Mami not to come?" I say. "You wouldn't take our calls, you didn't tell her anything."

"I told Eddie to tell her."

I make some noise like a cat coughing something up. "Oh come on."

We talk like this. My relief is harder to find the longer I look at her. On first walking in the room I was just glad she wasn't hooked up to tubes and supine, too weak to speak or something. I don't know what I expected but it was terrorizing to anticipate it; the reality of her seemed better than what was in my head. Now, though, she's so small in the bed that it's impossible to believe she has an adult daughter, Ezme, just out of college and working in Grand Rapids. Yet conversely she has lines around her eyes and mouth I have never seen before, as though in losing so much weight her skin collapsed. Where is the slutty Frida Kahlo? I don't want this shorn ghost. Isabel has always been shockingly, inappropriately beautiful, but now she looks something like a fifty-year-old baby. Three years ago, the last time I saw her, she was forty and looked twenty-nine and like she was in some faux-farm photo spread for one of those glamorously hypocritical simplify-your-life magazines. Simplify your life by working so hard on your environment that you and it will always look perfect. I had laughed at Isabel, gardening, making her own bread and yogurt, though really it filled me with sick envy—I had mocked, *You need to buy some goats to walk around behind you looking atmospheric*, and she had said back, completely deadpan, *I've ordered some chickens but you'll be gone by the time they arrive*. The woman in this bed is something it would be bad form to photograph. I could cry looking at her, except no one in our family spare Mami has ever been remotely capable of that.

"You need to get her out of my house," Isabel tells me. Her refusal to say *Mami* is conspicuous, like we are playing a party game where you aren't allowed to say a certain word or you lose. I want to ask her how she feels or what the game plan is but she won't let me.

"Isabel," I say, and I sit down on the bed, trying to indicate friendliness, trying to indicate some familiarity between us that doesn't exist. "I can't do anything with Mami. We have one car and it's in Charlevoix. Don't pretend like you think Eddie would ever actually tell Mami you didn't want to see her—if you really didn't want to see her then you should have called and told her not to come—you should have taken one of her eight million calls. There's one ferry a day, so if you want us to leave, you have to at least wait until morning."

"I didn't say *you* have to leave."

I will replay this moment for years, Nick. The way she thinks as she says this that she's conveying approval, maybe even love for me, but what she's really doing is revealing that I am nothing but a pawn. That she doesn't respect me enough to think that if she draws a line in the sand I'll choose the woman who raised me over her. Isabel acts like a victim, but I have never been in a room she occupied where she didn't hold all the power. I'd like to tell you that I didn't realize any of this until later but the truth is I knew it before I even entered her bedroom.

And still I say, "You have to tell her. You have to at least tell our mother herself that you want her gone." I think the word "our" can somehow put her in her place, without my actually having to leave.

"That isn't going to happen," Isabel tells me. "Close the door on your way out."

What do you do with someone who is always willing to lose? What do you do with someone who wins by losing?

We drive home, some twenty-four hours after our arrival, Isabel having never once come downstairs or spoken to Mami. We drive home like sole survivors of a lost battle, wordless in our shared disappointment and humiliation. This time I don't wear lipstick. This time Mami doesn't cry.

Isabel wants to wait until after the New Year to have her hysterectomy, but neither the doctor nor Eddie will hear of it. Her daughter, Ezme, comes in from Grand Rapids; I would only be redundant. The surgery goes "perfectly," according to Eddie—"as well as we could have hoped for." She will be home for Christmas.

Getting information is like playing Clue. Doctors speak in euphemisms unless asked extremely specific and direct questions, and Eddie is clearly not that guy. *You're talking to the wrong guy.* Eddie and Isabel are not the people who sit in their doctor's office with notebooks, writing down CA 125 levels and the names of specific chemo drugs and inquiring about new studies in which they might participate. Isabel being in the hospital is the first time I am able to obtain any concrete information, because I call and ask specifically to speak to her doctor. I say the sentence, "This is her daughter," for the first time in my life. My heart ricochets around like I'm afraid there will be some approved list of daughters stapled to Isabel's chart that will include only Ezme, and that security will be called and I will be arrested for fraud.

It turns out, of course, that the doctor thinks I *am* Ezme, whom he has met. He calls me Ezme throughout the conversation, and I do nothing to correct him. He seems fond of Ezme, although neither of Isabel's children is as beautiful as she. When I interrogate him, he never says, "We've already discussed this, Ezme." No doubt he thinks she has gotten on the Internet and suddenly realizes how paltry her questions have been up until now. I am worried, for the duration of the call, that the real Ezme will walk right by him, bearing flowers, on her way to her mother's room.

(Why don't I correct him? Why don't I just say, *I'm her other daughter, I live in Chicago*, and tell him my name? Why do I make everything harder than it needs to be, and insist on behaving as though I am an intruder in my own life? I accuse Miguel of acting that way, but the things we recognize in others, that drive us the craziest, are the ones that cut closest to our own bones.)

Isabel's CA 125 markers, going into the surgery, were over six thousand. The acceptable level is thirty-five. She is at Stage IIIC of ovarian cancer, the cancer having metastasized to her stomach lining, her colon, and her lymphatic system. Her ovaries are gone now, and they have removed as much of the cancer as they could from her stomach and colon; it's the lymph nodes that pose the most serious issue and that account for the "C" staging, her situation being as bad as it can get before she would be in the final stage. They'll be able to tell us the new CA 125 numbers as soon as they come in, the doctor says, but we should expect a significant lowering given the success of the surgery. The objective is to use chemo to put her into remission. "Yes," he assures me, "that's attainable. She's young and healthy, she was asymptomatic, she isn't coming to us compromised already—chemo is hard on the system and the biggest barrier to remission is patients not being able to withstand aggressive treatment, but your mother is as healthy as it's possible to be at this stage, at our starting point, and we have every reason to believe she'll respond well to treatment."

"But how long does remission last?" I ask. "It's in her lymph nodes—it's spread all over the place—she can't be cured at this stage, I know that. Realistically, what's the prognosis?"

"You need to stay off the Internet," he says. "You're reading studies that say the average survival rate is two years, but you need to understand that if those studies were published even a year ago, then they were following patients for five years prior to that to collect that median survival rate, so you're talking about people who were diagnosed seven years ago. Seven years ago were the Dark Ages when it comes to cancer treatment. Every single year is bringing radical improvements. Don't read the studies. Just think positively and help your mother do the same."

I hang up, shaking. I have not read any studies. Was this some arbitrary example? My brain cycles through its usual overwhelming desire to jump out of my head. Every single fiber of my body wants to escape itself. I'm having a hard time getting my lungs to feel full when I inhale. I'm not thinking that I want to be high so much as

I want to just feel different. A drink would do it. A pill would do it. Being tied up would do it. A lit cigarette against my skin would do it. I want to feel like anything other than myself. I'm not sure how long I sit there, wanting to be Not Me, falling into the familiar black hole of time suckage, the energy drain it takes to simply exist in my own skin, unable to rip off my head for relief, deciding (sometimes by inertia, by not moving toward self-destruction) not to detonate, one minute at a time.

The sun patterns are different on the wall by the time I get online. And there they are: the studies. Oceans of studies. Two years. Two years. Two years.

According to the Internet consensus, Isabel will be forty-five when she dies.

I call Eddie's cell. He answers, which at this point hasn't stopped surprising me yet. I know that Isabel takes my calls less out of love for me than as a way to hurt Mami—that even if Mami doesn't know I've just called, Isabel still gets a secret burning satisfaction from picking up the phone as though Mami is the invisible camera that follows her everywhere, as though Mami is the eye of God, and Isabel's main objective, even more so than remission, is to tell God to bend over.

"She's doing real good today," Eddie says. "They'll probably send her home tomorrow."

"I was thinking I'd come up again," I say. "Without my mother, I mean. For, you know. For Christmas."

Why would I say that, you wonder? Getting to Isabel's island is as complex and exhausting as flying overseas, and I just undertook the endeavor only to be sent away. Clearly, I would be exempt from another visit so soon, so why do I voluntarily enlist, like some desperate patriot in an unwinnable war? But really, how dare you ask me such a question—you, who left your mother behind in Ireland when you were not even eighteen; you who had the luxury of having something to, as in the proper order of things, grow out of and past.

"Oh, yeah, sure! Isabel would like that a lot," Eddie says, like a man who hasn't recently watched Mami and me flee his house in shame. "Ezme will be here, too, that's great."

I should be clear here that Eddie, to the best of my knowledge, has no idea that Ezme is my sibling.

"Fabulous," I say. "I'll make the drive Sunday. I could see if Miguel wants to come, too, if that's all right with Isabel."

"Sure, Miguel, yeah, Isabel will love it, that's great."

After I hang up, I think about calling Miguel. He hasn't been to see Isabel yet. I have no comprehension of why I said he'd come, when of course he won't, and the fact that Eddie didn't even miss a beat and acted like everything I was saying was perfectly normal just confirms to me that he is so over his head with my family that he's essentially inconsequential, like Isabel married the village idiot as some kind of grand subterfuge. This is unfair—Eddie isn't stupid—he's taken care of her and Ezme and he's actually less of a religious fanatic than she is. Still, it's like Isabel has led her entire adult life in disguise, on the lam, in some witness relocation program.

I text you: *You don't want to drive up to Charlevoix, Michigan, for Christmas, do you? It's not like you have two kids or anything. It's not like you have to play Santa. It's not like your wife is pregnant. You don't want to drive seven hours and wait for me in some motel while I go visit my secret mother for a couple of days, and keep me away from sharp objects on the way home? Wtf, it's not like you're busy—what kind of friend are you anyway?*

You don't text back right away; you must be with the boys. When you do, it reads, *I can be there on the 26th. Wherever "there" is. Whatever you need.*

You pick me up the morning after Christmas, to drive me all the way to Charlevoix, even though you are not coming with me to visit Isabel. You have told your wife and presumably your children and anyone else who asked that you are heading up to Minneapolis to check out the other version of your play. The fact that you have agreed to our actual journey makes less sense than anything other than that I would ask it of you.

I'm waiting for you on the corner, half a block from my apartment, in a fur-hooded coat that weighs as much as an infant. I have two take-away coffees in my hands, and when you stop the car and see my hands full you jump out and run around to the passenger's side to open the door for me. The chivalrousness of the gesture seems incongruous with everything I know of you—you are sweet but not chivalrous; you don't seem to understand, most of the time, how manners work precisely. I put both coffees into the tray cups between the two front bucket seats while you're going back around to your side of the car. You get in, and by then my hands are empty, and I take off my left mitten, red and wooly with a yellow flower on the front, and take your cold hand into mine, still warm from the coffee. The gesture doesn't seem so inappropriate given that you are taking me to see my cancer-stricken sister.

The first time we let go will be three hours later, when you have to stop for gas.

I painted my nails that morning—my usual color, like blood in a vial—and took them for dry enough to put on mittens. But while you are filling the car, when I look down at my hands, I see your fingerprint stamped into the polish of my thumbnail. You are outside, in your long sheepskin coat that I call Pimp, 1972, and I am inside the car slowly raising my thumb up to my lips, slipping it into my mouth and tracing the intricate design of you with my tongue: our first kiss.

We miss the ferry, of course. This time, I know the ferry schedule. This time, I made sure we would miss it. There's no other option, you see. On this trip there is no earthly reason for you to be on to begin with, now that we're here, what else can we do—there's no ferry, you see? We have to get a hotel.

I don't need to tell you about that night. I don't want to write about our first night because of what it means to me, and how schmaltzy, how cliché the narrative of adultery is, and how the act of pinning the words to the page like butterflies no longer in flight will cheapen them, will dissipate the power of what it meant the one moment I thought to roll away from you and instead your body moved fluidly in time with mine like we were liquids bleeding together, like a single energy coil, you winding around me, your every joint bent into my every curve, your head resting on my head. What does that mean, in words instead of motion? It says nothing, so fuck it, I refuse to try.

Rather, as some paltry offering in return for what that night meant to me, I'll tell you something you don't already know:

The first night I slept at Bebe's apartment, I was twenty-five years old. I had been clean and sober less than three months. Though I could only claim some eighteen months or so as a full-on heroin junkie, I'd been more or less fucked up on something since my freshman year in high school. I had never quite learned how to live as an adult, and now the world seemed like I had been in a coma or in prison for a decade, and had been suddenly re-released into a civilization that was vaguely recognizable, but inexorably different than I remembered it. Dazed and blinking like a time-traveler, I was perpetually stumped by minor details, like that everyone seemed to know how to surf the Internet and make dentist appointments and go shopping for clothes one could wear outside a strip club. But in other ways, quitting had made me reckless. Nothing could be harder than those agonizing days of withdrawal. I'd burned through two husbands and fancied myself someone who had nothing left to lose. So although I had a hard time ordering a pizza, I had no problems flagrantly picking up my female professor at a reading, even though I'd never done anything sexual with a woman beyond mild girl-on-girl stage acts just for show. In her car, Bebe called me a "bratty bottom" and I didn't know what that term meant. But when she closed the door of her apartment behind us and said I had a very spankable ass, I instantly said, "Prove it."

At first, she did the talking. She told me to strip, which by then I felt nothing much about doing, but when she fastened a collar around my neck, before she even touched me I was wetter than I'd ever been. She ordered me to my hands and knees, and then, wordlessly, cropped me until I could feel hot welts swelling on my ass that stretched the skin tight, like they might explode if I touched them. And it was like some dam had smashed and words bubbled out of me uncontrollably: I asked her to chain the collar to the leg of the sofa and make me sleep on her floor all night. When I said that for the second time, Bebe threw her head back and cackled. She cropped the hard welts again—her aim was so sure she could replicate the exact path of a previous stroke—and told me to beg to be chained up like her little bitch. I begged wantonly—the floodgates of me were so far open I spilled all over her living room. I called myself names I doubt she'd have dared approached on her own, but my doing so made her bolder and she told me to whine and bark for her, and for the first time she put on her strap-on and fucked my ass. I had never done anything like that with Javier, who would have thought it made him gay, or Todd, whom I'd barely noticed despite having somehow ended up married to him, and I grunted and moaned in pain and ecstasy and the wild terror that I would lose control of my body and have some horrific accident on the floor. I was completely out of my head with bliss.

I didn't know much about how to exist in the world, but I knew this was the best I'd ever felt sober, and therefore understood that I should not let Bebe slip away. I confused an act at which she was exceptionally skilled—a common set of desires—for love, and hitched my wagon to hers so quickly and over such duration that it became love.

Gloriously unrepentant, Bebe left me chained, naked, to her leather sofa ("It cleans up easy after sex," she said, and that, too, made me fall in love), just as I'd requested. She went into her bedroom and closed the door. I fell into a glorious subspace sleep, my last awareness being the helpless, goofy smile on my face and the way my ass burned while the rest of my naked body felt cool. With the typical impulsivity of an addict, I had not considered what to do when I had to pee during the night, which, as you know, I always do. When I woke in the dark, my bladder was nearly bursting; I'd been slamming club sodas all night to occupy my sober hands. Embarrassed, I called Bebe's name but she didn't respond, so I called out again, three times, so loudly that it seemed impossible she could sleep through it. I squirmed a long time in my desperation, waiting for her to come, but she did not. Finally, I pulled one of her potted plants close to me and pissed quietly into the soil, and then put it back where it came from so she would never know. I curled tight in a ball and cold on the floor, unable to reach the throw blanket on the other side of the couch. In the future, whenever I hit subspace with Bebe I would feel emptied out and clean, sometimes for days, but that first night on the floor, having pissed in her plant, I thought how I should have killed myself better the last time I'd tried. How I had just met this amazing woman but she would soon enough realize I was broken and couldn't be fixed, and I'd have to live alone in my head again. If I had not been chained, there is no question in my mind that I would have gotten blind drunk, though I never told anybody that.

In the morning Bebe came in the room bright from a shower and unlocked the chain and said, "God, last night was hot—you are so fun." I ate the spicy eggs she cooked and we went to the farmers' market in Wicker Park to buy vegetables so I could make her dinner. It turned out that the proverbial lesbo U-Haul was already metaphorically parked outside her door, and I was overcome with gratitude. I would realize soon enough, of course, that Bebe is the world's lightest sleeper—that she had to have heard me calling her name and was ignoring me on purpose, to heighten my feelings of helplessness either for her own gratification, mine, or both. I'm not sure how I feel about this. Probably I don't care anymore. I never asked her about it, whether she was in her room masturbating and silently laughing at me. The incident, in memory, has been robbed of its power, of the desperate humiliation I felt in the actual moment. It's been softened by retrospective eroticism or the indifference of cohabitation (I would later water those same plants daily, for years—somehow managing not to kill them though I had never tended a plant before) or some combination therein. All I mean to say is that suddenly it was daylight, and there was Bebe, with eggs, offering me a future inconceivable only a few months prior. And in the light of morning she seemed all-powerful: a hand that could push me to the edge and yank me back simultaneously, and there was never any decision to surrender. I was merely, all at once, hers. I don't remember thinking of suicide again.

The thing about psychotic episodes is that of course I can't recall them afterward. The last thing I remember from our night at Villa Moderne is my body twitching out of your arms to the edge of the bed—your voice telling me, "I didn't say anything," and the cold realization that I have been talking to the air.

Episodes are like a drunken blackout, except the beauty of a blackout is that you have to make the call to drink yourself into one. Addiction may not feel like a choice, but if you've ever had your brain chemistry go haywire despite every meticulous effort to keep it level, words like *choice* start to take on new meaning. My Lamictal is the first thing I pack when I travel. I'd taken it that afternoon, swallowing it down with my cold coffee once you let go of my hand, while you were filling the car with gas, before I noticed my nail. I see my shrink every month. I'm supposed to keep a journal of my sleeping and eating habits, of my moods, though I admit I don't really do this. Does anyone really do this? The Lamictal is heavy-duty shit, the best mood stabilizer I've ever been on. I haven't had a psychotic episode since my first six months clean—the last was when Bebe and I had only been together a couple of months, and when I woke in the hospital I was certain I would never see her again, but in the morning she arrived with wild, expensive-looking pink peonies like Mrs. Dalloway had decided to visit Septimus Smith.

After our night at Villa Moderne, my shrink would prescribe my Abilify, to take if I feel an episode coming on. It works pretty well, Nick—it's powerful shit. But even if I had it that night, I was gone too fast to help myself. You'd have had to know in advance the ways my brain is capable of breaking. Our first night, I didn't yet have a magic pill you could give me, but even if I did, the chances I'd have told you about it in advance are none.

So instead, the first thing I remember after the last thing I remember is my voice saying, "You didn't say anything, did you?" For me, it's as though no time at all has passed, as though we've circled back exactly where we began, and the loop of dialogue can be rejoined, with everything in-between edited out like splices of tape on the cutting-room floor. Except now, weak Michigan sunlight hits the gray motel curtains, whereas the last I knew it was barely past midnight. The last I knew we were in bed holding each other like drowning children, whereas once I become aware of myself again, I'm standing alone with a TV antennae in my hand, and nothing in the room seems like it's in the right place. I know right away what has happened except I don't understand the time schism. Because if I had really had an episode six or seven hours in duration, I would be in a hospital, wouldn't I? If for six or seven hours I have been talking to voices inside my head, taking things apart, moving furniture, tremoring and twitching and pacing, while you sat in a Michigan motel room watching me, I cannot think of any possible reason you would not have had me taken away.

Then I realize. I say, "Oh my god. Nick, fuck, I'm so sorry. You couldn't call anyone. You're not supposed to be here."

You look confused. "I'm sorry," you say. "Who was I supposed to call? Did you want me to call Bebe or Miguel? I didn't know."

It's like I'm still talking to voices in my head. "No," I try again. "I didn't mean to scare you. It's your car—you could have just called 9-1-1 and told them where I was and then driven away before they got here."

You're looking at me like I'm nuts, which is of course an entirely appropriate way to look at me. I watch your face, moving through stages of understanding. You try to smile but it doesn't happen exactly. You say, "Is it okay to touch you now?"

I can't be touched in the thick of them. Not just the episodes, but other times, too: sometimes my body just starts moving and can't stop; I have to pace or kick my legs, and any physical contact feels almost like an electric shock, too much—it hurts; I can't keep still or bear it.

"Yes . . . I mean, if you want to. You don't have to."

Your hand reaches out and strokes my back; I feel your palm traversing my vertebrae, warming me. I'm still in the kind of hangover that comes after the episodes and I won't remember any of this later; I can only write down what you told me we said to each other. But I do remember your hand.

The things you tell me you said: That I have twenty minutes to get to the ferry. That I must still be delusional if I think you would call 9-1-1 and drive away. That I kept wanting to go outside to smoke, and you kept having to go with me because you didn't want me to just wander off, and I smoked so compulsively that we only have one left, but I can have it for my trip. To hurry up and put on my coat if I want to make the ferry. That if I want to stay another day, I can go tomorrow. That you'll still be here waiting for me when I get back, either way.

That it never occurred to you to be scared.

"I just figured it'd pass," you say. "Was that wrong?"

And there are so many ways to answer that question. My shrink would say I was safest in a hospital. Bebe might even say it was arrogant of you to think you could take care of me with no training, and no idea what I might do, in a town neither of us knew, in the middle of the night. People who have seen me this way before—they loved me, too, in most cases they'd loved me longer than you have—not one of them would agree with what you did tonight.

"No," I tell you. "You weren't wrong."

While I am waiting for the ferry to leave, bundled below deck, you text me from Villa Moderne. You, Nick, with your pregnant wife and two sons, write simply: *I wouldn't change a thing unless it were everything.*

Ezme treats me like a visitor. Ezme, at twenty-two, seems a decade older than I am, all authority and reasonableness and understanding the protocol of having (somewhat distant) family visit for the holidays. Ezme does not talk or weep loudly. Ezme knows how to cook rice and beans just like Mami makes them. Ezme knows how to change a tire. Her hair is short and frizzy; there are no hair products in the guest bathroom. Ezme does not seem to drink, but for reasons clearly different from mine. Ezme never sits down, wakes up early, doesn't fidget or pace or smoke or swear or "work out." She does not talk about sex; she does not read novels; she does not bring music with her when she travels. It is clear that she wears underwear. Ezme was breastfed by her mother until she was almost three and slept in a family bed, which Mami always told Isabel would make Eddie divorce her, but apparently did not. Ezme majored in economics. Whatever the fuck economics is, they apparently have jobs for it in Grand Rapids, Michigan, even though nobody in the country, especially in Michigan, can get a job. Ezme wears glasses—her contact lens case in the guest bathroom remains untouched throughout my visit. I don't want to develop Ezme. Ezme exists in a place of *opposition to*. She is defined by virtue of what she is not. She is Not Me.

It turns out Mami and I were wrong about Beaver Island . . . collectively, Mami and I know very little about the ways the world functions. Naturally, there is a medical center on the island where people can get chemo: they don't, as it turns out, have some special ferry for bald and nauseated cancer patients, all of whom would, in this *Far Side* cartoon of my imagination, be hurling off the sides of the boat while dragging IVs on rollers. There's a communal section where people sit in chairs with their IVs next to them, chatting, but private rooms are also available, and Isabel requests one. They are standard-issue hospital rooms: a bed, a chair. Surely Isabel isn't the only person here who knows private rooms exist, yet other people are sitting upright getting their dosage of toxins surrounded by strangers. I am at a loss.

For a lot of people, you text me, *the desire for privacy isn't as strong as their need not to feel alone.*

I text back, *I cannot imagine anything more lonely than getting chemo surrounded by strangers who think they're kin. I'd feel like I'd been drafted into the Cancer Club without my consent, and the presumption that everyone else in the club understood me would be violating and humiliating.*

Isabel says, "Who are you texting?" and I say, "Miguel," because of course she doesn't want to hear *Bebe* any more than she wants to hear about you. Maybe less.

She reclines back on the bed. Ezme and I overlapped for only two nights; she left for Grand Rapids to be home for work this morning, and Eddie is working, too, so I am the only one here with Isabel. The little sister taking her big sister to chemo; the daughter taking her mother to chemo; the crazy bisexual stripper taking the righteous Christian to chemo. I of course don't have a job and you only teach on campus one night per week, so we aren't leaving until tomorrow, but already I regret that. Isabel and I don't know how to be alone together—alone is not in our repertoire.

She has brought two things with her to chemo: a rosary, and an Uglydoll.

"This is my good-luck charm," she tells me of the toy, her voice strained, though I don't know if that's because of me or because she's about to get pumped full of chemicals the nurses wear gloves to touch. "Good things happen when this doll is around." She waves the doll a little bit, like she's making it dance, the way she may have done to Ezme when she was small. The doll, small, green, and made of chintzy felt, with an X for one eye, looks like something cobbled together by a fifth-grade sewing class—it is an obviously ironic toy, but Isabel is using it un-ironically, and for some reason this unnerves me. She seems to me cutesy and earnest and gullible—exactly like the forty-something Midwestern mom with cancer she is—holding tight to her idiotic talisman like a child clutching a toy in the dark. Her sudden lack of nuance makes my heart pound.

I've been sitting there dumbstruck, but that's okay since Isabel never seems to care all that much what I say. She tucks the doll under her non-IV arm and closes her eyes.

Eddie is at McDonough's, buying overpriced groceries that have to be imported from the mainland, and Isabel is puking over the toilet. I thought I'd be gone by this part—they told her at the Center that she wasn't likely to get sick until a couple of days in; she's on steroids and Benadryl and IV anti-nausea medications, but . . . upstairs, the sound of her retching violently. I sit on the tasteful sofa, trying to be someone who doesn't hear her.

We are private beasts, the women—and one man—of the Guerra clan, so at first it does not occur to me to go to her. It's just that the vomiting goes on for such a long time. It's just that there seems to be no end, so that I worry by the time I get up the stairs, she will be turned inside out. When I peer around the corner of the upstairs bathroom, Isabel has her head on the raw porcelain bowl, and she is sobbing so nakedly that it's like she isn't wearing any skin. Vomit clings to the geometric edges of her flapper bob. What must Ezme have felt like, growing up with a mother so beautiful? "Isabel," I say, "can I help?"

She is looking right at me but it's clear she hadn't noticed me until that moment. Her eyes open wider, taking me in. Isabel has always stopped crying more quickly than anyone I have ever known. Some phantom has to have been doing that sobbing, not her—she is incapable, a wide-eyed statue of unfeeling stone.

"Can I get you anything?" I ask, and I hate myself, the way I approach her, my entire goddamn life, like one might a rabid dog, creeping, maybe she won't see me coming closer. I get down on the tile floor next to her, and she smells so much like the inside of herself that I want to lick her. My mother. My fucking mother. Die, you hateful bitch, go on and die. "Some water, or one of your pills," I explain, hating the tentative of my own voice. "Do you need me to call Eddie?"

"This is nothing," Isabel says flatly. She has become, you see, a woman with nothing left to lose—whose hand is already forfeit. "I'll be praying for the mercy of days like this when I'm in hell."

Miguel answers his phone, "Yeah." He can see my number, sure, but I suspect he answers every call like that. I tell him quietly, in the snowy parking lot of the closed Beaver Island library, what Isabel said.

My brother makes a startled noise of alarm in his throat. "What the fuck? Do you think she's cracking up? It's a . . . lot of pressure, you know? Knowing you're going to die."

I don't say anything for a while. Fat snowflakes like little shredded pieces of Styrofoam float down around me, stage props; I don't feel cold. At Villa Moderne, you are working on a new play or reading on the bed or sitting on the snowy bench outside getting your ass wet while smoking a cigarette or talking on the phone to Emily.

Miguel says, "I'm sorry—hey, Lina, I'm sorry . . . that was a really negative . . . I don't mean to be so pessimistic . . . I know we have to keep a good—"

"Come on," I say, "we all know she's going to die."

"Okay," Miguel says. I hear him dragging on a cigarette. "If by everyone you mean only you and me and that we'd better not admit it to Mami, then all right, sure."

"Something doesn't add up, though—it's not just me, right? This shit she's saying. The way she's been living her whole life in a kind of incognito . . . what does a woman like Isabel have to feel so guilty about? What does hell want with her? If it's me she feels so badly about, I'm right the fuck here, why doesn't she make her goddamn amends?"

We play a game of exchanging silences. The air crackles, a shitty connection full of loud static, or maybe it's just my head. Why isn't my big brother here? In what sick scenario would I be the only Guerra on the scene? But abandonment is like a game of telephone in our family; we all just keep passing it along.

"Miguel?" My voice is rising; the hairs on my arms stand up all the way under my ten-pound coat. "What don't we know?"

"I'm not sure how to bring this up." He barks a little laugh. "I think she was a prostitute for a while in Caracas. I could be totally full of shit, but I think . . . Isabel is the queen of the cryptic remark, but she said some things about having a police record. I think after Mami didn't come back for her, she ran away from Papi and that for a few weeks she must have been living on the street, turning . . . uh . . . you know, tricks to survive."

"Jesus! Why didn't you ever say anything about this to me?"

"Lina," he says. "Think about it. You know why."

"Great." And I'm crying even though I'm about to tell him how ridiculous it was to think I'd care. "So I'm not just the bastard she didn't want, I'm the offspring of some pedophile john, too?"

"It might not be that. It might not be anything. She's kind of . . .

Lina, she's sort of crazy, you know? It's not just us. She's crazy in a different way. She's crazy for real."

I think I could make a pretty good case for my own Crazy for Real, but I don't say that now. I just demur, "I know—I mean, poor fucking Mami. Isabel's going to die estranged from her, for what? What's Mami so guilty of? Raising me so Isabel didn't have to? If you don't want to go to hell, try not cutting off your long-suffering mother."

Miguel says, "If you don't want to go to hell, try not believing in your long-suffering mother's god."

I intend to be vigilant the rest of the time I'm here. In the picture of myself in my head, I have every manner of cathartic intention. I am going to somehow break through Isabel's reserves, which clearly she is beginning to allow to crack anyway. Maybe she *wants* to know me at last—to confess. All this time, I've felt like the black sheep of the family, when it turns out my biological mother was more of a sex worker than I've ever been . . . when maybe we should have been . . . bonding?

But of course it doesn't happen that way, Nick.

For the rest of my time on Strong's Landing—only that night until the morning's ferry—Isabel avoids me, is "resting." Eddie rushes around tending to her with one tea mug after another, mainly I think to create the illusion of movement and not have to sit down and engage in small talk with me, and then finally he disappears into their bedroom and closes the door, and I wait, I have silent conversations in my head in which I write both Isabel's dialogue and mine and they correspond perfectly, but soon it is clear no one is emerging from the no-man's-land of their marital bedroom and my head just buzzes, bounces, aimless. You and I sext until nearly morning.

By the time I am running late for the ferry the next morning, I am preoccupied and bleary and looking at my phone as Isabel and I say good-bye. She isn't making the drive, so I'm off alone with Eddie, in the midst of telling you about my arrival time and plotting how we can get a little privacy before we hit the road. The thing is: two years to live is not a long time, but it's not a five-alarm fire, either, exactly. I've seen more of Isabel this month than I had in the past four years. It seems like a trajectory we are simply on now, and that whether I like it here or not—whether I can *bear* it or not, even—I will soon be back. My eyes scan again for the pink bicycle as I'm leaving, but I haven't seen it since 2005; I don't even know whether it still exists. My eyes evade Isabel's face, which looks different already than the night before, being claimed by degrees. Whatever toxins she was vomiting into the toilet also seems to be trying to escape her pores, and she's broken out like a teenager, maybe the teenager I never knew her as, though the circles under her eyes are darker. It's like there's a bubbling kettle of toil and trouble under her skin, and all at once I imagine her darkly: a pimply, homeless, flimsily dressed streetwalker in mythical Caracas, which I have never even seen, getting into the backseats of old-fashioned cars. In my head, the cars in Caracas circa 1978 look like those in Cuba in the 1960s, because I don't know anything about anything. In one frame, Isabel is thirteen and wrapping her legs around a john, her beauty hidden behind acne and sweat in the backseat of a car; in another, Isabel stands in her wellies, the pink bike propped and picturesque, more domestic and appropriate and beautiful than I can ever be. In the final frame, as I wave to her weakly before she closes the heavy oak door, I'm supposed to be looking at my sick biological mother, but really I'm looking at the screen of my phone, where I don't have to look into the face of death or envy anymore, where nobody is in charge of the secrets except for me. Where you, quieting and quickening my pulse at once, are waiting on the other end of this body of water.

GRETCHEN

REQUEST FOR ORDER

PETITIONER/PLAINTIFF: Troy Fox Underwood

RESPONDENT/DEFENDANT: Gretchen Merry-Underwood

OTHER PARENT/PARTY: ____________

9. ________ I request that time for service of the Request for Order and accompanying papers be shortened so that these documents may be served no less than (specify number) ______ days before the time set for the hearing. I need to have this order shortening time because of the facts specified in item 10 or the attached declaration.

10. ______ FACTS IN SUPPORT of orders requested and change of circumstances for any modification are (specify):

__X__ Contained in the attached declaration. (You may use Attached Declaration (form MC-031) for this purpose. The attached declaration must not exceed 10 pages in length unless permission to file a longer declaration has been obtained from the court.)

I will be succinct here because this is really a cut-and-dry situation, as you will see. My estranged wife, Gretchen Merry, just up and decided one day that she would sabotage our whole entire lives as we had set them up. She was disruptive to our son Gray's therapists at his very prestigious school, which we had gone to great lengths to get him accepted at, and where Ms. Merry's own family all attended. She withdrew Gray from the middle of a therapy session and announced to everyone there that we were getting a divorce, which is not something I had ever heard her even mention until that day. I had no wish for this divorce, but before I even knew it was happening, she had kidnapped my son and taken him to her parents' house and on a dangerous excursion to Chicago with her family members, when I know that they were all drinking. They were driving drunk with him in the car. Gretchen and her parents, Charles and Elaine Merry, all drink alot and I think it is clear that Gretchen is an alcoholic and she is also taking prescribed psychiatric medication for her "stress." She pops Xanax like candy, which no one should eat, which Gretchen eats regularly!

As you will see from looking at her, Gretchen does not take care of her body. When I married her, she was an athlete. We both were in top physical condition and treated our bodies like temples. Now she will not even go to the gym, and she is always giving Gray Pop Tarts in his lunch, as though it is the 1970s and we live in the projects. Who, in Winnetka, gives their only child processed sugar crammed in to a weird fake-frosted square and calls that "lunch?" Obviously she not only doesn't care about Gray's well-being, she also doesn't care how she is being perceived by her social contemporaries and what impact that might have on Gray socially. She does not buy organic and makes fun of me when I suggest it.

She is a cold mother and you can ask anyone about this. She very rarely pays attention to Gray and is always working. She works maybe seventy hours per week, which is clearly unacceptable for someone with a young child with special needs. Her pattern of behavior just over and over again shows a flagrant disregard for her own offspring and for our role as a family in our community. Gray has pervasive developmental disorders NOS. It is hard for him to fit into our community, which is very high achieving, yet Ms. Merry sabotages all my efforts to get him to fit in and have a smooth, happy life. I did not even want to bring this up but as an example of what I mean, she has recently given her eggs (yes, her reproductive eggs!!!) to her gay brother in the city. This is apparently how meaningful motherhood is to our Ms. Merry, that she is just giving eggs away on the street corners to people who are not even qualified to be parents, who live an hour away from her where she would not see the child regularly. This would be my son's brother or sister, but does she consider that this might be an issue for Gray?! No, she does not. She is too busy drinking vodka in her sweat pants and stocking up on the fruit roll-ups that everyone knows cause cavities and harassing the school therapists who are only trying to help Gray. I implore an immediate shift to sole legal and primary physical custody in my care, so that Gray can have a reasonable upbringing befitting to his station in life and be a respectable human being in his community.

I declare under penalty of perjury under the laws of the State of Illinois that the foregoing is true and correct.

Date: 1/19/09

Troy Fox Underwood	*Troy Fox Underwood*
(TYPE OR PRINT NAME)	(SIGNATURE OF APPLICANT)

Gretchen walks in to Juko Nail + Skin Rescue, on uber-hip Division Street, with the same self-consciousness with which she enters clothing boutiques and hair salons. She does not belong in places of this nature, full of lithe sales girls or tattooed, terminally edgy aestheticians. She looks, in such environs, like she is in an improv group and is performing a skit about an uptight, middle-aged suburban mom: all khakis and button-down, crisp shirts topped by V-necked pastel sweaters, and sensible shoes that cost deceptively obscene amounts of money. She is always the tallest woman in the place, unless, God forbid, one of the staff "models" in her spare time. Instead of being all Asian, like most nail salons Gretchen sees, this one is a virtual United Nations of aestheticians: Black, Asian, Latino, Polish. This both complicates and alleviates Gretchen's discomfort. On the one hand, she is more comfortable than she would like to acknowledge with the dynamic of people (well, *women*, if she's honest) of other ethnicities serving her in some manner in exchange for money, and the implicit way in which this makes it seem that Gretchen is the important one in the situation, the one somehow more fully nuanced, like the lead in a movie rather than an extra. On the other hand, since the Cabrini-Green/Capital Grille incident, it has become abundantly clear to her that she and her entire family are racists . . . which sucks, and about which she is completely unsure what to do. Is there some sort of *Political Correctness for Dummies* book she is supposed to buy to rectify herself? Gretchen hovers near the sofas up front, staring self-consciously out the window and wishing she could disappear into the floor.

Chad is late, of course. When is Chad ever not late for anything?

He invites her here, after things have been kind of strained between them—he invites her here to a place she would never ever go on her own, despite that he grew up in a house with her and when did he ever know her to get pedicures?—he invites her here like a stranger of whose preferred recreational pastimes he has no prior knowledge, and now he is late.

Under her agitation, however, Gretchen is aching to see him. Her entire body strains with the hope of being around someone who *loves* her, even if he is a clueless dolt. She has told no one about Troy's petition for custody of Gray—has been afraid to speak the words aloud and make them real—and yet she knows she needs everybody in her corner she can accumulate. She needs her parents and all the force of their respectability; she needs her brother and his dimples and charisma, of which she herself is in short supply. She needs someone to tell her that this is going to be okay and she is not going to lose her baby boy to a jackass who will structure Gray's life like an endless series of adults volleying balls in his direction until he falls over his own feet, and then blaming him for it. *Gray!* Gretchen's eyes well up. If Troy tries to take Gray from her, she will murder him with the goddamn blue light and then use it to hide the evidence. Except then, what would become of Gray, visiting his mother in prison? Would her parents even take him in, or send him off to some "home" for children who don't perfectly live inside the lines of an affluent, suburban grid? Gretchen sits in the horrifying nail salon, silently weeping.

"Lady, you like some wine?"

A woman who may be Filipina—she is not, thank God, luminously gorgeous, but in fact rather chunky and no younger than Gretchen's age—stands in front of her smiling. "We give you wine, you wait for Chad."

Chad? This woman *knows* she is waiting for Chad?

"You like red or white?"

"Red," Gretchen says numbly. It's like she's fallen down Alice's rabbit hole and people are speaking a language she doesn't understand, but it is the dead of winter in Chicago and anyone who is drinking white wine is clearly insane.

Gretchen accepts her plastic cup of red wine. The shock of it has stopped her piteous weeping, thank God. She looks up, and there is

Chad at last, through the giant storefront window of the salon, striding happily toward the door, his scarf flapping in the wind.

Emily is with him.

Gretchen rises to her feet. The reaction in her is that strong, though she has no idea why precisely. Her impulse is to dash before they can see her—to get the fuck out of there.

Their cheeks are flushed from cold as they throw back the front door. Both the woman who gave Gretchen the wine and another woman immediately rush over to them, clucking, "What month now?" and, "Oh, pretty pretty!" at Emily, even though Emily is, at most, *mildly* pretty. Still, it is enough to make the inexplicable, Wonderland-meets-Kafka nature of things clear: Chad and Emily obviously come here *often*, and *together*. Only today has Gretchen been included for some reason, on this excursion that is normally *theirs*. She has not been invited to spend the afternoon with her brother, as she believed, but to join in Chad and Emily's preexisting plans: an afterthought, just like the day she arrived at her parents' home to find them all celebrating with cake. Well, no, of course she wasn't *any* kind of thought then—she just showed up on her own.

Chad and Emily both, hugging her, perhaps taking note of her stiffness, thinking Gray's apple doesn't fall far from the tree.

"Look!" the wine woman says to Gretchen, as the woman pours half red and half white wine into a glass together, like Gretchen is in on the joke, "we make her wine pink!" She hands the disgusting, pale-red concoction to Emily, who smiles affirmingly and takes a delighted sip.

Why is that stupid bitch drinking cheap mixed-up wine with Gretchen's fetus inside her?

Chad, however, is nonplussed, hooks his arm in Gretchen's. "I'm so excited you could finally come here!" he exclaims, as though invitations have been volleyed her way weekly and she keeps batting them away.

"I've never had a pedicure before," Gretchen says, for lack of absolutely anything else to say that wouldn't involve smacking Emily or her brother upside the head.

"Never?" Emily trills. "That's amazing!"

Coming from someone whose personal aesthetic would not have been out of home with the fucking Manson family, Gretchen finds it hard to swallow Emily's amazement.

They are all three led to oversized massage chairs, handed the remote controls to adjust their settings, and Gretchen mindlessly pushes "knead." *Knead, need.* Three women come back toward them with decorative bowls full of soapy water, help them to remove their boots and socks, usher their damp, linty feet into the warm water. The sensation is beautiful and uncomfortable simultaneously. Gretchen notes that her feet are larger than Chad's. Across her brother's body, in the massage chair flanking his left side, she sees Emily's dainty feet in the bowl, skinny like a girl's, at odds with the rest of her milk-fed figure. Manson-family snark aside, Gretchen also realizes that Emily is not dressed today as she has been the other times Gretchen has seen her, in what seemed to be tied-dyed rags. By contrast, she is wearing perfectly creased wool trousers and a black turtleneck that might actually be cashmere. The effect is . . . uncanny. Emily looks like she could be Chad and Gretchen's sibling, on her way to meet the Merrys at the country club. While Gretchen is no expert (despite Elaine Merry's consternation) in judging the expensiveness of fabric, these clothes were at the very least purchased at, say, a respectable mainstream chain like Banana Republic, and not at some hemp specialty shop that sells soap, patchouli, and earth mother clothing along with organic scones. Gretchen has met Emily only a handful of times, but the fact that Emily is dressed this way is even more inexplicable than "pink" wine.

"You look nice," she makes herself say to Emily, across Chad's body. "Pregnancy apparently suits you. Are those new maternity clothes, or ones you had from your sons?"

"Oh these?" Emily gestures her body carelessly. "They're new. After Jay, I gave all my old ones away."

"Don't you love your gloves?" Chad croons, as though Emily's hands are also in need of a maternity wardrobe. "Show Gretchen your gloves. They're delicious, Gret, you'll want to eat them."

Their coats are all hanging at the front of the salon, but to Gretchen's surprise she sees that Emily has a pair of gloves on her lap. She holds them up for Gretchen to see, though with far more hesitation than she accepted and downed her wine.

"We were walking down Damen and she didn't even have gloves on!" Chad cries. "Hello? It's almost February, in *Chicago*! We saw these in a window and they were so exquisite we couldn't resist."

Gretchen looks from the gloves to her brother, her brother to the gloves. It's as though there is a CNN ticker running commentary underneath her brother's moving lips. The commentary reads: *I bought this woman's new maternity clothes, and then, because she was too stupid to leave the house wearing her pair of cheap, fake-wool Target gloves, I also bought her a pair of $800 gloves from the kind of store she's never been in before in her life.*

The woman on her knees in front of Gretchen is scraping her feet with some kind of loofah stick, and it tickles so badly Gretchen's entire leg keeps twitching like she's having her reflexes checked. The woman beams at her and says, conspiratorially, "Tickles, eh?" but then continues her sadistic endeavor. Gretchen sits like a simmering cauldron. She cannot pinpoint her emotions. It is not like she wanted Chad to buy *her* a new wardrobe or expensive calfskin gloves. Gretchen has no shortage of nice things, and she could have more of them if she were that kind of woman, and does not require any man, much less her baby brother, to buy them for her. What, then, is the toxic brew boiling in her gut? Why does she want to scream?

"I told Chad they were too expensive," Emily says demurely, tucking the gloves back on her lap. The fact that she has kept them with her, instead of in her coat pockets, indicates clearly that she has never owned such an exorbitant item in her entire life and is afraid of losing them—Gretchen should feel touched. Here is this relative stranger, doing their family an almost unspeakable favor: why shouldn't the poor girl have a nice pair of gloves, for God's sake? But then she watches Emily's fingers caressing the leather, and something in her churns again.

The clothing. The gloves. The cake with the Merrys. Capital Grille. This salon at which Emily and Chad are apparently "regulars." There is something *Single White Female* about the way Emily is insinuating herself into Chad's life, on Chad's dime. Is she wrong? For perhaps the first time in Gretchen's life, she wishes Miguel were next to her, even if his own CNN ticker read things like, *See, Chad's secretly lesbian sister has never had a pedicure!* Miguel is no naïf. If something creepy is going on here, he would perceive it, too. She wants to ask him, though she isn't sure, really, whether she wants to be wrong or secretly hopes she is right.

While they sit with their toes under drying jets, Chad reaches over and takes Gretchen's hand. It's an odd gesture, even though Chad is an affectionate boy, but Gretchen feels something on the far-enough side of desperate that she doesn't pull away. She's said not one word about Troy or Gray, because it is none of Emily's business—Emily, who has Gretchen's egg inside her body, but that has nothing to do with familiarity, whether or not the others can see that clearly. Chad clutches her hand, his eyes wide and shiny and so happy Gretchen almost has to turn away.

"We should go have a celebratory lunch after this," he tells Gretchen. "Emily just had the amnio, and they told us the baby is a girl."

And then it is like being underwater. She sees Chad's lips moving, but all sound has left the room.

Muffled noise. Her entire head feels clogged with waves. He is speaking, but nothing he's saying matters anymore.

Emily has had an amniocentesis.

No one invited Gretchen to said procedure.

No one invited Gretchen shopping or bought her gloves.

No one invited her to her own fucking parents' house for cake.

Gretchen's egg is a girl.

Gretchen has a daughter, but she lives inside of Emily.

Emily had a fifteen-week amnio, to which Gretchen was not invited, at which they found out the sex of the baby, and Gretchen has spent approximately seventy minutes now inside of this idiotic pink-wined salon, but only *now* is anyone mentioning to her that her baby is a girl.

We're all the heroes of our own narratives. Gretchen knows this. There are no "villains" in real life sitting on a throne in a lair like a Disney movie, rubbing their hands together and cackling with glee over their own divine wickedness. In regular life, everyone thinks what they're doing is justified. Genocides, witch hunts, murders: all committed by people who were convinced they were in the right—so clearly, on the small, ordinary human scale of Gretchen's own First World, upper-middle-class, white-privileged reality, it is not so far-fetched to understand that, among her cast of players, *Troy* believes his actions are justifiable, that Gretchen is "wronging" him, that he alone deserves Gray. It is not so hard to understand that Chad believes himself a good brother, taking his sister out for a pedicure, offering a celebratory lunch in exchange for Gretchen's egg—for Gretchen's *daughter.*

And Emily?

What does *Emily* believe? In this story where Gretchen's daughter has somehow ended up the prize and the pawn, to what does Emily feel entitled? Gretchen stares at them both, their joyful faces watching her expectantly, and feels herself smiling, even emitting a small, very un-Gretchen-like squeal that Chad, were he a brother who paid attention to who she is instead of one who thinks pedicures are an appropriate celebratory outing for her, would realize was wildly fake. Her heart throbs all the way up to her ears, and she is glad she is sitting down. *Be careful*, she thinks slowly to herself, like she might if encountering a rabid animal. *No sudden moves.*

"A girl!" she squeals again, half expecting the floor at her feet to open and swallow her whole, because otherwise how can it possibly be that she will live through this impending lunch?

LINA

My brother's fetus, like most Guerra fetuses, is female, so I am going to Enemy Camp to celebrate. This makes me laugh, because I don't really feel that way about Emily, about your home. At this point, I think such infidelity stereotypes are hilarious because I don't believe they apply to me. This is during the Era of Our Spectacular Rationalizations. I have no problem with your wife, I tell myself. Your wife is a lovely person, doing a great favor for my brother. Your wife bore you two sons you adore. Your wife is someone who means something to you, I reason, and therefore she means something to me, too. I don't want to be her intimate friend, but I think of her as a kind of in-law about whose well-being it is incumbent upon me to care.

I am desperate to see the inside of your house. There is a quality to my curiosity of gawking at a roadside accident, but I don't care. I feel vaguely like a shitty person for my ability to lie skillfully enough to enter your wife's domain without blinking, but I don't care enough to change my behavior. You and I have been sleeping together for nearly two months. I would be hard-pressed to pin down five consecutive minutes that you have not been on my mind. Sometimes, on the precipice of sleep, I fear murmuring your name, like some cheating husband in a B movie. I want to see the coffee cups you drink out of in the morning. I want to see your marital bed.

I am so hungry for every scrap of knowledge about you that if I were permitted to watch you fuck your wife, I would. My ravenousness still exceeds my capacity for jealousy. I wear a black dress with the red strap of a bustier peekabooing under the sheer fabric, because you have touched these items. I wear boots you have licked. I am shameless. Heroin never made me this high.

"There's nothing in the world more boring than other people's children," Bebe says, dragging on her cigarette holder, watching me get ready. I keep a plastered smile and think, *Oh, yes there is.*

"So," Chad says as we all gather around your farm-style dining room table with the mismatched chairs and faded batik tablecloth, "I've been thinking. Since the baby's a girl, we should name her Isabel."

"Oh, come on," Miguel says, like he was afraid this would happen. "Let's not go overboard."

"Isabel is a beautiful name," Emily says. According to you, she and Chad have become very close. They talk on the phone every day, and go shopping and to lunch and for pedicures together; Chad gets his toenails buffed and shaped but doesn't actually have polish applied. I can't remember whether you or Miguel told me this—often, you cover the same Chad ground.

"Sure, it's a beautiful name," Miguel says. "And my sister Isabel is a beautiful woman. Who wouldn't come to our wedding—after she had agreed to be my best woman, may I add—and who thinks we're going to burn in hell. No bad omens in that or anything."

"There's such a thing as forgiveness," Chad says. "It's a virtue."

"Excuse me," says Miguel, "I seem to have found myself in a Hallmark card. Can someone point me toward the exit?"

You may not believe me, but this is the first time I realize my beloved brother must be a fucking bitch to live with.

I am seated between Miguel and Emily. Keep your enemies closer. Except remember: I don't think of Emily as my enemy. I keep touching her stomach, which seems to please her. Some women are fussy about it, but not Emily. She seems proud of her body being used as a vessel in this way. A breeder—my knee-jerk reaction is to assume this means she's no good in bed, but lately I've realized that a lot of these assumptions I hold about the "straight" world are either wrong entirely or could also be applied to me. Emily has no sexual dysfunctions of which I am aware. She orgasms from things that generally make people come. She doesn't dash out of the bed to gargle with Listerine. Before this pregnancy, you fucked about once every week or two, which puts your annual fucks per year at somewhere between twenty-six and fifty. You tell me that this is lower than the national "married people" average, but for a couple married for fifteen years, it seems almost fiendishly high.

Bebe and I used to fuck at least five times a week. Alone or with others joining us—though our rule was that guests never spent a whole night; that we woke up only with each other—our sex lasted for hours, like performance art. Miguel used to roll his eyes at me when I told him about it. He'd quip, "Don't you ever just get horny and rut around for five minutes until you're sweaty and call it a day?" And I explained, with an earnest solemnity people don't expect of perverts, that sex was "too important" to be trivialized in that way. Perverts, of course, are as earnest as any converts, any zealots. I worshipped at the altar of sex, though I rarely thought in terms of my own pleasure. Like a nun, what I practiced was closer to devotion.

"Where's Bebe tonight?" people keep asking me, but I'm not sure anyone cares.

Your root vegetables are perfect. The beets don't bleed at all into the parsnips, the onions, the celery—later, you will tell me that you cooked them separately, that that's the trick. In the serving bowl, they look as though they've all come from the same place.

"I never had an amnio with the boys," Emily is saying. "I was afraid it would increase the risk of miscarriage. But I haven't had any bleeding at all, and they said at Northwestern that you can't look at national stats for that stuff, that their figures don't look like if I were getting my amnio in Podunk, Idaho. I feel stupid now, like maybe it was never unsafe, and I should have had one. It's just . . . I was so much younger then, the chances of anything being wrong seemed so slim . . ."

You have Jay on your lap when she says this. You bounce him on your knee. He giggles. Your arm rests around his waist as easily as if he were part of your own body. He has no idea on earth that anyone is talking about him, or that the ensuing silence in the room is awkward, made more acute by his shrieking, gleeful laughter.

(Interior: motel room, curtains drawn.)

(Exterior: not visible from Interior, so what does it matter?)

(But: let's say through a gap in the curtain [there was no gap in the curtain], audience can see a motel sign reading "Heart O'Chicago.")

(What the hell, why not go for broke with an echo of Villa Moderne? We will give this sign missing letters, too, so that it reads Heat O'Chica.)

(Here in Chicago, we like our chicas hot.)

(Interior: a man—that would be You—lying on the bed in ripped jeans through which half of his right leg, bent at the knee, is visible, smoking a cigarette. In case the broken sign has not conveyed to the audience a state of retro disrepair, the fact that Hot Chica motel has "smoking rooms" ought to do it.)

Man: I'm starting to feel guilty.

Woman: (Looks unsure what to say . . . for the record, she thought that "guilt" was a given.)

Man: I didn't think this was going to impact things the way it has. Not that Emily and I ever had an open marriage or anything—it's not that I thought she'd be okay with my fucking around. It's just that in a way, how is this any different from, say, having someone else's baby? Right? No . . . I don't mean right, like I'm asking you to agree with me—I'm not even sure I agree with me anymore. I just thought, well, some men would object to sharing their wife's womb with another couple. Some men would object to their wife having another man's child, to her body expanding and losing energy and feeling generally shitty in the service of another man's sperm. But I wasn't that bloke, you know? I don't believe love is a thing that can be owned. I don't think there's just some finite quantity of ourselves and we'd better jealously guard how we spend it. Emily's never had an affair that I know of—okay, no, she's never had an affair—but I always thought that if she did, I'd be all right with it, maybe. I never wanted to deprive her of any opportunity for joy.

Woman: I think if not fucking another person equals being deprived of joy, there's probably a bigger problem going on than the fucking itself.

Man: How do you mean?

Woman: I mean—duh—that if Emily felt like she needed another man in order to experience joy, then it would mean that her feelings were way too contingent on that other man, and your marriage would already be in trouble, whether she fucked him or not.

Man: (Silent a long time.)

Woman: What? You disagree?

Man: No, that's the problem. I was just thinking how many times I . . . (a nervous glance at the woman, to see if she may be offended) . . . how often I *didn't* fuck someone, you know, when I could have—some actress, some student or other faculty—all these past seven or eight years, and how I've felt so self-congratulatory about it. But if we're going to go all Jimmy-Carter-I've-sinned-in-my-heart about it, thinking about those women, whether it was for a day or weeks or a whole semester, was a big part of what got me through days. It brought me joy, when home felt like drudgery.

Woman: Is there anyone married fifteen years and raising two kids who *doesn't* feel like home is drudgery? I mean, seriously—I'm curious. Do you think there is?

Man: I thought I'd drawn myself a line in the sand. Like I was allowed to get right up to the line, as close to the line as possible, but then I had to jump back, and as long as I did that, I was a good husband, a good father. I kept playing a game of chicken with myself and I thought I'd mastered it. But with you, I'm living without a net.

Woman: You used to feel like there was a net? That's unfathomable to me. I don't have a clue what a net would feel like.

Man: It felt pretty amazing. And also kind of awful. Like you're acting out a script and it's maybe method acting but still, what you're going to do next is always already determined.

Woman: Maybe you just don't like that Emily's less available to you now that she's busy being a saint for my brother and Chad. Men need a lot of attention. Maybe you just aren't getting the attention you're acclimated to getting from her, so—*voilà*—you crossed the imaginary line and lost your imaginary net.

Man: *Men* need a lot of attention? No offense, beautiful girl, but I've never met a woman worth knowing who didn't need five times the attention any man does.

Woman: You don't get out enough.

Man: (Laughs.) Well, maybe you're right! Like, the other day, I *did* feel angry about the baby—though it was the first time. Both other times Em was pregnant, I wanted it to be a girl. I don't mean I was walking around calling the fetus my little princess—I'm not even sure I admitted it to anyone. But I wanted a daughter. Obviously once the boys were born, I wanted them, not some other replacement kid. I wanted what I had. But now, my wife is having a baby girl, and giving it away, and I felt kind of . . . sick. Like, grief-stricken. I was jealous. It didn't make any sense.

Woman: You just explained it. You always wanted a girl.

Man: No, I just mean it doesn't make sense because here my wife is, pregnant, and I'm jealous I can't keep the kid, and kind of pissed at her for doing that to me—but meanwhile I'm shagging another woman like some John Edwards piece of shit.

Woman: (Cracking up, then looking away, ashamed of herself.) What's with the politician analogies tonight? Emily doesn't have cancer. She *chose* to get knocked up—it's not a disease.

Man: But she's pregnant with this . . . philanthropic spawn. (Flings himself back against the flimsy pillow, hair—like copper on fire—askew.) Anyway, if she had cancer I might *still* be here with you. Do you see what I'm saying? I reckon I'm just not a very good person.

Woman: You're talking to the wrong guy.

Man: (Laughs, but reluctantly.) It's not even just the pregnancy, or the "we have kids" thing . . . it's not even just *kids* kids. It's . . . Christ . . . Jay.

Woman: I know. I'm sorry. I understand the complexity of that.

Man: You know what my problem is?

Woman: That you're madly in love with me?

Man: Yes, well, that too—god, yes, that too. That's a problem I wouldn't trade. But I meant . . . it's dangerous, thinking we're entitled to things. Thinking the rules don't apply to us.

Woman: I don't know. Thinking you're not entitled to anything—being some martyr, living solely for other people, thinking we're lesser and our happiness doesn't matter, that's not any better, is it? Everything's dangerous in extremes.

Man: So, a life in moderation, eh?

Woman: I don't understand moderation.

Man: It's what I wanted. Growing up in the theater, my parents always thinking they were Dick Burton and Liz Taylor, all their messy affairs and reconciliations and my dad running back and forth to Dublin and London thinking he was such a big shot—it wasn't until I lived in London myself that I realized nobody knew who the hell he was, he was some character actor, the biggest fish in our pond so we all swallowed it whole, even my mum, even when she was disparaging him, it was always like . . . he was still the king. She idolized him, no matter what he did. I couldn't stand to see it. The way he strutted around. I hated how she'd even named me for him.

Woman: It's a good thing you were obsessed with Fitzgerald instead of, like, Melville, when you changed your name!

Man: Call me Ishmael, baby.

(Another cigarette has been lit, is being passed back and forth.)

Man: I admit it happened sooner than I'd have liked—Miles, I mean . . . I don't know that Emily and I would have stayed together if she hadn't turned up pregnant. But the thing is, maybe we would have. We might have ended up in the same place. It wasn't some shotgun wedding. I wanted to be a good family man. I thought I was happy.

Woman: If you believed you were happy then you were happy.

Man: Now it all seems black and white, though. I mean in black and white as opposed to in color. Muted instead of loud.

Woman: I know what you mean, you goof.

Man: I'm sorry I'm talking so much about myself.

Woman: (Cuffing him in the head.) You're a fucking idiot.

Man: (Passes her the cigarette.) I am a fucking idiot indeed.

Woman: But you're right. There were enough years between Miles and Jay. If you'd wanted to leave, you would have. You must have been happy. You stayed. A lot of people don't stay.

Man: Oh, I don't know. I thought about leaving plenty of times.

Woman: (Sitting up. She is wearing a vintage 1940s-style dress unbuttoned down the front, through which her black bra—which fastens in the front and is unfastened—can be seen.) You've never told me . . . you thought about leaving Emily, getting a divorce? Way before me?

Man: For over a year, I was just waiting for Miles to start school, and then I was going to tell Em, yeah. You know, that we'd given it a go but it wasn't how I wanted forever to look. I presumed we'd share custody of Miles, and go on our way, you know, lead separate lives as self-consciously hip divorced parents or whatnot, begin the sheer agony of dating again, and it would all be sad and thrilling and terrifying in a perfectly ordinary way. Then Miles started school and I didn't . . . go anywhere. I told myself I wasn't in a hurry. Why not wait a bit longer? Then we got pregnant with Jay, and it was . . . I don't want to imply that I didn't leave because of his condition. That's not true. I'd had my chances and didn't take them. I knew from the time Emily told me she was pregnant that my window had closed, and I made my peace with that before—my decision isn't on Jay. Still, once he was born . . .

Woman: You're the best father I've ever seen. You're so natural with the boys. I can't imagine any adult actually really . . . talking to me, when I was young, the way you talk to them. The way you all laugh together. It's like a foreign country.

Man: Here's the thing they don't tell you. A great deal of parenting, especially when they're young, is acting. People get confused on that point. They think they're meant to be totally genuine and authentic, for the sake of intimacy. But if you go that route, you're furious and frustrated, because kids are maddening and impossible half the time, so you're dragging round your own baggage, shouting and projecting your own tangled needs and issues everywhere. You try to be authentic all the bloody time and you end up a tyrant or a basket case. A lot of the intimacy is only possible if you know when to shut your mouth at other times, when they're driving you mad, and act the role of the good parent. For better or worse, I'm a good actor.

Woman: I'm an excellent actress, too, as it turns out. God, I really should have gone on more auditions—

Man: What's the point, though? Of your acting to get through your life? I'm not trying to be an asshole, honestly, but if you and Bebe aren't happy anymore . . . well, it's not exactly easy living a double life, being a liar all the time, is it? If you could get out cleanly and just live honestly, why do you stay?

Woman: I still wouldn't be honest—I'd just be a single woman clandestinely fucking a married man. (Stubs out cigarette, then, seemingly without thinking, fastens bra, begins doing up her buttons.) Right now I'm staying because of us, in part. I look less predatory as a coupled-up lesbian, right? It's a decoy. It's better for you if I stay. (Grins widely but unnaturally.) I'm like a double agent.

Man: (Deadpan.) That's not a good reason, Lina. I don't want to be responsible for your being somewhere you don't want to be.

Woman: I'm where I want to be right now, here.

Man: You know what I mean. I can't give you a whole life. I want you to live your life fully, not just . . . in some motel. I don't want to be the excuse for your not expecting much the rest of the time.

Woman: (Standing up, fully dressed now, turning in a half-circle as though confused about her body's intentions.)

Man: Are we going somewhere? Are your legs twitchy? Do we need to walk?

Woman: (Facing him.) So what are we?

Man: Oh, sweet girl. I don't know. Revelatory? The most beautiful thing that's ever happened to me outside of my sons? The surprise of my life? An adventure? A free fall?

Woman: Seriously? You're giving me the "I don't know" answer?

Man: I know we're best friends. Very . . . strange best friends.

Woman: (Doesn't even know how to format a script, anyway, so fuck off.)

Woman: (Tears in her eyes, unimportant since they can't be seen by the audience.)

Woman: (Touching the man's shoulder—please tell me that I'm right, that at least I touched you before my next line.)

Woman: Or maybe all I really am to you is another kind of moderation.

GRETCHEN

REQUEST FOR ORDER

PETITIONER/PLAINTIFF: Gretchen Merry-Underwood

RESPONDENT/DEFENDANT:

Miguel Guerra/Chad William Merry

OTHER PARENT/PARTY: Nicholas Owen Ryan

9. ___X___ I request that time for service of the Request for Order and accompanying papers be shortened so that these documents may be served no less than (specify number) ___10___ days before the time set for the hearing. I need to have this order shortening time because of the facts specified in item 10 or the attached declaration.

10. ________ FACTS IN SUPPORT of orders requested and change of circumstances for any modification are (specify):

__X__ Contained in the attached declaration. (You may use Attached Declaration (form MC-031) for this purpose. The attached declaration must not exceed 10 pages in length unless permission to file a longer declaration has been obtained from the court.)

I am filing for custody of an unborn female child, who is currently nearing the 21st week of gestation. I am the biological mother of the child. My brother, Chad Merry, had asked if I would donate an egg so that he and his partner, Miguel Guerra, could have a child. I was under a lot of stress as a result of deciding to divorce my emotionally abusive husband, Troy Underwood, and unfortunately I exhibited bad judgment and decided to donate my eggs. I love my brother, and he is a good person, but it has become very clear to me that I don't wish to have my daughter raised by people other than myself, and far away from her half-brother, my son Gray. I am trying to rectify this error in my judgment before it goes too far. In order to show my seriousness in wanting to make no further poor judgment calls, I have voluntarily given up all alcohol and am seeing a life coach, to help me understand why I would have done clearly detrimental things like marry an abusive man and give my immature brother and his partner, who I don't think even likes me, my eggs. It is clear to me that I was having some sort of midlife crisis. I would like to be able to get my life back on track by raising both of my children together as siblings, and providing my daughter with a more stable, normative environment, in a calm and tranquil suburb, near her grandparents, rather than having her grow up the daughter of gay men in a very chaotic and wild area of the city known for its bars, Wicker Park. I think I can provide a more stable environment for this little girl, and that if my brother and his partner really want to have a baby, they should adopt like other gay men often do, like from China or something, where the baby would otherwise be living in some third-world orphanage and my brother would be able to offer a better home. In this case, however, I am able to offer the better home. And, of course, the baby is biologically mine, not theirs. The sperm donor is a man we barely even know, who has no desire that any of us know of to claim or raise the child.

You will note, above, that I have asked for a very shortened period from these documents being served, which I am doing in the best interest of my daughter. I would like to have these papers served only after she is born, and for us to be able to immediately go to court to decide the matter at that time. If I were to serve these papers now, the gestational surrogate, who seems potentially a highly opportunistic person, could decide to sabotage the pregnancy, or my brother and his partner could pay her to go with them somewhere else to give birth, where I wouldn't know where they were. At minimum, serving papers at this juncture would be a significant stressor on the pregnancy if everyone involved knew a custody suit was pending. For the safety and protection of my daughter, I would like these proceedings to remain a secret until on or near the due date of July 16, 2009.

Thank you for your consideration and discretion.

I declare under penalty of perjury under the laws of the State of Illinois that the foregoing is true and correct.

Date: 03/12/2009

Gretchen Margot Merry-Underwood

(TYPE OR PRINT NAME)

Gretchen Margot Merry-Underwood

(SIGNATURE OF APPLICANT)

EMILY

Emily is standing up to get dressed, head still pounding and every breath a labor that doesn't hit bottom and make her feel air-full, when the doctor—about Emily's age and also pregnant, though further along—leans in toward her and says, urgent and conspiratorial, "Look, it's a noble thing you're doing, and I admire you. But you have two children of your own and this can be extremely serious. If you decide the right course of action is to deliver immediately, no one could fault you for that."

Emily blinks compulsively, which she has, in truth, been doing a lot of this week. Her vision is screwed up, which she thought was from exhaustion but—it turns out—is from this preeclampsia thing: a profusion of symptoms that had appeared unrelated, but turn out to be Bad.

"Deliver?" she says, hearing her voice as nearly a squeal. "But I'm not even in the third trimester yet. Do you mean . . . terminate the pregnancy?"

"We don't look at it as termination," the doctor says cheerfully. "We can try to treat this with steroid injections to help the fetus's lungs develop faster—we can give you magnesium and blood pressure medication to try to lower your own complications, but the thing you need to understand is that the only cure for preeclampsia is to deliver the baby. You're a mother. Your own children need you."

Under her blue paper medical gown, Emily's armpits leak conspicuously. She is not sure she has ever felt sweat dripping and running down her sides in such a manner. Her body has become a thing out of her control.

"I couldn't possibly do that. I've signed a contract. I have an obligation to these people. This is their *child*."

"Of course," the doctor says. "Whatever you decide. It's my job to make you aware of all your options. Most women with preeclampsia do deliver their babies past the thirty-seventh week, and everything works out, but some women have a more mild form of the condition, and yours is somewhat more serious at the onset, so it could be more challenging to get it under control. But that doesn't mean we can't achieve it."

She pats Emily's arm reassuringly, then retreats from the examination room. The stupidly green walls look blurry. How can this be happening? Emily glances down at the "Preeclampsia & Eclampsia" pamphlet the doctor has given her and the potential consequence of "cerebral palsy" for the infant jumps out at her as though written in 3-D. Could she have had this last time and never been diagnosed? But . . . her pregnancy with Jay seemed perfect. No one ever mentioned high blood pressure. She never felt like *this*. It seems to be a cosmic joke.

It's difficult to get dressed. Her abdomen isn't that huge yet, but everything else is swollen, too. Her shoes are hard to get on. Her hands feel bloated and tingly, like she's trying to work her zippers and buttons after a shot of local anesthesia.

If she terminates this pregnancy, everything she's been working toward will be lost.

Instead of being the hero, the saint, she will just be the failure, yet again. Chad and Miguel will mutter disappointedly to each other how she was too old—how she already had one disabled child and they should have known better. Nothing has been found wrong with their daughter on the ultrasound, but nothing was found wrong with Jay, either.

She sits, breathing hard, not leaving the exam room. Chad is in the waiting room, and she will have to face him. What will she say? What would he want her to do? If she carries to term, something could be wrong with the baby. She would have delivered them a damaged child. She wouldn't wish that on anyone, of course—but mostly, she wouldn't wish the stigma of a double-hitter on herself, and the terror of it makes her throat constrict. Her head buzzes and hums.

How to salvage this situation? What to do, who to ask? She clutches her referral to a maternal-fetal medicine specialist (whatever *that* is—if her existing OB-GYN isn't a "maternal-fetal medicine specialist," then why has she been handling maternal Emily and this fetus?), shoving it deep into her purse where Chad won't see it. She has to go home and begin bed rest, which is going to be hard to explain, since Chad will think they're going out for "just one glass" of champagne or (virgin, for Emily) umbrella drinks, and maybe even shopping, and Emily *wants* to go—wants to go so badly that it hurts worse than the pain in her head to think she has to deprive herself.

Chad jumps up when he sees her, all innocent gleeful smiles, and for the first time since she's met him, Emily wants to smack him. Usually, just seeing him makes her feel better than she does at work or home—but now he's become another male body she has to hide things from. Already her head is churning with how she's going to manage Nick, who she suspects resents her pregnancy even now, *before* he realizes she's about to spend the next three months in bed, while he will have to wait on her.

Which, according to the pink apron fantasy, he should get off on. But no, of course he will hate it. A pregnant woman with swollen hands and feet and dangerously high blood pressure is hardly the epitome of sexy. With the boys, Nick is a nurturer. He never snaps, never yells, never fails to say kind things or make Miles and Jay laugh. He fetches things for Jay like a personal valet. But when Emily has the flu or something, Nick never even thinks to get her a cup of tea. He says things like, "Don't worry, you just rest, I'll take care of the boys," but "resting" ends up meaning that she is stuck in the bedroom alone, starving and dehydrated and uncomfortable and bored. In no one's mind is *Emily* ever the one who needs taking care of—as though the epitome of any care they might offer is to alleviate her of the burden of caring for *them*.

"How did the appointment go?" Chad says, rubbing Emily's belly with gusto. "How's our little girl?"

"She's great!" Emily says, wishing she could pop about twenty Advil right now. "My blood pressure is a little high so they said I should rest a lot the next few days to bring it back down. I should probably skip going out to lunch."

"Your blood pressure's high?" Chad's voice fills the waiting room—people turn to look. "Should we go back and talk to the doctor some more? Is the baby okay? Did they take the baby's blood pressure?"

Emily forces herself not to sigh audibly. "The baby's heartbeat was just fine. Everything about the baby is perfect. High blood pressure isn't terribly uncommon in pregnancy. It's no big deal—I just need to take it easy."

"Okay then, all righty then," Chad says, still talking too fast and too loud. "No problem! We can get Barb to come to your house more regularly. We can order you some meals from First Slice Café—they donate parts of the proceeds to homeless shelters and have vegetarian options. We can order you HBO so you can binge watch all the shows you've missed. It'll be fun!"

Emily begins to exhale. He still seems stupid to her in this moment, but he is a stupid man who is going to buy her HBO and make sure her house is cleaned and the three males she lives with are fed. He is better than she can manage without him, and relief begins to sink into her bones like an analgesic.

"Hopefully the resting thing won't last that long," Emily lies. "I'm supposed to talk to the doctor again in a few days, to see if I need to be referred to any kind of specialist, but hopefully it's all just normalized by then."

There is no possibility this is true. The doctor, the pamphlet, have both already informed her that the only way this matter will "resolve" is to get the baby out of her body. But she has an innate instinct, uncontrollable, that makes her want to buy time, to figure out how to spin this, to figure out how to present it to Chad and Miguel in a way that assures their continued devotion and gratitude—to make sure she isn't a disappointment to them, of which they will wash their hands.

She can see the specialist on her own. After that—once she knows more—she will call Chad and tell him . . . something. Maybe the truth. Maybe some half-version of the truth. She can't avoid it entirely—he has access to the doctors, too. It's only out of respect for her modesty that he wasn't in the examination room with her. She can't hold him off forever.

They wouldn't have to return the ten grand, would they? She and Nick had twice that in debt, and the money is already spent. Emily makes a note to review her contract when she gets home. Surely, there must be some clause that provides for situations like this?

On the way back to the parking garage, Chad links arms with her, walks more slowly than his usual brisk pace. He hovers solicitously while she puts on her seatbelt, as though expecting to have to fasten it for her. She wishes, with a ferocity that makes her feel like the bottom has dropped out of her stomach, that he would just *take her home* with him. If she tells him—*once* she tells him—might that be an option? Might she just go and stay with them, and leave Nick and the boys to fend for themselves while Chad and Miguel minister to her every need?

Then, if they lose the baby anyway, it would be all of their shared failure and grief. It wouldn't be Emily, quietly letting them down on the west side of town, solely culpable, something to be forgotten.

Somehow, if the baby doesn't make it, that has to strengthen her bond with them, not eradicate it . . .

This is a long game. A marathon, not a sprint. This is still salvageable. It *has* to be.

Forbidden to return to work, confined to her bed, Emily will soon have ample time to figure out exactly how.

LINA

You've told me that one of the first rules of writing is not to be coy with the audience. Not to hold things back that the characters already know, for no apparent reason other than the value of surprise. You've explained to me that shocking the reader is cheap, that punchline endings are a cop-out and the real trick is creating something that feels new with each read, fresh points of entry invisible on the last round. For example, when someone writes a letter in real life, they won't rehash all the things the letter's recipient already knows, and that's why letters never look real in novels, because there's a difference in awareness between the story's players and its audience, and writers forget that. And so, Nick, under the laws of your universe I've already made too many fatal mistakes. I am still the girl who thinks I can turn this into a love story. I am still the girl who thinks if I say, "I don't want to talk about it," it will somehow go away.

There is still so much you don't know. Please be patient with me. I need to take this slowly.

I learned about the BRCA gene during my phone call with Isabel's doctor, way back in the late fall when I was masquerading as Ezme. The doctor said to me, "Ezme, did your mother talk to you, have you decided yet whether or not to be tested?" and when I said, to stall long enough to figure out what the fuck he was talking about, "No, I haven't made up my mind yet, what do you think?" he sighed into my pretend-Ezme ear and said, "It's a very personal choice, but I think it's better to have the information. You're so young that you wouldn't need to have a preventative hysterectomy immediately, most likely. You could still bear children, if that's what you're worried about." And I said dumbly, "Yes, that's what I was worried about." When I hung up, I wrote "Bracka Gene?" on the thigh of my jeans, before I called Eddie and invited myself for Christmas. I sat staring into space, in the screaming vortex of my own head, hating my existence and wishing someone would cane me within an inch of my life so I could feel different without having to take a new sober date.

Later, after the aforementioned phone calls, I would finally Google it. I would see *BRCA gene*. I would read about the time bomb possibly ticking inside me, potentially putting me at such an increased risk of both ovarian and breast cancer than the general population that the recommended course of action was a preventative hysterectomy and, in some cases, a bilateral mastectomy. I immediately went into my bathroom and took five Klonopin by chewing them to get them into my bloodstream faster, even though that would leave me short of pills by the end of the month.

So where was I supposed to drop this little tidbit of information in, Nick? Go ahead, go back over what I've written and tell me. Fuck if I know.

So here I am in our story, near the end of your wife's second trimester, and I've been sitting on this information for nearly four months. So what? That I'm capable of denial—that I'm capable of spinning while revealing nothing—is hardly news.

One thing's becoming clear, though. Yes, you're the *you* of this story, but just like it isn't all about us, it also isn't all *for* you anymore. I want to get everything down as I remember it. I want to understand things myself, as much as I want you to understand. I want something bigger than what I wanted when I started writing this, even if I'm not sure what it is.

Denial is easy when you have no actual information. It took me months to actually make an appointment to get the BRCA gene test, and—as with every terrifying blood test I'd ever had—I expected the results would be back to me within a couple of days. Only once I was in the lab with a needle in my arm did I find out it would take some six weeks for the results to come in, and that the anxiety I'd been facing wondering whether to get the test had just multiplied by about a million, and I was trapped, helplessly waiting.

In some ways, I don't know why I'm saying that. The truth is, I always knew what the results would be.

When the phone call comes, imparting the news that I tested positive, Isabel's toxic DNA making up the blood and substance of me, I feel, if anything, a powerful sense of déjà vu, my body long since a foregone conclusion. I think for a quick, violent flash of Miguel, and how his syphilis became some opportunity for a madcap communal adventure, and for maybe the first time in my entire life I hate my brother, who has always had more love and support circling him than he ever acknowledges, while I am here alone.

But wait: Can I scratch that? It sounds so self-pitying. The truth is that I am not alone even on a *literal* level, as in *in my apartment.* I could knock on the door to Bebe's office and tell her, and she would call me "pet" and hold me. I could call Miguel a few neighborhoods over, and he would meet me anywhere, might even let me pound a drink in front of him and not complain. I could, for fuck's sake, call Isabel and tell her off for not warning me herself, and perhaps derive some catharsis from that.

I do none of those things.

Instead I text you with the name and address of yet another motel, and a time to arrive. I mention nothing of the test, of my contaminated state.

And so I wait: naked, ass facing the door. You have texted back, to let me know you are on your way, and in what position you desire to find me. Waves of fear and arousal roil through me, starting at my core and rolling outward in both directions. Electric sparks shoot down my legs; my body feels plugged into an outlet. The curtains are drawn, blocking out spring sunlight. My phone lies next to me on the bed but I already know you will not text to signal your actual arrival: you will want to catch me unaware. I don't know what will touch me first: your hand, your belt, your cock, your tongue. What you don't know: I'm gyrating my hips uncontrollably, like something in heat, even before you're in the room. Later, you will think I'm doing this for your benefit, you will give a throaty laugh and say, "Mmm, very nice, do that again," but the truth is my body is already beyond performing, is a thing outside my control. I keep lowering my face to the scratchy bedspread, shy, exquisitely, intimately humiliated. Gooseflesh crawls on my skin. My stomach drops miles on a rotation of every few seconds. I feel hyperaware of air touching my splayed-open parts. A lump keeps rising in my throat. Wild, unrestrained joy.

Are there things I'm not supposed to want anymore? Am I supposed to be fixed, cured, healed? That's not what this is about. That's a punch line that isn't coming. I don't want to live in a world with those borders. *It would hurt me if you couldn't bear to hurt me*, I whispered to you, the first night I whipped you and showed you how a blow could feel like a caress. You had never liked pain. You didn't spend your childhood burning and cutting yourself like I did, and floating away on the sweet endorphin release. Pain was not your first morphine. You had always been "curious" but afraid. You had submissive fantasies, but not masochistic ones. The borders of sensation, though, are less neatly delineated than most people believe. The first time I saw you fall away from yourself into subspace, I felt like some combination of playground pusher and heart surgeon and god. You were smiling, no longer twitching from each strike, a quiet laugh rolling low inside you that sounded like a purr.

Am I supposed to stop needing what I need, just because I no longer need Bebe?

There are parts of every story that don't fit. The loose threads of a psyche, of a body, that won't pull taut. Here is the truth: I didn't tell you about the BRCA gene not because I had some nefarious plan (I had, I promise you Nick, no nefarious plan . . . not *yet*), but because I was afraid that if I told you I was radically predisposed to *cancer*—that I might even at that moment be "sick"—you wouldn't fuck me the same way anymore. I was afraid of your pity. I was afraid of Us turning into some sanitized, sad thing where you would make haltingly gentle love to me and your tears would drop down onto my face; I was afraid of doctors' offices and holding hands in waiting rooms; I was afraid—more than anything else—that you would hear this almost comedically hideous news and cut your losses and run, and here in this hotel room, that is the goddamn opposite of what I need from you.

I need you to take me outside of myself. I am a barn door you didn't open but cannot shut. It's more than that, too. I love you, which has both nothing and *everything* to do with this. With love, everything old is new again, the human heart so perilously capable of perpetual renewal. Every tree once eaten from fails to preclude a new tree never seen before, bearing new fruit. I wait for you. Your key card, your hand on the door, your skin like warm electric silk, your belt. Hurry. Arrive. Touch me. Thrill me. Hurt me. See me. Save me. Please, now, please.

A word about desire: there are no words about desire.

Later, I don't want Bebe to hear me making the call, so I park outside the apartment, my body still vibrating and rolling with you, and look up Ezme's number on my phone. I'm hoping for voicemail, though fuck knows what I think I would say to voicemail in a situation like this. Instead I get Ezme herself, businesslike and chirpy, near the end of her workday. I say things like, "How's your mom?" and listen to her answers: "Two weeks until she's done with chemo as long as her white blood cell count is high enough on Friday to get treated," and, "She had to have a blood transfusion last week before they'd give her chemo again," and, "She's on track for remission—if she can just get two more treatments on schedule, her CA 125 numbers are basically cutting in half after every treatment, and she'll be there." I don't say that, statistically, "there" only lasts a couple of years, tops. I don't say that the chances of Isabel living another five years are practically nil. Ezme isn't Eddie. She knows that.

"Has your mother," I begin—*your mother, your mother*—"talked to you about being tested for the BRCA gene?"

I don't know what I expect, actually. She could say, "What's that?" or she could say in a patronizing tone of voice that of course she knew and that she thought her mother would have told me by now. What I don't expect is for her to say, "Oh. I'm sorry, it's just my mother didn't think you would need to worry about that since your genetics only overlap by half."

"What?" I ask.

"Just, you know, because of only being her half sister."

"I . . ."

"She said that since nobody on Abuela's side of the family has ever had cancer, it had to be from her father's side, but Abuela had already left him when you were conceived. She said you knew that, that it wasn't a secret or anything."

I hold the phone away from my face for a moment, staring at it. I'm parked on Ravenswood, where there's not much traffic, warehouses lining the east end of the street and train tracks lining the west end. "Let me get this straight," I say to my clandestine younger sister. "Isabel says that since Mami was whoring around at the time of my conception, it was just fine to risk my possibly dying of ovarian cancer. Am I understanding this correctly?"

"Look," Ezme says, her voice perfect ice and poise, "My mother would never say that. She doesn't talk that way about people. I'm sorry you're offended, but this is between the two of you."

"Oh, it's between the two of us, all right."

"I've already been tested," Ezme says. "If you want to know, I didn't think she was making the right decision not to tell you, but it wasn't my business."

"I'm none of your business. I'm nothing to you so why should you get involved."

"I can see you're very upset, so I should really go."

It's on the tip of my tongue to ask why I should be upset that my actual whore of a mother is trying to pass my fake mother off as a whore, but instead I blurt out, "Wait! Ezme, wait. You got tested. Are you okay?"

"I tested positively for the gene," she says, calmly. "But it isn't really a big deal. I'll wait until I have children, and then I'll have a hysterectomy in my thirties. It really isn't an issue. I apologize for this awkward situation."

Our mother's memorial service will be the last time I ever see her.

I love you as certain dark things are to be loved, Pablo Neruda wrote in his "Sonnet XVII," *in secret, between the shadow and the soul.* This was one of my favorite poems even before I met you, Nick. I wanted to be the object of the poem, the way every woman wants to be Leonard Cohen's Suzanne or Bob Dylan's Sara. Later, I imagined that you and I might get matching XVII tattoos, or even *between the shadow and the soul* inked into our flesh, someday, when we were together officially. It didn't occur to me that if we were living in the light, I wouldn't *be* your "dark thing" anymore. I didn't let myself acknowledge that everything we did "in secret" was at Emily's expense. Or, fuck it, that's a lie—the truth is that I felt special in my darkness. I believed darkness more worthy of passion. This belief predated you, as though I conjured you into being with the force of it. If anything, after my genetic testing came back, this sense of darkness as privileged only amplified—made *me* the doomed heroine, while Emily—bland, breeder, blond Emily—was somewhere offscreen on her monotonous bed rest, languishing as boring saints do, never reaching the heights of experience reserved for those like us.

That you will wish I could have changed places with her by the time I'm done with this seems self-evident, so why fight it?

Something reckless sets in.

Is it the fact that I am secretly in the countdown to my surgery—the preventative hysterectomy that will take place sometime after the Community Baby is born and everything has settled down? I am keeping my breasts for now—Isabel's cancer hasn't spread there, so I'm telling myself this affords me time. The hysterectomy itself, though, will bring on premature menopause. I will no longer menstruate; I will become the target market for personal lubricants instead of being so perpetually wet since we began that I can drench your eyes in me until you cannot see. I will never have a baby. Would I *want* a baby? Although I am positively geriatric by the standards of my family's childbearing timeline, in my own adult tribe I am young—why would I have to decide such a thing right now? Bebe seems in a vague way to find maternal behavior an affront to feminism, but watch her go on to parent with her next girlfriend—isn't that how this always works? Watch her settle down into alternative family bliss with some nice stripper who happens to be a doula on the side.

I'm in a kind of diffuse mourning I can't talk about. You have two children. You are married. What am I supposed to say?

"I wish I knew Jay better," I say instead, and you tell me, "You could spend some time with him, you know—from the outside, we're practically family."

Recklessness has overcome us and I don't know how to tamp it down. Danger and longing electrify the air between us. Every moment feels larger than life. You are practically a single parent since Emily became preeclamptic. She is busy lying on her side, avoiding salt, popping steroids that make her moody and waiting it out until the baby is developed enough to be viable. Today, I am bleeding. I will have, if things go according to plan, three more periods after this one, and then I will be done. No more communists in the funhouse, as they say in Denmark. Sexton's *not a woman quite.*

"Jay and I are going to the Nature Museum," your voice says on the phone. "He loves the butterfly sanctuary." I don't know what you are talking about. I have never been to a "nature museum." This is not the sort of thing my childhood included, if it even existed then. "You could join us," you say, and I should refuse—I know I should tell you you're being careless—but I say immediately, "I'd love to."

The butterfly sanctuary is like a greenhouse, hot as a jungle inside. The air feels thick inside my lungs. At first, it doesn't seem real—doesn't seem possible—that so much flight can take place in one confined space. We sit on a bench while butterflies soar all over the glass-encased room, high above us toward the vaulted ceilings, then swooping back through the dense greenery, fluttering, to land on your son's arms. They are *everywhere*, mariposas, winged, fragile, wild. When I was younger I identified with the moth, perpetually flying into flames, self-annihilating. I wanted a tattoo of a moth on the inside of my forearm but I worried people might mistake it for a butterfly. Beautiful things annoyed and bored me. *Everything I love is ugly,* Ani DiFranco sang. Now, the butterfly and the moth seem like essential sides of a coin. Emerging in a new form from a cocoon—*reinvention*—seems the opposite of boring. I sit inside the sanctuary, our knees occasionally brushing, intoxicated on beauty.

"It would be easier," you say, "if Emily weren't such a good, solid person. All she's ever done is help and support me. I wish I had any justification at all for what I want."

For no reason anyone has been able to ascertain, your wife is using her body as a selfless vessel. If her life isn't exactly in danger, it's close. Emily is the Isabel of this story, saving everyone, but I am still on the outside, never among the rescued. Emily is the one who would throw herself on the pyre, while I'm not sure I have ever done anything altruistic in my life.

"Bebe supported me for years, too," I say, quietly. "She got me through college—given what I was like back then, she may have saved my life. She may not present as saintly like Emily does, but that doesn't mean she deserves to be lied to and betrayed."

You look taken aback. "I wasn't talking about meritocracy," you say. "I wasn't trying to make it a contest. I just meant—I love Emily, she's great, she's one of the most competent people I've ever met, but kind, too—a good mother. But I've never for five minutes felt around her the way I feel around you."

The thing about you is that your skin is white marble lit from the inside; the thing about you is that your eyes ignite things, and your lips are as crazy beautiful as your old lesbian posse said. The thing about you is that your tenderness toward me was instant and inexplicable, and I would spend these pages explaining it to you except I can't.

Your son comes over to you. It's impossible not to notice that, although the sanctuary isn't crowded, Jay is being covertly followed by the eyes of every child and adult in the room, as though he is on display alongside the butterflies. He seems oblivious, and maybe he is—maybe, being seven, he simply has no concept of what it would be like to move in the world without the eyes of strangers scrutinizing him. You, on the other hand, must be deeply, painfully aware, though your posture and smile give no sign. Jay's movements are jerky and his legs misshapen as he maneuvers the concrete path, but there is something airless about him, too, as though from his labored movements he might suddenly float away like the mariposas. The bones of his face are feline, sharp and delicate. His skin is poreless, but then so is yours. I am porous next to you both, leaking.

"Daddy," he says, "What if all the butterflies are pooping on me but I just can't see it because it's too small?"

I start laughing, and Jay's face blooms into an unbridled grin so like yours that my heart hammers. His fingers reach out to my bare arm, and there, right in the space I once wanted to camouflage with a self-destructive moth, he pokes his small finger into a subcutaneous skin-popping scar.

"What's this?" he asks.

"A mistake," I say. My hands brush, over and over, butterfly wings that seek to smooth.

"It's something Lina gets worried people will judge her for," you tell your son. "Like your braces."

"But it's just little," Jay says.

For months, I opened the abscess repeatedly, trying to drain it, too ashamed to go to the doctor, or maybe I didn't care enough to go to the doctor, I don't really remember now. I just remember that sometimes I could get puss out of it, and other times it was hard and merciless like a stone. I look at you above your son's head and I see just a flicker of a smile, like you're trying to tell me it's okay. And I touch the top of Jay's soft hand, and I say, "You're right, it's tiny—do you think maybe I shouldn't worry about it?" and he says, his voice suddenly one of I've-been-there authority, "My dad says it's what's inside that counts, but mean people don't think that, so if I were you I'd wear long sleeves."

"You're smarter than I am," I say, because it's the kind of joke adults make to kids for the benefit of other adults, and because he has, already at the age of seven, been through more than I have ever had to face. I think again about choice. Permit myself a self-indulgent moment of letting myself believe at least Jay will never know what it's like to have chosen his own problems, to be culpable in the things he's judged for. But that's just another junkie trick, another symptom of the narcissistic belief that we're the piece of shit at the center of the universe, that we're special and different even if it's by being worse than other people. You know my tricks, and you accept and forgive them, and I know it's time to do the same but I can't get out of my own way.

I wonder what your bedridden wife, having a child for my brother, would think of my desire to *accept myself.*

All around us, butterflies soar.

Days shimmer. We don't know yet what's coming. We are drunk on one another. I wake up every morning breathless, heart already gripped in a fist of anticipation of the next time I can hear your voice, the next time I can taste you, the next time I see your texts flash across my phone. I am thirty-one years old. I've divorced an ex-con who everyone in our old neighborhood feared, but who never caused me to so much as flinch. I've dragged my ass through rehab twice and detoxed alone four or five times until it finally stuck. I've been institutionalized three times for psychotic episodes and held myself together while people screamed and smeared shit on walls, refusing to succumb to my own hysteria, knowing it could keep me trapped inside longer. I came out as a lesbian to my Baptist family. I've been gleefully beaten and burnt and electrocuted in ways that might provoke the government of Singapore to complain of human rights violations. Yet somehow, here in the presence of your son—*of you and your son*—here in the presence of so much beauty and the lightning-bolt realization that I have not *quite* yet lost the chance to have a child of my own, I understand danger for the first time.

Your wife is at home, getting sicker by the day, but it's like we are the only people on some post-apocalyptic planet. We are hiding out inside the asylum, hoping the villagers don't storm the gate of our monster paradise. I would say, *I have never been so happy in my life*, but of course I have never been happy much at *all*, so my barometer for such quantifying is broken. What I know even that day is that our happiness is flourishing in the eye of a storm, and what I don't know even now is whether that was merely a coincidence, or a condition essential to its existence.

I lean into you as Jay ventures away, murmur into your ear, "What if we just . . . Nick . . . what if we just leave them, no matter how good they are? What if we decide to hold hands and jump off the ledge together into something new?"

It is the most terrifying moment of my life, and the most transcendent moment of my life. I tilt my face to look at you, to scan the reaction in your eyes, but before I can fully take you in, my cell phone vibrates in my back pocket, muffled buzzing against my ass, and I will never know why I reach for it, mindlessly, but I do.

That's when I find out Isabel is dead.

MIGUEL

Death is a battle cry. A predictable pattern of vultures fighting over remains.

In Miguel's family, nobody owns anything of value, so the bickering is particularly sad. Most likely in Chad's Merry Clan, there will be actual material bones to pick over: *I was promised the grandfather clock*, vs. *fuck the grandfather clock, I was promised the house in Scottsdale*. But while Isabel's house is kind of cool, it's in the middle of a lake and her husband is still living in it. Miguel, Lina, and Mami are so removed as to seem distant cousins. None of this, of course, stops Mami from having opinions that differ with Eddie's. This is always how it plays.

On the drive up to Beaver Island, Miguel sits in the backseat of Mami and Carlos's car with Lina, like they are children on a vacation their family never actually took. While Carlos drives, Mami rages that Isabel's funeral should be in Chicago. "Isabel's friends" should be able to attend, Mami insists, by which Miguel understands Mami to mean her *own* friends, members of the Baptist congregation to which Isabel has not belonged since the late 1990s. Eddie told Mami that Isabel didn't care about any of those people and that "her real community" on Beaver Island deserved the chance to mourn her. Miguel imagines that Mami kept right on making her point, though Eddie is the clear owner of Isabel's death—the proprietor of everyone else's grief.

"He says she *asked* to have her funeral at that little Catholic church in town," Mami says for at least the fifth time, "but I know she never said that." With this, Miguel cannot disagree. He doubts Isabel and Eddie ever talked about her impending death at all, mainly because Isabel never talked about *anything* real, especially to Eddie. But also because her death was not impending, exactly. She would have thought—if she was thinking this way at all—that she had months or years to plan.

Eddie came home from putting in some fancy kitchen on Donegal Bay and found Isabel dead on the floor, lying in enough blood to be a TV crime scene. Cancer is a thrombotic disease, and although Isabel's CA 125 levels were lowering in a steady and ideal fashion, on the fast track to "remission" (whether that meant six months or six years before things went south again, who knew?), she threw a pulmonary embolism, alone in her island home. The blood began to spurt (from her nose first? From her mouth?) while she was still in bed, and she stood, her blood trailing after her, grabbing the phone. She pressed "talk" but never, it seems, dialed—she must have realized, through her panic, that she couldn't speak in her state, and instead rushed toward the stairs—if Miguel knows Isabel at all, thinking to get to her car and take herself to the emergency clinic. In the end, she died before reaching the bottom of the staircase. She fell forward, sliding down the remaining stairs face-first, breaking her nose and crushing the bone beneath her left eyebrow. The blood from her nose and mouth pooled at the bottom of the staircase. When Eddie found her, Isabel's blood had leaked all the way to the front door, where it was trickling under the door and down the small step, but Eddie entered through the back door as always and didn't see Isabel until he was inside. Her head, from lying face-first on an incline, was the size of a watermelon. She looked like something that had been dead for days.

Eddie called Ezme. Ezme offered to take over the telephone chain, but to his credit, Eddie, still inches from Isabel's body, then called Mami. Mami had to choose between calling Miguel first, or Lina. She chose Miguel—Miguel, the Chosen One, who according to most of his family members is on a one-way train to hell for his gaiety, and yet is something of Mami's favorite. This has never made any sense, the way families never make any sense.

Hence it was upon Miguel to call his sister/niece/closest friend and tell her that her biological mother was dead. It took him two tequila shots to steady himself enough to dial. When Lina answered, she sounded unnaturally happy, like someone he didn't recognize, her voice high, devoid of gravelly cynicism. When he got the words out, she hung up on him without speaking, and for a few hours he thought maybe she wouldn't attend the funeral, and allowed himself to concoct fantasies in which he, in solidarity with Isabel's shunned daughter, also abstained. But now here they both are, meek in the back of Mami and Carlos's car, Lina's all-black garb for once suitable to the occasion.

"I can't believe she is being laid out in a Catholic church," says Mami, who of course was—like every good Puerto Rican girl in Chicago—raised Catholic, and married Papi, a Cuban Catholic, and baptized all her children Catholic, but now having been married to Carlos the Baptist for nearly thirty years has forgotten about all that.

Lina sighs long and slow. She seems reluctant to say what she is about to say and fiddles around with the rings on her fingers and the hems of her sleeves. Finally she says, "Mami, they converted back to Catholicism almost as soon as they moved to Beaver Island. That Eastern Orthodox thing was just a phase. She never really felt Baptist, she said—she's always felt she was Catholic, really, because it's how she was raised. By *you*."

The car sits silently. Isabel abandoned Lina thirty-one years ago—or, no, maybe it's that Lina was *stolen* from Isabel thirty-one years ago; Miguel can't be sure—and in the brief time they did live together under Mami and Carlos's roof in Chicago, Isabel took barely an interest in Lina's existence. Now, Mami, who bore Isabel, and Miguel, who slept in the curves of Isabel's body as his only solace for years, are hearing about her deepest feelings from the daughter Isabel never quite acknowledged. Everything has turned upside down. At least Mami *tried* to go visit Isabel on this godforsaken island, only to be sent home. Miguel didn't even try. Lina said that Eddie told her Isabel was hoping Miguel would come, but he didn't. Why *would* he? Lina isn't the only one Isabel abandoned. She left him, too, long ago.

When he asked Isabel to be his best woman, she immediately began to cry. Miguel understood the sound: silence. She switched to English: "I have to talk to you. About the ceremony." Previously, she always said wedding. *Miguel waited. He knew what was coming. Though it had not been made official, Isabel was about to confirm that Mami and Carlos would not attend. He could already hear her platitudes,* You know Mami loves you, *and,* She thinks Chad is such a nice boy. *Oh, sure, his mother would pray for him; he was welcome for dinner anytime. She would not turn her back. Yadda yadda. He felt agitation at his sister for ruining what should be* their *moment, but nobody had a moment—nobody in the Guerra clan—had a moment without Mami.*

"I can't be the matron of honor," Isabel said, as though Miguel were the bride. "This is the hardest decision I've ever made. You know I love you . . ."

Miguel was uncontrollably smiling, waiting for the punch line.

"I just can't support something I don't believe God supports—not in public. I can't act like the union is binding in the eyes of God. I'm not saying the right thing would be to marry a woman if you just can't love her that way. I know you were born . . . I believe God made you like you are."

Explosions. Small fireworks going off behind his eyes.

"But He gives people tests, Miguel, like some people are born without a leg or without sight, to see how you'll handle adversity. You

could still choose not to give in to the limitations you were born with, not to take the easy way out."

"What," he stammered, "are you talking *about? Wait. Did Mami put you up to this?"*

"Mami's God is meetings and potlucks, she doesn't know what she even believes." Isabel paused, snuffling. "Mami doesn't know I'm talking to you. Her religion is about finding a new man who doesn't drink liquor, you know? I don't go to her church anymore. I don't want Ezme growing up like we did—I've been taking her to Eastern Orthodox church for a few . . . I feel it there, what I've been looking for."

Two weeks until the big night. Miguel should have asked her long before this, but hadn't—Chad kept asking why, What are you waiting for, do you think she's a mind reader and is just going to show up? *and Miguel had reasoned he was just being typically reticent about actually expressing to another human being that he gave a shit about them—that asking Isabel to stand up at his wedding was tantamount to saying* I love you *aloud, a display of emotion of which he was positively horrified. Then he thought,* We've grown apart, *as though that explained it, as though perhaps his older sister would think he must be a loser if he had no one closer to ask. Now, he saw all at once that none of that had been* it, *even if it were all completely possible of him—him and his backward, stilted emotional range, his crippling fears of being* noticed. *That it was all true but not The Truth, and that the real truth was darker, buried deep inside Isabel and her insatiable longing to betray.*

"Being Baptist wasn't restrictive enough for you?" Miguel asked incredulously. "I mean, they wouldn't want you to be best woman, either. You don't have to change religions to get out of standing up at my wedding."

"That kind of thinking," Isabel said quietly, "is exactly what I'm talking about. You know, the world does not revolve around individuals, Miguel. Mami married a Baptist, so bam, she became one—you feel attracted to men or whatever, so you think you can marry one like

a man and a woman marry. Everyone does whatever they want—Papi did whatever he wanted and he had bastard children running around Caracas and us with bruises starving to death while he partied. The Orthodox Church and its rituals have been around a long, long time—it's not about what you or me want. It's about what is."

"Or maybe its just you wanting morality prescribed in clear, unchanging terms. Maybe traditional ethics is about cowards not having to choose. There's a thought, too."

"You can't change good and evil by changing your opinion!" Isabel flared. "Christ taught us the difference, and if you found Him, you'd know what I'm saying is true. I'm not denouncing you or Chad as people. I love you both as children of God and I'll always stand by you and hope you find your way."

"You'll always stand by me unless I ask you to stand next *to me on the most important day of my life?" But why was he doing this? He heard his voice: all rhetoric, like hers.*

"This is useless." Her tears had noise now, the sound of a common cold, his warrior sister a nasal congestion commercial. "I've been meaning to tell you there was no way I could attend the ceremony, but I'd been putting it off. I'm still new to the church and I was hoping to have my cake and eat it, too. I didn't want to sacrifice. But I've spoken with my priest, and I can't make exceptions just because I love you—"

"God forbid anyone make exceptions for love."

Isabel's tone was somber. "God does *forbid it, Miguel."*

He sat stunned, still holding the phone gingerly. How could this be happening? Isabel, joining the ranks of the earnest, all humor sucked from her pores by a vampire more powerful than their father ever was. Nothing left to say. At the dial tone in his ear, he wondered if a union between two men was more or less morally right when based on the kind of compromises mainstream heterosexual marriage also extolled. Would marrying Tomas for hysterical lust have been more meritorious? Or was marrying Chad, with whom he tended a litter of bulldog pups whose butts need wiping in the middle of the night; with whom watching The Simpsons *at 10:00 p.m. was a far more regular ritual than sex, exactly the kind of circumstances that would, someday in the future, convince the religious right that gay love was not so different after all? If he had pleaded:* I thought about killing myself for years, and only this man with his lightness and entitlement and oblivion has pulled me out of the depths of my own narcissistic despair, *would Isabel consider the mortal sin of suicide greater or lesser than that of loving a man? Would she take pity if he had confessed,* I'm not sure I even am *in* love with him—I'm not sure he's anything more than a survival tactic?

Next to him in the backseat, Lina so strongly resembles the Isabel he remembers that Miguel cannot stand to look at her. Soon, he will become a father—will grow old—but Isabel will remain frozen in time, still in her early thirties the last time he saw her with any regularity. Lina looks over at him, her eyes widening with motherly concern at what must be his stricken expression, and slides her hand along the seat to grasp his, but Miguel manages to choke out only, "I'm sorry," before he recoils, turning to look out the window and pressing his pulsing temple against the coolness of the glass, not looking back until the car stops in Charlevoix.

"My mother was a traditionalist," Ezme says into the humid air of the sanctuary. Her voice is too soft to project well, and she is too short to reach the microphone properly, so the collective energy of the room is one of straining toward her, to hear. "These days, families often don't have time for one another. The television is the babysitter for the kids. They go from daycare to school to the TV and the computer. Families don't talk together or do activities together or pray together like in former times. But my mother preferred the old ways, when families were tight-knit. I wasn't allowed to watch television until junior high. Mom homeschooled me, giving up her salary and living more simply, making many of our clothes herself, and cultivating a vegetable garden. She valued motherhood more than money or her own ambition. She gave me all of her time, and made me into who I am."

Miguel squirms in his Armani suit, leans down and whispers snidely into Lina's ear, her cartilage piercing brushing his lip, "Yep, just like we grew up, a real traditionalist."

It's true that his family owned no television until Carlos came into the picture. It's true that there were long periods in Caracas when they didn't attend any conventional school. Mami had a vegetable garden, of course. But it's almost as though Isabel took the bare-bone details of their childhood and dragged them from a hellscape straight into *Leave It to Beaver.*

"Why didn't Chad come?" Lina mutters back, her lips unmoving, like a ventriloquist.

"You don't get it," Miguel says back, also side-mouthed like a spy. "All Chad does is work. That's why we haven't killed each other. Why would I want to drag him here, to this? But what about Bebe? Are you guys okay?"

"Sure," Lina says, "we haven't had an argument in months. We barely talk, so that makes it hard to fight."

These are the "marital rights" he and Chad and Lina and Bebe are emulating then? This is what it's all about? *I, the undersigned, vow to stay out of your way as much as possible, so as not to get on your nerves. I, the espoused, vow to occasionally laugh at your jokes, not gamble away our money, stay away from needles, not beat our children, and thus present you with a relentless lack of Real Problems so you can never justify leaving. I promise to make being with me simple enough that the thought of being single again will give you a headache. Till death do us part.*

The official story on Bebe is that the hybrid battery in her car has rotted from the inside—that she was planning to come, but as soon as she learned they couldn't drive their own car and she would be stuck in a car with the other Guerras for seven hours, she bailed. This is plausible enough. There *is* no official story on Chad. In reality, Chad's barely been working since Emily developed preeclampsia—he's been spending all his time bringing her gifts and hanging around her house all day until Nick comes home to care for her—but none of that is applicable here, because Miguel didn't *want* him to come to Beaver Island anyway. He can't feel any of the things he's supposed to feel—his reactions all feel off-kilter, inappropriate, and he didn't want Chad as a witness, so that he would have to feign some kind of normalcy in his grief. He doesn't have to pretend in front of Mami and Lina. They're used to him. Besides which, they are probably both so self-involved they're taking very little notice of the fact that he's carrying a flask of tequila in his suit jacket, and that he's rolling his eyes a lot rather than crying. Mostly, he's numb and sick and bored.

"She was my best friend," Ezme tells the congregation. "She was the love of my life." Clusters of women in the audience begin to weep openly, no doubt thinking of their own departed mothers, of their young, trusting daughters at home. The mother-daughter bond is supposed to be . . . well, Miguel is not sure what it is supposed to be exactly, but something like what Ezme is describing here: primal, proprietary, primary. What is a lover, really, or a spouse, compared to a mother? A spouse can file for divorce. A lover can change his mind. Romantic love comes with boundaries on the blueprints. Isabel threw Mami out of her house in the pre-winter chill and refused to ever talk to her again, and still, Mami is here, deferring to Eddie, standing sentry over her daughter's bloated, unrecognizable body.

The child Emily is carrying will not have a mother. Is what he and Chad can offer enough to transcend that loss? Is something a loss if it never existed in the first place? Isabel never even held Lina—Miguel remembers with utter, shocking clarity, the way she refused to pick the baby up, and Mami and Tía had to buy expensive premade formula for baby Angelina because Isabel could not be forced to nurse, would not even listen to the reason that it was "free," and the family needed the money for Miguel and his food and his schoolbooks. Isabel was unmoved, held her arms fast over her too-young, too-ripe breasts, saying, *Get her away from me.* Miguel shivers in the chilly white sanctuary. All her years with Mami still, somehow, could not make up for Lina's loss of Isabel. Or is that a fair assessment? Lina is . . . well, she's *sick.* She has a diagnosed mental illness. Maybe she would be the way she is no matter who had mothered her. Maybe it means nothing about what Miguel and Chad are withholding from their own unborn child.

He needs another deep pull from his flask but the fucking thing is empty.

In the church basement, after the service, Eddie wanders around blank faced, blank voiced. The small white church is packed as though Isabel were an archbishop—the largely Irish-Catholic community of Beaver Island must have welcomed her and Eddie with open arms. Eddie looks, to Miguel, as totally over his head in Isabel's loss as he did when she was alive. He doesn't cry, but then again, this is a man who always seemed like he might claw his own face off with discomfort whenever Mami hugged him. He is not That Kind of Latino, as Miguel and Lina always joked. Still, every once in a while, Eddie seems to forget the mask of grief he is supposed to have plastered on his face, and his laughter dashes out like thunder in a quiet sky, talking with neighbors and island friends. At times, he looks like a man sprung from prison. What could it have been like being married to beautiful, formidable Isabel, the double agent, the emotional terrorist, the heroine and martyr? Maybe Eddie has a lover in the wings. Later, Miguel sees Eddie leaning against the wall of the sanctuary, his hands in his hair, and guilt impales him. Eddie will be remarried in less than six months, but of course Miguel doesn't realize that at the time, and even if he did, it wouldn't prove much. Men, all studies will tell you, prefer marriage if they've had it once. Men are happier married, while women are less happy and live less long inside long-term marriages. Widows often choose the single life. But who knows what that means about anything?

Miguel sat in his parked car, completely flummoxed as to what to do next. It was a Wednesday night, September of 1999, and he had to be up at five to get ready for work, but his baby sister Angelina, to whom he had almost never spoken outside of the confines of Mami and Carlos's home, had called him and asked him to come to this . . . place . . . *and meet her. "I have to talk to you," she'd said urgently on the phone. She must have had to call Mami for his number, because they had never before, to his recollection, spoken on the phone. Still aching from Isabel's spurning of his commitment ceremony, it wasn't in him to reject Angelina in turn, so he'd gone out to his car and driven to some obscure west-side intersection at which she'd said he'd find the bar where she was "working." He had expected to find his underage sister tending bar, expected it so without shock that he had not even considered she might be a hostess or waiting tables. Now he sat parked outside looking at the signs that proclaimed "All Nude Revue" on the chintzy marquee, his heart seeming jammed and throbbing inside his esophagus.*

He called Chad on his cell. "My sister is working at a strip club," he said. "The place is called Aphrodite's, but it's spelled A-p-h-r-o-d-i-t-y-s, with no apostrophe, even."

"Um," Chad said.

"I can't go in there. I'm coming home."

"Honey. If you were really leaving and not going in, you would be driving home right now, not calling me."

"What if I go in there and it's, like, the wrong place?" Miguel persisted. "What if Angelina isn't even there?"

He heard Chad take a breath. "Okay," Chad said slowly. "So are you more afraid of seeing your sister shimmering in pasties on the stage, or are you more afraid of being in a strip club alone and being mistaken for, you know, a heterosexual man who likes to look at tits?"

Miguel was silent for a moment. "I don't know," he admitted finally. "I think I'm humiliated in either scenario. Can you just drive out here and come with me?"

"Right," Chad said. "That is not going to happen."

Miguel hung up the phone.

Inside the club, the woman onstage was not Angelina, thank god. Miguel had no idea what to do with his body. The room was dimly lit and generally in the sort of disrepair of a typical corner bar that catered to old men who had been boozing together for thirty years. It seemed safe to assume that the smallish stage had once been for bands, and that only the pole was a new addition. There weren't that many customers—maybe twenty, all male except one middle-aged blonde smoking at a table with a bald man; she looked a little old to be one of the dancers, but if she found the venue a shitty choice for a date, she didn't show it, laughing and throwing back her head in a horsey way. Miguel stood there, thrashingly embarrassed to be so visible just loitering alone, but hesitant to commit to sitting down in a corner if maybe—please, please—he was in the wrong place and would have cause to make a speedy exit.

Then he saw her. She wasn't at one of the tables, but rather at the bar, alone. Her feet dangled from the barstool like a child's; she was wearing Chuck Taylors, which seemed so out of place with anything Miguel had ever imagined of a strip club that it was as though her shoes glowed conspicuously. Onstage, the dancer, also Hispanic, as were most people in the bar other than the blonde and her date, hung upside down on the pole, but her breasts, large enough that Miguel half-expected them to smack her in the chin, didn't seem to respond to gravity. He scurried desperately to the barstool next to Angelina, slid onto it.

Acne still littered the sides of Angelina's chiseled, Guerra jaw. She had Isabel's features, but larger, and her skin seemed thicker, less delicate. She was so tiny she could pass for a high school freshman—he did a mental math check and was pretty sure she was now twenty and had been married for two years—but despite her girlish appearance, there was something worn about her. She looked to Miguel, with her ravaged little nut of a face, like a member of a girl gang in a 1980s made-for-TV movie. Tough but somehow already ridden too hard, and achingly vulnerable.

She blew smoke from a Marlboro Red into his face. "I know we haven't talked in a while. I just want you to know two things. One, nobody is coming to your wedding 'cause Isabel's gone crazy and shamed Mami as a bad Christian if she shows up, but fuck them, I'll be there. I won't have a date, so maybe you can tell some of your cute flamer friends to take pity and dance with me."

Miguel said, "Thanks . . . but I already knew all that. Isabel called me. I guess she wanted to do me the courtesy of telling me I was an abomination in the eyes of god to my face. Well, not my face *exactly, but . . . I never expected Mami and Carlos to come. Yeah, I'll make sure you have people to talk to, I didn't imagine Javier would want to go to a gay wedding, it doesn't exactly seem his style."*

"Two," Angelina said, as though he hadn't spoken, "I'm getting a divorce."

"Did he hit you?" Miguel demanded, his voice too loud.

Angelina pushed his arm. "Are you on crack? Javier knows better than to be raising a hand to me. He's just, you know, set in his ways. He doesn't want me going to school, which I'm gonna do. He wants to, like, have a gazillion babies hanging off my boobs and shit, but I'm gonna be a nurse. Or a teacher. I don't know. Something."

He wanted to say, Be something that pays better. *Instead he said, "So this place is giving out teaching degrees on the side then?"*

She was drinking a whiskey or scotch, neat. A strange drink for a young girl, but she gulped it with the kind of desperation that transcended age. Under the too-long arms of her shirt cuffs, he saw that her nails were bitten down so low the fingertips were scabbed: picked over, re-scabbed again, mutilated and made sport of, just as he had done at her age. He guessed that she tended to torment the skin, forbidding a quick healing, perversely fascinated with damage. He wanted to put his arms around her, but he had never known how to do that, not with anybody—which was why he needed Chad.

"Uh, are you still working at Dominick's Deli counter?" he asked lamely.

Her eyes met his. Mocking, the eyes of a mother, except his mother had never teased, always wore a sheepish expression, embarrassed for her mistakes, for what her children had seen. Angelina lit another cigarette, rubbed up and down on his leg like a lover—no, like a sister, except in his family, nobody ever touched anyone anymore, love too close to violence.

"Does this look like the Dominick's Deli counter?" Then simply, "This is where I work now. I'm better than that puta *up there. I make more money than anyone else here. This is just temporary."*

"Temporary? For tuition, you mean, to pay for school?"

"Temporary," she said, "until I can get a job at a better club. This place is a dump. I'll earn four or five times as much if I can get in somewhere like The Dollhouse."

They looked at each other through the wispy smoke. Broke, undereducated, on the verge of divorce, and working in this almost unimaginably sad shithole, she gave off waves of nervy confidence that baffled and eluded Miguel—that felt utterly inaccessible to him despite the armor of his math degree, his job at the Board of Trade, his "marrying up." She seemed to be sizing him up.

"Look," she said, "can I be your best man or what?"

So many people are milling around downstairs, eating handfuls of oil-slick peanuts and drinking cups of Sprite, that Miguel and

Lina have taken refuge in Isabel and Eddie's bedroom, which has a window seat where they can sit, window cracked, smoking. Miguel vigilantly blows smoke out through the window, his lips almost making out with the screen, then passes the cigarette to Lina every few drags, and watches her flagrantly exhale her smoke straight toward Isabel and Eddie's bed. Her black stockings are torn in a way either purposefully punk or accidental, and Miguel, with his utter lack of fashion sense, can't discern which. Still, it makes her look even more delicately ruined than usual, her knees drawn up sideways on the seat next to her: she's all hair and bones and kohl-smudged eyes and snags. Miguel feels an urge to protect her, when of course he can't even protect himself—he can't even protect his unborn child, inside Emily's preeclamptic body. It strikes Miguel hard that he should have been telling people that Chad wasn't in Beaver Island because they didn't want to abandon Emily and the baby, with the pregnancy so high-risk, but of course it never occurred to him to say such a thing.

Two days ago, everyone was still wearing light jackets, but now the world feels like a hot, dry bone. There's no wind, and with the greenhouse effect of afternoon sun bearing down on the window, Lina's face looks shiny with sweat so that she resembles Isabel—who always seemed glossy in a way that was somehow hot—even more. Lina prods him with her foot, gestures with the cigarette so that smoke waves around their proximity. "Look at that."

Boxes are piled up near the closet. It would have been impossible not to notice them, but Miguel humors her and nods.

"No, dickwad," she says, "*That.*"

Miguel snatches the cigarette from her fingers as she approaches the boxes. There are seven of them in all, full of Isabel's clothes, neatly folded, Miguel suspects by Ezme. No doubt they will be donated to the church. Lina starts shoving one box out of the way with her leg, revealing another box behind it on which the word is written in black sharpie: *Guerras.*

"This one's for us," she says. "I saw the G-U in the gap. All these boxes, and we get a whopping *one*, to split between us and Mami."

Miguel thinks to say that maybe there will be more boxes for them by the time Eddie and Ezme finish going through the house, but in reality he's stunned that anything's been set aside for them at all.

Lina lifts their box, which is so conspicuously smaller than the others that it was only even elevated and visible because it was sitting on a bigger, not-for-them box. She carries it over to Eddie and Isabel's bed. Mami and Carlos are downstairs, abandoned, but no doubt they expected nothing more from either Miguel or Lina, both of whom have made familial careers out of being useless. Back when he and Isabel were still talking regularly, when she lived in Chicago, the few times she visited his various apartments she would always suggest that he should "bleach his walls" to mask the discoloration his smoking caused. *Bleach his walls.* Miguel is not even sure how such a thing would be accomplished. His guilt at smoking in her bedroom is both nauseating and triumphant, but both feelings leave him desperate to get out of this room.

Lina has a bunch of papers and relics, not a single one of which Miguel recognizes, spread out on the bed. She's shaking her head, and then she begins to cry outright. He cannot remember ever having seen her cry in their entire adult lives, and despite the stifling heat of the room, his sweat breaks out cold.

"These aren't even for us," she says thickly.

"What are you talking about?" Miguel says. "Who else would they be for?"

Lina thrusts an envelope at him, so hard its corner knocks him in the cheek as he bends to retrieve it. The outside of the envelope bears Isabel's own name and address, but the sender is "Pilar Guerra," with a return address in Miami.

"This shit," Lina says, "it all belonged to your father, I think. Look at it! It's this old, creepy, pointless, male, Cuban shit."

Miguel blinks, trying to take in the plethora of stimuli. He's on the verge of being offended by Lina's words, but . . . well . . . she's right. On the bed is a smattering of utterly pointless male, Cuban shit. A Zippo lighter. A few photographs of what seems to be pre-Castro Cuba, boasting American casinos, with no actual humans in the photos. A cigar box. Some cufflinks that are actually pretty cool and that Miguel would pocket, had his father been even marginally less of a scumbag. A very old copy of Cortázar's *Hopscotch*, in the original Spanish, which Miguel read—also in the original Spanish—while living in Barcelona with Tomas, and the sight of his vicious father's copy on the bed taints his romantic memory so much that bile rises in his throat. What *is* this shit, and why did Isabel have it?

"Listen to this," Lina says, opening another of the letters. "She calls her, *Mi hija*."

"Who?" Miguel stammers. He tries to focus his eyes on Lina, looking like the Ghost of Isabel Past. "Who's calling Isabel that? I have no idea who Pilar Guerra is."

"She's related to your father, obviously," Lina snaps back. "His first wife? His sister? His mother? Why don't you people know anything about anything?"

"You people?" Miguel mutters.

"You and Mami," she snaps. "Why is, like, the very existence of this—" she waves the letter around—"Pilar Guerra like an Illuminati-guarded mystery? Why are you all like this?"

"I'm not like anything," Miguel says back, his own voice rising. "I was ten years old when we left Caracas. You think anyone told me anything, either?"

"Why was this woman writing Isabel?" Lina demands.

"Lina." Miguel exhales slow, though stars are popping in front of his eyes and he has to sit down on the bed. "You're asking me things I don't know. One day we were all in Caracas and Isabel and you and Mami and I lived with some old woman called Tía, whose real name I never even knew, and then suddenly—Christ—we were all in Chicago, except for Isabel, and Mami was your mother, too, and our only relative was Mami's mother—you knew Abuela as well as I did. I have no idea on earth how Isabel ended up corresponding with some Guerra in Miami or owning stuff that looks like it was Papi's. Maybe it isn't even Papi's. Maybe it's just *stuff*."

Lina is scanning the letter furiously. "This just talks about a bunch of artists, like Isabel's taking some art correspondence course. Then she's asking about Ezme and gushing how much she loves Isabel and thinks of her all the time and how she should bring her *precious daughter* to visit."

Miguel scans the outside of one envelope she's thrown his way. It's dated 1998, when Ezme would have been . . . what . . . maybe eleven years old? It's right around his wedding, but he doesn't imagine Isabel mentioned *that* in in the letter."

"Look," Miguel says, "the box is probably for Mami, not us. Clearly Mami will know who this woman is. Mami will know if this stuff belonged to Papi. There's no big mystery here, just because we're too young to remember things."

"Why does this woman love Isabel?" Lina counters. "Why does she even *know* Isabel, and doesn't know us? Why is she thanking Isabel for her 'wonderful letters'—did *you* ever get a wonderful letter, or any kind of letter, from Isabel? She lived in Caracas for the first six years of my life, and then she lived *here* for the last eight or nine years of hers, and did she ever once send you a goddamn letter? Because she sure didn't send one to me."

Miguel says nothing.

"I'm going to Miami," Lina says. "I'm going to knock on this bitch's door and find out what's going on."

"Lina." Miguel's flask ran out too long ago; he is not nearly drunk enough to be having this conversation. "Look." He flicks through the envelopes, roughly, and Lina jerks to grasp a few back. "Some of these letters are nearly twenty years old. The latest ones are over a decade ago. They probably stopped because this woman died—she could have been Papi's *mother.* No matter who she is, she probably doesn't live at the same address. I know we're all upset. I know Isabel was . . . an upsetting person. But you're talking crazy."

Lina puts all the envelopes but one back into the box, but empty—the letters themselves, plus the most recent envelope containing Pilar Guerra's address, she shoves into her handbag. She arranges the remaining pointless, male, Cuban shit back on top of the envelopes, carries the box back to where it sat atop the others, in the back: unimportant.

"Fine," she says to Miguel, folding her arms across her chest. "You don't have to come with me. You don't have to get involved."

Miguel thinks of Emily, one last time, with her high blood pressure, her anticonvulsive medications, her bed rest. If they induce delivery right now, the baby will die. But Emily, despite doing everything right, seems to be getting worse instead of better, and Chad is living in a dream world, in which bringing her copies of *People* magazine and fancy cupcakes can somehow make everything all right.

"Okay, okay," he says to Lina. "I didn't say I wasn't coming."

LINA

Miguel and I barely speak on the plane. Inside my carry-on, a bundle of letters wrapped in a rubber band. They are effusive, full of love, assurances of the good things life holds in store for Isabel, but they say very little of any use to us, and I keep thinking, again, of how you would tell me that people who both *know* how they know each other, who both know what the other already knows about of their shared history, don't rehash all these details for the benefit of some outside reader of whom they're unaware. Aunt Pilar's letters are both tender and innocuous, with sparse concrete information or nostalgic recollections, and I might as well have thrown them out, but I couldn't. Miguel and I both seem to be holding our breath until we can get to Papi's sister's house—like we have a finite number of words and don't want to waste them on each other anymore. What I mean is: there is a sense already, in the air hurtling toward Miami, that we are all running out of time.

We Googled Aunt Pilar before we left, of course, mainly thinking to find a current address on her, in an era where it is virtually impossible to be untraceable, and indeed we did. What we found in addition was that, in accordance with all the chattiness about art shows in her letters, she is . . . moderately famous, if visual artists can be "famous" anymore. The Internet holds a variety of photos of her: a heavyset, openly lesbian sculptor who looks nothing like anyone in our family. In every picture she displays a penchant for fringey scarves. Her sculptures blend burned books and parched tree branches and amber, and to say they are staggeringly beautiful and haunting sounds cheap. To my knowledge, Nick, no one else in our family has ever *made* anything besides children.

Despite our theory about the impossibility of anonymity in 2009, Miguel and I are not on the Internet at all. When we Googled ourselves, it yielded nothing except the revelation that people who are not us have our names, and are referenced on Spanish-language websites we don't bother to decipher. Miguel and I live unambitious lives, off the grid. He's loaded and I'm broke but the result is the same.

Aunt Pilar doesn't expect us. We find her condo easily but no one comes to the door when we ring the buzzer. She could be having an exhibition in San Miguel de Allende, in Antigua; she could be *anywhere*. Our lack of forethought would not serve us well if we were applying for work as private detectives. We sit on the front steps to her condo, in the blinding sun, our suitcases in front of us, saying things like, "She's an old lady, she has to come home sometime." We both know that *sometime* could be in a week and a half, but neither of us says it aloud. Miguel seems patronizing or bored, I can't tell which, and as the afternoon wanes so that the sun grows weak and the orange sky is tinged with gray, it occurs to me that my brother is too smart to have not planned this trip better—that he must have expected and *wanted* me to fail, and is only here to keep me from doing something crazy, though I have no idea what that might be.

A white van pulls up in front of the house, and simply because it's the first vehicle to park directly in front of the condo in the last four hours, I mutter to Miguel, "Look, Auntie drives a rape van." "Rape Van" is one of the fake band names Miguel and I have made up over the years, and whenever we see a white van we say things to each other like, "Rape Van opening up at the Aragon Ballroom." I don't think either of us expects the driver of *this* rape van to actually be Aunt Pilar, but it is. She looks at us carefully from across a stretch of lawn and driveway, and then drops a canvas she's holding and breaks into a clunky, inefficient run that lists to one side, stopping several feet away from us, a look of grief and confusion contorting her face.

She says plainly, as though the possibility that we are not family has already been excluded, "I thought you were *them* for a moment. I thought I had died and my Javier and his beautiful Isabel were waiting for me."

"Wait," I said, "you *knew* Isabel had died?"

And at that, she sinks to her knees on the unfeasibly smooth Miami concrete, that does not at all resemble Chicago concrete, and begins to wail.

I don't know whether Aunt Pilar eats Cuban food from the hood every day of her life, or if it's for our benefit, but before Miguel and I have been in Miami for twenty-four hours, she has taken us to the same hole-in-the-wall for two meals. Miguel is happy as a pig in slop. My brother could live on *ropa vieja* and *arroz con pollo*, and never want for anything. This is the only indication, really, that Miguel grew up in a Latino household. Of course, if you say things like that around him, he will promptly inform you that when he lived in Barcelona, he read all of James Joyce in Spanish, thank you very much.

Um. I rest my fucking case.

We sit on purple benches at picnic tables in a parking lot. The place looks like it used to be a gas station, and I can smell the ocean but can't see it. Seagulls circle and call overhead, and Miguel says several times that he loves "water birds," though it's a phrase I've never heard him use and a fact of which I was unaware. Miguel is the only member of my family with whom I have ever shared anything resembling intimacy, yet he seems, comfortably chatting with Aunt Pilar about ducks and cranes and geese and swans and loons, like a complete alien to me.

Aunt Pilar has a tendency to break into rapid-fire Spanish, but Miguel knows I can't keep up, so he vigilantly answers in English. If she is disappointed in us, she has not let on. She keeps hugging us, and Miguel and I have banded together on one side of the picnic table, with her on the other, in an unspoken agreement between us to stay out of her arms' reach. Thus far, we've said virtually nothing that needs to be said.

"You look so much like your papi," she says to Miguel over and over again. "Your eyebrows, this arch here, so strong—it's like he is looking back at me, the last time I saw him."

Papi was two years older than Miguel when he died. His sister had not seen her brother, it seems, for two years prior to his death. This coincidence was, obviously, unplanned.

There's nothing truly vegetarian on the table. I stir food around and separate it with my fork. It is something like 111 degrees outside. Miguel is drinking beer in a rapidly condensing bottle. I could maybe kill him just for the dregs and feel no remorse, but I don't even like beer. If I go out, it will be for something better than Corona.

We have looked at photo albums. Aunt Pilar is not lying about Miguel. He and his father could be the same man. I have seen very few photos of Papi—a fact that never concerned me much since he was only a reminder that the other children in the house were full siblings, whereas I thought of myself as something like a half blood, though technically I was no kind of sibling at all. Papi, in photos, looks like Miguel has put on period clothes and been filmed through gauzy light. His handsomeness is conspicuous, like a costume he was forced to wear everywhere. It may be because he is my brother, but Miguel, although beautiful, isn't a particularly *sexy* guy . . . there's something of Eeyore about him, some glum, shuffling, pessimistic quality that makes it hard to imagine him in sexual ecstasy. Papi, though—no. Papi smolders. He has a wicked, easy grin. The angles of his body are almost feminine in their grace; he has the habit of leaning on things in photos that makes him look languid and come-hither. He looks like a good time, not just in bed, but in general—the people standing with him in photos are always smiling in a spontaneous way, often looking at him. Nothing in these photos indicates that his children were starving, apparently eating sticks of butter to survive. Papi's clothing is somehow both drab and debonair at once, as though in this period picture he's been cast to play the poet revolutionary. He *wrote* poetry, Aunt Pilar has told us. She showed us some, though it was from his youth outside Havana, before he moved to Chicago or Venezuela. Miguel is spending a lot of time sitting on his hands.

"Eat," Aunt Pilar urges me. "You're too skinny!"

I think of Isabel, of the last time I saw her alive, a brittle stick about to crack. In her casket, her face and neck were swollen like melons overripe to splitting. I think of the sides of my ass that you grab and hold on to when we fuck—of the way you take my inner thighs inside your fists like you are crafting me from clay and every handful of me is precisely as you would form it. I say, "I'm not too skinny," and Miguel says, "Well, if you're dieting, fattie," and starts shoveling my beans into his mouth without moving my plate in front of him.

"Grief," Aunt Pilar says. "It is hard to eat. When your father died, our mother wasted away. Six months later she broke her hip and caught pneumonia in the hospital and that was the end. Javier was the sun around which our mother revolved. Always, even from South America. Her precious Javier."

Miguel and I bob our heads. To some extent, we are both lost to the discourse about suffering mothers, about all-powerful motherlove.

"And what about *your* mother?" Aunt Pilar asks, furrowing her brows the way a stage actor would do to indicate concern or having eaten something unpleasant. "Did she and Isabel ever come to peace? Are you two in contact with Wanda?"

I watch my brother's eyes spring to life, almost like the rattling of a snake's tail just as it prepares to strike. He's woken up. He doesn't care about the "water birds" anymore. I open my mouth to speak, and Miguel, very calmly, under the table so that Aunt Pilar cannot see, lays a hand on my thigh solidly, to silence me.

"Well," he says slowly, as though measuring his words with great emotion. "We saw her at Isabel's funeral, of course. It's been very difficult, though."

Aunt Pilar's eyes shine. Prisms of the purple bench catch in the water of her eyes, or maybe I'm just starting to see things. My tongue tastes metallic, feels thick. It's good Miguel is doing the talking because sometimes I can't make words form when this starts, if something is starting. I should take an Abilify, but I don't have one in my tote bag. Maybe my brain just feels like a wet rag because my brother is clearly *up* to something and I can't tell what it is—his superior brain has left mine behind.

"You can probably imagine," Miguel says. He is speaking in a tone I've never heard from his lips. Maybe you'd call it a "vulnerable" tone in a stage note. "I mean, Isabel practically raised us," he says, and I kick his ankle not lightly under the table but he doesn't flinch. "She protected us," he says. "But then after she became so religious, she abandoned us, and I see—I hope you don't mind my being this blunt, but I see from the dates of your letters, and when they all stopped, that she must have done the same to you. Lina and I were left without a mother."

My heart pounds so hard it's like a stopwatch in the middle of the table. What is he doing? *What is he doing?*

But Aunt Pilar reaches both plump, strangely smooth hands across the picnic bench, and Miguel and I quickly, like joining hands to pray around Mami and Carlos's table, have to grasp her hands or lose whatever inexplicable moment Miguel has created.

"I loved Isabel as a daughter." Tears roll down her face. Her eyebrows, I see now, arch identically to her brother's and to Miguel's; the effect is just different on a woman. "It tore me up when she told me her views on my . . . lifestyle . . . and stopped answering my letters. I was hurt and even angry—I'm sorry to say, angry—for a long time. I spent years meditating on it, and I understand better now. Isabel had not been given the freedom to choose. She spent her childhood covering up for your mother's actions, facing loss after loss, and she needed the structure the church provided her. I am a believer, too—I tried to help her to understand that there is more than one way for faith to manifest. But such is the nature of the world, no? Everyone has a monopoly on faith. Everyone's god hates everyone else's. It broke my heart."

"I'm surprised Isabel told you those things about our mother," Miguel says, and for the first time, I understand clearly how he managed to get double promoted inside of a year of his move to Chicago, even though he barely spoke English. "Isabel was a deeply private woman, as you know. I didn't think she had *ever* spoken of any of that with anyone but me. Lina knows, too, but not from Isabel—Isabel thought she was too young to handle the truth. But once she was grown, and Isabel had turned away from us, I thought Lina deserved to know her own past."

It's clear to me all at once. Miguel thinks Aunt Pilar is going to tell us who my father is.

"I'm so sorry," Aunt Pilar says instead. "To have to wonder all these years if your mother got away with murder, and then was able to exile her own child because that child knew the truth. Isabel probably didn't want to put Lina in danger."

Miguel chokes on his beer. Aunt Pilar yelps, "Aye," so identically to the way Mami says it that tears spring to my eyes—or maybe that has nothing to do with what is happening with my eyes, which have started to uncontrollably water, spilling down my face. My brother seems speechless, gaping—his plan has clearly been derailed and neither of us has any idea what's going on. I'm crying like a ninny, and apparently this only lends credibility to whatever ball Miguel has set in motion, as Aunt Pilar strokes my hand tenderly. It is everything I have in me not to pull away, not to run from the table.

"That man they thought shot him," Aunt Pilar begins, "he was nothing but a drunk. He had an alibi at whatever bar those men—your father among them—went to every night. He was there that very night, raving about Javier—about his wife bedding Javier, and I'm ashamed to say that everyone at the bar apparently knew this was true. They knew of this affair, and that the man's wife was with child and it was Javier's. The drunken man was shooting his mouth off—Wanda must have found out. Word travels quickly in such places."

"But," I begin, and I realize I need to say something to avoid tipping my hand. "I never really believed that story, Aunt Pilar. It sounds like some folk legend. If the man had an alibi in the bar, how would Mami have heard so quickly that she ran over to Papi's house and shot him? With what gun? She didn't even have a car."

"I don't claim to know," Aunt Pilar says. "Only that it's what Isabel believed, and is why she fled the house and was living on the street instead of going to your mother."

"Then why wasn't Mami ever arrested?" I demand, angry now. Not at Mami, to be clear—my pseudo mother barely has it in her to kill a housefly; she didn't have it in her to protect her children; she didn't have it in her to stop her husband from beating her or drinking; she is a wringer of hands, a weeper of crocodile tears, and also, *fuck you, Isabel, you spiteful lying bitch*, a peaceful, gentle woman. But Isabel already threw Mami under the bus to Ezme, passing her off as a whore who bore me out of wedlock. Why not a husband killer, too?

Aunt Pilar merely shrugs. "Caracas," she says. "Who understands? Maybe the old woman your mother was living with gave her an alibi, just like the men at the bar gave the drunk his. Maybe Javier's mistress had no alibi—maybe it was her. But your sister claimed it was your mother. She said the man had come by waving his gun, but Javier wrestled it away from him easily, and then when your mother arrived, there was the gun, poised for Wanda to act. It wasn't premeditated, Isabel said, and your mother didn't know Isabel was in the house. Then Isabel had to run, and she kept running until the police found her."

Miguel and I sit, stunned. Whatever artifice and smoothness we were collectively mustering is gone.

"So wait," Miguel begins at last. "So . . . you say my father was shot in our *house*, with Isabel right there in our old bedroom hiding? You say it was the gun of some man who later gets an alibi from fellow cronies at the bar, or maybe his wife did it, but Isabel says our *mother* did it . . . you're saying . . . just . . . holy shit." My brother's head sinks into his hands. "There was no bridge, is what you're saying. Nobody's car, in this story, goes off any bridge."

Aunt Pilar looks at us with surprise. "This isn't Hollywood," she says. "No, no bridge."

MIGUEL

Miguel's body bobs like a buoy: on autopilot, senseless. As long as he stays out here in the ocean, he doesn't have to go *back there.* To the women. Neither Aunt Pilar nor Lina has accompanied him to the beach, so theoretically he is safe from them even on his flimsy towel on the sand, but it wasn't enough. He felt driven—almost pursued—into and under the water: the imperative to submerge, to block everything out. Lina's neediness for answers that are impossible to excavate, Aunt Pilar's crack-brained theories, are as relentless as the sun. He knows he should call Mami and say, *Hey, what the living hell—did you shoot my father?* But of course that is preposterous. Mami did no such thing. In his grief over Isabel, in the unwelcome chaos of Guerra urban legends, Miguel isn't sure he's ever been more exhausted in his life.

Clearly he and Lina should have stayed home.

Clearly, going on some investigative mission to visit a family member of his crazy, violent father could not have been expected to yield anything . . . easy. Anything good. Poor Aunt Pilar doesn't deserve his evasion—he and Lina came looking for her, and she has been remarkably hospitable, open, even loving. Especially considering that she seems to believe their mother is a killer. *Their.* Even that's a lie. Aunt Pilar clearly has no clue that Lina is Isabel's daughter, which is the one thing Miguel had assumed she *would* know. How does one embark on a fact-finding mission when "facts" are relative?

The waves. His body, bobbing. Spinning: shore, horizon, shore.

In two months, Miguel will be a father. Back in Chicago, that is Chad's problem for the moment. Chad, who is ministering to Emily like a wounded bird, who talks to their surrogate—*Miguel's* high school friend—far more often than he talks to Miguel, and who can blame him? Emily is kind; Emily is cheerful and interested and doesn't rub salt in everything she touches. But Miguel was right from the get-go that Guerras should not be allowed to breed. With all the focus on what it took for a gay couple to have a child—on their *right* to have a child—somehow Miguel lost sight of the fact that his family tree is rotten from the roots, and everything it grows is poison. Isabel knew, but she distracted herself with fairy tales about sin and hell. She couldn't face that god doesn't have to be real for their family to be doomed.

Even the ocean feels a little ominous today. The current is strong for the onset of May. Miguel is a confident swimmer, though, even if his swim team days in high school were mainly a ruse to see other boys in speedos and naked in the locker room. Still, he lifeguarded one summer for the eye candy, and actually saved a life one day, a kid: for years afterward, whenever he felt worthless he would go back to that day and remind himself that if he had never been born, the kid would be dead. But of course that was a false dichotomy: if Miguel had never been born, there would just have been some other Chicago teenager perched on the Foster Beach lifeguard chair, who most likely would, also, have rescued the kid. Only now, of his impending progeny, can Miguel finally say with certitude that *if*: I had never been born or I had committed suicide, *then*: this child would never have existed.

Is that a *good* thing, though? Is that supposed to justify everything?

His throat feels tight. The moment this awareness filters in, scattered by other awarenesses, it occurs to Miguel that his throat's tightness has been the case for a while. How long? He can't say. But it's been growing, unnoticed until he finally noticed it; until he finally *noticed that he had noticed it.*

The thing about breath is that only its absence seems to matter.

The tightness in his chest. His tongue, like a slab of cold beef in his mouth. His limbs electric, like he's stuck his fingers in a socket under water.

This is crazy. This cannot be happening. The water isn't cold enough for this to be happening.

Then why are his teeth chattering?

Nothing like this has happened since midwinter. Then Miguel, with his constant companion of the EpiPen, learned to *be careful.* He wore hats and scarves and even one of those full-face winter masks that made him look like a bank robber; he hasn't had ice cream since that night at Emily and Nick's. Under the waves, Miguel frantically feels his own bare arms, chest, for the hives that characterize his allergic reaction, but there's nothing he can find, no sensation of itching. His throat has only swollen this badly once in the past, that night in early December, back when everything still felt like a wild, reckless game, like they were playing *The Big Chill* and even at forty it was possible to just be on the verge of the most exciting Act of their lives unfolding. His throat had closed, *haha,* it had been just part of the madcap adventure of the evening, of the strange collusion he and Chad and Emily and Nick were entering into together. He remembers making jokes before his heart rate had even returned to normal. He remembers the strange, blissful connectedness he felt, standing on their porch with Chad's arm around him, calling out farewells into the night, while Isabel, seven hours away, was already doomed.

He is swimming to shore. His body has always understood more about survival than his brain. His strokes have been solid, certain . . .

it's just that he can't bring in air anymore, and suddenly a flailing is upon him, unbidden: he did not authorize this flailing. He did not give his body permission to behave this way, this graceless, this desperate. For forty-one years, he has lived on the precipice of a willingness to die—an unobtrusive, low-key consent; a passive hurry for it to all be done with already, this sublimated shame and confusion and monotony and anger. *Nobody is looking.* He could go down silently under the blanket of the ocean, and maybe his body would be washed to sea and no one would ever even know what happened. He would not be blamed. Chad has more than enough money. He can step out of the picture, and just like Lina never mourned or celebrated Papi's death the way the rest of them did, *his* child will never miss him. Miguel will be only an idea to his daughter, and children's ideas are invariably better than the real thing.

Why can't he will it? *Stop moving. Stop thrashing. Stop.*

The shore seems only farther away. Cupping the water, *help, help*, but his throat can't get in any air. Starbursts pop before his eyes: a loss of precious oxygen. He can't move forcefully enough to get back to land. Mami's red curtain in their old shanty in Caracas, his body on the other side, desperate to push back the soiled fabric and climb into her bed, but too afraid of Isabel's disapproval to act. His father's purple knuckles. Isabel's cotton underpants as she leapt like an airbender. Tomas's lush mouth, a pillow made of wine . . .

Coughing, but into the water, water into lungs into water. We are dust and unto dust we shall return. His father, breathing in the water of the Guaire River, trying to open the car doors against the current—why didn't he swim through a window, was he too drunk? But no—it's because *that never happened*; it wasn't real. Water to water to water. The way Isabel used to hold him while he slept, her arms a thing that would never, ever betray. And that is the thing, *isn't it, Isabel*, about all this beauty, all this miraculous pain, all this poisonous life. It is somehow always too short.

LINA

Aunt Pilar and I are sitting on the balcony facing the street, smoking a pack of Delicados she brought back from her last trip to San Miguel de Allende, when an SUV pulls up in front and Miguel, still in swim trunks, soaking wet, inexplicably gets out of the stranger's car. He looks up at us, and his face looks masklike and frozen as he raises his hand quickly as if to wave, then lets it hover in the air and lowers it. I say to Aunt Pilar, "Do you know those people?" and she says, "Your brother must know them," and I say, "No, he doesn't," even though really how would I know, and Aunt Pilar says, "Well, he does now," in a tone that makes it clear she thinks Miguel has just picked up a man at the beach, and raises her Guerra eyebrow at me as if to say, *Men*.

To her implied moral superiority of the lesbian caste, I say, "You're talking to the wrong woman," and laugh to myself. She looks confused and I'm trying to figure out whether to attempt an explanation (and what that would sound like) when Miguel—who has come inside the condo—flings the French doors open widely and stands between them, shirtless and drippy still, saying, "Jesus Christ, I almost drowned. Some guy in a boat had to pull me from the water—if he hadn't come along, I'd be dead."

Aunt Pilar and I talk on top of each other, yelping the things people exclaim in response to such news.

Miguel waves aside our clucks of concern, collapsing into one of the wicker balcony chairs.

Aunt Pilar is looking at us strangely. We have not, it could certainly be argued, presented in a particularly *How to Win Friends and Influence People* manner since arriving in Miami. All said, though, she has handled it pretty well, even thinking we are the progeny of the woman who murdered her beloved brother. Now, though, she looks at Miguel as though maybe—despite his overwhelming resemblance to Javier—he is not supposed to *be* here, as though he is some kind of mistake.

We are, all three, silent. Miguel reaches out to the railing of the balcony, where the Delicados are resting, shakes one out, and lights it. His hands are trembling. He drags deep on the cigarette with his waterlogged lungs, and I think of Isabel, choking on her own blood, suffocating on a bursting dam from inside her own body. I listen to the roar inside my own head. One reason I love the beach is because the natural world and my brain seem, for once, in harmony. If I focus on it closely enough, the sound inside my head is the din of voices, but on days like this, on *most* days, I can't make out any individual words; it's just a dull roar of a crowd that, when I tune it out (which after thirty-one years I have become mainly good at doing) sounds almost like surf pounding against the shore. If you want to know the truth, the first thing I think is that if I went into Aunt Pilar's house and got out a bottle of rum or some Mexican tequila—my brother's poison of choice—picked up on the same trip as the Delicados, maybe Miguel would be too shaken up by his near death and Aunt Pilar's wild proclamations to care that I was pouring a double shot. He looks at me, and his eyes are searching, vulnerable, like he wants me to say something to save him, the way the stranger in the SUV saved him from drowning, but nobody in our family has ever been able to save anyone from anything. I shrug, looking away from his eyes.

"I'm having a baby," Miguel says. "I'm going to be a father." And for the first time in my life, I watch my older brother begin to cry.

After Miguel has retired to his guest room, Aunt Pilar stands and pours us, as though reading my mind, two tequilas. She brings one over to me. She has no way of knowing I am a drunk. Why would she know this, any more than she knows Isabel was my mother? Why would she know anything about me? But she is looking at me with a kind of naked love, like staring at a ghost she believes may dissolve if she touches me, Miguel and his wild drowning episode already forgotten. She takes a long swig from her drink and I pick mine up and I am about to pretend to sip just to be polite, but instead I do what of course I would do: I drain the entire goddamn thing in one gulp. My head spins, in the most pleasant and beautiful way imaginable, and I want to bolt up and grab the bottle by the neck. In that moment, I love Aunt Pilar more than anyone on earth, even you.

"I was just about to tell you something," she says to me, "before your brother, he comes in with his dramatic story, and interrupted us."

I'm not thrilled, to be blunt, about the fact that she's trivializing Miguel almost dying while accompanying me on a trip he didn't even want to make, but I am not one to question the woman who owns the tequila, and I say nothing.

"I want you to know that Isabel loved you very much. That she talked about you to me frequently. She couldn't admit it to herself or to you, what it really meant to her to have had you so young, and to be unable to care for you, and to have to rely on her mother. I believe how much guilt she felt, in allowing her mother who had committed such an act, to raise her own *hija*—I believe this is what drove her to assuage her guilt in Church and with so much dogma. She felt she could never be forgiven for what she had done to you."

Cruelly, it's as though the alcohol has all evaporated. I am reeling, sober, everything in laser focus and surreal at once. "She *told* you that?"

"She told me many things," Aunt Pilar says. She stands with some labor—despite her active lifestyle, she seems to be nursing a bad hip—and goes to a cabinet, a drawer, like somebody in a movie, withdrawing a key. She brings it over to me—without a second drink—and presses it into my hand, caressing my skin as she does so.

The key has a number taped to it. A safety deposit box key, I realize instantly, though I have never seen one before. I close my hand around it.

"She would have wanted you to have this," Aunt Pilar says. "To keep her things safe."

I stammer. "What's in the box?"

"I have never looked in the box," she says, with some surprise, as though I should know her better, when of course I know her not at all. "Isabel asked me not to."

I must be shaking. This oracle woman in her fringed scarves and secrets of gunshots to the chest brings me another drink after all, and I down it in one sip, once more.

"Go now," she says, "before your brother wakes up." She begins scribbling directions down for me. "Whatever you find there," she says, "remember that even though there is no statute of limitation on murder, Isabel never told anyone what your mother had done. I don't believe the information in the box is about Javier. I believe it is about you."

It is only then that I think for the very first time, Nick: *What if those are one in the same thing?*

I rush out the door, into the Miami unknown, alone.

It is the very definition of irony, of course, that on my way to the bank, in the back of a taxi, I nearly throw the key out the window and ask to be taken back to Aunt Pilar's—to Miguel—to everything I know and don't know. Whatever I thought I was coming here to uncover, it wasn't *this*. This isn't what I want or need. I don't want to open the box. But my hand—steady now after two tequilas—won't roll down the window, won't dispose of the key. Instead, on my cell phone, I call Mami.

"I'm in Miami," I say, after her depressive, my-daughter-is-dead *hello.* "I'm at Aunt Pilar's house."

"How . . . ?" Mami stammers. "I don't understand, what are you doing there?"

"We found letters from her to Isabel," I explain weakly. "Miguel is with me, too. We wanted to understand the nature of their relationship. We didn't even know who she was, really—Aunt Pilar I mean . . ." I laugh too loudly. "But Isabel, too, of course. We wanted . . . to understand."

"What would that woman understand?" Mami demands. "She never even met any of you! She never spoke to us again after her brother died."

"You're not listening," I say. "She had an extensive correspondence with Isabel. She knew her very well—better than any of the rest of us did, it seems."

Mami harrumphs.

"She also says nobody ever drove their car off a bridge," I say recklessly, though I can't get the rest out, quite. "She says Javier Guerra was murdered—shot in the chest."

At this, Mami actually laughs.

"Oh," she says cackling. "This is priceless. This is just . . . Angelina . . . what are you doing? Who is this woman, even? The sister of a madman who terrorized us? Where does she get a story like this, from Miami? She never visited us once in Caracas! She wrote us off like dogs once he was dead."

"No," I say. "She says Isabel told her this is how it happened."

"Your sister never said that," Mami says, just like she insisted Isabel never asked to be buried on Beaver Island, even though she obviously did.

"She did say it," I insist.

"Oh yes? You heard her say it? You know this because some strange lesbian beatnik tells you this?"

"*I'm* a strange lesbian beatnik!" I shout into the phone. The taxi driver peers back into his rearview mirror at me.

"Aye, the beatniks are from the 1950s," Mami says, sighing with exasperation at me. "You're just copying your brother, like you always did."

"Look!" I demand. "Did your husband's car go off a bridge or what?"

"Of course it did." Mami sighs. "Why wouldn't it have? But what does it matter anyway? He was an unimportant man. We were all better off without him. I can't for the life of me understand why you—and Miguel, of all people, who saw what Javier was like—would be down there on this . . . what? Criminal investigation of a non-crime, that didn't exist? And you don't tell your own mother and then you call me up and say these strange things?"

"Isabel was my mother," I say. "Not you."

"*Entonces tu no sabes lo que es una madre*," the woman who raised me says, her voice cracking hard.

It is a day for firsts. My brother has wept. And Mami hangs up the phone loudly in my ear.

But I have forgotten to mention why the irony is ironic, haven't I? I don't throw the key out the window. I stand in front of a box, untouched since Isabel was younger than I am now, breathing hard, seeing shadows in my peripheral vision, but naturally, inevitably, being who and what I am, I turn the key.

Then: only the small rectangle of space, absent of light. Absent of answers. A trickster to the end, a woman on the run from something I will never pin down, Isabel's box is empty.

And so you see, Nick, there are only so many variables. Maybe variable A goes like this:

A mother and her beloved son flee the abusive, drunken, mentally ill man of the house, who has been holding them hostage to beatings and borderline starvation for years. The only catch is that one child—the daughter—remains behind, the way people in ancient times sacrificed virgins to volcanoes. For some days, let's say, Papi expects his good-for-nothing wife to come back in an attempt to claim the little brat. He beats the brat nice and hard so that when his wife sees her, she will cry and gnash her teeth and wring her hands with guilt; she will think twice, looking at those bruises, before leaving him again.

Why he wants to keep the wife in the first place is an eternal mystery we cannot engage here—why do any such men so desperately need to possess women they seem to despise?

Papi—*Javier*—has such women all over Caracas, like a junkie sometimes has numerous dealers. Somehow, though, this one, his *real* wife, the one he had before the dark days came, doesn't return. She and his only son are gone. Javier is left with the smart-mouthed daughter, of whom apparently his bitch wife has also washed her hands. How can this be? What is he supposed to do now? Oh, but he is not a stupid man. Soon, the possibilities begin to register. He hasn't been able to work in some time thanks to his bottle, thanks to his moods, but the daughter who caused his wife and son to leave is pretty. She is young, but built like a woman. Even Isabel knew this, the day she refused to peddle Mami's homemade bouquets door-to-door and made Miguel go alone. *I'll find some man to buy my flower instead*, Miguel told me she screamed. Maybe *every* girl is born with the knowledge, the possibility, inside her skin.

(And you would tell me there is just no point to wondering about Variable B. No good to be gained by wandering the dark alleys of: *Was Javier Guerra my father, too?* Safer to just leave it the assumption that I was spawned by some anonymous john. So let's say)

Javier begins to rent his daughter Isabel out. The money pours in, and Javier celebrates with his favorite lover, perhaps buying her a dress, a splashy night on the town. The lover's jealous husband gets word, comes to the house waving a gun. He and Javier fight, but the man is distraught and weak-willed—the kind of man whose wife carries on with a bastard like Javier—and easily overpowered. Say that Javier refuses to return the gun, mocking the man, telling him to go home to his empty bed and look for his balls. He rests the gun on some table, flopping back in the chair he was lounging in when the jealous husband arrived. Drinks from the same bottle he was drinking from before the interruption. Laughs to himself. His daughter Isabel hides in her bedroom, heart on fire. Soon enough, Javier passes out in his favorite chair, bottle thudding to the dirt floor.

How easy would it be to leave the bedroom, to walk as if on anesthetized legs to the exact spot where the jealous husband once stood, waving the gun? Look, this gun, still in the room. Isabel stands, holding the gun in her thirteen-year-old hands. She is the top student in her class, her baby brother's hero. She has saved her family, but somehow she ended up still here. Some people, from the moment of their birth, are made for something greater. Isabel: homeschooler, gardener, church-hopper, warrior. On her first try, she shoots her father in the heart, from the angle at which the jealous husband stood an hour or two earlier. It would be better if she had done it only moments after he left, but she needed to wait for Papi to pass out. In this window of time, the jealous husband has acquired an alibi at a nearby bar, but Isabel knows nothing of that. She flees the house, never to return.

When the police find her, living on the street, she tells them she ran away in fear for her own life after seeing a man shoot her father in the chest. That she was afraid to go back to the house, because maybe someone would kill her, too. Or maybe she says none of this. Maybe she only later tells Aunt Pilar this tale about Mami, when she visits Miami for the first time six years later, en route to Chicago to live with us, perhaps hoping for a better option, somewhere else to go besides to Mami and me, but somehow despite seeing Aunt Pilar and forming a relationship with her that would span years and letters, she decided to head to Chicago anyway . . .

The thirteen-year-old Isabel wouldn't have owned gloves, would she? What did she hold the gun with, such that her prints were concealed? Never mind: she managed to hide the evidence.

If you'll hear me out, though . . . just one more moment about Variable B:

My biological mother never suffered a psychotic episode. Nor, for all Miguel's charming babbling about being "crazy," has anyone else in my family. *Except* Papi.

So you tell me: What are the chances that anonymous john did, too? What are the chances that none of Javier Guerra's offspring inherited his "black fits," but that it skipped a generation, landing instead on me?

I am the motive, Nick. I am the one piece of evidence Isabel couldn't hide.

EMILY

Every morning, Emily wakes up and thinks to herself, *This is what life is like on TV, and now it is my life, too.* Not the retro network TV she grew up on—shows that earnestly attempted to reflect the gritty reality of blue-collar single parenthood like *One Day at a Time* and *Alice*—but like the cable shows Miles has grown up on, where teenagers are all played by twenty-seven-year-olds wearing Prada, or like a soap opera, or *Friends*. Shows where everyone lives like money is a nonissue even though hardly any characters appear to work. Emily is on medical leave, and for the first time since she was seventeen and started putting in hours at a dry cleaning business after school every day to help her mother, she does not have to wake up and go to work. At 6:00 a.m., her body jolts with a start even without her alarm clock, but instead of being disruptive the feeling is glorious: she stretches like a Disney princess in her high-thread-count guest bed, rolls over (albeit uncomfortably) onto her other side, and falls promptly back asleep.

At 10:00 a.m., Chad arrives with her cup of decaffeinated coffee, which comes from such a high-quality bean that Emily cannot even taste the difference. He has the coffee on a wicker tray along with some sort of pastry, because his assistant arrives with coffee and pastries every morning, not even from a chain like Starbucks but from some quirky Bucktown European café, and Chad has the timer on his phone set so he can bring Emily her treats at 10:00 a.m. sharp.

Until she came to stay with Chad, being an invalid was merely inconvenient, frustrating, lonely. She lay in her and Nick's unmade marital bed, watching chaos explode around her. The house smelled like a locker room. Nick and the boys did nothing but watch TV and "funny" videos on YouTube that contained an inappropriate amount of swearing for Jay, and that involved entirely unfunny things like one teenage girl kicking another teenage girl in the head while her friends shouted at her to stop. Nick, Miles, and Jay would roar, and yell "Stop!" at each other in the intonation of the videoed teenage girl; they would watch the clip eight times in a row, convulsively laughing on the living room sofa, just out of Emily's range of vision. They ate frozen pizza every night, offering her one slice. Her head hurt, and she thought she would claw her eyes out with boredom, and despite doctor's orders she kept getting out of bed to try to straighten up, or to make herself something decent to eat before she murdered Nick in his sleep, or to help Jay with something while Nick was elsewhere, always allegedly on some domestic errand that would have taken one-third the time to fulfill than the duration he was actually out of the house.

Emily was supposed to be on bed rest, but obviously when a rich doctor imagines bed rest, the bed is clean and made; the food automatically appears; the children continue to practice basic human hygiene; there is a flat-screen television in the bedroom on which all the high-end cable channels play. Emily spent her hours staring at the cracking Moroccan-blue paint on her bedroom walls and recalling all too acutely studying "The Yellow Wallpaper" in college and how histrionic the story had seemed at the time, how almost tacky in its heavy-handed points . . . now, like to her (also tacky, but in a different way) mother, she related to Charlotte Perkins Gilman. She spent her hours staring at the oversized armoire Nick once thrilled her by making for them, but which in reality is too large for the room and has a rack too high for Emily to reach without standing on a stray dining room chair that clutters the bedroom further, and is not safe for her now, in her "condition."

During her bed-rest days at home, she kept playing over and over again in her mind what the doctor had told her: how nobody would blame her if she induced labor now to end this nightmare, to reclaim her body, to put herself out of danger. She thought over and over again, *I clearly tried*. The phrase *too much* came to her on repeat like the YouTube videos. It was only Chad's daily visit that kept her from calling her OB-GYN and saying, *Clearly this isn't working*. But every single day like clockwork, Chad arrived with flowers or chocolate or stacks of magazines or an artful throw blanket from Anthropologie or unbelievably delicious-smelling Chinese takeout in giant paper bags with the sauce leaking through, which Nick proceeded to not allow Emily to eat because she was supposed to be avoiding salt. Nick actually said, to Chad, who at least *tried*, who at least brought her gifts to make her smile, "That's, like, the whole basic tenet of preeclampsia, mate, the high blood pressure," and shamed Chad, who stammered, "Oh God, I know that, I knew that, I wasn't thinking about the soy sauce, I forgot, I'm so stupid," and Emily wanted to shove a chopstick into Nick's smug eye while he and the boys chowed down on her dinner.

That turned out to be the night Nick unwittingly saved her, though. He said to Chad, "Yeah, it's bad enough she keeps jumping up trying to do shit. I can't keep her in the bed. She's incorrigible—she won't listen!" And Chad, the second he and Emily were alone in the bedroom—Chad perched on the edge of the bed like a mother: not Emily's mother, but some mother, some Florence Nightingale kind of mother who would make pancakes when you were home sick—leaned into her ear and whispered, "Do you think he'd be offended if you just came to stay with us for the rest of the pregnancy? Then we could take care of you."

Offended? Emily had no illusions that Nick would be anything but indifferent at best, possibly thrilled.

Some pang in her rose, thinking of Jay. She had never, she realized with some shock, spent more than one night away from Jay, in all of his seven years, and even a one-night absence had occurred only twice, both times for overnight conferences Emily had been obligated to attend for work. She had, a few times when Miles was young, gone on girlfriend getaways for a weekend or to visit her same-age cousins in Rochester on her own, but nothing like that had happened since Jay. Seven years. She had for seven years barely left her home except to go to work, like she was under house arrest. And just like that the pang snuffed out, leaving in its wake a hunger, an inevitability.

Jay asked, as Chad was helping her out the door, "Will you call me every night, Mommy?" and Emily kissed his pale cheek and promised, "Of course, little man!" But the first night she forgot, and the second night when she called, Miles talked to her cursorily, and then said Jay wouldn't stop playing on his DS and kept saying "Later" when called to the phone, and could Emily call back?

Emily did not call back.

At Chad's house—Miguel calls it "Termite Mansion," though everything infested has been gutted and replaced with shiny, new-smelling materials—just being in her guest bedroom is like being on an episode of *Friends*. Mugs of coffee appear, and though Chad runs a large business, his office is just in the basement, so it seems like both he and Emily lead lives of leisure, job-free. People "drop by" all the time at odd hours of the day, mostly women her own age, though a few gay men, just to *hang out* with Chad for an hour or so. They bring him pita sandwiches, and Chad parades them all to Emily's room, where she has been watching *General Hospital* for the first time since 1986, and they all sit around talking about the baby excitedly, eating nice things, dressed in fresh, fashionable clothing. Emily herself wears revolving pairs of maternity pajamas Chad and

Miguel purchased—at home, she just wore sweats to bed. The only thing missing is a delivery of fresh flowers to her room daily, but of course even though Chad and Miguel are gay, they are still *men*, so one can only expect so much.

In the evenings, she and Chad and Miguel all recline on her California King bed in a happy row, binge watching shows on HBO that she and Nick could never afford. Chad and Miguel act as though Emily having never before seen an episode of *The Sopranos* is a cultural travesty they must immediately rectify under penalty of a steep fine. Had she watched *The Sopranos* at home, Emily would have been sick with envy at Carmella's cushy life, but here, under the auspices of Chad and Miguel, she feels a detached amusement that Carmella, despite all her money, still has certain "Guido" tastes, just like Emily's mother did. Emily's mother wore gold chains with charms that dipped into her conspicuous décolletage: a gold horn, a gold cross. In the California King, watching Chad and Miguel carelessly order dinner delivery every single night as though the food arrives for free, Emily can hardly believe her mother was real—her gold horn, her selfishly guarded orange juice that she never let Emily or her friends drink because it was "expensive." On Mondays, the boys' cleaning lady ("Hi, Barb!" Emily calls out, delighted to already know her name, to already be somehow an insider) works around Emily in cheerful silence. The few times Emily and Nick considered spending up for a cleaning woman, Nick always concluded that he "couldn't take" someone poking around his things and cleaning his house while he sat there. "It'd be too embarrassing," he insisted. "I'd feel like some bourgeois ass, picking up my feet so she can dust! I'd have to evacuate the house, and what if I don't have anywhere to go? It's not worth it—we're capable of cleaning our own house." But of course Jay doesn't even have chores, and Miles always just claims Emily is "too type A" whenever she asks him to do anything more complex than dishes, and Nick takes Miles's part, maintaining amidst the utter disarray that the house is "fine."

Here is her secret: she is *supposed* to be sick, but other than symptoms that are not uncommon at this stage of pregnancy anyway, she feels perfectly fine. Her head hurts some; she is swollen . . . but she's also getting used to it. It seemed strange and disconcerting in the beginning, but by the third trimester most women—especially at age forty—don't feel so fabulous. Pregnancy is tough. This bed rest business—this everyone-would-forgive-you-if-you-induce-delivery-and-kill-the-baby business . . . it all feels *excessive*, honestly: out of proportion to the situation. Not that she is complaining—but it feels like something extoled by the sort of OB-GYN Chad and Miguel would choose. Bed rest! At Northwestern ("Prentice Women's Hospital," they call the wing where she will give birth—they've just done some multimillion-dollar renovation and the food is allegedly gourmet), these doctors are probably acclimated to litigious rich ladies who sue for malpractice if their blood pressure spikes ten points above normal. Emily's grandmother had high blood pressure her entire life and worked every single day as the secretary at a roofing company until she was seventy-five. Imagine calling your boss and saying you have to lie in bed being fed European pastries and watching *The Sopranos* because your blood pressure is high! This is the United States of America, land of the obese! Half the country must have high blood pressure, and they are all still at their jobs. But now, in this strange new world, Emily is here, in her silk maternity pajamas, not among the suckers anymore.

Just when it seems impossible that things can get any better, Miguel announces that he is taking a trip to Miami with his wretched whore of a sister. He's only barely returned from his *other* sister's funeral—Miguel always had a dramatic family—and now he and Lina are off to Miami, to see some relatives or something, and Chad, who has to jump through a fair number of hoops to keep moody Miguel happy, is undividedly Emily's. He even arranges for their usual pedicurist to come to the house and do their nails right there in Emily's bedroom! At night, he falls asleep watching *The Sopranos* ("This is such a great episode!" he always enthuses, just before passing out), and sometimes sleeps there in his clothes, over the duvet, happily through the night, as though even in his slumber he is standing sentry watching over Emily. He would be the perfect husband, she thinks. He is the perfect man. Not so much because he doesn't want sex—that's not it precisely—but because the things he offers are infinitely more important than the things he doesn't. Emily chose unwisely. She chose with her pussy; she chose with her thrashing desire to not be her mother. Only here in middle age can Emily see that there are thousands of different ways to not be her mother, and she chose the most obvious, the whole Superwoman lie, the perfect mother, the ambitious career woman, the driving of herself into the ground to prove some point to an audience that has long since left the theater. She didn't understand, in her twenties, what options were even on the table. If she had it to do again, it seems unlikely she and Nick would even end up on a *date*, much less married. He must feel the same way, or maybe men don't think about such things. Maybe most men don't think about *anything*, and that's what makes Chad so rare.

The thought to be glad that Lina is out of town while Emily is otherwise occupied at Chad's and Nick has more than his usual excessive freedom occurs, but only occasionally, like breaking through fog, unbidden and unwelcome. Emily has trained herself not to think about Lina anymore, like the pathetic woman she *used to be* did. The Emily she is becoming would not lose a husband to a tacky stripper . . . or rather, if she did, it would not even be humiliating so much as it would be a pathetic cliché over which everyone would shake their heads in mystification, and castigate Nick. She, *Emily*, who had Chad and Miguel's baby—she, Saint Emily in her silk pajamas with her perfectly groomed feet—is clearly in the right in all matters now. Nick would have to take the boys 50 percent of the time, and during that time Emily would be *free*—free to go to Chad and Miguel's vacation homes and to be their guest at the opening of every hot new restaurant. She would still have to work, of course—she isn't delusional!—but she would come home to an empty apartment many days, and could clean until her heart's content, her own mess. It sounds like a form of heaven.

Who cares, then, if that stupid, déclassé tramp from the hood is in Miami or not? Emily is the goddamn assistant principal of a school. Emily has babies for one-percenters out of the goodness of her heart and barely accepts payment. Emily is "sick," but heroically forges on to protect the pregnancy, despite the "hardship" of extended bed rest. Emily has nothing to fear from a girl like that.

On the ninth day of her stay, Chad arrives in her room with his usual flair. He pulls back the curtains like a ladies' maid, letting in the paltry daylight and singsonging, "Rise and shine, sleepy head." He puts the wicker tray with her brioche and oversized coffee mug (he apparently cannot bear to serve her coffee in its original paper container, so it arrives daily in a different artisan mug, perhaps freshly reheated, always steaming just a bit too much) toward the foot of her bed, where she can't disturb it while struggling to sit up. He sits down next to the tray waiting patiently, a big smile on his face.

"Tonight," he says, "Miguel's coming back."

"Oh," Emily says, disappointed. "That's fabulous—yay!"

"Yeah," he agrees, though he doesn't seem to think it is any more fabulous than she does. "I guess things didn't go well there."

"You mean with the relatives?" Emily says. "Did they fight? Or do you mean things didn't go well with Lina? I know she's . . . kind of eccentric."

"Oh, no." Chad waves his hand absently, too close to Emily's coffee. "No, Miguel thinks Lina walks on water, he's mad about Lina. I mean just other things. Various things. A plethora of Guerra things, that went, apparently . . . wrong."

"Oh," Emily says.

"He's such a private person," Chad says. "You must remember that, from high school. He's just such a freakishly private person, Miguel. He would find it unbearable for anyone to know if he so much as had a hangnail. Everything is always top secret, like the CIA is wiretapping our home and we have to speak in code. That's the only reason why. I love having you here, it's just that things apparently didn't go so well."

For someone indicting another person for speaking in code, Chad's words would seem to be unintelligible. But they are not, of course. Emily understands instantly: she is being kicked out.

"There isn't any hurry, of course!" Chad says, and now he looks down at his excessively gesticulating hands and picks up Emily's mug and hands it to her, then sits down on his knuckles. "His flight isn't due back until five or something."

"Am I . . . ?" Emily realizes there is no way to ask the question, because if the question had an affirmative answer, she would already have been informed. Still, she hears her voice saying anyway, "Am I supposed to come back? After you two have a chance to talk? Tomorrow or the next day?"

"I just don't know, is the thing," Chad says. "Sometimes when things have gone wrong, you have to batten down the hatches. Miguel has to, I mean. I'm not really that sort of guy."

"The sort of guy to batten down the hatches?"

"Right," Chad says. "Except I guess I mean . . . the sort of guy who always has things going wrong."

"Of course you aren't!" Emily agrees. Though then tears spring to her eyes, because she is praising a man who just threw her out of his house, which makes her what her mother would call a chump. Her eyes fly around the room almost madly—she imagines herself sneaking back in somehow, hiding herself, indeed, within the walls, behind the paint, pulling this perfect world inside behind her. She swipes at her eyes, a laugh catching and cracking in her throat. "I'm sorry," she mutters. "Pregnancy hormones." Even though they have been each other's nearly constant companions for the duration of the pregnancy, and he has never once seen Emily cry before now, which is because Emily *doesn't* cry, pregnant or otherwise, because what is the point of crying—when did crying ever aid anyone with anything, except maybe helping women get out of traffic tickets if they're under thirty and hot?

Lina probably never gets a traffic ticket.

Emily stands up. She's so swollen and clumsy that she displaces the heavy duvet and upsets the brioche. "I should really give you a chance to prepare," she says to the walls. "I'll be ready to go in five minutes, really—I just have to put on some clothes and . . ." It's suddenly unclear whether she should presume she is packing everything they gave her and bringing it back to her own stupid house—but of course! They bought these things for her. It's not like there is another pregnant woman in the wings to whom they would give her pajamas. These things are hers now.

Pedicures that wore off her toes. "Pink" wine she drank and pissed out; expensive dinners she digested. Expensive maternity clothes she'll never wear again once she isn't pregnant. Sporadic cleaners and work teams who cleaned and fixed things that will only mess up again. A pair of gloves so soft Emily wanted to lick them, one of which has already been lost in the bin of constantly disappearing gloves, hats, and scarves that sat in their foyer all winter, and that Emily will, for the rest of her life, berate herself for having left in there. She accepted only $10,000 to carry this life-threatening fetus inside her, on the urgings of Nick, who wouldn't take more—Nick, that genius about money. All in, Chad has spent maybe seven or eight grand on her—a lot!—but nowhere close to the some $20,000 in extra cash a professional surrogate would have in her hands right now. Emily has been playing a long game. She has been placing her bets on summers in Scottsdale, calculating what renting a comparable house would cost her family year after year; she has been counting on theater subscriptions and nights on the town and bottles of hundred-dollar wine brought to every dinner party. She has been banking on the fact that in-kind money would hypothetically add up and exceed, over the years, what she would have earned with a one-time fee, but she has also been banking on something less precise—on the improvement Chad and Miguel meant to her emotional *quality of life*.

That somehow, when they battened down the hatches, she would be one of those left *inside*.

"I can call Nick to pick me up," she says, though who the hell knows if Nick will be home or have his phone on or will say he has somewhere else to be. "I know you need to work, you don't need to bother about me."

"Don't be silly," Chad says, and his tone is some awkward mix of jocular and shrill. "You're supposed to be in bed—I'm not sending you home alone. I'm taking you home myself and putting you into your own bed and making sure you're comfortable."

The shame of it is too much. She can't bear for him to see the inside of her house, even though he has been there dozens of times.

"I'll come by tomorrow or the next day to check on you," Chad promises. "As soon as things here have cooled down."

What is it that needs *cooling* more than her hypertensive body, carrying their child? What is it that is more important to Chad Merry, perfect man, perfect traitor, than that?

"I'll let you get changed," he says, dashing out of the room.

Emily pulls out her phone. It would be that easy. That easy. All she has to do is call the doctor and calmly say, "I'm too sick, this is dangerous, I can't do this anymore." All she has to do is say, "I'm a mother, and I can't orphan my sons for someone else's child." All she has to do is press the number, wait for them to answer, and that will be that: Saint Emily, making the only call she could make for her own children. Just like that, Chad and Miguel will be punished, and her body will be her own again, and only Chad will ever understand that it was retribution—that he could have played things another way, but he didn't, and now this is what he drove her to do.

For a moment, the thought satisfies her so much, she feels half-drunk. She sits at the edge of the bed, imagining, not getting dressed, not packing, paralyzed with thrill.

Only once Chad knocks timidly, saying, "Just call me when you're ready," does she realize she's being insane. She can't call *today.* She can't fall prey to relishing Chad's understanding the causality of the situation. She can't leave an A-leads-to-B trail of any kind. To do so would ruin everything. No . . . what she has to do is wait, continue to act just as she's been acting: so grateful, so desperate. She has to continue to crawl on her belly before them just a little while longer, long enough for Chad to believe completely that everything is all right. Only then can she do the deed, and no one will be able to blame her, even Chad and Miguel themselves. Only then can she call them weeping, can she say words like *postpartum depression*, can she talk about how *We all lost a baby together*, and they will, she understands fully now, not want to have that conversation with her, will not want her in their inner sanctum of grief, and so they will give her things, throw things her way to make *her* go away, and she will continue to receive the rewards, only they will not have their baby, and nobody will ever be the wiser or blame her for anything, because why on earth would they?

She has no choice. It's what any mother would do. It will be the doctor's idea.

She just has to wait. A week maybe? That will do it. One more week stuck in bed in the fraternity house she lives in, biding her time. The fetus isn't viable yet or they would induce. She will only be *sicker* by then, if things keep going this way. The Prentice Women's Hospital doctors will be having their aneurisms over fear of lawsuits and the fragile state of Emily's health. They will pop champagne in the break room after they get this toxic fetus out of her, that she is fine and no one can sue them. Never mind that her grandmother delivered her mother in the back bedroom of their old apartment alone, while her husband was at the factory working. Emily is a white lady walking around with two rich men paying her bills. The doctors cannot let anything bad happen to her.

She loves her own children, after all. Her own children come first. What else is there for her to do?

LINA

The night of my return from Miami, you lick my eyelids. Your tongue lightly traces the sockets, the bones of my nose, and then, like a mother lion cleaning its newborn cub, you suddenly begin to lick my entire face, long and hard and claiming and ferocious, until my smile threatens to split my skin in two. I have never felt this *nurtured*. I'm floating, flying, without even having to feel any pain at all first, half-moaning, half-sobbing back at you, "I love you," wet inside and out with every liquid of you.

"Fuck moderation," you promise.

Lucy Grealy wrote:

When I dream of fire
You're still the one I'd save
Though I've come to think of myself
As the flames, the splintering rafters

Grealy was an undergraduate. By age thirty-nine, she'd be dead of a heroin overdose.

We all have our demons. Pain doesn't make anyone special.

I am tired of being the splintering rafters.

So what, in the end, is there to even say about the day of leaving my lover of six years?

You probably think you have Bebe figured out. You are still assuming I am a reliable narrator, even though you should know better by now.

How it starts: I leave my pregnancy test in the bathroom for Bebe to find.

I don't *have* to tell you this part. You will grant me that you were not likely to track Bebe down, follow her to work or stalk her at our old haunts, and interrogate her about the monstrous manner in which I ended the relationship. You will grant me that I could have told you, here, that she simply got tired of me (I was tiresome after all: my cheating, my petulance, my facile remarks about the Patriarchy, my failure to earn a dime) and said, *Honey, it's been sweet but I think it's time.* I could tell you anything, but I'm trying to do this right, even if I'm not sure why.

I leave the pregnancy test on the bathroom counter. Then I nonchalantly sit around painting my nails, waiting for Bebe to come into the kitchen saying, *What the fuck is this?*

Except she doesn't. Kudos to you if you can see what I was incapable of seeing: that, of course, Bebe would never do that. She goes in the bathroom; she comes out again. Nothing.

I called her name, over and over again, before giving up with humiliated defeat and pissing into her potted plants. I called her name like my life depended on it, and the next day she looked at me with clear eyes and talked about eggs. And for that, I loved her.

My nails are the color of blood in a vial, that deeper, less-oxidized red. "Lincoln Park After Dark," the color is called. It is my signature color, one might say. *You* might say. You love the color. You love to see it when I'm clutching your prick. Sometimes you call me your vampire girl. I am painting my nails for you, even though I've been setting the stage for Bebe. Even though she left the theater months ago.

"So I guess you know I'm pregnant," I finally tell her. It takes me five or six hours to get there, from the staged pregnancy test in the bathroom to finally confronting her, to accusing her, as though I am the wronged party. "I'm a month in, though that part seems confusing to me." I desperately want her to cut me off, to *say something*, but I'm so afraid of her potential silence that I can't stop talking. "I conceived two weeks ago, so I don't know how that means I'm already four weeks pregnant—you're two weeks pregnant before you're pregnant—that's stupid, don't you think?"

It's only once I shut up, Nick, that she looks up from her book and I see she has been crying.

"Do you honestly think I haven't known, this whole time," she says, "that you've been fucking him?"

(*Did* I "honestly think"? I don't know, even now. Perhaps appallingly, I hadn't "honestly thought" about it at all. I was too busy inside my own head to contemplate what this narrative looked like to Bebe.)

But I'm not ready to own that yet. Instead I demand, "Why didn't you say anything then?"

"Fuck that—why didn't *you*?"

"Because I knew you'd lecture me," I shoot back. "I knew you'd have a field day judging me. Not only am I failing to claim my power by subverting the male gaze, I'm actually—gasp!—*sleeping* with a man."

"Oh, you're not sleeping with him," she corrects. "His wife is sleeping with him. You're using him to knock you up. Let's at least be clear here."

"I was not!" I shout, outraged, scandalized, except of course, yes: when I got home from Beaver Island after the funeral, I bought an ovulation kit. Except, yes, that is in fact *exactly what I have been doing*, if only for three weeks. They just happen to have been three perfectly timed weeks, and I just happen to come from a family that gets pregnant if sperm is released into the air in the same building. "I know you won't believe this," I tell Bebe, but I can't look at her eyes, the red rims, "but I love him. We're in love. You don't really love me, so as sorry as I am that I lied to you, I don't see why you'd even really mind."

What is she reading, you may want to know? Or rather, you don't give a shit, but only then do *I* realize that it's *Lithium for Medea*, my favorite novel. Maybe she is only pretending to read, a prop like my pregnancy test and my toenails. But the sight of it makes me sob.

"Why did you have to be so cold?" I blubber, covering my face to hide from her. "Why couldn't you love me?"

And she stands, shaking. She's grown too thin in the past six months or so—from glamorous to drawn—did I do that to her? "Your family," she says, "thinks love is a nonstop parade of noise. What's the *matter* with you? I knew you were fucking that married man, that . . . that guy with a disabled child, for fuck's sake . . . and I just sat here, patiently, waiting for you to come to your senses. What about *loyalty*? What about not falling to pieces every time the wind blows? You spend all your intensity like some kind of burning star that's going to crash to the ground—no one can move at your velocity forever, Lina, even you. You crash and burn and do it all over again with someone new. What the hell do *you* know about love?"

I'm throwing clothing into a bag. I'm crashing and burning. I'm shooting.

Bebe, watching me, starts to laugh. "Look at you," she says. "Look at yourself! *You're* going to have a baby? Are you going to show up at that poor pussy-whipped man's house and show your flat little belly to his gargantuan wife and tell him how you're knocked up? What, are they going to invite you to move in and support you? How the hell do you expect to take care of a child without me, anyway? You don't even have a job! Besides the small matter of your being crazy!"

"You liked me crazy just fine when I was doing whatever you wanted me to do!"

And Bebe sinks onto the bed. She sits down next to my open suitcase. She says, "Yes, pet, I did. I know I can be controlling, and I'm sorry. But what are you *doing*, Lina? You don't have to go anywhere. Why are you behaving so melodramatically? I don't want to live with a baby, but for god's sake, be real. You're not really *having* that baby, Lina. You know that. You don't have to move out. Relationships can be redefined. You were always free to see other people. I never tried to restrict you. I was trying to give you perimeters you could live with, within your limitations. You're not . . . that stable. You can't live alone. Where do you think you're going?"

I don't know where I'm going. Somewhere a pregnancy test in the bathroom merits comment. Somewhere I can be unchained when I call out. Somewhere I wouldn't leave the test to be discovered to begin with, hoping to provoke some emotion. But does such a place exist, or is Bebe right about me?

Crazy. Not that stable. My head is loud, even for me. I take a benzo and half an Abilify to stave off an episode in case one is starting, then slam out the door with my bag full of useless shit. Bebe and I only have one car between us, so I can't just drive it away—I drag my bag around the corner and lean against the building, out of the line of sight of our windows, texting you the first of the desperate, frantic texts:

I need you.

Then: *Bebe and I are over.*

And after no reply: *Please don't feel guilty, you know that train had so already left the station, even if you and I had never met. It's just that before you, I wouldn't have believed I could sustain more than she offered. You make me believe, Nick. Not in some white-knight version of romance, but in ME. When I'm shaky, like now, I try to look at myself through your eyes, and it helps.*

I lean against the wall, the voices in my head racing against the letters flying from my fingertips. Sometimes the Abilify knocks me out, and here I am out on the street with my luggage, no car. I'm not tired yet, am wired, if anything, too much energy, but before I crash I'll have to get somewhere, probably one of our habitual motels. After my slip in Miami, though, I want a drink too badly to go somewhere that solitary: somewhere I can get away with anything and nobody will ever know. My bag isn't that heavy—I don't own much—so I decide (I am impressed with myself for this decision) I'll go to a meeting first, and by the time it's over, you'll have gotten in touch with me and we can figure out together what to do next.

We are going to hold hands on the ledge and jump, Nick. This is what I still believe, voices like an ocean's roar in my head, and the first spark of everything that was between us growing in my borrowed-time ovaries. I have not exactly made a career of optimism, but there, in those moments, as desperate as I have ever been, wanting the burn of Jameson running down my throat, no idea where I am going from here, I need you to understand that I truly *believe*—that it has never yet occurred to me otherwise—that your call is coming, and that I am only this close—this close—to finally becoming a *mariposa* and sprouting my wings.

Except three meetings later, I'm still trying to reach you. More than four hours have elapsed since my first text, but you are, for the first time since I've met you, unreachable.

Staying for numerous meetings in a row can be meditative, almost spiritual—I've done it on holidays, and felt, in that shimmery, momentary way, transformed, useful, *hearing* other people, being of service, inching through the minutes together on a hard day. Tonight is not one of those times. I stand in this church basement, in front of a room full of struggling people, and say for maybe the thousandth time in my life, "I'm Lina and I'm an alcoholic," thinking about the ritualistic words Isabel and Mami have recited over and over again in church, looking for some kind of salvation.

I'm Lina and my mother who abandoned me is dead. I'm Lina and my ex-lover says I'm crazy. I'm Lina and I've barely ever held a real job, but I played a shrink in a burlesque about mentally ill zombies.

I'm Lina and I'm in love with the playwright, who is married and not returning my texts. I'm Lina and I'm supposed to get my ovaries ripped out before they kill me, so I don't have much time. I'm Lina and it's possible that I'm a product of such violent, ugly inbreeding that I should have been born with two heads.

The Abilify has utterly failed to knock me out, or even take the edge off my feeling like my brain is a spinning hamster's wheel, although I'm not feeling on the brink of an episode anymore—the voices have lulled to their usual dull roar. Still, I chew another two Klonopin in the church lobby and don't even care who sees me. *It's not heroin. It's not Jameson.* I want to drink more badly than before I came.

Bebe called me crazy and unstable, I text you. *Not that I didn't deserve it. Still, I have to admit it took me by surprise. If I'm so crazy and unstable, what was she doing here all this time? Why did she want me to stay?*

Then, *I hope everything's ok. I'm worried about you.*

Do you see how you are too good? Not answering a text within an hour makes me afraid you're dead in a ditch. Because you're always so Here for me. How can you be possible? I love you. I love you, my bright red meteor boy—I wish we could be sitting outside of Villa Moderne, smoking on the wooden gliders, our knees brushing as we rock.

Where ARE you, baby? Fuck. I have something so important to tell you.

Nick? I need you.

Usually, I know people at this six o'clock meeting, but none of my friends are here tonight. One other person, a man about your age, is sitting through consecutive meetings, too—maybe he is three days sober; maybe he will be here all night; maybe I should talk to him, but I don't. It's dark when I get outside and I have nothing but an overnight bag with some black clothing and embarrassing lingerie in it and nowhere to go except Mami's. I am thirty-one years old but here I am again.

It's past nine when my phone vibrates. I have it in my back pocket, close to my skin, not in my handbag, so that I can't miss you. This gesture of hope humiliates me, even though the phone is ringing now, even though my hope has been fulfilled. Your name flashes across my phone and I clutch at it like a sweating glass, ready to gulp you down.

I want Isabel not to be dead. I want my ovaries not to be a detonating bomb. I want any woman in my life to have loved me enough. I want *you* to love me enough to make up for it. I want to be somebody else.

For a moment, as desperately as I've been waiting to hear from you, I almost hang up my phone.

"Oh god," you say, and your voice is all wrong. Despite the Klonopin I can hardly breathe. "I'm so sorry," you say, and I get ready for the blow: you have reconsidered everything, reconsidered me, reconsidered whether I even have the right to be alive much less whether I have the right to steal your good wife's man, *go ahead, hit me, bring it on*. But then I'm crying, too, because I know you'd never do that, Nick. I know that isn't what you've called to say. I know you're not capable of hurting me on purpose, and if you aren't calling to break my heart then it has to be even worse if you sound like this.

"Emily had a seizure."

I cry out to try to comfort you. I still believe, with my newfound hope, the hope you accidentally taught me, that maybe I am now in the role of the comforter, that maybe everything will be okay.

"She was alone with Jay—the ambulance—he called. I didn't even know he knew how *to* do that—I was at the stupid fucking gym, my phone was in my bag, the boys kept trying to call me—I got home . . . the ambulance—I thought it was Jay—I thought—"

"Nick, oh god, I'm sorry—"

But you cut me off. "No, you don't understand—" Your voice clogs, raw again. "They don't know if she's going to make it . . . Emily, the baby . . . *anything*."

Of all the things I wanted, one thing I never thought, precisely: *I want to take care of an infant.* This thing, this clump of cells inside my stomach, could be just another grasp at salvation. Maybe a baby could love me enough to heal me. *Me.*

And I never say to you, *I'm pregnant.*

Perhaps that is my one humane act.

If this were Caracas, circa 1978, maybe someone would be en route with a gun, ready to shoot me in the chest. But three decades have passed. I'm a bisexual adulterer in a Blue State whose lover's wife is having my gay brother's child: that's not how we do things in our tribe. If I want to go down, I'm going to have to do it myself.

I'm sorry, Nick.

This is what we've wrought.

MIGUEL

Once again, Miguel is outside his body. He watches himself walking through tiled corridors, playing the role of ambassador. Other people litter the halls, strangers, but they do not register. Hospitals are like miniature worlds in that sense: so many life-and-death dramas playing out in tandem, adjacent but never touching. For that man at the vending machine, talking to the air, one reality; for the woman with balloons in the elevator, another—Miguel, too, is trapped in his inviolate, singular experience. He can see himself moving and talking, the way he remembers witnessing, from somewhere skyward, his nine-year-old self peddling chintzy faux bouquets door-to-door. He can *still* see himself there on his old Caracas street, the view of the basket in his hand as though he was looking straight down on it, even though he cannot envision the face of a single neighbor who pressed money in his hand, or remember what his house looked like from the outside, or recall the color of the car Papi allegedly drove off a bridge, or that they even *owned* a car. His childhood seemed a universe traversable by foot, as though if you ended up farther than your body could carry you, you would simply fall off the edge of the earth. Tía's, which had seemed so far away from their own block that it might as well have been Chicago or Miami, was, Isabel told him many years later, barely half a mile away.

The NICU at Northwestern is the new ground zero of his life. Entire years—decades—feel like they are falling away so there was only ever That, the interior of his tiny house in Caracas, and This: the incubator where his daughter Imogen is, according to popular vernacular, "fighting for her life." Language is coded with violence, with blame, with platitudes. Three pounds of existence and in a listless magnesium fugue, not breathing on her own, Imogen—a mass of cells now coded and quantified by the label of the name Miguel and Chad slapped upon her to pin her down and in place—is beyond their desires for sentience and intention. She has no awareness of "life" for which to "fight"—no pride to surrender in "losing." He thinks of Isabel, and the way people spoke of her *battle with cancer*, a disease *less* sentient, even, than this small mound of humanity that is Imogen. Language, doctors, mothers, lovers, religion—everyone assigns *meaning* to everything. Christian mothers battle with cancer and bad drunken men drive their cars off bridges and newborns too small for the world are presumed valuable and hence fight the good fight of survival. Miguel's head swims. *God is love; God hates fags; Jesus loves the little children; there is a season for everything; when a door closes another opens; God is forgiveness; thou shalt not kill.* He feels he will somehow die if this clump of neurons and fiber and beating heart does not survive, but what does his survival matter, or hers, or any of it? There is no arc to any story; there is only a beginning and an end and a million moments in between, adding up to nothing.

His body goes on, plodding from the NICU to the waiting room where Gretchen and the Merrys huddle together, a unified front of civilized WASPs still muted in their crisis mode. He goes from there to the room where Emily is being closely monitored, Miles at bedside vigil clutching her hand while Nick seems to have fallen apart and is leaning against a wall at the end of the hall looking deranged. Miguel goes back to the NICU where Chad sits gazing at Imogen with a singular attention, occasionally raising a hand to cover his mouth, his eyes above his left hand—above his wedding band—brimming up and then freezing, static, the tears not falling. He brings the Merrys news of Imogen; he brings Chad news of Emily; he sits next to Chad while the movements of nurses lurch on around him.

He can't feel his own skin.

Chad has his arm linked through Miguel's, and slowly Miguel forces himself to concentrate on the pressure of Chad's meat-slab limb against his own. They are all fragile meat. He imagines Imogen, her unfathomably tiny striped hat covering her head that is smaller than his palm. Her entire body is the size of a large animal's heart. What kind of animal? Surely an elephant's heart is much larger—a tiger, perhaps? Is his daughter the size of a Siberian tiger's heart? He watches his hand close into a fist, comparing the size of his own heart to the size of Imogen by closing one eye and holding his fist out toward her incubator.

"I can't believe this is happening to us," Chad whispers, leaning against him.

It seems impossible to reply to this. Miguel thinks, but every possible response would be biting—*You can't? What kind of life have you led?* Or, *When will you understand that life's teeth come for everyone?*—and he does not wish to bite.

"I didn't understand," he manages only, "how instantly you *love* them. Like . . . the second they come out . . . how the world would be different."

Chad looks at him, his expression naked and cracked apart in a way Miguel has never seen. "I knew it would be that way. I loved her when she was inside Emily—I didn't even *know* Emily, but I loved her, too, I couldn't get enough of her, because the baby was inside her."

"I don't know how to do this," Miguel says. "I've never been so afraid in my life."

"She's going to be okay," Chad says, but turns his eyes away. "We have to think positively. Everything will be *fine*. We'll be taking her home soon."

Everything Chad is saying right now is like some distilled essence of exactly why Miguel fell in love with him once—exactly why he wanted to make a life with this man, this person so capable of incautious love and hope—yet in this moment he understands fully that his youthful delusions that this would somehow rub off on him, change his own essence, was folly, and that he and Chad will live forever on opposite sides of a certain divide. Miguel cannot climb the fence, cannot claw his way in the dirt beneath it to live on Chad's sunlit side. Inside her incubator, Imogen looks to him like a broken newborn bird on the sidewalk, shorn even of protective feathers. She looks like a thing not made for this world.

"I don't know if this is the right time to mention this," Chad says. "But have you noticed that Gretchen hasn't come in here once? She isn't acting normal. It's freaking me out."

Miguel says mildly, "What are you talking about?"

"You don't think she's going to try to *take* her, do you? What if she's planning to take our baby away from us?"

Miguel's hand rubs Chad's arm, close to the space where their bodies are linked. The machines hum and beep, the digital sound of life. "You're just stressed out," he says. "You're just worried about Imogen."

"No!" Chad stands up, and Miguel starts, dizzily. Chad's back is to the incubator, and Miguel sees a couple of nurses eye him, though surely meltdowns are not uncommon in here. "Imogen's going to be *fine*," Chad says, too loud. "I'm not talking about that. I'm talking about my *sister*. I know her, and she's not acting right."

Miguel takes Chad's wrist and tries to pull him back down to his seat—*he* has become a civilized WASP too—hissing, "You're losing it. Maybe you need a break—get some air. Gretchen loves you . . .

and look, she has her hands full with Gray and that shitstorm divorce. What you're saying makes no sense."

Chad yanks his wrist back. "Since when does common sense keep anyone from wanting to keep what's theirs? Look at Troy! Look at *your* family!"

Miguel's nerve endings race back to life with pinprick electric sparks, his entire body a foot that has fallen asleep and is now being stomped on. "Okay," he says, trying to steady himself, "I hear you, but . . . I just don't know where this is coming from. Just because she hasn't come to see Imogen—people get nervous, Chad . . . around a baby who . . ." He wants to say, *Around a dying baby.* But he can't—not to Chad, not even aloud for his own ears to hear.

"It's not only that." Chad sits down now, voluntarily, lowering his voice. "She's been acting skittish and cagey for a long time, almost the whole pregnancy. I just didn't want to believe what I was seeing. I think we need to go see a custody attorney, and I mean, like, *today.*"

"I'm not going anywhere," Miguel says. "I'm not leaving Imogen."

"I think we should go together," Chad presses. "You're the biological father, I have no rights here at all. Our marriage isn't legal. I'm the *uncle*—I'm nobody."

Miguel's eyes lock on Chad. He can see Chad now, not himself—he's snapped back into his body, though he wants out again. "I don't want to leave her," he says urgently. "I just . . . *can't.*"

Chad stands. "I don't want to leave her, either. But while you've been running around with Lina playing detective about shit that happened thirty years ago, I've been here, slowly figuring out that my sister is planning to steal our baby." He closes his eyes briefly, inhales slowly, as if he's counting inside his head. "I'm sorry," he says when he exhales at last. "I didn't mean it like that. I'm sorry about Isabel. I know she practically raised you. But she wrote us off a long, long time ago, and it's like—ever since she got sick, and especially since she died, you just seem . . . checked out. You seem like you're not even here.

We're having a baby." Abruptly, the tears that have been brimming in Chad's eyes all day spill. "No . . . we *had* a baby. We *have* a baby. Imogen is going to pull through, and she is *ours*."

Chad's body, when Miguel embraces him, bristles at first like an electric spark, then releases and he grips the back of Miguel's shirt tightly in his fists. Miguel stands firm, Chad leaning into him so hard that if he were to move, Chad would fall over. He keeps his feet solid, absorbing Chad's weight. "Listen," Miguel murmurs into Chad's neck. "You go . . . contact a lawyer on our behalf, get some information, and don't tell anyone, you hear me? Don't tell a soul." He kisses Chad before pulling slightly back. "I understand that you're doing what you need to do, and that you're doing it for us. But I'm not afraid of this. I have to stay here, with our daughter." He thinks, suddenly, of the Judgment of Solomon, throat constricting, staring down at baby Imogen, a world unto herself, indifferent to their cleaving.

He is afraid there won't be a baby to fight over.

Chad has been gone some two hours, texting periodically, when Miguel has to leave Imogen for the first time to take a toilet break, and collides straight into Mami in the hall, rounding a corner. He was looking down at his phone and didn't see her coming. She yelps, and he knows the sound of her distress call before his eyes focus on her, which he has little chance to do since she immediately swoops him up in her arms, keeping him stooped over to allow her embrace.

Then her short arm reaches up and cuffs him in the head. "So, you don't even call your own mother when you have a baby, that's how it is? I have to hear from your sister?"

For a moment the words don't connect. *My sister is dead*. Then he realizes that of course, Mami means Lina. Nick must have called her, amidst all his hall-pacing. Miguel supposes he should be surprised at this, but being surprised at the things Lina circuitously knows about their pregnancy has gotten old, and he can only pretend to himself for so long that he can't connect the dots.

Lina herself is nowhere to be seen, hasn't called—to congratulate him or express concern, Miguel isn't sure which would be appropriate.

"I'm just going to the bathroom," he tells Mami, the side of his head still smarting. "But listen, could you sit with Imogen while I'm gone?"

"Of course, of course, where do you think I'm going?"

"I guess Lina told you that she's . . . that Imogen is . . ." He finds, though, that he has no words for what Imogen is. "She's delicate," he settles on, carefully extracting his arm from his mother. "You need to be prepared, before you go in there."

"She will be fine," Mami proclaims, clap-sweeping her palms together cleanly. "God will watch out for her."

It is as though everyone he knows is suffering from some collective cultural and personal amnesia. *If there were a god, he would be a sociopathic serial killer who pulls the strings while Rwandan children get hacked with machetes and Jewish children are rounded up for gassing and Thai children are washed from their mother's arms in tsunamis . . . if there were a god, he watched my father beat you while Isabel and I starved.* The hall seems to narrow. Miguel's hand gropes the wall for balance. When is the last time he's eaten?

"How is Chad?" Mami, like the hallway, seems to be growing even smaller, though she has already, at sixty-six, shrunk below five feet tall. She is still lovely beneath the worn surface of herself, but it is getting harder and harder to see through the cracks. "He isn't as strong as you. He has no callouses on his hands."

"Chad is . . . optimistic," Miguel says dizzily. "Like you."

"I was thinking," Mami continues, like a woman who has all the time in the world, "how you maybe need a nanny, and, you know, why hire a stranger? I was thinking, I can come, I could go to your house, I can ride the Damen Avenue bus straight down."

They bought Termite Mansion before Emily was even inseminated, but Mami has never seen it. Now she is planning to bus there daily to take care of the baby she couldn't even acknowledge aloud the night he broke the news, stuffing her mouth with hamburger?

"You don't have to pay me, of course! But I'll let you buy me the bus pass. Carlos was right, I should have learned to drive."

"I was thinking I'd leave work," Miguel says, though he has never thought this before, for even a fraction of a second. "I was thinking I'd stay home with her myself. I've never . . . liked my job."

"Aye," Mami says, frowning, "they pay you good money there. Babies are expensive."

"I have to go," Miguel explains desperately, scanning the fun-tunnel hallway as it expands and contracts. "I have to . . . I'll be back in just a few minutes." His mother's face collapses and he quickly adds, "Maybe when I'm at home, I'll need some time to myself so I can run errands, and . . . uh . . . go to the gym." He wonders for a brief flash why he is placating her, this woman who couldn't be bothered to come to his wedding or get it up for Imogen's sonogram, this woman who abandoned Isabel and borderline kidnapped baby Angelina. And then he remembers, like an echo in his head, a heartbeat pulsing slow, *Because Isabel is dead. Isabel is dead now. Because Isabel wouldn't even see her. Because whatever our mother's crimes, she has paid and paid some more.* "I could bring Imogen to you, at your house," Miguel says through his blocked throat. "It's smaller so she can't get into as much trouble." But when Mami goes to embrace him again, he steps back so sharply he knocks into the wall.

"You have to be strong," Mami says, eying him as though really looking at him for the first time. "You're a father now. I know you're strong. You were always the strongest of any of us, and your daughter needs you now."

"I really have to go." Miguel sidesteps away from her waiting arms. "If you can sit with the baby, you would . . . you'd really be helping me."

As soon as he is far enough away that she must have rounded the corner to the NICU by now, Miguel breaks out in a run. He dashes down the corridor, toward the elevators and the men's bathroom, flings back the door too hard and stands inside, the row of sinks wavering in his vision. He doesn't even have to piss anymore, though back in the NICU, the need was urgent enough to drive him away from where he could keep Imogen in sight. Why did he flee here, then? He scans under the stalls for feet, but he is alone, ducks into a stall, bolts its flimsy door, sinks onto the cool tiles, trying to let the cold seep into his skin, his breathing fractured and thin.

Isabel seated calmly on Tía's worn sofa, her back straight, a pile of blankets beside her.

Isabel staring, straight ahead, past Miguel as he raced through the front door crying, yelling at her, *No one will play with me because you're a whore with a bastard!*

Isabel's voice, far away, *Go back outside and leave me alone, nobody cares about your little problems.*

Miguel's arms lurch forward, pushing the empty air.

The pile of blankets beside Isabel was red, like the curtain on Mami's bedroom door in the old house. Or maybe Miguel's memory only has one color . . .

Images flood and overlap. His arms pawing through the blankets as though they reached to the ceiling, when of course it was usually hot out and the house couldn't have had more than a few blankets in it to begin with. In his mind he rummages through the pile eternally, as though he has to climb to the center of the earth to reach what he is searching for—the infant's leg he finally touches, slippery and slick. She is crying, as wet with sweat as if Miguel pulled her from a lake. Her black thatch of hair soaking, her face as red as the blanket . . .

Isabel hit him hard on the side of the head. "Go outside, mind your own business, go back outside."

Miguel pushed her hand away, held Angelina's leg firmly in his slithery grasp as the baby still screamed. "You can't do that!" he shouted at his sister. "You're not allowed to do that. Look at her—she's crying. You're not allowed . . ." He sounded like an imbecile; he was embarrassed of the way he was crying. "It's not allowed," he finished, lamely.

"What do you know about what's allowed?" Isabel countered, her voice utterly even, calm. "Fine, I'll just drown her in the bath next time you're out. What do you care, anyway?"

"You can't do that," Miguel screamed. In a lifetime of feeling helpless, of feeling young, of feeling small, he had never felt so much of any of those things. He was a gnat around Isabel's head, easily batted away. He went to school every day while she was here with Angelina. He was inconsequential—nothing—next to the insurmountable will of her. He never had been. And he was nothing *to her, either. That had once been different, but now, for reasons inaccessible to him, he was as expendable to Isabel as the baby screaming with her will to live on the couch.*

"Don't you dare tell Mami," Isabel commanded. "You owe me. You left me there, with him.*"*

Miguel cannot breathe.

"Why are you dead?" he shouts into the echo chamber of the small bathroom. "*You* left me, Isabel! *You're* the one who left, over and over again."

Don't you dare tell Mami, his once-beloved sister had instructed him. But he must have, though he has no recollection of that conversation. He *must* have. Because his mother took Baby Angelina and Miguel and fled to Chicago for good, leaving Isabel—Isabel the savior, Isabel the warrior, Isabel who may have killed Papi—behind.

His air is gone, the flashbulbs are popping. He hears his jagged breath fading. He's going under. The EpiPen is in his pocket—he carries it always. But *there is no cold*. Just like in Miami: no stimuli, no causal force. He fumbles for the pen. Does it stop a histamine response, or does it just stop his own brain?

You were always the strongest of any of us, Mami told him. *Your daughter needs you.*

He doesn't feel strong. He never has. He has substituted cynicism, sarcasm, anger, denial, sublimation, *Chad* . . . anything at his disposal, anything he can find, in the space where his strength should be, just to keep himself alive, sometimes without even knowing why being alive was the goal. Only that the will to keep going was primal, like Angelina's smothered screams, like Imogen still hanging on by an invisible thread . . .

You're a father now. But fathers are the opposite of strong. Fathers are the ruin of everything. Still Mami believes. In Carlos, who drank and seemed a train wreck, but then got sober and took care of them, who still takes care of Mami, who parented Lina the best he could amidst the maelstrom of her, and is a good man. Still Mami believes, in Miguel who saved baby Angelina's life, and on whom she has never turned her back despite his deviance from the rules of her god. Still, Mami believes, still Chad believes, still Lina believes, and Emily believed, enough to offer her body up to his dreams. Now Imogen, too, if only she survives, will have no choice *but* to believe. He has not been worthy of their belief—of *any* of it—but somehow, unless he wants to leave wreckage like his father did, somehow he will *have* to be.

He poises to stab the pen hard into his leg. He has come to love the rush of it: his breath, his heart, sounds and colors and walls popping back to place. But his hand stops mid-thrust, less than an inch above his thigh. *There is no cold.* Whatever this seemed at first, cold urticaria, a real condition apparently, Miguel does not have That Thing. Miami, here—*there is no cold.* There is no bridge. There is no Isabel. There is no resolution. All he has is this bathroom. All and everything he has is his newborn daughter, fighting for her flimsy beautiful life.

The still-full EpiPen clinks to the floor, rolling away like from an unconscious junkie. Miguel watches it depart. Hears his own sobs, wrenched up from the center of the earth, the center of him, filling the bathroom, stripping back everything but this.

If he can sob this way, it means he is breathing. On his own steam, he is breathing.

"Please," he begs god and the walls and his dead sister, "you don't owe me anything, but please let her live anyway."

He can't sit here much longer. He has to compose himself, accept the air into his lungs as, if not his birthright, if terrifyingly impermanent as all things are impermanent, then at least, today, under his own control. He has to check in with Chad, to take the threat his husband has perceived seriously. He has to go back to the NICU and sit with his mother and his daughter, bearing witness to whatever is about to transpire—he cannot hide from it any more than he can fix it. *Fixing things* was supposed to be Isabel's job, but she was only thirteen, and it broke her. Miguel is a grown man—a father—but nobody can fix unfixable things. He can only stand by the people he loves, and brace his feet against the ground to absorb their weight the best he can.

Even knowing this, he remains immobile on the cold tile until he hears the bathroom door open. The stranger, some other man dragging his own scars and demons through the world, upon hearing Miguel's private, wracked sobbing, rushes off, the door closing slowly on its springs. Only then, once there has been some kind of witness to Miguel's memories, his moment, his existence, is he able to get to his feet and make his way back down the corridor toward his daughter, and whatever the future holds.

GRETCHEN

Gretchen's efforts to see Emily alone feel as complex as robbing a bank. She isn't even sure why she feels the need, but it scrapes away at her, makes her leave her parents sipping their Au Bon Pain lattes with their shallowly funereal air, and wander to where Emily can only have one visitor at a time—where clearly there is no reason, amidst chaos and emergencies, that the one visitor would ever be *Gretchen*.

Emily's freakishly good-looking son, who at fourteen is already taller than Gretchen despite the fact that neither Emily nor Nick is tall, sits at his mother's bedside clutching her hand. It seems impossible to imagine Gray behaving so protectively, even as a near adult. Gretchen is aware that she has become one of *those* people—that just a year ago, she was not someone who immediately translated every situation to her own, so as to compare and find her life lacking. There is a word for this, she knows: *bitter*. She is on the brink of forty-three, still young enough that a baby born of her egg has now joined the world (but for how long?)—still, she feels so bitter she could pucker faces. So brittle she could crack into jagged pieces and make Miles, the handsome, devoted son, sweep the shards of her into the trash so as not to disturb his saintly mother.

Gretchen loiters. Nick, who Gretchen takes for being, as a matter of course, a shiftless good-for-nothing and probably a cheat, will be expected to put in appearances in Emily's room, too, so at some point Miles has to leave and there will be a changing of the guard. She waits, pacing, finally sitting on the scuffed tiled floors in a way that would desperately alarm Elaine Merry were she here, and so Gretchen doesn't get up, even though the floor is uncomfortable and she feels silly. She can't bring herself to go to the NICU with Miguel and Chad—she's festering in the juices of her own shameful duplicity—so instead she sits on the floor outside Emily's room and, sure enough, eventually Nick himself comes and asks, in a voice that seems theatrically reverent and sad to Gretchen, if Miles would be willing to "come talk privately for a minute." Miles makes a big show of kissing his mother's forehead and assuring her that everything will be all right before he walks stiffly away with Nick, leaving Emily unguarded, alone.

The truth is, Emily is barely conscious. She may not even know Miles has been there so long. She may not even *recognize* Gretchen, who hasn't seen her in months and has been a pretty insignificant player in this Community Baby drama—*never mind me, that's just my egg.* Ever since getting the call down to Northwestern, to Prentice Women's Hospital where Emily was already in distress and being loaded up with magnesium, Gretchen has had the sense of herself as being in the late stages of a film, when one of the good guys suddenly pulls off a mask or steps forward with a gun and reveals himself for what he really is. Her legal paperwork could scorch right through the tasteful beige Italian leather of her handbag and drop out onto Emily's thin white blanket. It has never occurred to Gretchen before: the balls-out courage it takes to be the Big Bad Wolf. Everyone rallies blindly around the pigs. No one cares that a wolf needs to feed, too.

Emily is watching her with eyes swollen nearly to slits. Gretchen smooths the legs of her pants compulsively, trying to think of what to say, before she realizes that—no—Emily isn't *looking* at her at all. She is just one of those people who sleeps with her eyes partially open, or at least she does right now, from all the drugs. Gretchen smiles forcibly at her, but Emily does not respond. She waves her hand in front of Emily—far enough away to pass for an actual wave—and it clearly doesn't register. What passes over Gretchen is such a mixture of disappointment and relief simultaneously that it feels like her skull could split in two with the fracture. She is here for a reason, though she has no idea what such a reason might be. She wants to talk to Emily, though she does not *like* Emily, and has not one single thing to say for herself that anyone on earth would want to hear.

She slinks into Miles's abandoned chair.

She is a sham.

Even being here, out of . . . what? . . . *concern* for Emily? . . . is flimsy at best. She should be in the NICU with her brother and Miguel; this subterfuge is nothing but a clutter her splitting head is creating, to distract her from the fact that her daughter is probably going to fade quickly from the world, and that Gretchen will have spent Imogen's brief hours of life hanging out with her parents in a "family lounge" like a freaking distant relative from out of town. She can't face it, not any of it: her own intentions if the baby lives, or the baby's *death*, either, on top of so much else gone wrong. Imogen's dying before even living would be the pièce de résistance of Gretchen's every shattered dream.

What *were* her dreams even? It's impossible to remember. The woman she used to be didn't think of such things often, didn't want—in Gretchen's memory of her own Former Self—anything all that intensely. It was more that she took for granted certain unalienable rights that . . . included things many people want intensely. A well-mannered husband who would treat her in the decent way people were supposed to treat each other—who would earn money and not attempt to steal hers. A child who would behave like an adult's concept of "a child," who would love her with a childlike ferocity that it would be her prerogative to entertain or dismiss as her busy adult schedule allowed, the way her parents once had with her and Chad. A home in which all these unalienable rights of hers would live, under one roof that no one was trying to sell out from under her and keep the spoils. She does not suppose that this Former Gretchen thought much about whether or not she would feel passion for her job—it seemed lucky that such a thing had been entertained in her brief foray as a professional athlete, though if she is real about it she never *loved* tennis, either, it was merely something she was good enough at to enjoy the praise until she proved not good enough and smoothly detoured into some alternately acceptable route. Her life was meant to follow a formula, and when Gray arrived and deviated from that formula, the fissures beneath the surface immediately began to show. His Grayness brought out the truth of her and Troy, which was that they were nothing at all.

Gretchen doesn't know how it can turn out to be a "mistake" that she dared to want out of a marriage in which her husband not only didn't love her but seemed to actively dislike her, but it has been the worst mistake of her life. Troy is trying to bury her, and she was unprepared. She didn't know anyone would dare *act this way*, publicly, without regard for how he was perceived, for how they as a family were perceived. She thought she was safe behind some screen of propriety, but the notion that her reputation was once her biggest concern is laughable to her now.

In the world of divorce, everything is inverted.

Troy's shiftlessness translates as: Stay-at-Home Parent. As: Primary Caregiver. Gretchen has worked seventy-hour weeks, supporting the family alone, and that translates as Troy having the right to long-term alimony ("maintenance," the courts call it), and half of everything she is worth even beyond her income. Russian escorts, it turns out, are fairly irrelevant in the world of divorce—though in fairness so are the darts Troy has attempted to hurl her way about vodka and psychoanalytically distant mothers; about embarrassing wardrobes and high-fructose corn syrup. The law is cut and dry, and if you *work*, if you have money, if you are out of the home more often, you are fucked. Troy is bound to end up with at least fifty-fifty custody of Gray, but he is aiming for more and could, conceivably, get it, and she will be separated from her son and have to pay Troy child support for the privilege.

This is true: that asshole actually got to stop fucking Gretchen for years, spend that time insulting her makeup and making snide remarks about her weight, and now he is going to waltz away without ever having to work again, because everything she owns is a joint marital asset. The house will be sold, the proceeds divided.

The only thing they may not split straight down the middle is *Gray*, who Troy wields like a blunt instrument, tormenting her son in various fashions to torment Gretchen vicariously, like some dictator who does not know he has already won the war. Troy's latest fetish has been to trot Gray around to new doctors, claiming to be a widower and solely responsible for Gray, and asking for strange medical tests that terrify Gray and expose him to X-rays, blood work, and radioactive dye, for symptoms the hapless boy does not possess. This seems to be some kind of game to Troy, who knows Gray will not speak up in the doctors' offices. Gray is barely able to convey the facts to Gretchen when she interrogates him, driving her to a hysteria that makes her weep and then feel like a heinous monster for badgering her already-terrified son. Last week, *still* on his soccer kick, Troy called Gretchen from Gray's soccer practice and told her in a frantic tone that another child had accidentally knocked Gray's eye out in a particularly vigorous game, and that they were all searching the playing field to find the eye in hopes of saving it—Gretchen, in the dentist's chair waiting for her cleaning, started screaming, only to hear Troy cackling on the other end and calling her "unstable" for her inability to take a joke.

It cannot be real. This cannot be real. This cannot be her life.

Every night Gray is gone, Gretchen is awake until 3:00 a.m., spinning with worry, with grief over the loss of his precious, eccentric presence she so long took for granted. Every night Gray spends *with* her, she is awake until 3:00 a.m. with the dread of returning him to his father. She has—Jesus, the pitiable fact that she once would have *loved* this—dropped twenty pounds from stress. The bags under her eyes are deeper than her father's.

"You probably don't want to visit me," Emily says, and this jolts Gretchen so she actually makes a squeak of fear. She is not just bitter, but jumpy—she is something not fit for public consumption. Emily sniffs and wipes her eyes, and it's clear to Gretchen she's been crying quietly beside her—possibly for some time?—and that Gretchen, in her self-involvement, didn't notice.

"What's the matter?" she tries now, touching Emily's arms as if looking for something broken. "Are you in pain?"

"Ha," Emily says, her lips tight. "Why yes, I am."

Gretchen squirms, unnerved. "Do you want me to get a nurse?" She adds, "Or Nick," if somewhat reluctantly.

Emily looks confused. There's a blood pressure monitor attached to her, a giant white clip on her finger, and an IV in her arm. Her heartbeat ticks away noisily on the machines. "Nick . . . no. Wait, did you talk to Nick?"

"Me?" Gretchen doesn't know how to explain the utter improbability of that—the way Nick walked right by her in the hall, as though they had never met. *I'm invisible. Men like your husband look right through me. You see*, she might say to blond, innocently pretty Emily with her milk-ripe boobs and glowing skin, *It served Troy's purposes that I didn't feel desirable, because it would never confuse me when, as soon as the ink was dry on our marriage certificate, he didn't desire me. That would just confirm my worldview and keep him safely milking my money . . .*

Gretchen tried—in her outrage, her shame and humiliation—to mess up Troy's plan. But no, he is getting everything he planned on anyway, except the one thing he never wanted: her.

"I waited too long," Emily says, her head lolling a little to one side in a way Gretchen wants to correct. "I was going to call it weeks ago, but I just . . . didn't."

It takes Gretchen a moment to catch up, to cleave from her own anxiety and bile . . . to realize she has no idea what Emily means.

"I changed my mind," Emily tells her. "I kept changing my mind. Then *this* happened, and I thought, great, it'll just kill me and then I can rest. Everyone will be better off." Jarringly, Emily cackles. "But look! Not so much! So much for best-laid plans."

Gretchen doesn't know how to process what she's seeing, this cracked-mask version of the self-possessed earth mother she has previously known. What is Emily even referring to, in her confused state? Should Gretchen give her some lecture about postpartum depression, like an infomercial? *Some people experience radical fissures from their normal personalities,* Gretchen imagines herself reciting. *Talk to your doctor if you're experiencing* . . . But she chews her chapped lower lip, mumbles only, "Is there anything you want me to get for you, to make you more comfortable?"

"Your brother doesn't deserve this baby," Emily says coldly.

"What?" Gretchen's body pricks upright, shocked.

"He's a phony. Don't pretend you don't know. He tosses around every excess and charm, and then takes it all back. He's glib—he's a *careless* person. You know it's true, he does it to you, too."

Gretchen's mouth fills with saliva. "Okay," she says quietly, then feels instantly guilty for having given even that much. Is *Emily* planning to sue for custody of this child, too? Somewhere in that crappy west-side house of hers, are legal papers already drawn up, just like Gretchen has? Nick is listed on the birth certificate as the father—Emily almost died giving birth: Would they have a claim? But no . . .

of course Nick *isn't* the father, and Emily has no blood shared with the baby, and they have no money and no chance. Gretchen's spiked heart rate leaves her dizzy in her chair, but she tries to breathe slow and long, calming herself. Only *she*, the biological mother, has a legitimate claim on Imogen, no matter what any papers she signed through the attorneys or the fertility clinic may say. Biological mothers have fierce precedent in the law. Still, poor Emily must have fallen in love with the baby inside her and wanted it for herself, and for a moment, Gretchen wants to be the kind of woman she has never been: the kind with scads of girlfriends she easily hugs and reassures. She wants to put her arms around sick, weeping Emily, who seems to have grown in energy through her agitation—it can't be good for her blood pressure—and assure Emily that once these hormones die down, she will probably go back to her own monkey-sphere, her own family and career, and forget about the whole lot of them—that it will all probably pass.

Except of course maybe it won't. Just like for Gretchen, maybe it won't.

And she is a bitter woman, apparently. So instead of going to Emily and holding her, she says, "You were supposed to be the hero in this story." As soon as the words are out she thinks, *Don't you mean heroine*—but no, heroines are always given the shaft; they never save anybody. "You came out of nowhere and offered my brother and his husband your womb. They trusted you, against all my better judgment. They said you weren't like the rest of us—that you were idealistic and selfless and didn't care about money. But I knew it was bullshit. Nobody's like that."

Now Emily is the one to look confused. "But . . . *you're* like that. You're the one who offered your egg. It's *your* baby."

Gretchen's hands grip the arms of her chair, as if the rollercoaster she has been poised precariously atop for nearly a year is finally going down. *Her baby.* Not Saint Emily but Saint Gretchen. Nobody has ever suggested that possibility aloud except perhaps her clueless parents, who were communally understood to be offensive and homophobic for doing so—lauding Gretchen an affront to Chad and Miguel. Nobody has ever—not once, especially not Chad—spoken aloud that this was . . . an extraordinary thing to do . . . perhaps even a crazy one, in its kindness. Nobody has ever suggested to Gretchen that her generosity, her genuine love for Chad or maybe even her own careless nature, similar to that of which Emily has accused her brother, would come at such a cost.

She lets herself look, hard, searching, into Emily's slitty blue eyes. But what she sees isn't what she carries in her mind when she thinks about Emily—Emily as a concept. This woman in the hospital bed, who gave an emergency, medically induced birth last night to a potentially unviable infant in order to save her own life, doesn't *glow* like usual. If anything, her skin has the consistency of a sauce that's cooled and hardened unappetizingly on a plate. Emily: the sort of woman who attracts charismatic assholes like Nick and keeps them; Emily, the usurper of an egg that was supposed to be Gretchen's, and with her swollen stomach began to steal not just the baby but Chad, even their parents. But that Imaginary Emily is gone. There is only this sick, depleted person in the bed—middle-aged, body swollen and slack. Only another mother of a special-needs child, who may have longed for a do-over, just like Gretchen did, and did something heroic, not for the right reasons but rather to avoid the life she had. What Gretchen would give to get back the life she had, once—how inconsequential Imogen feels, truly, compared to what Gretchen is facing with Gray. What she would do—God, what she would only do, to *go back* . . .

But if that's true, what are these papers in her handbag? If that's true, why is she prepared to put Chad, Miguel, and Imogen through what Troy has been putting her through? If she isn't doing it out of blind love, as a mother lion claiming the cub she would die for, then why is she doing it?

Imogen as payback. Imogen as consolation prize. Gretchen was the heroine of their story, even if nobody recognized it, but she has ruined all that. She has become the Wolf. She brings her hands to her face, begins to cry quietly alongside Emily, who actually sighs impatiently and says, "Oh, calm down. I didn't mean it about Chad. I like Chad. I like him better than just about anyone else I know, that's the problem."

"I do, too!" Gretchen sniffs, muffled, into her hands.

And she thinks of Chad, then, at last, though she has been trying vigilantly for the past twenty-four hours—maybe for the past few months—not to linger on him, not to remember the brother-ness of him, not to recognize his humanity at all. All at once she sees him, behind her determinedly shut eyes. Not her brother *now*, the adult Chad with waterlogged blue eyes as he traverses the halls from the NICU to waiting rooms to fill everyone in on Imogen . . . no, if anything, she has barely looked at that man, has not imprinted him on her brain, too preoccupied has she been with trying to find the courage to pull off her own mask. Instead she sees Chad as he was at four or five, when Gretchen painted his fingernails sea-foam green, and dressed him in the fairy costume she'd worn to her dance recital, and Chad—more euphoric than Gretchen ever saw him again until he began his obsession with historic-building preservation—begged their parents to let him go to school that way. Maybe it was even class picture day, Gretchen thinks, though she may be embellishing that part, and Chad, more delicate and fine-boned and ethereal than Gretchen would ever achieve, flitted around in the fairy costume yipping, *Please please please*, like an annoying little dog, until finally their mother shouted "Charles, make him stop, make him act normal!" and Charles Merry strode across the room on his impossibly adult legs and picked Chad up by one arm, yanking the fairy leotard with its attached skirt off his skinny body with one rough tug, and left Chad standing there, naked, in their kitchen. Although Gretchen saw Chad naked all the time—sometimes they even took baths together still, she abruptly recalls; they were practically babies, for God's sake—the shame of Chad, stripped of his fairy costume, rang through the cavernous kitchen like thunder, so Gretchen felt too afraid to cry. How long had Chad stood there before—what?—had he run weeping from the room like a shorn animal? What had Gretchen and her parents said to one another in his absence? She would like to believe she stood up to Charles and Elaine Merry, but get real—what would she have said? She was six years old at most. She didn't know anything about gender roles or sexual identity. She only knew she had witnessed something not meant for her eyes and had failed to come to her brother's defense the way big sisters were supposed to.

"*I'm* the one who could sue for the baby," she says preemptively, looking up from her hands and putting on the steely face her father gets sometimes. "If you make a move, even if your husband really were the father, even if my brother and Miguel were no match for you because they're gay and you were willing to put all your so-called liberal idealism aside to snatch their baby right out from under them, all I would need to do is walk into that courtroom as the biological mother, with my parents standing behind me, and we would have any judge in this country signing Imogen over to us by the end of the day. And then all I would have to do is give her right back."

Emily's eyes have grown wider. "What are you *talking* about? You'd do that to your own brother, just to prove you can? What kind of monstrous family are you?"

And most of the time, in life, things just *happen* to you, Gretchen knows. They happen and you react. You do the things you do and suddenly that's the kind of person you are, even if you never planned it that way. So, Emily is not the Wolf. Whatever she has been talking about is outside Gretchen's range of vision, is not a mirror held up to Gretchen's own plans. Gretchen says to Emily, "I didn't mean that—I don't know why I said it—I was just afraid."

"Afraid of what?" Emily asks. "Of . . . me?"

But where can Gretchen even begin in chronicling her fears? Of the loss of her son, of the loss of her daughter who is not hers to grieve, of the loss of some fragile identity she took for granted her entire life that can be so easily stripped by someone who hates her on his own endless steam. Of forty-three years of invisibility and the uncertainty she can ever manifest herself properly—that she can ever be seen. Of how alone she is in the world outside of a family she often doesn't entirely like, who don't seem to have her back. She has, if she is honest with herself, no idea if she is even the kind of mother Gray, in his luminous specialness, needs, but she knows she is a better choice than Troy so she will fight him tooth and nail—still, she could end up losing.

"I could end up with nothing," she says to Emily, and though she explains the context of none of this, surprisingly Emily nods.

"Why did you do it then? Why would someone give away her own baby?"

There isn't any one answer, though. "I love my brother," Gretchen tries. "It's not fair that he can't have what other people get to have without having to justify it in any way. He and Miguel have been together for over a decade—they're making a better go of it than I did, in my marriage. Why shouldn't they be able to have a baby, if they want one? They'll be good parents."

"They could have adopted," Emily insists. "The baby is *yours*."

"Stop," Gretchen begs, and the plaintiveness of her own voice both surprises and shames her. "Please. You have to stop saying that. She's not mine. She really isn't."

It isn't often that you have a moment when you get to choose, once and for all, *how far you will go*, how much you will let *reacting* determine who you're going to be. "You did a good thing," she says to Emily, who shrugs wearily and looks done with Gretchen, turns her face toward the door. Gretchen knows she is being signaled to leave, but instead she grasps Emily's hand for real, the way a friend would. Emily twitches with shock, but then seems to tune this out, too, falling silent, relaxing into Gretchen's touch though with her face still toward the door, eyelids shutting. Gretchen's skin is dry and cool, Emily's alarmingly slick and hot. The light outside the hospital window glows a gray-yellow amber of waning day. Now that Gretchen knows with bone-thudding clarity, a clarity that *hurts*, that she is not serving legal papers, she wants to jump up and bolt—not to the NICU where Imogen hangs in the balance, but all the way back to Winnetka, to gather Gray up in her arms and promise him, *There is no replacing you. Not with Carrot. Not with Imogen. You are my baby. You are the ship I will go down with if I have to.*

Instead, for the moment, she clutches on to the mass of secrets and desires that is Emily—who knows if she will ever even see her again? Soon she will *have* to go to the NICU and face whatever hell or beauty is about to transpire there, that belongs to her brother and Miguel, not to her. There are only so many moments of truth a person is offered in a lifetime, and it is a fleeting miracle to recognize one for what it is—a miracle so slippery and tenuous that Gretchen supposes it must be false: surely poor little Imogen will die, and all this drama and epiphany will have been for naught, and they will each be left alone with the lives they tried to change or flee by conjuring her into the world. They wanted—six adults—for this three-pound infant to save their lives, and in return they can do nothing for Imogen except to wait it out and try to do no harm.

"Do no harm," Gretchen whispers under her breath like a prayer. Emily is breathing sleep-breath, and Gretchen releases her hand onto the bed to reach into her own handbag, taking out the neatly clipped legal documents and ripping them harshly down the middle, then again. Some stray scraps glide down to the floor, and Gretchen awkwardly bends to pick them up, gathering them in her fist and placing them, neatly, under some discarded plastic and cups in Emily's trash, where no one will ever notice. Emily still doesn't look so good, and Gretchen wonders if she should ring for a nurse—get up and disappear, ending their temporary Venn diagram of overlap—but instead she merely sits there in the weak amber wash of light, keeping vigil until Emily's people return, counting the seconds until she can go back to her son.

EMILY

This time, the house is clean. Although they seemed to spend every waking moment at the hospital, except Jay, who has been with neighbors, Nick and Miles have inexplicably pulled off a spotlessness in their home that Emily has never previously beheld. They help her not to her bed, where she will fester in exile like before, but to the sectional sofa, handing her the remote control for her own discretion, rushing to make her a cup of the Ginger Peach tea she loves, that they both ordinarily claim smells like wet dog. Flowers are everywhere around the house—it resembles a funeral parlor, really. Most are from Emily's colleagues, but some are from families at Jay's school, one is from Emily's best friend from college who now lives in Baltimore, and a few are from couples she and Nick used to socialize with regularly, before Jay was born—people Emily would have figured had long forgotten about them. Emily doesn't like the overwhelming smell of the collective bouquets, but she is stunned—moved, but mainly *shocked*—that so many people . . . give a shit that she was in the hospital, that she had a "close call." She is perplexed, honestly, how so many people even knew.

Miles is snapping photos of her with his iPhone, no makeup, her hair in some three-days-in-the-hospital nest, and suddenly Emily realizes: social media. She is not on Facebook—not as a vice principal, wherein nothing she could possibly post would seem professional enough unless she were updating her "status" with cutting-edge curriculum and lectures about upstanding behavior. But everyone else in the world seems to have joined the craze—certainly her son, and even Nick, who claims he uses it to "network" professionally, though Emily suspects he uses it to keep tabs on old girlfriends.

He also, perhaps . . . she is not sure what to feel about this (flattered? violated?) . . . uses it to tell the world that his wife has had a medical crisis. Did he mention on Facebook that she "had a baby" that isn't theirs, Emily wonders—though of course all her colleagues already know this, seeing her as they do every day. Miles, who is normally so secretive about his phone that if Emily so much as lifts it up to dust a table, he accuses her of leading a spy ring against his top-secret teenage life, sits next to her on the couch, scrolling down the sixty or seventy people who have wished her well on Miles's profile page, offering "prayers" and "white light" and "love" and heart emojis.

Who *are* all these people? Some she knows—without knowing they were "friends" with her son. Friends of the family who must mean something to Miles, if he has let them into his online domain. Others, Emily has never heard of, but Miles seems not to mind her reading their messages, too. *She must be a great lady if she has a son like you!* someone named Caitlin writes. *Hoping your kick-ass mom makes a full recovery, brother,* writes a long-haired kid named Tomer. Tomer is her son's "brother"? Where has Emily been?

Jay sits so close to her it hurts her tender body, and she cringes. He keeps putting his head on her overripe breasts, which are bound so they will dry up more quickly, from the child she is not going to nurse. From the child who is probably not going to *be* . . . Imogen in the NICU, not breathing normally, no corners turned beyond the point when they should have been. Miguel and Chad are still there with her round the clock, Gretchen still wandering the corridors, too, the Guerra-Merry clan an ensemble group of Penelopes, waiting attentively for a boat, a love, a hope that will probably never arrive. They are all there, even Miguel's mother, so much older than in Emily's memory that it makes *her* feel ancient—she is roughly the age, now, that Miguel's mother was when they knew one another in 1985, 1986. There they all are, standing vigil, Imogen's extended clan, but Emily . . . Emily was pronounced "out of the woods" and sent home.

"Careful with your mother," Nick tells Jay. "Her body is sore right now. You can hug her all you want soon."

"It's okay," Emily says, and Jay looks perplexed between her and his father, then settles back firmly against Emily. She doesn't want him there, but she doesn't want him to *leave*, either. It's unclear what she wants, what she feels. It's like being at her own funeral—fascinating, giddy—but at the same time an incredible letdown. *It's all over now.* She did all that, for *what*? The baby probably won't live; nothing in the fabric of the world has changed. She wasted so much of her family's time, told herself so many stories that were false, and now here she is again, the house cleaner for the moment, but of course that won't last—nothing will last. Here she is again.

Lina wasn't at the hospital. Not once, that Emily knows of. She even asked Nick at one point—she asked Gretchen, since Gretchen insisted on visiting her periodically for reasons utterly mysterious. But no, everyone said (her husband with an air of false casualness): no Lina.

How is it possible that people are so stupid?

If the thieving bitch had shown up, Emily might have concluded that she herself had miscalculated. There would be Lina, visiting her distraught brother, not conscious of or worried about Nick's or Emily's presence. It's via her conspicuous *absence* during a crisis every other Guerra and Merry in the Chicago area has converged for, that Lina might as well have hung a banner over the doorway of the NICU proclaiming, *I am fucking your husband and have the decency not to show my face while you're sick.* There, it is out in the open, confirmed—in Emily's mind, at least. Nick, of course, is clueless.

And what is Emily supposed to do with all this, now? Now that the surrogacy is over, a failed experiment? Now that Chad and Miguel are likely gone, at least in any significant way, from her life? Now that Nick is what she's left with, puttering around her acting solicitous as a suitor—is she supposed to confront and divorce him, go on Match.com and meet some other troublesome man? Live alone? Trust, as wives have done throughout history, that this is all nonsense, just sex, and that her husband—an intelligent man, after all; she will give him that—isn't planning to leave her for an unemployed stripper, and therefore hold her tongue? These are problems for another day. Emily's body feels all wrong—she feels all wrong *in* her body. She wishes they had kept her in the hospital, where she had some privacy and calm and people tended to her without expecting anything in return. She has to go back to her regular life now, and she isn't ready—the whole idea had been to leave her regular life behind, but that was only ever some silly idea her mother would have clicked her tongue and lit a cigarette below rolling eyes and chided Emily for believing.

Is she supposed to be torn up, texting Chad every fifteen minutes, frantic about Imogen? Is she a bad person because that already feels so far, far away, like someone else's ill-conceived notion? If she could fast-forward ahead six months, have her body back, have some semblance of her equilibrium back, Emily would.

She couldn't go through with it. In the end, she couldn't go through with her plan. Every single day she woke up, that week after Chad spurned her and sent her home, intending to telephone the doctor, to call it all off, but she never did. Always, she came up with something pressing she needed to do that day (even though she was supposed to be doing all of nothing); always, she thought *tomorrow* sounded better. She waited too long—or is that even the truth? Maybe she was never going to make the call. Maybe she would have waited all the way through the thirty-seventh week, when the fetus was unquestionably viable, and gone in meekly to do the duty she'd signed on to do. She was on bed rest, festering around her unsatisfactory house, with nothing better to occupy her time, yet failed, day after day, to call the game, to end it. Her eyes were bigger than her stomach in terms of her own capacity to lash out, though the fantasy—taking entitled Chad and Miguel's bubblegum-baby fantasy away from them—continued to give her pleasure in those days, to help her bored-stiff hours pass. In the final analysis, however, she lacked the guts, the agency, the malice to put it to action . . . she lacked *something.*

She didn't sacrifice the baby on the pyre of her hurt feelings. Isn't that enough? But . . . enough for *what*?

She waited two weeks, when she barely meant to wait one. She had a seizure, then another at the hospital, and her kidneys were acting up and it was a whole passion play Emily spent drugged up enough to barely remember most of it, but never drugged up enough that it stopped the splitting pain inside her head. She "almost died," everyone kept claiming. And the absurdity of it all was that that option had seemed—maybe it was the drugs talking, though Emily doesn't feel far on the other side of that veil even now—like not such a bad thing, either: that maybe she would just drift away, and be done. In the hospital, blinding white lights everywhere as she lay on her back on stretchers, on tables, noise and doctors in blue paper shower caps hovering above her, it had seemed an acceptable thing to just close her eyes and not open them again—to be free of her own angry heart. Nobody would miss her.

Except, apparently, people had. Her lazy men have cleaned the house; her youngest son clings to her like a rhesus monkey to a plush, comforting, false mother who gives no food and will starve it out. Apparently she *has* been missed, by strangers on Facebook and neighbors who have taken Jay and delivered food and parents and colleagues and students at her school. Apparently there is an

Emily-shaped hole in the world that she leaves in her wake, and here she is again, expected to fill it.

"It's so good to be home," she says to the three male faces surrounding her, because that is what people are supposed to say, whether or not it is true.

They beam back at her, all three. Their relief that she is not dead comes off of them in waves, like steam from a sweltering sidewalk. What does she mean to them, these three people? Is she capable of giving them what they need? Does she *want* to anymore?

Save the baby, she told the doctors desperately, in her quasi-suicidal delirium. *Don't worry about me, save the baby.* But she woke up anyway, she and Imogen both alive, and outside of the closed box of Emily's body it was no longer in her control whether Imogen stay that way. Surprise.

She is glad not to be dead. Clearly, that much is true. Of course. *Obviously*, she is glad not to be dead. That was madness—hormones, her compromised blood pressure and various obscure organs, *something.* She is not Anna Karenina. She is not some crazy bitch in a French film from the nineties, when all they ever did was off themselves in the end. She is a *mother*—an entire school depends on her—and here is Nick, too, still hovering, not going anywhere no matter what he's up to when she's not around. He is nothing to live and die over anyway. That's just something people like to think—that romantic love could matter *so* much. Of course she is thrilled to be alive, to have it all behind her. She is still . . . not old, even if she is no longer young. If she is dissatisfied with her life, she is supposed to just change it, right? That is what people are supposed to do; that is the American Dream. Emily has done it before. She is a master of reinvention, or *was*, before motherhood, before economic responsibilities. Maybe this is it for her, then—but would that be so bad? People have worse lives! Most of her students' families have worse lives. What was she so unhappy about, anyway? Everything is fine.

"Please," she says to Jay, "enough now. Mommy needs a little space and air."

And nobody looks at her twice. It is her *right*, it seems, to say that, even if it *feels* wrong.

Everything is all right. Even if it all feels wrong.

That night, Emily rolls onto her side, spooning Nick, her hand grazing his cock, and murmurs "Nicky" into the back of his neck. She is in no condition, physically, to have intercourse yet, and she looks, she knows, far from her best—still, if she is going to *be here*, if she is going to *do this*, it feels as though she must offer him something: a gesture, a return.

"But you're sick," Nick protests. "You just got out of hospital."

"I'm fine," she soothes, despite the pain in her head that has been her constant companion now since before the preeclampsia diagnosis, that has not faded even as the doctors checked all their machines and pronounced her good to go. "I'm not building a house with my bare hands, I'm giving a hand job."

He half-laughs softly. "Okay. Okay, if you think . . . if you want."

They have not been sexual since before she was inseminated. What at first seemed a mutual nervous reverence for "someone else's fetus" potentially getting knocked around soon grew into an uneasy stalemate: for the first time, Emily allowed herself to behave toward Nick with as much disinterest and disdain as had been slowly festering, but unspoken, for years, and Nick—Nick whose sex drive had always been consistent—gave no complaint or coercion about her closed candy store, it growing increasingly obvious that he must be getting it elsewhere. *But he didn't leave*. It has been nearly a year since Emily first began to suspect his affair with Lina, and here he still is, cleaning her house, caring for her sons, so he must not *want* to go. Emily isn't sure *she* wants to stay—maybe?—but it seems imperative to keep her options open, and sex is part of that imperative, part of *this*, here, remaining a viable, livable option.

As someone who grew up pretty and female in America, she has always understood and experienced her body, even as it changed and morphed over the years, as a reward of sorts: a gift. She has internalized a narrative in which women, as a matter of course, control the flow of sex in the world, except in aberrant instances of force, and from this position it has been her prerogative to allow or deny Nick admission, and Nick's position to be grateful or frustrated in turn. This is how the world works, from everything Emily has ever known and seen. If you screw the landlord, he will give you a discount on the rent—Emily learned these truths from her mother, early on, and even having married a man who is arguably more attractive for his gender than she is for hers cannot alter certain immutable biological truths.

Nick's cock, however, will not conform to her narrative—will not obey. It curls, soft and shrunken, in her hand, humiliating them both: a rebuke.

Tears clog Emily's throat, though she is not even sure she *wants* him. Their sex since Jay was born has been merely perfunctory, whereas Nick used to be creative; dispassionate where he used to be so intense it sometimes made her nervous. She has told herself that this is just what happens after some fifteen years of marriage. Still, the reliability of Nick's cock has always been like Old Faithful, whether or not the sex that ensued was anything to shake the rafters. Emily is not sure—she can't recall (though if it *had* ever happened she's sure she would recall it) this happening to her in her entire life, not only with Nick but with *anyone.*

"I don't know what's the matter with me," Nick says into the darkness. "I've been so worried for days, and I've had a bit more than usual to drink."

It's not true exactly. He had three beers earlier, yes, but while he's no hard-drinking Irishman cliché, that's hardly aberrant.

"Don't worry," Emily says, forcing her voice to sound cheerful. "I'll blow you, just relax."

He used to tease her about these little Chicago dictions of hers—*I'll blow you*—he found her white-trash ways charming. He used to say things like, *If the other teachers could hear you talking this way, but they can't, only I know the Emily from the hood.* He *likes* girls from the hood, she suddenly, disturbingly remembers—she was one once—she was not so different from Lina, only with a different skin tone. She was not always a vice principal and mother of two; she grew up worse off than Lina and Miguel did with their mother's second husband buying them a sweet little house in a safe neighborhood without gangs and roaches—and maybe Nick liked her better back then. Emily can't shake these thoughts, her own graceless slurping pounding in her ears, the repetitive, unvaried bobbing of her head striking her as rote and bloodless. His cock isn't exactly recoiling but it's not standing at rapt attention, either, noncommittal. She pulls back, her chin wet from her own spit in the darkness. "Nicky?" He used to love it when she called him this in bed, but it's been years and the double-hitter of the endearment tonight feels self-conscious and cloying from her lips. "What's wrong?" she dares, when really she doesn't want to dare—she has been *right* all this time, not to dare. "Are you mad at me? About . . . all of it? About Imogen?"

"Imogen?" He sits up like he's overcome with shock, but she thinks he probably just is trying to remove his dick from her proximity. "What . . . why would I be *angry* about Imogen?"

"I know you regret our ever having done it," she says. "I know it's been a huge inconvenience to you. I know I've been . . . preoccupied and sick and no help around the house. I know I've been . . . different."

"Honestly, Em, I don't even know what you're on about, why you're saying this. I don't feel those things in the slightest. You couldn't help getting ill. You were pregnant—of *course* you were preoccupied. I'm . . . confused."

"Things just haven't been the same between us," she says, voice faltering. But she isn't sure what *the same* means anymore, in this context. The same as seven years ago, before Jay? The same as a year and a half ago, before he knew Lina? The same as fifteen years ago, when they were only sleeping together with gleeful abandon and she had not yet gotten accidentally knocked up? She hates the timidity of her voice, the begging of him to want her. Where is the girl who dropped her recent abortion on the table between them like a ticking bomb on their second date and dared him to flinch? How did they grow into these awkward people whose inner lives feel sealed in separate vaults? "Since I agreed to the surrogacy," she finishes, because she needs the time period she's talking about to be finite, short. She can't face the excavation that ambiguity might invite.

"That's ridiculous, Em. I agreed to it, too! We made the decision together. You're imagining all this . . . I had no idea, honestly—I don't know what to say."

"But . . ." she tries. "But."

If he's going to deny it all—if he's going to refuse to blame it on the surrogacy, then how will they explain it all to themselves? She is giving him an out—she is giving him a way to avoid saying, *I've been shagging a younger woman and that's why I've pulled away*—but he refuses to take it. What story will they tell themselves about how their marriage has arrived at this pitiable condition, if he won't accept the one she is handing him like an apple, so easy to bite from then toss behind them and move on?

"Have you ever wondered," he begins, his tone as painfully careful as hers, "why we agreed to it? I mean . . . I don't regret it, really, that's not what I mean. I swear to you I don't feel the things you just said. But why *would* we have done it, you know? Am I making any sense? It seems . . . like we must have been raving fucking mad. We barely knew them."

"I knew Miguel." She doesn't counter, *We needed the money.* She doesn't explain, *It seemed a ticket out.* None of those things ever made sense to Nick, and wouldn't tonight especially.

"You knew some guy called *Mike*, in high school, Em. You hadn't seen him in twenty years. You hadn't even known he was gay, for Chrissakes—you didn't know anything about him. What were we thinking?"

She emits a weak laugh. "You're right, I guess. It was the sort of people we wanted to be—people who would do something like that. It was . . . what we used to talk about, when we were young . . . we wanted to be part of something larger, to do something good."

"We were looking for something," he concurs. "We were looking to feel something that was lost."

"Lost? I wouldn't say lost." It is all she can possibly risk, and she decides, here in the aftermath of her alleged almost death, to risk it. "I'd say we—I—wanted to feel something I'd maybe *never* felt."

"But what?" He touches her face, a tenderness she can't recall the last time he offered. "What did you want to feel?"

"I don't know, Nick. I don't know. Maybe I just felt like my body always betrayed us—I got pregnant too soon, and then somehow I'd made Jay sick . . . like I was broken, and this was a chance to fix myself and do something right. Maybe I just wanted to feel like I mattered."

"But Jay isn't broken—you didn't *cause* any—"

"You don't think I hate myself for feeling that way? But *feelings* aren't always something that can be controlled."

"I know, I know—it's just . . . you already mattered to the boys—you mattered to everyone in an entire school—you mattered to *me*."

"It's not something I can explain rationally. You *asked*."

He falls into a familiar, taciturn silence. This is where he goes when he isn't sure what to do with her—when she's said something he doesn't know how to easily tamp down with his charm. Why couldn't he have *pretended* to understand precisely what she meant, even if he didn't—even if it scared him? He should know that *marriage* is partially acting, too, just like he likes to say about parenting. He should *act like* someone who doesn't leave a gaping part of her empty, waiting to thrash out in ways that have terrified her lately—but who can ever be that, fully, to another person? How could he fill every gap in Emily, every place beyond language and her own darkest impulses? No one can do that for anyone. No one.

And then, inexplicably, Nick's erection is strong, visible in the street-lit room, even though Emily is on the other side of the bed. He opens his arms to her, whispers, "If you still want to . . ." Moves toward her in that languid, almost feminine way of his and kisses her long on the mouth, deeper than since she can remember, refusing to come up for air until she laughingly turns her face away, gasping a little. Her head is still pounding; she can't remember a time anymore when her head didn't hurt; she can't remember a time anymore when loving her husband and trusting his love seemed simple. She goes down on him, though it is honestly the last thing on earth she wants to do now, grateful only that it's not real sex, where she has to worry that Miles would hear the bedsprings and be repulsed—why, really, why is it a *necessity* that sex continue on and on this way, beyond the point when two people can possibly see each other in those terms anymore? Why is it part of the intricate artifice of life that, all combined, has worn her down to the bone? Nick comes, empties emptiness into Emily's mouth, but silently, whereas she used to have to beg him to quiet down, *The boys, they'll hear us!* Nothing now but the pounding of her head, the illusory satisfaction that she managed to make a man's penis rise and shoot something out its end—a task even easier, more commonplace, than *having a baby*, yet she can't seem to manage either thing—she can't seem to manage anything properly anymore.

She rests her head on Nick's chest obligatorily. The rapid pulse of her own heartbeat against her cheek disquiets her. It is too fast; her head is too loud.

"Nick. I don't feel so good."

He strokes her hair. "You've been through a lot."

"No . . ." She means to say more, but can't, the words aren't coming. She tries to move her right arm, slung over his body, but nothing is *happening*, it's like when they slide the epidural needle into your spine and suddenly your body is gone—you can't even feel yourself breathe. What comes from her mouth is a guttural sound, and then there is Nick, at attention, kneeling over her, his face over her, then dark, in, out, where, how? She is . . . somewhere. Screaming that cannot belong to her. The world is an accordion, contracting and expanding, her eyes and brain with it.

"Emily? Em, baby, stay with me, stay with me now."

"Mommy! Daddy, what's wrong with her?"

Nothing's wrong, my little bird. It's all right, put your head on my chest. I just needed a bit of air, that's all.

"Ma'm?" It's someone else's face, someone not of their Home. "Emily? Emily, how many fingers am I holding up here?" But that is impossible since she is in her bed, since no time has passed. "Emily, can you squeeze my hand?"

She is squeezing as tight as she can.

"Can you try squeezing my fingers with your right hand?"

"Look at you, so hoity-toity," her mother drawled, cigarette burning too close to her fingers, long fingernails filed to nearly a point. "Since you have contempt for everything I do and say, what is it that makes you think you're too good for me and your shit doesn't stink?"

Where is the bed? She was in the bed, and Nick was there, Nick has always been there. Flawed, maddening, hers to hold cheaply. After all these years they are almost like brother and sister, and isn't that what siblings are entitled to: to take one another for granted—to not have to be careful? How did they become so careful?

I want to show everything to you, and have you love me anyway. You were supposed to be the one who knew where all the bodies were buried. How could you make it seem, Nick, like I was never, never enough to hold you in place? Take me back to bed, make this stop, stop this.

But of course, she never showed him everything. She never showed him much of anything at all.

"What do you even want, Emily?" her mother demanded. "Money? Fame? With a teaching degree? Who are you kidding? Those who can't do, teach."

I just wanted a normal life. I just wanted a family, and respectability, and love. But that can't be true, because she has those things and the world has felt cavernous and lacking in oxygen anyway.

"I'm tired of leaving," Nick, so impossibly young, promised, gripping her hand. "I want a home. You'll see."

"She can't squeeze my hand," the strange voice says, even though Emily *is* doing it, even though the stranger lies.

"Mom? Mom, we're right here, we love you, we're right here, we're coming in the ambulance with you."

You're not coming with me.

"Mommy, stop it! Stop it now, be regular!"

"Please, Miles, please take your brother. Em—Em, can you look at me?"

Where is the bed? Why can't she see through her eyes? Where are her eyes?

Save the baby, Emily thinks, but no, that's already done. That happened in some long-ago time. That's not what she meant to say anyway. That baby was not her People. *Save me*, she thinks, *I meant save me.*

Save me.

ACT IV

STRONG'S LANDING

WHEN I BETRAYED, I LOVED CHAOS,
LOVED MY CRAZED VERSION OF SANE.
WHEN I WAS BETRAYED, I LOVED FIDELITY,
HOME. I LOVE MORE CAREFULLY NOW.

—STEPHEN DUNN

Nick has been bracing himself for the Villa Moderne sign since Traverse City, but when he rolls their SUV right by it without fanfare, too quickly to even scan for the gliders he and Lina once sat on, his stomach still drops like he has stepped into an empty elevator chute by mistake and is falling down, down. Miles has his headphones on; he hasn't spoken during the seven-hour drive except to occasionally tell Jay to shut up. Nick talks to Emily privately about this: how to handle Miles's newfound rudeness to his brother, whom he used to coddle and baby and defend. *It's healthy*, he's convinced himself at last. Jay is treated as fragile by enough people. They need brotherly strife. It's normal. So Nick holds his tongue. The myriad manifestations of Miles's anger seem part of an intricate web of things he cannot possibly explain, that might merely be part of his imagination anyway, just like he can imagine his body next to Lina's, casually draped over those hard wooden rockers outside the rooms at Villa Moderne, smoking cigarettes they'd torn the filters off of, her tiny leg slung over his, nearly weightless but possessing a kind of tingling heat from within. Miles does not ask once, in seven hours, to use the toilet. His seventeen-year-old son is a camel. A mute camel. His taste in music is equally problematic. His son mocks Wilco, says they are "too old to tour." His beautiful son, whose face could launch ships, is full of livid, wordless rage. It is age appropriate. It is generationally appropriate, having grown up in an era of multiple wars, of Occupy Wall Street. It is gender appropriate: another angry young man. It is situationally appropriate. Who can presume the things for which Nick may or may not be to blame?

This ferry used to seem like magic to him, when Lina rode it out alone in the cold, that giant hooded coat covering her like she'd been swallowed by an animal. He would sit inside the chilly motel and text her things, stupid things, *I'm imagining you now like that famous shot in* French Lieutenant's Woman, *with your hair blowing across your face*, romantic nonsense. The weather is beautiful in June, and he could have a beer and sit out on the deck while Jay tools around exploring and Miles covertly checks out the local girls from behind his Malcolm X shades; it could be that sort of shimmery summer day, but Nick doesn't know how to give that present to himself, so instead they sit indoors, where the loudness of the other passengers ricochets off the ceilings and walls like the inside of a fishbowl, and they eat shit from the vending machines and he feels seasick, yet vaguely happy somehow, to have ruined their ferry ride. To have allowed the moment just enough promise not to bring down his whole house of cards, but to have denied himself some fundamental poetry or kismet that would feel like healing. He doesn't want to heal. Except, of course, he does. The island is visible in the distance now. If he were some nihilist, he wouldn't be here. This is a loop that never stops. If he were a braver man; if he were more selfless; if he were a hedonist: *if if.* He can play the game with himself endlessly.

"There they are!" Jay shouts, pointing at the dock. On the dock, Miguel and Chad wave back, Chad with considerable more enthusiasm, which makes Nick laugh. At first he doesn't *see* Imogen, but then her fathers pull her up, one holding each arm the way Nick and Emily used to do to Miles—never Jay—a three-year-old suspended in midair, her yellow and blue sundress billowing in the wind. Imogen Strong Merry-Guerra: a Provençal sunbeam.

"What," Miles says finally, nearly hissing at his father, "am I supposed to do here for a whole week?"

"You're new blood," Nick promises—he knows this part well—"the girls will take care of that for you. Just go where they can see you."

Miles rolls his eyes. Then, suddenly, his voice pitching almost like it used to when they were friends: "Can I fake an Irish accent?"

This is their third summer at Strong's Landing.

The year the baby was born, Miguel went to Beaver Island alone to settle the sale, but at that time, of course, Nick knew nothing of it. That was his Summer of Chaos.

The world burnt to the ground that summer. He didn't care about Isabel's house, or even about Imogen, as the infant slowly—then with herculean strides—began to defy the doctors' every expectation, her lungs growing and functioning normally, her appetite insatiable. Miguel's and Chad's lives revolved around feeding their daughter with a dropper, around each gained ounce of weight and hope, but that might as well have been happening in China for all the attention Nick paid it. His eldest son was barely communicating, seemed coiled inside himself perpetually ready to strike, while Jay's health suffered—mild setbacks, ultimately, but Nick fixated on them to avoid facing Jay's emotional free fall. Despite his braces, his odd gait, his undersized skinniness, Jay had never been much teased at school—he possessed, Emily often said, Nick's "charisma," and for the most part had been taken in by his peers, usually as an equal if sometimes in the condescending manner of a mascot. That summer, however, Jay grew clingy as a toddler, had night terrors, and when school began Nick knew in the deep marrow of himself that his son was entering the lion's den of childhood poised differently now: a target. That horrible summer extended into a fall of fights, of visits to the principal's office, of discussions of "special schools." Nick took Jay to a therapist, thought he'd sit in the waiting room reading, stewing, hating himself, while someone else patched up his son—but in the end he was called in, too, every other week, until some numb peace was forged. Jay returned to his own bed at nights; the school stopped calling; birthday party invitations again began to arrive.

And Lina? As summer wore on, Nick was unclear whether anyone else *realized* that she had evaporated—gone up in smoke. Where *was* she? Even Miguel, who probably considered Lina his closest confidante, was so preoccupied, and how often did he and Lina really talk anyway? From the night of Imogen's birth on, Lina's mobile number went straight to voicemail until voicemail was full; soon the number was disconnected altogether. She didn't answer Nick's emails. Was she just avoiding *him*, or was something bigger . . . wrong? Did she think she was torturing him emotionally "for his own good"—some misguided notion of simplifying his already enormously complex situation by removing herself from the equation? Where was she *living*? With one angry and one traumatized son, mounting bills, and a new play to finish, Nick wasn't seeing Miguel—was barely leaving the house—and had no one to ask.

He and Lina had not, since before Imogen's conception, gone more than nine hours without contact. It was like there had been a horrifying global disaster and he was quarantined. Phones and computers looked hostile, broken, if they didn't lead to her. They were *best friends*. Best friends first, before everything else, above any lover's drama—she would never do this to him, would never make a unilateral decision to remove herself at the worst juncture of his life, not allowing him to so much as weigh in. He would not consent to it. Except, of course, his consent had not been sought. Lina had simply *done* it, the thing of which he believed her incapable. His life—each expanding day and week without her—was proof of her capability.

When Imogen turned three months old, her dads brought her by, unbidden, uninvited. They had some preposterous bow around her peach-fuzz head, and she looked five times the size of the misshapen walnut she'd been in NICU. Miles seemed to resent the child's presence, could barely bring himself to buck his chin in a nod at Miguel and Chad before sequestering in his room, but Jay was entranced. Nick waited, sick to his stomach, for Jay to lose interest and leave, but only when Jay squirmed enough that Nick was able to chase him off to the toilet could he ask Miguel, "How's your sister doing—I haven't heard from her in ages?" Miguel quipped, with only cursory interest, "Oh, that crazy *flaca* left town and we didn't even know she'd gone! She dumped poor Bebe and moved out."

By Halloween, Nick had dropped thirty pounds. What few friends he managed to see urged, "You need to take care of yourself, man, for the boys." They said things about "self-care" that made him murderous with sarcasm, but yes, *for the boys' sake*, for the sake of what community they had left, he held his tongue, thanked people for their help. He'd always considered himself a nurturing person—the gentle one, between himself and Em—still, for months he ordered pizza almost every night in an effort to keep his sons alive, incapable of cooking, of eating, of sleeping. He drank to excess, as though this were a way to keep vigil to either Emily, whose mother had been a vitriolic drunk, or Lina, who'd exerted massive will every single day to stay clean and sober. Paradoxically, though, a blanket of oblivion made him feel connected to them both, like fucking an ex's toxic best friend. His behavior was a sick, desperate homage that manifested as an affront—he was a specter in his own life.

Most nights, he passed out on the basement couch. Other evenings, he went for long walks—he never smoked in the house, still, even though he could now—and talked to Emily inside his head, a few times aloud, wondering if he'd cracked. *What should we do about Jay, Em, should I put him in private school—how will we afford it?* And, *Do you think Miles blames me, Em? Do you think he knows?* He caught himself asking her, *Did you see Jay at school today, did you watch over him for me?* and after that he wouldn't go on his Emily walks anymore, smoked on the porch like in times past. He wasn't willing to go down the rabbit hole of magical thinking that wholly: his dead wife their personal guardian angel, causing a bully to trip over a shoelace en route to Jay, capable of fixing their lives. Emily was gone. She couldn't help anyone. The dead don't care.

Meanwhile, every time his cell phone rang or beeped, he nearly threw up in anticipation.

It would never again be Emily—he knew that much. Her voice was beyond him.

It was never Lina, either.

Being at Strong's Landing always feels to Nick like he is in some Ann Beattie story. Pretty-but-faded middle-aged people engaging in what Lina would call "quaint WASP activities" like softball in the backyard, the smell of barbecued meat wafting in the air. Miguel, slightly paunchy now though his hair-thinning has plateaued, presides over the grill. Gretchen, who has lost the weight Miguel gained, hurls pitches too good for Chad, Gray, or Jay to hit, so mostly it is Nick, and Gretchen's bohunky boyfriend Ron, dashing around the makeshift bases, trying not to fall over toddling Imogen. Ron works with Dead Isabel's widower, who took the profits on the sale of the house and got married to someone else, but "never comes over when we're here," Chad complains. His new wife has a son Gray's age, and she and Eddie have a baby just a little younger than Imogen, "but we never see him. This island is the size of Wicker Park, but so help me I think he avoids us. We barely even run into him at the grocery store—it's like he has spies out telling him when we've left the house so he can go into lockdown."

"I have no idea why you're complaining," Miguel says from the grill. "Like we were best friends when he and Isabel were married?"

"The kids are practically cousins!" Chad protests.

"Our kid has absolutely none of Eddie's genetics," Miguel corrects him. "They are nothing like cousins. They're more like descendants from prisoners in the same POW camp."

"I thought we bought this place because it was so important to Isabel," Chad says, and Nick wishes they would keep their marital bickering to their room at night—he can't bear anymore the way he and Emily no doubt used to sound, and what this pecking does or doesn't mean about a marriage. "I thought the whole idea was to preserve Strong's Landing as a place for family, in a way Isabel wouldn't have allowed, and try to unify and come together here. Heal old wounds."

Miguel shakes his head, like Chad is reciting from a script written in a language Chad doesn't understand. "Look around you," he says quietly. "What do you think we're *doing*? What the hell does Eddie have to do with any of that?"

They talk this way in front of Ron, who drinks his beer jovially, not contributing. Every so often, Ron makes his way over to Gretchen and kisses her full on the mouth, or slings an arm around her the way Nick imagines football stars at American high schools do with their cheerleader girlfriends, and Gretchen, who looks her age more than the others, giggles like a schoolgirl. Their passion is clumsy, a little embarrassing, but that doesn't mean it isn't enviable just the same. It makes Nick think of Lina, though it has nothing in common with the way they were together; though Lina would probably not even consent to this Kennedys-on-the-lawn jocularity. If she were here, they would be somewhere else: in a dark bar while she nursed a soda water and covertly kissed Nick's Jameson mouth; riding bikes through early-evening pockets of mosquitos on their way to the weird little airstrip restaurant she loved; lying together on a blanket on the beach reading; smoking on the back-porch rockers, ignoring everyone else. But Lina isn't here.

"I think Gretchen's going to *stay*," Miguel mumbles low when Nick makes his way over to the grill. He flips the last of the burgers onto a plate, then ambles a little toward the apple orchard near the woods, cigarettes extracted, so Nick follows, the *thwacks* of the softball popping as they walk, no one keeping score anymore. "This whole last year she talked to Ron on the phone every night. He wants to marry her. He's good with Gray."

"Isn't her ex some sort of psychopath?" Nick asks. "Would he go along with her taking the kid out of state?"

"Well." Miguel shrugs. "The thing you need to understand is that Chad and I have been paying that asshat off for the past three years. Gretchen thinks Troy must've gotten Kumbaya therapy or something, because he was on the warpath about custody, and then he suddenly backed off. Suddenly he started agreeing to whatever Gretchen said about Gray—pretty soon, he was virtually gone. All the Merrys think we were crazy to flip Termite Mansion like that, to sell so fast after we'd put so much work into it, but the profit from that house—and about twenty other properties of Chad's, plus my bonus from my last year of work—pretty much all that went into the Bribing Troy Fund."

"Holy shit," Nick says. "That's beyond generous, man, to do that for Gretchen."

Miguel clears his throat. "Not really. She was at a breaking point. She was just coming to terms about Gray's Asperger's, and he wasn't doing so hot, with the custody battle and all. I don't know whether Troy's chances of getting Gray were realistically ever very high, but he seemed to be in it . . . for him it was a vicious blood sport. He didn't care if he won, he just wanted to torment Gretchen. I mean, desperate people do desperate things. If Gretchen lost Gray, or even *feared* she might, she could have started looking for some kind of shared custody of Imogen. Or more. We paid that piece of shit to back off so we didn't end up in court over our own daughter. Simple."

"But Gretchen's so involved with Imogen now," Nick says, perplexed. "She and Gray live out here all summer with you guys. Practically every time we see you in Chicago, they're around."

"Exactly," Miguel concurs. "Gretchen is a super-involved *aunt.* Gray and Imogen are *almost* like siblings. Chad and I are very welcoming. And the terms are dictated by . . . magnanimity, not the courts." Miguel leans against a tree, and Nick thinks of how, the first few times they met, Miguel always looked on the verge of crawling out of his own skin with discomfort—how now there is something fluid and relaxed about him that's new, even with his bulkier form. "It's easy to love someone who gave you an egg to have your daughter," he says, blowing smoke like some noir Humphrey Bogart in a borderline-Hawaiian shirt. "It's impossible to love someone who's tried to take your daughter away. Like I said, simple."

Nick takes a long swig of his IPA. He likes Miguel—has always liked him, but more so now, as the closest person to Lina, the most palpable, breathing reminder of her. He doesn't want to think of her beloved brother as some Machiavellian weirdo. Miguel has a degree in actuarial mathematics; he used to be an options trader. Maybe people look like equations to him. Probabilities. Variables. Playing the odds.

"But you don't tell Gretchen what you did?"

"It wouldn't do for her to feel . . . manipulated."

"What if Troy tells her?"

"Then we only kept quiet because we didn't want to damage her pride. We were only trying to help her and Gray. Which, of course, happens to be true."

Nick looks back over the tall grass, where Ron is helping awkward, brilliant little Gray hold the bat properly. How will a kid like that survive on Beaver Island, if his mother moves him here? Nick knows from his own Universe of Jay that the city offers "different" kids a certain anonymity, a certain weirdo-among-many-weirdos ease that small-town life—like the life *he* had as a boy—doesn't. There are no Northwestern University computer classes for gifted eight-year-olds on Beaver Island. Jay says Gray already creates his own computer games. Nick knows he goes to some swanky private school, sees various "specialists." He feels like taking Gretchen aside and saying, *Hey, can't the carpenter move to Chicago? You're the one with the child—don't sabotage your son for some guy.* But who is *he* to talk? Maybe the simplicity of life here would be the best thing for Gray anyway—for any kid.

What does Nick know about anything?

Miguel and Chad have never apologized. They never made their amends. They never said, *What we asked was too much to ask of another person, we miscalculated. And because of that you lost your wife.* They never said, *We felt so blinded by the desire to have what other people are permitted to have that we didn't really consider anyone else.* They have never said, *We wouldn't do for you what Emily did for us, so we don't know why we felt entitled to it.* But what does it matter that they have never said these things? He and Emily were consenting adults. Both mistakes and flagrant acts of generosity were made all around, and now a little girl is alive and adored. *History is written by the victors.*

Miguel drops his cigarette into a coffee tin at the base of a tree. Nick scans the orchard; almost all the trees closest to the house have them! He imagines Miguel, over the past four summers, saving every coffee container, walking it out to a new tree, creating some kind of performance-art statement about his own life in cigarette butts, stabbed out alone under blue-domed skies and relentlessly starry nights. The tins strike Nick as heartbreaking—tragic even—though Miguel seems, for *him* at least, to be a happy man.

"Your hair," Miguel says to Nick, heading back to the rest of the group. "You're looking awfully . . . adult."

Nick runs his fingers through his newly shorn hair. He did it on a whim, but since, he's found himself less conspicuous in the world, almost like he is able to wander through walls without being spotted: an invisible man. He'd never realized how glaringly *visible* he was, until some of the visibility was gone: the haircut, maybe age, too. He says to Miguel, "Mr. DeMille, I was ready to end my fucking close-up," and Miguel snorts indelicately and says, "Amen." They walk in silence for a moment, back to the picnic table, where people have started eating. Nick's veggie burger is waiting, because who the hell else would want it?

"I'm making sure we save a couple for Miles," Gretchen says when he sits down next to her.

"Great," Nick says, though surely Miles doesn't care. He is out somewhere on the island, meeting people, making his own shimmery memories, filling his own future with ghosts. His close-up is just beginning.

And: "You and Jay are *everything* to me," Nick swore to his oldest son in the hospital's Au Bon Pain the day after Imogen's birth—two and a half days before Emily's death. Emily and Imogen were both upstairs, struggling for their lives, and Miles hadn't wanted to leave Emily's bedside, but Nick, under the pretext of making him eat something, needed to get the words out, to hear himself say them. "I'm here and no matter what happens, you'll always have me. This family is my *country*."

Parenting is largely acting; he'd always believed that. But when he said these words to Miles, nothing about them was feigned. He meant them with a singular ferocity. Lina meant nothing to him in that moment; she was a thing that could be thrown to the lions and disavowed. How could it *be*? He loved her as he had never loved anyone. They had clicked like some complex machinery that could only fit together in one possible configuration out of millions, and *they*, their bodies and brains, were it: that one shimmery moment of synchronicity. Had he been planning, before Emily's initial seizure, to leave once she gave birth, to move out and abandon his sons' home? In his memory, this was his intention—it was what he and Lina had started, haltingly, to plan. Would he have done it? The world is overrun with people who have made both choices: to go, to stay. If Emily had recovered, as the doctors *said* she was going to, would Nick be here with *her* now on Beaver Island? Would he be with Lina, wherever she fled? Would he be on his own, forging a new life someplace like New York? Did he lie to Miles baldly, before he had even ascertained what he might be capable of—before his options were stripped from him by Emily's stroke, by kidney failure, by the cessation of her heart?

He honestly doesn't know.

There was no way for Lina to ever learn about the conversation he had with his son. Still, even up to the night Emily came home from the hospital, he'd intended to admit it to her—to admit his own confusion, to apologize, to beg her to give him time to work it out. But then there was Emily in an ambulance; then the overlapping sounds of sirens and Jay's sobbing and Miles's stony silence, all an interactive screensaver in Nick's brain now, stuck. Lina would have heard from Miguel what had transpired, would understand that he *needed* to retreat with his sons and would call her the moment he could. But he waited too long, and she was gone. It was almost as if she *knew* what he'd said to Miles, and believed him.

Now, Miles will be off to university in just over a month. Jay is still at home for eight more years, leaving Nick only fifty once he's gone. *We give our lives for them*, Nick thinks, *but if we've done it well, they don't return the favor.* In the end, it's never any different than it was for Emily or Gretchen, handing Imogen over to Chad and Miguel, who believe that makes her *theirs*. But our children are never ours. We belong to them, but they belong to themselves. They belong to people not yet born.

A bustling day at the beach on Beaver Island, unless it's "Homecoming Week," might mean eight families on the sand. There's a 1970s-styled playground, further from the water but still on the sand, full of unsafe metal and spinning and too-high equipment Jay and Gray both love, and this year Imogen is running around, too, fearless and squealing, though Nick expects her to go flying backward off something any second now and Chad and Miguel can rack up their first ER visit. Or maybe it wouldn't be their first. He has the illusion of familiarity with them but little idea what their day-to-day lives entail. Once, Miles vomited twelve times in under an hour, when he was smaller than Imogen. Nick and Emily finally gave up entirely and stopped even attempting to change the sheets, sat naked and covered in puke until at last Miles's body ceased its wracking spasms. Jay, when sick, is able to go four days without eating *or* drinking: the pediatrician always demands that they give him Pedialyte or Gatorade or popsicles at least, and at first Emily and Nick would become frantic, pinching his skin for signs of dehydration and taking him to the ER asking if he needed to be on an IV, but eventually they accepted the fact that, for Jay, this was normal, his body's autopilot survival mode. Children are primal, Darwinian beasts. There is only so much you can do. Chad constantly looks behind them to the playground, checking on the kids, but Nick can't claim it's his impulse to check much.

Gretchen wears a one-piece, sporty suit. She's taller than Nick and looks like she could take him in a fight. She is eating fried cheesecake on a stick—what passes for a Beaver Island delicacy—from a joint called Daddy Frank's. Miguel's not taking off his T-shirt, Nick notices, though he's got his own cheesecake stick, too, unrepentant. Nick has his shirt off—he's thinner than he was in university, what Lina would call "junkie thin"—but his skin is nearly translucent, and Chad's not much better. Ah, fortysomethings on a beach. Fuck.

Why are they *here*? They all live in Chicago—he doesn't need to travel seven hours by car and another two by ferry just to spend time with Imogen, whom Jay regards as his baby sister but whom Miles, with little give over the years, clearly resents for . . . existing? Killing his mother? Still, Miles doesn't all-out refuse to see her, drawn as he must be—as they all three are—to this one thing Emily left behind. The doctors who treated Emily the night she delivered have told Nick how she kept ordering them to "save the baby"—though Nick was so preoccupied with Lina he hadn't even noticed, Emily must have come to love the child inside her as she did her own sons—enough to offer up her life. And so, Nick and Jay and even Miles forge on with this makeshift family: they go to Guerra and Merry birthday parties; they exchange Christmas gifts. They placate themselves that Emily would have wanted Imogen happy and healthy, even at the expense of what those who wanted *her* have lost. If Emily loved this baby, it is the least Nick can offer, retroactively, to love her, too.

That doesn't explain why he comes *here*, though, to this island of ghosts. Here on Beaver Island, his brain fills in the blanks of every empty space: there, propped against the side of the house, would be Dead Isabel's pink bicycle that Lina used to borrow; there would be Isabel's wellies near the door, the ones Lina said looked "sexy" on her somehow; there is the canopy of trees arched above the gravel road, reminding Lina of the South of France, where she had never been. Is Chicago not enough of a ghost town for him? The moment the wounds start to scab over, he has to open them with fresh salt? He comes here for Lina, plain and simple, not his wife, not Imogen.

"We'll all fly to New York together and stay at the same hotel!" Chad is enthusing. He's pulled out his iPhone to make some note of it. "When does the play open, Nick?"

"It's November," Nick tells them. Does Chad mean Gretchen and Ron, too? Ron's at work now, but has this surrogate family become such a given that even Gretchen and her new man would drag themselves off their idyllic little island, truck it to New York to see Nick's first play at an off-Broadway theater? Why would they care? He doesn't tell them that, once Miles is away, he is considering moving with Jay to New York in earnest. It's been nineteen years since he moved to a new city. In New York, who would he be?

How exotic Emily was to him once, when he first arrived in Chicago. A skinny, lost-looking, vaguely Goth girl in a bar who drank too many amaretto stone sours and told him about her jailbird father, whom she hadn't seen since she was three; who told him on their second date about her recent abortion and then challenged, "Aren't you going to run?" He loved the bones of her—used to cup her shoulder blades in his hands and call them her "wings," kissing the space between while she fell asleep in his arms. These people here all think of her as some selfless earth mother, "Saint Emily," and maybe they have good reason, but he should be ashamed for his own willingness to simplify—to reduce—her that way. "Do you *want* me to run?" he'd asked that long-ago Her, and she said, "There's something about you—I'm afraid if you don't leave right now, I'm never going to want you to," and Nick, twenty-four years old and having lived in five cities and two dozen apartments since fleeing home at seventeen, said, "Great, because I'm tired of leaving," and believed with everything he then knew that he meant it.

Is Emily less worthy of poetry than Lina? Was his wife, his winged creature, his jailbird's daughter, the mother of his children and bearer of Imogen, too, any less a Phoenix, less deserving of his passion, of his vigilance? He mindlessly slathers sunscreen on Jay, watches him move with such extra effort through the sand, staring after his son: *Emily, what will become of him—will he ever be all right without me? There were meant to be two of us, Em, to make sure he was never alone*. Impossible, of course—children are *supposed* to outlive their parents. Jay will have Miles. Jay will have himself.

"My ring." He's said it aloud, so the others turn to look at him. He feels his face reddening. "It must have slipped off when I was putting the lotion on Jay—it's gone."

A polite murmur of feigned interest from the others; a half-hearted sifting into the sand of their proximities.

"My wedding ring," he finally clarifies, unsure even why it's so hard to admit. Instantly, their energy shifts to high alert—from Gretchen, a gasp.

"Don't worry," Chad cries, jumping to his feet so that sand only shifts further around him; Nick wants to knock him over and keep everyone still. "We'll find it!"

Gretchen digs in the sand like a gold miner. Nick stands by, paralyzed, as she chases the others off the blanket, turning shoes upside down. Gretchen, on the romantic mission of a woman on the verge of engagement, doesn't ask why he is still wearing his wedding ring after three years—no one does, though Nick realizes now he feared their response, that they would find him . . . *hysterical? a fraud?* He feels himself lowering to the sand, too, helping Gretchen, but he can't find anything. How can such a small, simple thing have tunneled to the middle of the earth on its own steam? Why isn't it here?

Emily didn't want an engagement ring when she was pregnant with Miles; they needed to save money for a baby. Later, after Jay's birth, when they were in that precarious stage—both afraid the other would take them for "disappointed" in their son, so neither could articulate their fears, their grief—he found himself suddenly dropping thousands they didn't really have on the first expensive piece of jewelry he'd ever bought in his life: Jay's birthstone. And later still, Emily twisting the ring around and around her finger as they drove in their old car, headed somewhere Nick can no longer recall, she turned to him and said, "Thank you for my ring. I thought he might be too much for you. I thought it might be more than you had signed up for." Nick said, "What are you talking about? He's my *son*!" and Emily replied simply, "Men are fragile." And there could have been so many responses to that—so many retorts about war and sports and every other stupid goddamn thing, but instead Nick merely pulled the car all the way over to a curb to kiss her, and said, "Not me, I promise."

The things we say to one another. The way the most beautiful moments of our lives become lies.

He is on his feet. "I'm going to find a metal detector."

Squatting, kneeling, they all look up at him as though he has snapped.

"This is the United States," he says. "Every city, town, and island in this country's bound to have one."

"I doubt that," Gretchen says skeptically. "You probably can't just go *find* a metal detector."

"Sure I can," Nick says, walking away.

"Oh, great!" Chad calls after him. "Leave *us* to dig in the sand. Great ploy—a metal detector—right!" It's a play for levity and Nick actually appreciates it—doesn't want to be the afternoon's tragic figure—but before he's even out of earshot he hears Miguel reprimanding Chad.

He keeps moving. Walks across the sand to the grass, the parking lot, and beyond. Wanders in one of those hideous little souvenir joints that doubles as a bait-and-tackle shop and asks the kid behind the counter, "Hey, you wouldn't have a metal detector, would you?" and the kid, like it's the most normal thing in the world (god bless America) says, "Nah, but you should try the police. They're practically next door."

And so it is that Nick, some forty-five minutes later—because even the smallest police station on earth is a place you have to *wait* for everything—retraces his steps to where the others have reassembled the blanket and are sitting in some tentative state of collective disappointment, a metal detector in his hands.

"I can't believe this," Gretchen says, and she is actually smiling; Nick hadn't noticed until he sees her beaming that she often scowls when talking to him.

When they've all stood up once more, Miguel dragging the blanket, Nick begins moving the detector around, slowly, in circles, patient, trying to cover every inch of ground.

"You're going to find every beer tab and bottle cap every underage Michigan kid ever threw in this sand," Miguel warns. Nick pushes over and over and over again, the mood thick with anticipation. Even

Jay and Gray wander over, thrilled by the detector, asking to hold it, and Nick decides in a split second not to refuse, to let them, *process before product*, Gray stumbling around almost as much as Jay, before Nick can't go through with his good intentions and takes the detector back abruptly, continuing his mission. Again. Again. Again. His shoulders ache.

The afternoon's black flies have started biting, but still Nick keeps going, keeps pushing—he has, for Chrissakes, a *metal detector*, and there is no way that ring can hide from him forever. The detector is bound to sense it: that's how this *works*—the ring didn't get up and fucking walk away; it's here, and he is going to find it.

Except he's pushed the detector around for so long he's not sure he's even in the right spot anymore. So long that in the end, Chad and Miguel have to go back to Strong's Landing alone, for Imogen's nap, and Gretchen soon follows, not asking Nick's permission to take Jay along but merely co-opting him, citing that the kids are beat and have had too much sun. Except that finally, the sun beginning to set, the cop who loaned Nick the detector shows up, not in a squad car but by foot, as if it's just now occurred to him that maybe the Irish dude who came by with such a weird request was actually a terrorist or something, and is using the detector for nefarious purposes, and needs to be checked out—the cop, seeming giddily excited to find Nick there as promised, actually combing the beach, even makes a couple of rounds himself before saying he needs to take the metal detector back; it's gotten late, and he can't let Nick have it overnight. And there is Nick: stranded without a car, the cop carrying the detector away with apologies. Nick: alone on the beach, ringless, as though it is possible for the world to simply *eat* things, to devour all traces of the past. And he's crying, recklessly, foolishly, walking around in circles kicking up sand like a prat, making a complete ass of himself even though it's gone late and there's no one here to see him. He's cursing and ranting and can't stop, throwing a tantrum like Miles the year Jay was born and every night brought these jealous, infuriated theatrics, Emily and Nick so worn down they didn't know how they'd live through the year—when Emily was at work, Nick sometimes wanted to hide under a bed to escape Miles's wrath and Jay's constant, fragile need. In the dark—even Miles may be back at Strong's Landing by now, come home to feed—Nick punches a tree, the jagged bark immediately gashing his knuckles so he bleeds, and he'd like to hit the tree again except it hurts and he can't make his hand complete the mission. That ring is *here*, and if only he had longer—if only he had more time—he knows he could find it.

"I would have worn it forever," he promises the empty beach, despite all his firmly held belief in Emily's nonexistence. He's crying stupidly, his hand hanging bare and pale at his side, scarcely even a tan line where the ring spent nineteen years. No proof of history but the extra-smooth indenture of skin that will plump back to shape against Nick's will. What would his ring-wearing vigil have meant to Emily anyway? He was planning to leave her when she died—or *was* he? He isn't sure anymore. All he knows is she's gone, and he misses her, he wants his sons to have their mother back, he feels so guilty he'd gladly trade places with Em instead. Still, *Lina's* the one he can't stop spinning to after all this time, can't stop wanting in the night.

"Forgive me," he whispers against the night wind, to his dead wife, his lost mistress, his sons. Hand pulsing like a bass beat, his throat raw from sobbing, Nick begins the two-mile walk (Lina said, he's never measured it; *Lina said*) back to Sloptown Road, with nothing to show for himself. Back to all the people who do and do not belong to him.

* * *

Being on Beaver Island feels like being in an Ann Beattie story, I texted you the first time I came here to see Isabel after her diagnosis, *except we're all spics.* You said you had never read Ann

Beattie, though in my imagination, Nick, by now you have. In my imagination, you have pored over every text I ever referenced, looking for traces of me, underlining passages you think I'd have liked. In my version of your life now, you cry when you hear Cat Power's cover of "The Dark End of the Street." But just in case none of that is true—in case your life, raising two sons alone and teaching playwriting and getting shows picked up off-Broadway—does not permit this sort of flagrant vigil to me, I will use an example with which I know you're familiar, since Hanif Kureishi is a favorite of yours. In his short story (have you read his short fiction and his novels, Nick, or did you only mean you loved his films?) "With Your Tongue Down My Throat," the narrator appears to be a fucked-up teenage girl, a cutter and a slut, basically someone not dissimilar to me except at a more appropriate age for such thrashing angst. But in the end, the girl's quasi-stepfather (Howard, I think his name is—he's a playwright like you) steps forward from behind the veil, revealing that he is really telling the story, appropriating the young girl's voice, mocking the reader for believing she would even know certain words he's used, would say things in the sophisticated way he's phrased them.

And so what I mean to say is that, for a long time, maybe the entire time I was first writing this when I was pregnant, I thought I would "pull a Howard." I wanted to be writing myself *as you*—making myself into your creation, in a sense, to feel closer to you. I imagined myself as you might imagine me, trying to recapture our old symbiosis. I thought that, in the end, I would stage that kind of reversal and "unveil" you as the author—even if it wasn't *you*, of course, just some narrative device—so that when you finally read this, you would be reading the inside of your own head.

And then somehow you would know me, from the inside out.

But here we are, finally at the end ("nothing really ends"; "narrative arc is an illusion"; "life doesn't have a plotline"—the things you taught me are useless here, and I was a terrible pupil)—and I can't give you the gift of yourself. There is too much at stake and you can never read this now. I walked away; I forfeited that ending.

I might as well tell you, then, that when I first arrived at Aunt Pilar's, I had the same recurring dream over and over again. In it, I go to you and Emily and ask you to keep the baby and raise it for me. The dream was so strong, and possessed such a perfect symmetry, that it seduced me, until what had risen from my subconscious at night became an obsessive daydream, conscious. In the fantasy, phantom Emily would even forgive me, because I was giving her back what she had just lost to my brother. But Emily can never forgive me in reality, because she's busy being dead. Your wife *died*, Nick. I don't know what that fallout looked like, but I knew the moment I heard the news that I would never be like her or Gretchen or Isabel: One who bears gifts. One who sacrifices.

Only later did I stop thinking of myself—*my* role, my "destiny"—and start thinking of our actual baby. I always envisioned her as a girl, maybe because of Imogen, or because you wanted one. Only later did the recurring dream of turning her over to Emily—the good mother, the respectable woman—leave me with nothing but a blinding clarity, a force different than my shimmery fantasies, that I could never do to my daughter what Isabel had done to me. I could neither let her slide away into the ether of unrealized possibilities, nor could I let her come into this world to grapple forever with the immeasurable gap where I was supposed to be.

You don't deserve to be kept from the child we made together. Whatever "crimes" you have committed, my redheaded meteor boy, they were never against me. This isn't punishment for anything. But a baby would have forced your hand, when you were already living on top of a landmine. How (please tell me how) could I walk into that explosion and somehow claim my place at your side, affront everyone from your sons to my brother with my swollen body? Tell me how I could ask you to focus on my child, on *me*, when your sons had just lost their mother and needed your undivided presence. Tell me how else I was to stop being the wrecking ball, except to carry this one last secret, and leave you all where you rightfully belonged. We were fucking atop Emily's grave, whether we knew it or not. What was there left to hope for, for either of us, except a fresh start?

And so, I'm trying. Here I am in grad school, even, bolstering up the spectacular false economy of need that drives us. After I healed from childbirth and my BRCA-induced hysterectomy, I even stripped again for a while—a whole other economy of need, this one quite real—since being Aunt Pilar's assistant, a strangely glamorous gig at times but mostly just sitting in her house doing her correspondence, sending slides of her work to people around the globe, pays like shit because that's Art for you. I've walked away from dancing again for the time being, but I'm not promising you or myself that someday I won't go back. I'm *trying*, Nick, to be the person you—and even Bebe—would have wanted me to be for myself, to be a person I can be proud of, a person a daughter could be proud of someday. But if I think about that too long it feels like quicksand, so really what I'm trying to do is get through the day.

You are nothing I ever owned, Nick, but for a time you were everything I ever loved and wanted, and everything I ever hurt, and every mistake I made, and every decent gesture or incongruous act of grace, and I still carry you inside me even though I let you go. I'd beg for your forgiveness, but since you have no idea what to forgive me for, since your heart is too forgiving anyway and you always saw me as better than I really was, I know that's way too simple.

Maybe I still wish you were telling this story so I could be the me inside your head instead of *me*. But I'm not taking that cop-out, so here I am: not a gift to you or anyone else, except maybe, finally, myself.

So it was that when I gave birth, I wasn't thinking of you anymore. Only my daughter.

Now three years old, with the incongruous blend of your meteor hair and my brown skin, she is beautiful, she is herself. She is loved.

* * *

It's been a night of Nick's mourning, of making everyone uncomfortable. Chad and Miguel always retire early anyway; Nick hears them upstairs reading *Everybody Poops* to Imogen and laughing, and waits for them all to silence before he can scuttle upstairs to his solitary guest room. Miles and Jay share the twin-bedded room downstairs, but despite there being plenty of beds to go around, whenever he's here it feels like too many people in one shared space, breathing each other's air: no privacy. It isn't until Nick's in bed reading, reaches mindlessly over to the bedside table to put away his book, that he sees his ring, right where he left it, unscathed.

"No."

He says it aloud. He isn't happy to see the ring—precisely the opposite—he is horrified, ashamed. The trouble he's caused everyone! The disquiet he brewed in his own head! The ring stares back, round and endless and mocking in its unsullied solidity. He took it off last night to jerk off with some lotion he found in the guest bathroom, though the lotion was sticky and his orgasm furtive and regrettable, and he'd forgotten, when he woke this morning, that the whole sour endeavor had even occurred. He wasn't wearing his ring at the goddamn beach when he was chasing his son down with sunscreen. The ring was *here*. God. He touches the ring gingerly, as though it may disappear or set off a siren. He can't put it back on now, for fuck's sake—can't explain to the others how it was just sitting here. He puts it in his pocket, then panics and realizes it'll only fall out, gets up again and shuts it away inside his toothbrush case, the only place where it cannot fall out and escape.

Once the ring is silenced, Nick sits at the edge of the bed, cringing, loathing himself.

He hasn't slept with a woman in so long—there were a few, always when he was drunk, the first year after Emily's death, but no one since—that it's become embarrassing to masturbate: a stand-in for actual adult sexuality, like when he was a pubescent boy. His memories of Lina, that fuel him on toward his climax, crush him immediately afterward to the point that, at times, he's wept on the heels of coming. Christ, how disappointed in him Lina would be. In this dimmer switch he's come to use on his life for so long he doesn't know how to turn himself back up toward *living*, with all the risks and desires that entails—he isn't sure he wants to. Anyway, who is Lina to be disappointed in anyone?

He thinks of that one night at Villa Moderne, of Lina lost for hours to the voices in her own head. Of the way she tried to take the room apart, clocks and televisions, as though at her center existed an impulse to break things down, to get inside, her constant interrogation of the world more important than whether anything could be reassembled. And that, in a strange way just as beyond language as whatever hole Emily was trying to fill with Imogen, was the wild beauty of Lina: the way she seemed closer to her core than other people—some raw, stripped-down essence of herself. That night, caught in the vortex of a brain-chemistry misfire, she was unable to in any way cloak herself in the artifice, the performance that permeates human interaction so completely that we don't even question it anymore. She was locked inside herself, and there was something shockingly intimate about witnessing her in that place. She would never have believed him, maybe, but although he'd been infatuated with her for months, *that* was the moment—the moment in which she was not even conscious of his presence—he really fell in love.

Lina, whom he loved for her lack of artifice, enabler of his artifice.

Miguel says she is getting a PhD in literature, a pursuit both perfect for her and yet unfathomable. He says she only emails, won't tell anyone where she is living, that he hasn't seen her and she doesn't want visitors. *She's become Isabel,* Miguel told Nick, maybe a year and a half ago, the last time they discussed it. *She's become the woman who tormented her. I've humiliated myself and groveled and begged, but I'm done. She wants to be gone, she wants to abandon everyone and everything to appease some demon in her head, fine, I love her, but I'm not going to stalk her.*

Lina throwing her arms around him, biting his mouth like he was her sustenance.

Her body, the tattoos and burnished skin of her, is hazier than it used to be, and that terrifies him. Unlike Emily, of whom he has framed photos and several albums and thousands of iPhotos, he has only a couple pictures of Lina—cast photos where hers is one face in a sea of faces, before they'd ever so much as kissed. *His* Lina exists only in memory. What will happen when he can't see her anymore?

A word about desire: there are no words about desire.

She is the one who left. He has to let her go—he knows. What might have been romantic at first has become dysfunctional, self-destructive. He needs to move on. She wouldn't want this for him—though part of "moving on," he realizes, is it no longer being about what Lina would want.

New York looms, a promise or a taunt.

On their last night on the island, Nick, Miguel, and Miles sit out on the back porch, looking at the stars. The girl Miles met his second day on the island went home today—just to Ann Arbor—and Miles has been loitering around the house, bereft, in a way Chad and Gretchen have been calling "adorable." Now, he's left the porch and is stretched out on his back on the picnic table, texting her unremittingly. Nick wonders how soon they will run out of things to say, knowing each other a scant five days on an island where neither lives, their reference points and contexts so disparate. When Nick was Miles's age, he was already studying in London, had already left his home country in a day before cell phones and email and texting and Facebook and whatever the hell else the kids are doing that makes even those things half-obsolete. People touched and then just disappeared, no awkward fading away.

"There was something about her," Miles tells Miguel, in between texts. He has to speak loudly, since he's in the middle of the yard, and it surprises Nick, frankly, that he's making the effort. "She's so different from the girls at home. She's mellow and real, not all competitive and snarky. Maybe I should have gone to college in Michigan."

"Yeah," Miguel calls back, "you should have chosen Michigan—I mean, Julliard sucks, who'd want to go there?"

Miles laughs, but already he's looking at his phone again.

Miguel goes into the kitchen, then returns holding up a bottle of tequila like a question, and Nick nods. Then, remembering, Nick pulls a joint out of his pocket and says, "I'll raise you one," and Miguel looks nervously out toward Miles, though Nick shrugs.

Miguel says, "I don't know if I can—it makes me paranoid."

"Nah, this is the good stuff. Medicinal."

They pour; they light.

This is one of those moments Nick used to fantasize desperately about orchestrating. Miles is far enough away that Nick could ask discreet questions; the kids and Chad are already upstairs in bed. But the truth is that there isn't anything more Miguel can tell him without Nick having to admit things he suspects Miguel of suspecting but can't bring himself to confirm. *Letting go*, he reminds himself, and he waits for Miguel to steer the conversation elsewhere.

"It's so weird, isn't it?" Miguel says, obligingly. "Gretchen and Ron?"

"I don't really know her that well," Nick hedges, "but yeah, she didn't seem like the romantic type to me, I'll give you that."

"It's strange being around it," Miguel says. "I mean, you expect it from Miles—you remember yourself at that age and how big everything seemed. But it's hard to believe Gretchen, at our age, can really buy into all that all over again."

"If you don't buy in," Nick says, "what else is there?"

Miguel drags on the joint, awfully deeply for a man who's claiming paranoia. Maybe the Guerras have a certain hunger for numbness—for altered states—in their DNA. *I want to feel different,* Lina always said, whenever she was stressed. *I just want something to make me feel different.*

"But all that . . . passion," Miguel continues, handing the joint back to Nick. "It seems like so much effort. It seems so *tiring.*" He actually shudders. "I'd rather just fall asleep in front of *The Daily Show.*"

"You've got a toddler," Nick says glibly.

Miguel looks at Nick with a half-formed disappointment on his face, like he expected more of him. Nick shrugs, downs his tequila, says, "I don't know, man. Marriage is hard. I don't know anymore how people keep going at it. At least two men speak the same language."

"No one speaks the same language as anyone," says Miguel.

From the bench, Miles rises up on an elbow. "Are you guys getting high? Jesus, fucking hippies. Can I have some?"

"I feel dirty," Miguel says. Then, "Aren't you supposed to be bringing us Molly or something? Or . . . wow, do kids still do cocaine? I loved cocaine."

Miles leans through the open window of the enclosed porch and reaches for the joint. He takes two long hits, passes the joint back to his father—not even touching the cocaine question—and walks back out into the dark night. The stars pop violently in the sky, in constellations Nick couldn't identify if his life depended on it. The world is full of things to know, and you reach an age when mostly you realize all the things you planned on learning are things you've gotten by fine without. Miguel leans forward, looking after Miles as if to see how far away he is, then says, in that conspiratorial way of his, "I used to think . . . I thought Chad was mainly a surface person—I don't mean that the rude way it sounds, I actually loved that about him—but watching his friendship with Emily, I realized no, that's not exactly it. He was just surface *with me*."

Did Emily tell Chad the thing about feeling broken after Jay? "There's more than one kind of intimacy," Nick says, and he plans to leave it at that. But instead, a short beat later, he hears himself ask, "Would you ever have an affair?"

Miguel, even stoned, looks startled. He grimaces a little, like he knows he started this and now he has to see it through. He drops his voice even further, says, "I used to think, maybe I should just go out to Barcelona—I used to live there—once a year, go to my old haunts, just . . . get together with old friends. I thought, maybe that kind of thing is even good for a marriage. Chad and I—sex isn't the most central part of our bond, you know? We enjoy it, it's not like, some problem . . . but . . . it's not raw animal chemistry. I don't mean now—who has that after almost fifteen years? I mean it was never what we were really about, even when we were young. I thought, maybe no one can be everything to another person, and we're all responsible for our own needs."

"Fair enough," says Nick.

"But the thing is . . ." Miguel reaches for the bottle, then places it back down on the wooden slats of the floor, puts his hands back on his lap. "When it came right down to it, I've been cheated on, and I know what it feels like, and I couldn't do that to Chad. Attraction is cheap. What we have is more than that. Not just Imogen but . . . I mean bearing witness to each other's lives. That's bigger than sex. Without that, we're like the tree in the woods. Life is about compromises. Chad and I make each other real."

Miles, lit by starlight, laughs in the distance. Is he eavesdropping on them, laughing to hear two old men talking this way, or is he oblivious to them, laughing at his phone screen, at the words floating in intangible space between himself and his Michigan girl?

Who will Imogen be to Nick's boys, when he and Chad and Miguel and Gretchen are all nothing but stardust? Family? A story for the therapist's couch? *Anything*? What does this cruel, achingly luminous world have in store for the men Jay and Gray will grow into, carrying the albatross and gifts of their diagnosis around just as Lina carries hers? It is dizzying not to know—not to be able to control any of it. *Em, you needed to help me, you needed to stay, it's too much.* But Emily is still gone, along with everything he should have said to her to make it right, or everything in her that might have been better off without him. All of her but what remains in the children has disappeared into the great non-sentient unknown. Nick is free, and whether that is what he wanted at one time, or only another game of chicken he'd have pulled himself back from the edge of before the fall, doesn't matter anymore. He stretches his hand drunkenly toward the Nothingness as though he can grasp it, then relinquishes the attempt, reaches out and touches Miguel's arm instead, firmly places his hand there despite the way it makes Miguel twitch in alarm before slowly relaxing into something like solidarity in the vastness. Nick keeps his hand there, one moment longer, touching Lina's shared DNA, touching the father of the baby his wife carried, touching his friend, holding on just one, two, three seconds more—and then slowly, gently, letting go.